# AN EDGE
# IN MY VOICE

# EAN EDGE IN MY VOICE

## Harlan Ellison

The Donning Company/Publishers
Norfolk/Virginia Beach

AN EDGE IN MY VOICE

These columns appeared originally in
*Future Life,* the L.A. *Weekly* and *The Comics Journal*

A Donning book/published by arrangement with the Author

PRINTING HISTORY
Donning Edition/March 1985

The letters reproduced in **An Edge In My Voice** are with permission from
the L.A. *Weekly* and *The Comics Journal*

Editor for The Donning Company: Kay Reynolds

*An Edge In My Voice* is one of the many titles published
by The Donning Company/Publishers. For a complete
listing of our titles, please write to:
The Donning Company/Publishers
5659 Virginia Beach Boulevard
Norfolk, Virginia 23502

**Library of Congress Cataloging in Publication Data:**

Ellison, Harlan.
    An edge in my voice.

    I. Title.
PS3555.L62E3      1985              814'.54              83-16298
ISBN 0-89865-342-8 (lim. ed.)
ISBN 0-89865-341-X (pbk.)
ISBN 0-89865-373-8 (hrd. cov.)

10   9   8   7   6   5   4   3   2   1

Printed in the United States of America

# Books by Harlan Ellison

Web of the City (1958)
The Deadly Streets (1958)
The Sound of a Scythe (1960)
A Touch of Infinity (1960)
Children of the Streets (1961)
Gentleman Junkie *and other stories of the hung-up generation* (1961)
Memos from Purgatory (1961)
Spider Kiss (1961)
Ellison Wonderland (1962)
Paingod *and other delusions* (1965)
I Have No Mouth & I Must Scream (1967)
Doomsman (1967)
Dangerous Visions [Editor] (1967)
From the Land of Fear (1967)
Nightshades & Damnations:
     *the finest stories of Gerald Kersh* [Editor] (1968)
Love Ain't Nothing but Sex Misspelled (1968)
The Beast that Shouted Love at the Heart of the World (1969)
The Glass Teat *essays of opinion on television* (1970)
Over the Edge (1970)
Partners in Wonder *sf collaborations with 14 other wild talents* (1971)
Alone Against Tomorrow, (1971)
Again, Dangerous Visions [Editor] (1972)
All the Sounds of Fear [British publication only] (1973)
The Time of the Eye [British publication only] (1974)
Approaching Oblivion (1974)
The Starlost #1:
     *Phoenix Without Ashes* [with Edward Bryant] (1975)
Deathbird Stories (1975)
The Other Glass Teat *further essays of opinion on television* (1975)
No Doors, No Windows (1975)
Strange Wine (1978)
The Book of Ellison [Edited by Andrew Porter] (1978)
The Illustrated Harlan Ellison [Edited by Byron Preiss] (1978)
The Fantasies of Harlan Ellison (1979)
All the Lies That Are My Life (1980)
Shatterday (1980)
Stalking the Nightmare (1982)
Sleepless Nights in the Procrustean Bed: Essays
     [Edited by Marty Clark] (1984)
An Edge in My Voice (1985)
Medea: Harlan's World [Editor] (1985)

# ACKNOWLEDGMENTS

During the three years, off-and-on, that these columns were being batted out, many people provided assistance: some in small ways, as with reference or research efforts; some in large ways, as unnamed sources of information who preferred to be kept on "deep background," or as messengers, delivering my copy to the offices of the *L.A. Weekly* in the small hours of the night when I'd fall asleep over the typewriter. The proofreaders and typesetters at the *Weekly* who knew of my pathological desire to have the pieces published sans typos, who looked after the copy with special care. My office staff, who tossed an occasional grilled cheese sandwich at me as I labored. And most of all, the concerned readers whose suggestions as to subjects they wanted investigated or commented upon, who turned out for marches and at artistic events the column championed... those nameless dozens deserve my thanks. And yours.

But here are a few of the most important names, because they were invaluable: Sharon Buck, Ms. Marty Clark, Joanne Gutreimen, Barbara Krasnoff, Ed Naha, Stephanie O'Shaughnessy, Debra Spidell, Hank Stine, Sarah L. Wood and Bob Woods

And *very* special thanks are herewith extended to Gil Lamont, Shelley Levinson and my two most significant editors, Kay Reynolds of Donning and Phil Tracy of the *Weekly*.

# FOREWORD

by Tom Snyder

In *Shatterday*, Harlan Ellison assured all of us that we share the same fears. That the one thing none of us have to be afraid of is admitting that we are afraid of the scary dreads that lurk inside us all. I have been sitting staring at the keys of this machine since three months ago. Then, Ellison asked if I would write a foreword to this book. A collection of more of his rantings and ravings that I first experienced very late one night on a defunct television program named "Tomorrow." I liked Ellison then and I like him now. He honored me with his request. He flattered me. I accepted. And for three months I have been staring at the keys on this machine, in stark terror.

For years, I have written for television news programs. I think much of it has been pretty good, but if I set it down right here in front of you, few would remember a word of it. That's because television news writing disappears rapidly. It comes on, it goes off, and it disappears. It doesn't lie around gathering shelf dust for years and then one rainy night beckon your curiosity from the booktable. I called Ellison three days ago and confessed to him I didn't have the foggiest notion of what a foreword to a book was all about. That I was terrified to think whatever words I strung together would be available for the jeering and ridicule of the audience forever. The good pieces I wrote for television would always be a private satisfaction to me. The dumb ones—the really horrid crap I had dashed out with no thought and less preparation—those were gone and forgotten and nobody would ever know of them and thank God for that. But here I was facing a foreword to a Harlan Ellison book.

Ellison has written forty-some books, won every award his peers can give him, has legions of fans around the world who hang on his every word as if they were struck in stone, and he—he who has taken to college lectures and Trekkie conventions so he will never again have to write for television because he hates it so deeply—wants a "television schlep"—as he loves to define us—to write a foreword to his book. For me to write *anything* in the same book with Harlan Ellison makes about as much sense as having me hit tee shots for Jack Nicklaus. I confessed that to him, and he laughed and said to make believe the whole thing was writing a letter to a friend; simply to have fun.

I think Harlan Ellison has fun. Here's a little guy who every now and then drops into my life and points out that humans are the craziest people. We go absolutely nuts when New York State offers a winner $22,000,000 (that's right folks, *twenty two million dollars*) in a lottery. But New York State doesn't have the money to fix the highways and keep the bridges from falling down. Ellison has made me aware of things like that—the great contradiction between what we are and what we think we are. I want to believe that most of us have had sufficient of the current diet of news slime: How a Kennedy really died; are Brooke Shields and Michael Jackson more than good friends; is Boy George really a boy; and so on and so on and so on until your brain can't stand it any longer. Ellison delights in cutting through all the smarm. He fights battles most of us haven't even thought of, much less cared about. If you know anything of Frances Farmer, you'll recall how she challenged *everything* hypocritical about God and Country. The so-called guardians of the public good cut her brain out to rid us all of cynicism and skepticism but it didn't work. Watching a movie about her reminded me of Harlan Ellison. He fights the wars that aren't even worth fighting, and delights in our frustrations when we finally figure it out. Guys like Harlan know we can't win 'em all, but we sure-as-shooting better win some, or else the guy who said, "Life's a bitch, and then you die!", will wind up being right.

The writer in the book follows. Along the way, you'll hear him say that he wrote much of this a long time ago, and that when he asks you to write him about certain things, he meant for you to write him *then,* but that he doesn't want to hear from you now.

He's just kidding.

—Tom Snyder
29 May 1984

To the Memory of Charles Beaumont

(2 January 1929—21 February 1967)

Prince From a Far Land

# Introduction

## Ominous Remarks For Late In The Evening

Both Hemingway and Scott Fitzgerald discovered a peculiar syndrome that affected critics of their work. They learned in the roughest way imaginable that if they were praised as great, fresh talents early on in their careers, that as they approached the middle years of writing they were "reevaluated." The second guessers and the parvenus who could not, themselves, create the great and fresh stories, made their shaky reputations by means of pronunciamentos that advised those few literati who gave a damn, that *les enfants terribles* were now too long in the tooth to produce anything worth reading; that they were past it; and in the name of common decency should embarrass themselves no further by packing it in and retiring to the cultivation of Zen flower gardens. So they both croaked, and did the heavy deeds of assassination for their critics. But had they somehow managed to overcome cancer and alcoholism, had they managed to squeak through for another decade, they'd have found themselves lionized. Each would have made it through the shitrain to become *le monstre sacré*. Grand old men of letters. National treasures. Every last snippet they'd tapped out on yellow second-sheets sold at Sotheby's for a pasha's weight in rubies.

They never made it. Not rugged, spike-tough old Ernest, not lighter-than-air Scott. Time and gravity and the nibbling of minnows did them in. And so they don't know that they are still famous—though seldom read—in the way that talk show guests are famous: you know their names and often their faces, but you can't quite remember what the hell it is they did to make them "famous."

The lesson we who work behind the words learn from this is that if your life is as interesting as your work, or even approaches that level of passion, there will be those who are not-quite-enough waiting in the tall grass, waiting to compound your fractures when your brittle bones splinter.

1

Never get too fat, never get too secure. The rat-things are waiting. Just hang in there long enough, like Borges or Howard Fast or Graham Greene or Jean Rhys, and the sheer volume of accumulated years will daunt all but the most vicious (who quickly self-destruct when they try to savage the icons).

The fine novelist Walter Tevis, a sweet man who died on August 9, 1984, knew more than his share of pain. Walter once told me, when I was bitching about constantly being pilloried for trying to startle readers into wakefulness with fiery prose, "You can't attract the attention of the dead."

I am well in mind of that epigraph as I sit here writing an introduction to a book of occasional pieces, essays, columns done to a monthly or weekly deadline, that passed along to my readers the world I observed at those times. In the words of Irwin Shaw: "He is engaged in the long process of putting his whole life on paper. He is on a journey and he is reporting in: 'This is where I think I am and this is what this place looks like today.'"

Well in mind of Walter's consoling observation as I consider a scurrilous bit of business published in a jumped-up comic book called *Heavy Metal* last October 1983. A vitriolic hate-piece accurately titled "Hatcheting Harlan," as written by one of the universe's great prose stylists, Gus Patukas. If the name rings no carillons, don't go searching through THE READER'S ENCYCLOPEDIA or WEBSTER'S AMERICAN BIOGRAPHIES. Turns out Gus is a kid who lives in Brooklyn; buddy chum of a *Heavy Metal* editor whose own literary accolades are on the level of sucking fish-heads. They're into swagger, but not much into writing anything that will outlast the paper it's printed on.

But the best part of the attack came several issues later, in the letter column of this illustrated irritation dedicated to drawings of women with breasts the size of casaba melons and comic strips in which people get their heads blown open like overripe pomegranates. Rather than admitting that they'd received several hundred outraged letters from readers who thought I might have a few good minutes left in me, they presented a "balanced response" by dummying up a couple of letters saying good for Patukas and ever-vigilant *Heavy Metal*, for bringing to his knees that fraud Ellison, who never could write for sour owl poop to begin with. One of these letters contained the statement that *Ellison is an enemy of the People.*

> "Liberty is better served by presenting a clear target to
> one's opponents than by joining with them in an
> insincere and useless brotherliness."
> *Benedetto Croce* (1866–1952),
> Italian philosopher, historian,
> statesman & literary critic

2

I thought about that one for some time. And then I had to smile. The author of that letter, someone who signed himself "William Charles Rosetta, LA, California" (though no such person—as one with the "Jon Douglas West" you will encounter in these pages—seems to exist in Los Angeles or anywhere else), had miraculously stumbled on a hidden truth.

I am, indeed, an enemy of the people.

Ibsen, who noted that "To live is to war with trolls," codified the "enemy of the people" in his classic drama about a courageous man who tells the truth about a public menace—the contamination of the town's famous healing spring waters—which will bring about the community's economic demise. This honest man, Dr. Thomas Stockmann, plans to shut down the springs to make improvements for the public good. But when "economic realities" dictate otherwise, Stockmann's brother, Peter, who is the mayor, undercuts his efforts by turning him from a hero in the eyes of his neighbors, into "an enemy of the people."

"If fifty million people say a foolish thing, it is still a foolish thing."

*Anatole France*

The sixty-one personal essays that make up this book are my proud statement of enmity toward the people. Not just to people like Patukas and "Rosetta" and the pinheads at *Heavy Metal* whose dreary little lives move them to such ignoble attacks of foaming idiocy against their betters, but enmity toward the censors and the pro-gun lobbyists and the filmmakers who brutalize women in the name of "art" and the smoothyguts politicians who secure their futures with arms manufacturers by stealing money from the schools and the lousy writers who monopolize the spinner racks and their venal publishers who have destroyed the mid-list in search of bestsellers and the bible-thumpers who want prayer in the schools as long as we pray to *their* God and to the gray little bookkeepers who know their dancing decimal points cheat honest men and women out of their annuities and the garage mechanics who lie and tell you they can't repair that thingamajig unless you buy a new whatzit for seventy-five bucks and the headless snakes that are the multi national corporations that remove products you like from the supermarkets because cheaper items move more units per capita and the terrorists and the zealots and the true believers and the insensitive and the dull-witted and the self-righteous. All of whom are parts of "the people."

"I have sworn eternal hostility against every form of tyranny over the mind of man."

*Thomas Jefferson*

You'd better believe it, I am an enemy of the people. The people who stand by and do nothing. The ones who don't want to get involved, and the ones who don't want to risk a dime of their money; the ones who permit evil to walk unchecked, and the ones who abet the monsters because "If I didn't do it, someone else would"; the ones who beat up their kids because they're part of the household goods, and the ones whose rapaciousness gives them coin to bully the weak. I am foursquare and forever till the moment I go under, an enemy to the people who lie to you and want to keep you stupid. To those who sell you shitty rock music and drive classical and jazz off the FM dial, to those who tell you wallboard is better than lath and plaster, to those who say bad grammar is okay as long as you understand (however vaguely) what's being said. To the ginks and the creeps and the trendies and the destroyers of the past, who deny you your future.

I am a yapping dog with mean little teeth. I am as often as wrong as you, as often silly as you, as often co-opted as you, as often sophomoric as you. But I maintain. As do you.

And here, in these sixty-one personal essays that need no introduction because they are, themselves, introductions I pass along what I saw and wrote about for three years, from August 1980 to January 1983. (With a one-shot relapse in August of 1984.)

They were written with an edge in my voice, and they may make no more profound statement than to assure you that for the duration of this book you are in no other hands than that of an enemy of the people.

4

"Look for a long time at what pleases you...and longer still at what pains you."

*Colette*

"Common sense is instinct. Enough of it is genius."

*George Bernard Shaw*

"...the main purpose of criticism...is not to make its readers agree, nice as that is, but to make them, by whatever orthodox or unorthodox methods, think."

*John Simon*
6 Feb 84

"By the great might of figures (which is no other thing than wisdom speaking eloquently), the orator may lead his hearers which way he lists, and draw them to what affection he will; he may make them to be angry, to be pleased, to laugh, to weep, and lament; to love, to abhor, and loathe; to hope, to fear, to covet; to be satisfied, to envy, to have pity and compassion; to marvel, to believe, to repent; and briefly to be moved with any affection that shall serve best for his purpose."

*Henry Peacham*
*THE GARDEN OF ELOQUENCE*
1577

# INTERIM MEMO:

In this first installment of the column, I solicited letters
from readers. This comes solidly under the heading of *Yes,
of course I'd like an enema with a thermite bomb, Monsieur
de Sade.* Later, in Installment 7, and every six weeks when
the column moved to the *Los Angeles Weekly*, I would
attempt to answer those whose letters were something
more than deranged vampire-bat gibbering. You'll read all
that lunacy later. But I drop the notice here, that this is a
*book*, not a periodical, and I truly really honestly don't
want any more mail on these columns. Not that I don't
love you all, but the subject matter has been dealt with
fully; and Monday morning quarterbacking now that
these words have been collected will only chew the meal
twice. So, though we've decided to let the material stand
as it was published (with typos corrected, of course), just
forget it when you encounter a solicitation for comment.
Let me say it again, just to get through to that one twit out
there who *never* gets the word: Don't send me letters
asking or commenting. I'm dead, the magazines were
bombed out of existence, this publisher has gone into the
grain and feed business, and you'll only be wasting your
time and money.

Michael J. Elderman

Darkness falls early. From the horizon comes the wail of creatures pretending to be human. The red tide has come in, and shapeless things float toward the shore. He stands before the altar of Art, naked and with fists raised, and he vows: *I will not be lied to.*

Hello. My name is Harlan Ellison and I am a writer. This is a new home for my words and I'm in the process of moving in. Much of my personal furniture has yet to arrive. I'll be furnishing this space from month to month and though I'm aware some of my taste may not parallel yours, I bring with me several items whose beauty I do not think you will contest. The first is a determination to entertain you.

No matter what comes past my window, no matter what doings and philosophies and people are trapped for comment, I will bring to any discussion of them a resolve to keep your attention. Entropy is fed by boredom; and I am anti-entropy.

The second item already installed is a sense of ethics. I cannot be bought. This magazine has rented my words, but by contract they cannot edit them or change them or try to sway me to say things I would not say of my own volition. Truth is the greater part of these ethics and I will do my best to tell it as I know it. Sometimes I'll be wrong—I can be fooled as easily as you—but I have no doubt you'll let me know when that happens.

The third item I bring to this new residence is taste. Some have said I have good taste, high standards, a sense of what is worthy. Others have disagreed. I cannot espouse the taste of others, only my own. But I'm told it is that special view that is required here. I seldom agree with the mass, I despise bad writing, meretricious film-making, appeals to the lowest possible common denominator of cheap titillation, attempts to package snake-oil as a cancer cure, and I reject the notion that you are a vast audience of dumb, gullible children who will endorse even the shabbiest product if it comes heavily advertised.

And finally, I bring courage and my talent to this new place. They are as integral to what I will do and say here as are the walls and

9

ceiling of this magazine, the print and paper you hold in your hands.

The courage to defy many of you in your pet obsessions; the courage to consider only the work and how it was produced, even when writing about my friends; the courage to take risks with my own self-interest. I make no grand statements about my fearlessness; it's simply the way I've always done things and I have no control over it. Backed, however, by my talent. I will not dissemble: if I didn't have the ability, you would not now be reading these words. There are many things in this life I cannot do, but there are a few I do very well indeed. One of them is write. I will expend the fullest measure of that talent in your behalf.

It is my intention to write a column each time that will reflect the Real World through a lens of fantasy, that will, I hope, give you a different view of what others try to hype you into accepting uncritically.

That's okay. Millions are spent every year to get you to attend inferior movies, to believe talentless actors are Laurence Olivier, to sell you cheap goods and to bastardize your taste in food, art, life-style, goals and personal relationships. Those millions go to maintaining the status quo, also known as entropy. I am foursquare for chaos; I am anti-entropy. We will have wonderful arguments.

In the months to come I intend to write pieces on the arcologies of the visionary architect and dreamer Paolo Soleri, on the magnificent new PBS series *Cosmos* created by Carl Sagan, on the antic sense of humor of fantasy novelist Stephen King.

I know all three of these men, and have shared space and time with them. They may have said something to me they haven't said to others. I'll try to pass those new thoughts along to you.

In future columns I will review some films. I have written for television and films for almost twenty years, and much of the amateur nonsense you're asked to believe prevents you from critically judging what is thrown at you by powerful and monied corporations. My critiques of these films will attempt to go behind the sound and fury of the publicity machines that grind on through the night.

There will be essays on new writers you should pay attention to at risk of your mortal soul, there will be encounters with celebrities and with everyday men and women like yourselves, there will be anecdotes of craziness and danger and even low and high comedy. There will be views of the world around you that will propound the theory that reality and fantasy have flip-flopped; and I will do my best to aggravate you. Not because I am mean of spirit, but simply and directly because *nothing* should be accepted without considering it fully.

In some ways I'm an Elitist. I do not believe that we are all entitled to our opinions. I *do* believe that we are all entitled to our *informed* opinion. George Orwell once wrote that "The great enemy of clear language is insincerity," and to the end of providing you with clear language that informs and elucidates, I will be sincere at risk of bringing down your wrath on me.

Because, as an Elitist, I believe that each of you has the spark of nobility and change in you. I believe that it is the remarkable men and women in every age who alter the condition of life for all of us, who move us away from the pit toward the stars. I cannot be convinced that Einstein and Elizabeth Cady Stanton and Galileo and Mary W. Shelley and Ralph Nader and Marie Curie were not *better* than those around them when they made their contributions to the human race. And I cannot be convinced that among you reading this there are no incipient Einsteins, Stantons, Galileos, Curies and Naders. In each of you, in some way, is the fire that we need to change the course of history. And to stoke that fire I will try to write of things and in ways that will get you aggravated enough to *think.*

All the while keeping you entertained, because that's my job, and I've contracted to do it the best way I know how.

I'll expect your help.

When you stumble across something interesting you think you'd like to see discussed in this space, drop a *short line* to me in care of this magazine. Don't bother sending letters of praise telling me what a swell guy I am. I toss that kind of stuff in the waste basket. As many of you will think I'm terrific as will think I'm a card-carrying creep. Half of you will be right.

Don't bother sending crazy letters. You know the kind I mean: Jesus loves you, I took a ride in a flying saucer, JFK was assassinated by aquatic killers from Atlantis, have you read your I Ching today, didn't we know each other in a previous life, are you the Messiah, Marilyn Monroe is still alive and living in sin with James Dean in Madison, Indiana, will you marry me, are you my long-lost brother, *Star Trek* is greater than *Hamlet,* you are a Communist, how many angels can dance on the head of a pin or the head of Ronald Reagan, whichever comes first and is smaller. You know the kind.

From time to time I will pass among you, my people. I go out into the land frequently on lecture engagements, and I expect many of you to query me about whatever column has most recently come before your bright little eyes. Make yourselves known to me, but be polite. I have this cranky manner when rudeness manifests itself.

I'd thought perhaps I'd open my first column with a conversation I had with Ridley Scott, the director of *Alien* and *The Duellists,* when he came to visit a few months back; but something he said, about the time being ripe for a John Ford of science fiction films, has stuck in my mind. And I think I'll go into that theory in depth next time.

Or maybe I'll conduct the first interview with Marilyn Monroe and James Dean, direct from Madison, Indiana.

And if you conceive of this opening installment of the column as being terribly mild and polite, reassure yourself that it is only misdirection. From here on in, kiddo, the gloves are off. And so are we. Next time we set fire to the Welcome Wagon.

**INSTALLMENT 2:** 5 May 80
(published 22 July 80
in *Future Life* #21
cover-dated September)

I despise writing obituaries. Nor had I intended this second outing to be any such thing: I had intended to talk about Ridley Scott and an interesting conversation we had a few months ago.

But George Pal dropped dead on Friday, May 2nd; and in the torrents of sorrow that wash over me at his passing I find myself unaccountably, against my will, clinging to a sharp, black rock of bitterness that prevents me from being swept over the falls and down the cascade of maudlin sentiments certain to present itself.

If you never met George, you are the poorer for it. He was a dear man. Beyond his unquestioned vision and expertise in matters cinematic, he had a genuine love and understanding of fantasy and science fiction at the highest levels. He was kind, he was gentle, he was conscientious; he was a *gentleman.* A word fallen either into ill-repute or into ridicule: the former because duplicitous thugs like Nixon or David Begelman have hidden behind the term, using it as misdirection while they carried on their criminal activities; the latter because it bespeaks a mien, a sense of personal integrity that doesn't sit well with an encroaching cultural scene festooned with boobs who pierce their earlobes with safety pins and consider more than one exposure to bathwater every fortnight a social gaffe.

And it is George Pal's unrequited devotion to gentlemanliness, to *personal integrity,* that causes the bile of bitterness to rise up in me as I contemplate his death by heart attack at the age of seventy-two.

Because for the last decade and a half, Hollywood let him languish in outer darkness.

That obsidian rock of bitterness will not allow me to weep the fat crocodile tears currently sweeping through the often-linked worlds of science fiction and motion pictures. Now that he's gone, it's warming and succoring to remember dear old George and how much he contributed to the melding of sf and movies. It's charmingly hypocritical but nonetheless guilt-assuaging to talk about *Destination Moon* and *War of the Worlds* and *The Time Machine,* his box office triumphs, while ignoring the fact that it was seven years between the successful *The Power* (1967) and the even more commercially disastrous failure of *Doc Savage, Man of Bronze* (1974). Seven years during which, in the vernacular, dear sweet old George couldn't get arrested in this town.

15

Seven years of hustling, of trying to put together a deal, of taking ideas from studio to studio, trying to "blue-sky" them so he could get development money. Seven years trying to do what he loved to do...make movies.

And six years after the failure of *Doc Savage*, George was still hustling like a newcomer; having to talk sweetly to the much-vaunted "baby moguls" one-fourth his age and one-millionth his talent; having to eat the corporate rudeness and offhanded treatment; having to make appointments to visit these ex-agents, ex-time salesmen, ex-pr men, ex-vacuum cleaner salesmen who have jumped up into executive status; having to smile when the appointments were broken because something "more important" had come up to turn the executives' attention, usually to the latest "hot" director or producer; having to smile when not even the executive but the executive's secretary called to say, "Mr. Mogul will have to cancel his meeting with you next Thursday, Mr. Pal. We'll call you when another, later date opens up." Having to smile and bear the thousand insolences of the untalented, the dull and the meretricious: simply because they were the conduits to the development deals.

God, the ugly irony of it! That the one man who should have most benefited from the current boom in science fiction films became the man most excluded. The man who took the risks thirty years before the conservative second-raters began gorging themselves at the troughs was the man they chose to ignore to the point of total dismissal.

How it must have pained him these last fifteen years. How his soul must have cried out—not for victory, or triumph, or great wealth—simply for the *chance*. For a decently financed opportunity to get in there and create something fantastic with the new technology, the liberality of subject matter, the budgets that produced for twice the money, half what *he* had done on a shoestring.

And I sit here three days after learning of George's death, choking on black hatred and rancor at an industry too quick to dismiss its pioneers, too busy to be kind, too self-involved with its little rodent games of power and prize to honor with another chance those who were there before it was trendy. And here I sit with guilt, because I was in a position to help him...and I didn't go all the way.

I cannot hide from the nasty truth that I am one with those of whom it can be said dealt him "more honoured in the breach than the observance." There is a coppery taste of self-hate in my mouth as I cling to the black rock.

One with the approximately 140 others who attended the 1976 Nebula Awards banquet of the Science Fiction Writers of America at the Century Plaza Hotel in Los Angeles, I too stood and cheered, leaped to my feet and applauded as George Pal was given a special plaque by David Gerrold in behalf of the SFWA; a chunk of wood and a

16

chunk of metal to honor George's achievements in film that predated the birth of the Nebulas. It was easy to stand and cheer, and it seemed to make everything okay.

But it was merely another manifestation of the ways in which we liberalize our responsibilities to those who seek no honors but ask only for the chance to *produce*, to be allowed to work at their craft. It was eyewash, no matter how sincerely tendered. Because George was still beating the pavement trying to get a project on the wing.

And when he began calling late in July of 1979, asking me to come in on a project to do an updated version of *When Worlds Collide*, I thought only of the book I was writing, of the film I had just contracted to script, of all the deadlines I'd missed and the scarcity of time in any given day.

But he persisted. He honored me in the highest fashion by wanting to work with me. And finally I said I would try to help him get a deal going. Big man proffering largesse.

He had Universal interested. A young executive named Peter Saphier had expressed interest. I agreed to have a meeting with George and Saphier, but I said it was twenty-eight years since the original film, times and the way we look at films had changed, and to make simply an updated version of the old Wylie–Balmer book would be to stalk once again across terrain already scorched by *schlock-meisters* like Irwin Allen. I suggested he get a copy of J. T. McIntosh's excellent 1954 disaster novel, ONE IN THREE HUNDRED, which I felt could be combined to salutary effect with *When Worlds Collide* to humanize and make more contemporarily relevant, to make more suspenseful, the skeleton plot of the original.

George found an old Ace paperback of the book, read it, and called me to say he thought it was a terrific conception. We had our meeting at Universal's Black Tower on Friday, August 3rd, 1979. And I pitched the combined concept to Saphier. He seemed interested.

He took the two books and said he'd read them, and then we would meet again. When we left Universal together, George was like a kid again. He was up, he was ebullient, he saw a chance emerging. And I dashed his hopes by saying that I was so tied up with commitments that I wouldn't be free for perhaps a year. He smiled. Gentleman to the end, he smiled and said, well, we'll see...maybe you'll get finished sooner than you think. I smiled back, but I knew it couldn't be. But I didn't want to hurt him. But I didn't want to feel guilty. So I smiled and said, maybe, we'll see.

On Tuesday, August 28th George and I met Saphier for lunch at Musso & Frank's Grill in Hollywood. The Universal executive—a better man than I because he was willing to give George the *chance*—said he would be willing to enter into a step-deal of development. But only if I'd be part of the package.

George looked at me, oh God I'll never forget that look, and I think in that instant I saw his future in his eyes. And I didn't say okay I'll do it. I said I was up to my ass in work and was sinking fast and I didn't think I'd be free for six months or a year. And the smile held on George's dear face, but the light died a little.

It never came to be.

We never made the deal.

Universal thought of him as an old man, past his prime, not one of the new wave of hotshot director/producers. He was an ancient stone unfit for splendid new monuments like *Jaws II* or *1941* or *Meteor*.

George Pal died on Friday, May 2nd with his integrity intact, with a half dozen projects proposed and none in work.

He called me on the evening of April 28th, four days after the jury in Federal District Court delivered up its judgment in favor of Ben Bova and me to the tune of $337,000—final vindication for me in my four-year battle to prove plagiarism on the part of ABC-TV and Paramount Pictures and a man named Terry Keegan. He called to congratulate me, to tell me how pleased he was that we'd won. His suit against Paramount over *The Time Machine* ripoff was still dragging on. He called, because he was a friend and a gentleman, to say he was proud of me, that I'd struck a blow for writers everywhere and he held me in esteem.

I didn't take the call. I was having dinner with friends and my assistant, Marty Clark, took the call. "Be very kind and gentle to him," I said. "He's a dear man and a friend."

But I didn't speak to him.

And four days later he was dead.

Seventy-two years old, a gentle man with talent to spare right up till the end, who was shunted aside by those who could have cared a little more.

And I cling to this black rock of self-loathing and detestation of the industry in which I serve my time, and I'm not entitled to cry for the loss of George Pal.

But you are. Because you've lost more than you know. As they say, usually with as much guilt as I say it, his like will never be seen again.

**INSTALLMENT 3:** 9 June 80
(published 2 September 80
in *Future Life* #22
cover-dated November)

# Interim Memo:

In this column, I wrote "The going rate for a sixty-minute teleplay these days is $9972 with a raise expected after the upcoming Writers Guild contract negotiations later this year." That information is four years old. We had a strike, we lost some things and we gained some things; and the going rate is higher as this book is published. Initial compensation (that is, not counting subsequent residuals for reruns) for a sixty-minute teleplay in the categories of drama or comedy, for either network primetime or pay-tv, is $14,318. And they *still* bust your back and make your life a living hell. One should remember that there are *some* filthy jobs for which *no* amount of money can compensate. Not that it'll put off by even thirty seconds those of you all too willing to fling yourselves under the behemoth wheels of tv writing. (Have you ever noticed how anxious some people are to sell their souls, and would do it if only there were buyers?)

If this guy was a Director, then I was the reincarnation of Charles Dickens. It was years ago, and he's probably still feeping around in the television graveyard sucking the marrow out of scripts like some hideous Lovecraftian creation, a nameless horror of the coaxial wasteland, so I won't name him.

Wouldn't matter, anyhow. You'd say *who?*

Which anonymity is probably the most benign justice that could be meted out to a man of such impoverished talent. There were moments, however, when he was allegedly directing a script I'd written, during which I would have appealed to the Revolutionary Council to have his hands or his viewfinder loupe lopped off in the time-honored manner of Islamic justice.

He had raised hell with the producers of the series because I'd written such an exhaustive teleplay: all the camera angles and specific shots detailed for the cinematographer.

But that's the way I work. Always have, since I got to Hollywood in 1962. Never felt that a scenarist was doing the job properly unless the script was written *visually*; and that always meant to me the process of *visualizing* what the camera would see. The process was effectuated by my actually closing my eyes and running the movie in my mind. Then I'd open my eyes and describe in cinematic terminology what I'd seen in the viewing room of my mind.

But the price one commands in this town, whether writer, actor or director, is linked with how much clout one can summon up; and for years now the directors have used the myth of the *auteur* theory as their most powerful negotiating tool. The theory, for those who have been living in a sensory deprivation tank for the last two decades, is one propagated first by the *nouvelle vague* French directors, post-1959. Stripped of superfluous rationalizations, the theory says that the director is the *author* of the film, on the basis of his or her "personal style" brought to bear on the material.

The material, you must understand, is how the original conception, whether novel or short story or original screenplay, is depersonalized in directorial euphemism. Sometimes the dream of the writer is referred to as the "property." (A writer of my acquaintance once stood up at a seminar where a producer was blithely talking

21

about "properties" and denounced him as a fatuous martinet, advising him that she wrote *screenplays* and *stories* and an occasional *novel*. She did not write "properties." "Properties," she snarled, "are empty lots in the San Fernando Valley or condominiums in Malibu! I don't write those!")

But pollution of the language, employed in the service of those building clout translatable into percentages of gross profits (what we out here call "points" in a deal), is only one of the meretricious expedients used by directors to assume control of a project, to establish the *auteur* clout, to put his or her personal stamp on the creation of a writer.

Most of you actually go for that okeydoke.

Like studio executives and producers in Hollywood, you actually believe the credit line preceding the title of a movie that proclaims it A FILM BY PETER BOGDANOVICH or A FILM BY HAL ASHBY. The Writers Guild has been fighting that form of screen credit for years. They are not films *by* Bogdanovich or Ashby (to select just a pair of obvious miscreants in this respect); they are films *directed* by Bogdanovich or Ashby. Bogdanovich did not write *Paper Moon*, Alvin Sargent did, from a novel by Joe David Brown titled ADDIE PRAY. Hal Ashby didn't write *Harold and Maude*, Colin Higgins did.

But seldom does an audience remember the actual author of a film—and how many of you can remember the name of the writer of a television segment you enjoyed just last night? That serves the end of reducing the writers' creative and economic clout in Hollywood; and it always has. Writers, for the most part, are chattel in the film/tv industry. They have no more say over what happens to a script they've written than a prisoner in Raiford State has over the license plates he stamps out every day.

While that has traditionally been the invidious nature of the industry, for the last twenty years it has been insufferable for writers who give a damn about what they write. (The hacks, the "creative typists" who fill most of those empty hours of primetime, don't give a hoot. The going rate for a sixty-minute teleplay these days is $9972.00 with a raise expected after the upcoming Writers Guild contract negotiations later this year. Good or bad, inspired or donkeywork, *that's* the rate.)

Insufferable because of the *auteur* theory and the considerable clout directors now possess. We're not discussing here those six directors worldwide who are the best, the six whose individual voices—whether you like their films or not—set them apart from all other directors who are merely craftspersons of greater or lesser ability...from, let us say, Spielberg and Walter Hill and Ridley Scott at the pinnacle to, again let us say just as a rule of thumb, Eliot Silverstein, Otto Preminger and Irwin Allen in the pits...but *all* directors have that clout by implication. The myth has become the

22

reality.

Studio heads who are, for the most part (as Pauline Kael has termed them) businessmen running an art, are the most insecure and superstitious lot one could ever meet. They have no idea whom they can trust because they simply do not understand the creative act; and since they cannot read a script—they have assistants read them and prepare one-paragraph synopses—they fear and distrust writers. Treating writers as equals, listening to their ideas of how a film should be made, is about as salutary an idea to a studio executive as taking a ball peen hammer to every mirror in the house.

But directors are the *auteurs*, they believe that. And directors can be wonderful salesmen. They come in with all that freighting of *auteur* myth going for them, and they simply dynamite the producers or execs into believing that *they* have the vision. That *they* know just how to revise and reshape and mold and twist and disembowel the script created by a single intellect, to make it a fifty-million grosser.

We're not talking about the six real directors in the world; we're talking about guys so lame they cannot direct themselves to the toilet on the sound stage.

Like the guy who was directing that script of mine years ago, who complained about how fully written it was.

So he conned the producers into believing that he was an *auteur*, this dreary wimp, and he established territorial imperative, and he ignored the shots that might have given the show some vestige of originality, and he restaged most of the shots so they didn't work, and the segment looked like an outtake from *The Terror of Tiny Town*.

But here's the part that convulsed me.

The story took place in 1888, in the American West. I had extrapolated history of the period and come up with the not implausible concept that Jack the Ripper, having ceased his rampage of slaughter against the whores of London's Spitalfields, had fled the country on an immigrant packet and, working his way westward in America, had finally come to the Cherokee Strip where the same conditions of poverty and libertine living that had prevailed in Whitechapel manifested themselves. And his psychopathic nature reasserted itself, and he started killing the prostitutes who filled the nautch houses lining the Cimarron City staging area where thousands waited for the opening of the Strip so they could stake land claims.

So in an early sequence of the script, the Ripper is stalking a woman down the night-shrouded streets of Cimarron City; and I'd written it in ways that would heighten the terror by having it shot strictly in misdirection: in windows, in the eyes of a night owl on a building, in pools of water.

But the *auteur* gave all that a pass. He shot the usual cliché sequence with closeups on running feet, using an Arriflex, a hand-held camera.

23

But here's the part that convulsed me.

Picture it in your skull, if you will: the woman's feet running down the wooden sidewalks of Cimarron City...*fast!* A goddam blur of speeding tootsies. What I'm talkin' here is *mondo speedo,* gang! Cut to the feet of a man in tailored black pants, a Gladstone bag dangling from his hand so it's in the shot. Slow. Veeeery slow. A stalking, measured pace; the stealthy walk of the mad killer. But slow. Veeeery slow.

And it speeds up. The woman goes faster, faster, faster, running like a bat out of hell. But the Ripper keeps on stalking her slowly, slowly, veeeeery slowly.

And he catches her.

Don't ask me how. If we could judge by the real world, anyone running as fast as that woman was running would have been not only out of the town, but out of that *time-zone* before a guy pacing along that slowly could catch her.

But he caught her. Don't ask me how.

So what is all of this about directors in aid of?

Well, directors are much on my mind these days. Prominently so, since I caught the press screening of *The Empire Strikes Back* in London on May 19th. I was on a breather in England and France—while the attorneys settled the lawsuit against ABC-TV and Paramount Pictures about which you've read in *Time* magazine—and finishing up a new novel; and Craig Miller, who was then with Lucasfilm, set it up for me to see the press screening at the Dominion Theatre in Tottenham Court Road.

(And just to set at ease all you incipient werewolves out there, poised to spring at my jugular, though I still maintain that *Star Wars* had all the smarts of a matzoh ball, I was more than pleasantly surprised at *Empire*. In fact, not to put too fine a pernt on it, kids, I thought it was a helluva piece of filmmaking. Enjoyed it enormously. Even said so to Mark Hamill who, if you recall an interview he gave last year, was not terribly happy about my *Star Wars* remarks. Nice chap, actually. We had a cheery conversation. The war may be over, friends.)

And I don't think that it was because I saw the film in London, a town I dearly love, that the film impressed me so much. I think it's a superlative job because of the director, Irvin Kershner. And I don't think Kersh did a creatively sensitive job of expanding the concept and the content just because he's the director Warner Bros. is trying to sign to direct my script of Asimov's I, ROBOT. Would I be that shallow, come on!

To tell the truth, I had nothing but feelings of utter trepidation when I first learned that Kershner wanted in on the *I, Robot* project.

Back in 1961 when I first paid attention to Kershner's work, on a film called *The Hoodlum Priest,* I thought he was a director to watch.

Felt that even more strongly after seeing a film he directed in Canada with the late Robert Shaw called *The Luck of Ginger Coffey,* which was a superb piece of cinema. But as the years passed and Kersh added stinkers like *Up the Sandbox, S.P.Y.S., The Return of a Man Called Horse* and the despicable *Eyes of Laura Mars* to his *oeuvre,* I came to think of him as a man who had done as much as he could, a man who would never hit the first rank of craftsmen.

Then one director after another balked at the enormity of the project that *I, Robot* presented. Ridley Scott came to see me and wanted me to do the rewrite on *Dune* and I said no thankyou, but offered him a look at *I, Robot* and he took it away with him and decided no. I wanted Carroll Ballard—director of *The Black Stallion,* an astonishing piece of work—but he was off in Italy and Switzerland and, though we talked long distance about it, and he finally saw the script, he said no to it, also.

Then Eddie Lewis, the producer of the film, told me Irv Kershner had read my script and loved it and wanted to direct the film. And I panicked. Oh, God, no, I thought. Not the guy who directed *The Eyes of Laura Mars,* one of the most evil films of all time. Oh, help!

But Kershner was the only director who wanted me back on the project. Warner Bros. was less than happy with me, for reasons that may well have been valid. Or might not. It's late in the day and I'm not up to going into all *that.*

So everybody said, "Kersh wants you back on this film. Go see what he did with *The Empire.* You'll be amazed, it's so good he's the hottest director in the business." And I swallowed hard because I'd *hated Star Wars* and I couldn't see *anyone,* not even one of the six I mentioned earlier, doing enough with that sophomoric story to convince me I should be happy about someone *potschky'*ing with my beloved script, which had taken a year of my life to write. But Eddie Lewis said stop being a *schmuck* and go see the film, and Craig set it up in London for me, and I came out of the theater with a wide grin on my elfin countenance.

And when Kersh called me and said let's get together and talk about *I, Robot* I was jubilant. And we did, and we did, and last week *Variety* and *The Hollywood Reporter* had a page one announcement that Warner Bros. had signed Irvin Kershner for the *I, Robot* project based on Harlan Ellison's screenplay and it looks like that might even be a reasonably accurate statement of how things are—even though we all know out here that the "trades" as we call them usually run hype and idle wish-fulfillment.

So I'm thinking about directors these days. I'm thinking about Ridley Scott, who has made two films that knocked me out; and I'm thinking about that lame who directed my Jack the Ripper script years ago; and I'm thinking about how the promise I saw in Kersh's first films has suddenly, after a bleak interregnum, burgeoned anew;

25

and about how I may, after all these dreary years of waiting for my scripts to be done decently, have finally lucked out.

Because Irv Kershner talked to me not as if I was a beanfield peon, a scribbling toady with no stake in the creation of a beautiful thing that would enrich and uplift, a hack who would alter anything just to get the film made. He talked to me like a man who disavows the *auteur* theory.

Which is why I'm feeling pretty damned good today.

And just by way of closing, I'll let you have that list of the six directors in the world. I don't want any arguments about it. Don't bother writing me saying I left out this one or that one, or how could I include such-and-such whose films you don't understand. Just take the list and remember I'm never wrong, and shut up.

And they are: Kurosawa, Altman, Coppola, Resnais, Buñuel, Kubrick, and Fellini.

What's that?

That's *seven*, not six?

Well, jeezus, nobody's perfect!

**INSTALLMENT 4:** 20 July 80
(published 21 October 80
in *Future Life* #23
cover-dated December)

# 4: 20 July 80

It was one of those weeks, gang. Finished the new novel; had a lady visit from England who refused to speak, so after three days of catalepsy I asked her to give Freddie Laker some return business and she went away (Ms. Marty Clark, my adroit and highly efficient Executive Secretary, opined that the Limey Lady was in awe of me and was thus rendered *tabula rasa*, or more precisely, *tace*; I have come to an irrevocable decision about that cop-out; for years I've heard disingenuous excuses for obdurate silence—shyness, didn't know the people everyone was discussing, wasn't familiar with the subject matter, felt uncomfortable in such a large crowd, felt uncomfortable in such a small, intimate crowd, in awe; have heard all those bullshit rationalizations and have come to the irrevocable conclusion that I'm not going to feel sorry for them mutes no more; not going to "try and draw them out," not going to "try and pull them into the conversation," not going to feel guilty or even the tiniest responsible for them; it's *their* problem and it's a kind of selfishness and attention-seeking even worse than that practiced by those of us commonly referred to politely as "high verbals" or impolitely as "loudmouths"; just ain't gonna slow down or cripple the goodtime talk with bright friends and snappy strangers to *schlep* some semi-narcoleptic self-server into a conversation clearly too fast and complex for him/her to dog-paddle through; piss on'm. . . and the snake they slithered in on); and I got knocked off the *I, Robot* movie project again. Even before I was rehired. Kershner told Warner Bros. he wouldn't direct the film without me and they told him okay, take a hike; their words were (and this is an approximation, but veddy veddy close by reliable report), "We'll close down the studio before we rehire Ellison."

So when I got the word, I told the producer, Eddie Lewis, and Kershner, go ahead and do it with another writer whom they'll approve. It doesn't upset me, oddly enough. I wrote the hell out of that script—took me a year to do it. They tried other writers once before. . .after I refused to do the nitwit revisions suggested by Warners. Three subsequent passes through the typewriters of three other writers, and each one, by report, was worse than the revision that preceded it. So they came back to me. Noise of 5'5" Jewish writer chortling in glee.

But I got the head of the studio pissed at me; had this alleged "story conference" with him a year or two ago, and discovered in the middle of the meeting that he hadn't even read the screenplay he was advising me how to rewrite. Called him on it, proved to my satisfaction that all he was doing was spitting up bits and pieces of a synopsis one of his readers had given him; and he fumfuh'ed and harrumph'd and told me what a busy man he was; how he didn't have time for little pisher problems such as reading the screenplay it had taken another human being a year to write, on a project his corporation was contemplating backing to the tune of forty million dollars; and *I* responded that not only wasn't he functioning in any creative capacity but he wasn't even being fiscally responsible; also suggested he had the intellectual and cranial capacity of an artichoke.

Think I pissed him off.

So this week Kersh and Eddie will have a group of (how shall I put this to avoid the redolence of blacklist?) more or less "acceptable" writers presented to them; and they'll pick some dreg who'll change the names in my script and try to think his/her way around the deranged inventiveness in my screenplay; and it'll be muddled up again; and when they've wasted another batch of thousandbuck months they'll either shitcan the project as being "unworkable'" or come back to me once more. If the latter, we can assume a certain sense of utter desperation. That, or more pleasant concept, the executive in question will have been sent back to the mailroom of the showbiz agency from which he slithered lo these many moons ago.

Ho-hum.

And maybe Asimov's I, ROBOT will get made; and maybe it won't. As for me own widdle self, gang, I stand quietly up here on Elitist Mountain watching the clash by night of ignorant armies, as Matthew Arnold phrased it. (If the allusion escapes you, go look up "Dover Beach.")

All of which brings me around by the side portal to the more-or-less topic of this issue's screed, which is: my readers.

You see, I'm told that the executive in question isn't ticked off at me *just* because I compared his ratiocinating abilities with those of a vegetable. He is even *more* mightily hacked at letters sent to him by "fans" to whom I appealed at an sf convention several years ago, to write *polite* letters to Warners suggesting they not make the robots in Asimov's story-cycle cute little R2D2s. Should have known better.

The letters—carbons of which I've seen—frequently began with such encomia as "Dear Asshole" or "Respected Tertiary Syphilis Victim." And they spiraled down into snotty arrogance and idle threats from that already subterranean level.

One should *never* ask sf fans to attempt a little Machiavellian manipulation. They have all the subtlety of an acrobat in a polio ward.

30

Suffice to say, added to my own lack of tact, it suitably bent the executive in question, and his entire staff, so far out of shape that steaming them for a week wouldn't have put the puff back in their egos.

Bringing me to observations of the pragmatic realities of having a readership like some of you out there. (No, not you, kiddo, and not you, sweetie, *you're* okay; this is only intended for the escapees from the chipmunk factory.)

As an artist who (in the words of Dame Margot Fonteyn) doesn't take himself very seriously but takes the *work* very very seriously, I spend most of my waking hours writing stories and books and movies that I hope will have some lasting import, work that I slave over and put most of my daily energy into. Posterity stuff, know what I mean? The real goods. The forms I use and the styles I adopt are changing; approach is malleable, it mutates. I seek to produce a variety of textures and velocities, densities and rhythms of movement. I wish to sink no roots but rather to displace air, to create a sense of something abundant and prodigious having passed.

Imagine my consternation when I go out in the world—dressed even as you, I pass among my people, unseen and unheard yet I see and hear and remember—five bucks to the first reader who spots the cinematic source of that line—and meet my readers.

Jeezus, it is to chill the blood.

The word *weird* ennobles some of you.

Look: I realize a lot of you have problems...it has not escaped my notice that many of you have French Fried your brains sitting in front of the Sony...life is tough, I got that, honest to God I *got* that...the specter of Reagan and fighting for Dat Ole Debbil Crude in Iran or Kuwait or South Philly rises up in the night to make us whoopee our Hydroxes...few of us will come through the sexual revolution unscarred, if not emotionally then certainly with herpes simplex... your father is going through menopause, your mother did a weekend seminar in est and she's driving you buggy with psychobabble, your sister wants to be a Clayton chassis dynamometer technician and your brother hangs around the meat rack...the new Heinlein ain't terrific and the new Bester is an old short story pumped full of air and when the hell is Poul Anderson going to get back on track and is Spinrad becoming a crypto-reactionary and how much more of this obscure twaddle by Ellison can we stomach...I know it's tough, folks, and we have about as much chance of bolting down our sanity as the ghost of Django Reinhardt trapped at a Billy Idol recording session...but WHY ARE YOU SO GODDAM WEIRD!?!

Honest to Skippy, I'm not saying this to rile you. Believe me, in my squishy little heart of hearts I have nothing but respect and admiration and unquenchable love for every last screwloosed one of you. Even the one who calls from New York three times a day and then hangs up without saying anything. Even the one who sends me drawings in magic marker that I couldn't tell top from bottom if she didn't sign them with a signature that dwarfs the art. Even the one who writes me long poems in Esperanto, which I don't understand, without return postage. Even the one who teaches college in Pennsylvania and spends his off-hours making up the most incredible lies about my private life, based on old vaudeville routines. Even the one who named her firstborn after me. Even the one who found out I've been looking for a Dell Book (not a Big Little Book, a similar species published by Dell in the 40's) titled FLASH GORDON AND THE EMPEROR OF MONGO for about ten years and can't get my hands on one, who sends me hand-drawn pictures of Flash performing hideous obscenities on Dale Arden. Even the one who sends me religious tracts that assure me I'm going to Hell. Even the one who wants to buy my used Jockey shorts. Even the one who shows up at every autograph party in the Southern California area to ask me why I hate Barbra Streisand's voice. Even the one who swears I knocked her up last year even though I had the vasectomy *five* years ago. Even the one with the bird calls; the one with the right blue eye and the left green eye; the one who wants to pay me to let her read tarot cards over me; the one with a voice that could stun a police dog; the one who asks me why I don't stop the draft registration. . .the one. . .the one. . .the one who. . .I stagger, I falter, I fall in the traces. . . .

I love you all. May Yog-Sothoth hit me with a bolt of lightning in the pancreas if I'm not strictly wild about the whole slobbering, warbling pack of you.

Nonetheless, it *is* a bit disconcerting to get out there and meet all of you. And when some of you come to visit, unannounced and imprudently, sure I have the doorknobs cauterized. But does that dismay me. Not on your autographed Luke Skywalker hologram. Steadfast, thass me.

But just to make it a little easier for those of us you seem to consider great gurus, here are some tips of etiquette. How to talk like a writer. Things not to say. (I glean these tips after consultation with others of my genus who have begun to twitch prematurely: Frank Herbert, Poul Anderson, Larry Niven, Bob Heinlein, Mary Wollstonecraft Shelley, Ambrose Bierce, George R. R. Martin, Ursula K. Le Guin, Bob Silverberg and Stephen Donaldson. Jack Vance still refuses to speak to me because I voted against Goldwater.)

First tip: never say to a writer, "You know, I've looked in every bookstore in the state of Washington, and I can't find one single copy of any title you've written. Do you know they're not distributing your stuff, huh, did you know that?"

Yes, you insensitive lump of yak dung, I know it. And so does every *other* writer. We are as closely aware of where and how our books sell as you are of how much cash you have in your funny little change-purse. It is a constant anguish with which we suffer. There are something like 500–700 new paperback titles issued every month. Take your average paperback "spinner" rack in, say, a 7-Eleven. It has, what, forty, fifty pockets? Say fifty pockets. That means only fifty titles get full cover display. Anything behind that facing book is a lost book. And so if a writer is lucky s/he will get full-face display in one of those pockets above knee-level where the few remaining members of the reading public can see it...for about seven days. Then comes the new batch of titles, the writer's book is pushed to the back, and ten days later it's gone off the rack entirely.

Which means that unless one has written something of classic stature such as THE SECAUCUS NEW JERSEY FAT DOCTORS' DIET or JACKIE O'S SECRET SEX LIFE or a smash bestseller such as the latest plastic offering from Judith Krantz, Sidney Sheldon, Harold Robbins, Rod McKuen, Richard Brautigan or one of those pseudonymous lady writers with three names who prate endlessly of throbbing bosoms and bold highwaymen, you are in the toilet within two weeks. Even a brick as thick as the fan who tells a writer his/her books can't be found, should know that this means distribution kills *all* of us, no matter how well-known or unknown, no matter how talented or inept, no matter how beautifully-packaged or uglified. And we spend several hours each week on the phone to our publishers, demanding information or explanation—why ain't the books out there?

So don't do that to us. If you want to indicate your love for what we write, then lie to us: Tell us you were in the B. Dalton or the Waldenbooks flagship store and they had three huge stacks of our current title, right there beside the cash register at point-of-sale, and people were kicking shins to get at the copies before stock ran out.

On the other hand, if you *want* to annoy us, go ahead and tell us we can't be found anywhere. However, having been warned, and knowing that you're doing it to bug us, the shins likely to be kicked are thine own.

Second Tip: don't intrude your personal needs or problems into the lives of writers whose work you admire. That means, when you write a letter, don't babble on for three pages about how you simply *adore* every word we've written and how you're our *biggest* fan (my biggest fan weighs four hundred plus pounds; the only thing that beats him is the Goodyear Blimp); don't waste your time and ours telling us how we've changed your life; don't preamble a simple request with a tearjerking story of how you can't get an A in your CompLit course if we don't answer the 77 essay questions you've posed in the accompanying questionnaire; don't ask us to read your stories, novels, screenplays, poems, essays, reviews, interviews or idle ruminations for comment; don't send us baked goods by fourth class, they're always maggot-ridden by the time the Snail Mail gets the crap to us; don't ask us to help you get into publishing, writing, the movies or the plumbing industry; and for God's sake don't ask us to reply even though you *know* we're up to our *tush*es in work but any kind of hello how are you will suffice (if we answered all the dumb mail we get, we'd never be able to write the stories you liked in the first place that made us worthy of your notice).

In short, keep it short and simple, and try to do for yourself all the things you want us to do. Self-reliance will give you regular bowel movements. Most of us have neither the time nor the facilities nor the inclination to save your lives, remove you from the clutches of your rotten parents who do not understand why you spend all your time making models of Darth Vader and Close Encounters motherships, give you summer jobs working in our offices, forward your illiterate manuscripts to agents or publishers who would think we were nuts if we bothered them with amateur efforts, meet you for a cup of coffee or a quick roll in the hay, or sign autographed photos which *we're* supposed to provide. And for God's sake stop asking us where you can buy our books. That's why the Sentient Universe created bookstores, newsstands, and a reference work called BOOKS IN PRINT.

Third Tip: brush your teeth.

Oh, come on, now, don't get all guppy-faced on me. None of the other writers will tell you this; they're too polite. Most sf writers are destitute, and they don't want to offend their readers. With me it's a different matter; I'm loaded, so I can tell you the truth.

And the truth is that some of you who come up to us at conventions, lectures, lunchrooms where we're trying to eat a nice chopped liver on corn rye w/Dr. Brown's Cream Soda, autograph parties, etcetera...well, some of you smell like the butcher's mallet after a hard day bashing in horses' brains.

I realize it's bourgeois to suggest that maybe there are a few body odors, such as those produced by dropped-dead bacteria or as a result of eating human flesh, that might be less than salutary. I appreciate your need to remain "natural" by avoiding underarm deodorant, Bounce in your wash, aftershave lotion, Dr. Scholl's foot fungus powder, Handi-Wipes for your baby bottom and suchlike... natural is naturally best...particularly if you're eating Pringles, McDonald Toadburgers, Diet Pepsi and chemically-augmented yogurt. Nonetheless, I would be less than candid were I not to confess that when some of you lurch up and stick your gaping pudding-troughs at us, all rotted fangs and green ichor, it fwankwy make me wanna womit.

Fourth Tip: stop reading our personal lives into our stories. Hate to shock your nervous system, but the Artist is not the Art. Just because Ted Sturgeon once wrote a story about homosexual aliens does not mean he is necessarily gay or alien. Just because Bob Bloch— one of the gentlest men who ever lived—wrote PSYCHO is no touchstone to a perception that he is secretly a deranged mass-murderer.

Just because I write stories filled with senseless violence, incredible brutality, endless debasement of human beings and twisted, diseased, horrific concepts of sexual atrocities does not mean I gave to the March of Dimes last Christmas. On the other hand, it might.

The point is, kiddo chums, we are *interpreters* of reality; not recorders of same. Journalists do that. We simply take bits and pieces from here and there and reorder them. That means we deal with the basic materials of the human condition, and that which looks interesting to us gets into the stories. Writers are also, as Mario Vargas Llosa has said, exorcists of their own demons. So *some of us* is in there. But it ain't one-for-one. Trust me.

And on that uplifting note, I'll take my leave this time, reassuring you (as I whistle down the walk) that this has been something of a preamble to the column-after-next, which will be my sixth installment. Because, as promised, every sixth column will be responses to as many of the warm, wonderful, intelligent postcards you've sent as I can stomach, er, as I have room for.

Just to keep us in touch. Usually, I wouldn't touch some of you with a leper's claw. But then, I'm seldom invited back to the same house for dinner, so who's to say.

**INSTALLMENT 5:** 8 September 80
(published 9 December 80
in *Future Life* #24
cover-dated February 81)

# INTERIM MEMO:

In this column I suggested readers write to me for a copy of an Asimov essay on anti-intellectualism and ignorance that had appeared in *Newsweek*. It was one of my public service gestures in aid of the commonweal. Hundreds of readers wrote me for the piece, and like a good guy I sent them along. The date of expiration has passed for that offer. Also on the Ovaltine Little Orphan Annie Shake-Up Mug. And the End of the World Life-After-Death Placemat and Bidet Set. Don't write me for none of that there product, folks. (And that goes for the twit who never gets the word. Would one of you *please* slap him across the back of the head and wake him?) Go look up the proper issue of *Newsweek*, or go buy one of Isaac's essay collections that includes that piece. Or ask Jimmy Swaggart or Jerry Falwell for a copy. They've got anti-intellectualism and ignorance down pat.

Every now and then, when I'm confronted with one of the seemingly endless manifestations of obscurantism and institutionalized superstition that pass for "common knowledge" in our ever-increasingly complex world, I grow despondent and find myself thinking unworthy thoughts about the wad that we call the Human Race.

I find myself shrugging and saying (inwardly), well, hell, we've had our shot, now let the cockroaches take a whack at it. God knows they've been around a lot longer than we have. So what if they haven't produced the orthopterous version of *Hamlet*, or invented the aerosol spray; neither did the saurians and they maintained occupancy for 130,000,000 years, give or take a wild weekend. Maybe, like the dolphins, cockroach art and society function on levels non-interpretable by limited human minds.

The word *limited* persists in these reflections when I lay out the cards of contemplation and consider how many people believe in irrationalities like alien spaceships that kidnap Georgia rednecks just to tell them Jesus Saves; that fluoridation of city drinking water is a Communist plot to pollute our precious bodily fluids; that skyscrapers "sway" in the wind as much as eight feet; that Shakespeare's 16th century rival, Anthony Munday, wrote THE BOOKE OF SIR THOMAS MORE rather than The Bard; that great and original art can be created while the artist is doped out of his brain on Quaalude; that Ernest Angley, Oral Roberts, Jimmy Swaggart or any of the other members of television's God Squad can cure cancer or even a hangnail through Divine Intervention; that jogging for anyone over the age of thirty-five will produce any systemic health benefit except a tragic and painful osteomyelitis; that the actors on the soaps are actually real and living those lives of endless *sturm und drang*; that Atlantis still exists in a sub-oceanic cul-de-sac waiting to be discovered; that est or Self-Realization or Scientology or any of its whacky clones can do anything more for you than separate you from large sums of money; that Nobel prize-winning physicist William Bradford Shockley's naive and simplistic (but nonetheless mischievous and racist) theory of dysgenics, "proving" blacks are inferior to whites, is any less wrongheaded and damaging to the human spirit than Anita Bryant's contention that all Jews are doomed to Hell from birth; or that

Marilyn Monroe was murdered as part of the assassination conspiracy that punched JFK's ticket.

To this admittedly inadequate catalogue, by no means even the apex of the pinnacle of the tip of the iceberg of fallacious codswallop proffered or swallowed whole hookline&sinkered by a distressingly geocentric human race, can be added to your own freighting of favorite misconceptions and irrationalities. I urge you to make a list of your ten favorites and send them along *on a postcard*, no letters, postcards only...and I'll put them together some time soon so we can all share each other's craziness.

What brings all of this to mind right now are two stretches of writing that have come under my gaze, and a snippet of television news footage I caught the other night.

The writings are: first, a splendid book titled ASTROLOGY DISPROVED by Lawrence E. Jerome; and second, two entries by the indefatigably logical Dr. Asimov.

Of the former, I cannot say enough. Jerome is listed as an engineer and science writer who had done extensive research in astrology, but such usually thin credentials don't bother me one whit as regards this extraordinarily sensible and powerful weapon in the ongoing war against the forces seeking to keep us stupid. Why? Because Jerome is the co-author of the "Objections to Astrology" statement signed by 192 leading scientists whose credentials *are* unassailable. The statement, incidentally included at the end of the volume as an appendix, contains signatures by 19 Nobel Prize winners, among which are those of Sir Francis Crick, Konrad Lorenz, Linus Pauling, Harold C. Urey and Sir Peter Medawar. And the statement says, in part:

"Scientists in a variety of fields have become concerned about the increased acceptance of astrology in many parts of the world. We, the undersigned—astronomers, astrophysicists, and scientists in other fields—wish to caution the public against the unquestioning acceptance of the predictions and advice given privately and publicly by astrologers. Those who wish to believe in astrology should realize that *there is no scientific foundation for its tenets.*" (The *italics* are mine.)

I won't quote the entirety of this wonderful, responsible document, but will merely add this part...

"Why do people believe in astrology? In these uncertain times many long for the comfort of having guidance in making decisions. They would like to believe in a destiny predetermined by astral forces beyond their control. However, we must all face the world, and we must realize that our futures lie in ourselves, and not in the stars.

"One would imagine, in this day of widespread enlightenment and education, that it would be unnecessary to debunk beliefs based on magic and superstition. . . . This can only contribute to the growth of irrationalism and obscurantism."

. . .and having put down these words by scientists far more knowledgeable than I, will urge you to get hold of this book. Knowing the usually slovenly practices of many bookstores, when it comes to ordering a book not presently vying with Judith Krantz or Harold Robbins for a spot on the bestseller lists, it behooves me to advise you that Jerome's book can be ordered through the publisher: Prometheus Books, 1203 Kensington Avenue, Buffalo, New York 14215. It was published in December of 1977, runs 233 wonderful pages, and costs $14.95—which is a chunk of change, I'll agree, but is one of those books into which you'll dip again and again, especially to get rid of the twinks, flakes and oddballs who ask you, "What's your sign?"

(I make a practice of answering that question, at parties or when confronted by people who put themselves instantly beyond any consideration of friendship by the mere asking, of saying, "I'm an orphan. I was left on the steps of a foundling home. I don't know when my birthday is; so I celebrate it every day of the year." Or I simply lie and tell them I was born in September or February. Then I let them run those dumb numbers about how they absolutely *knew* I was a Pisces or a Leo or whatever because of this trait I manifest or that attitude I display. And then when they're all puffed up like pouter pigeons with their perceptive insight, I knock them in the head with my actual birthdate. Try it sometime. Watch how they back and fill and blame it on *you* that they made an ass of themselves.)

Now you may feel that attacking something as patently ludicrous as astrology is a waste of our time here; but I submit the undercurrent of belief in the irrational that astrology contributes to our society, speaks directly to the scientists' assertion that such things keep us from facing the pragmatic realities of our complex and demanding lives; that in a time of widespread education, of availability to *every-one* of the data that tell us how the world really runs, relying on bugaboos like astrology is one more manifestation of our refusal to deal with the materials at hand, to put our fate in the grip of irrational, non-existent forces.

And in so doing, we become powerless. We tend to feel inferior, helpless, manipulated. And we become pawns. We find ourselves hustled into jobs, life-styles, relationships, situations we despise, which debase or use us. And as Louis Pasteur said, "Chance favors the prepared mind."

Meaning: there is a lot less roll-of-the-dice in what happens to us than we care to admit. There is a power inside us, having nothing to do with The Force or Zen or God or any of the other names we give to self-determination, that can help us order lives and rule our own destinies. It is called, surprise surprise, intelligence and reasoning.

Look: I know what you're going through. You're not alone. They're all around you, trying to divert your attention, trying to convince you that you can't make it alone, without their help. If it's not the clowns on the religious television network haranguing you that you aren't decent enough or clever enough to get through life nobly on your own without slavish bondage to an ancient bearded myth, it's some peer-group Mephistopheles telling you ludes or free-basing is just what you need to get your head straight. The lame love to try leading the halt. Misery loves company.

And television and movies—the two most effective handmaidens of institutionalized obeisance to the existing power-structure—don't give you much help. F'rinstance, consider these two items:

(From the AP wire, out of Detroit, dated 16 December 1977): "A Detroit newspaper thought it had an offer few could reject—$500 if a family agreed to turn off its television set for one month.

"The *Detroit Free Press* approached 120 families with the offer. And 93 turned it down.

"The paper said it was trying to study 'television addiction.'

"Only 27 of the families that were approached agreed to exchange their TV viewing for the $500, the paper reported. A typical response came from a Romulus (Mich.) woman, who said: 'My husband would never do it. He comes home from work and sits down in front of the TV. He gets up twice—once to eat and once to go to bed.'

"The newspaper selected five families that agreed to accept money in exchange for television and sent TV repairmen into their homes on Sept. 19 and 20 to disconnect their sets.

"The paper reported these results:

"Two people started chain-smoking—one going from one to 2½ packs a day.

"While some children played together peacefully, others became cranky, bored and begged to have the set turned back on. Most of the fathers said they got to know their children better, men and women alike said they had gone back to reading books for the first time in years, and four families said they were drawn closer by the experience."

Huddling against the terror of ostracism, no doubt.

(From the Los Angeles *Times*, datelined 8 January 1978):

". . . 'the movie house has become the sacred church' for the pseudoscientific faiths, said Paul Kurtz, head of the Committee for the Scientific Investigation of Claims of the Paranormal.

"The movie *Close Encounters of the Third Kind* strikes Kurtz as 'extremely religious,' involving 'semigods from outer space.' Kurtz believes the entertainment media are abetting 'attacks on rationality' by presenting various speculations as scientifically possible. . . .

"Finding the terms adequately to cover the range of new beliefs is difficult, Kurtz admits, but he lists three categories:

42

"1: Space-age religions. By-products of actual ventures into space—UFO-ology, astrology revival, Scientology and the genre pioneered by Erich Von Daniken's now-almost-universally-debunked book CHARIOTS OF THE GODS.

"2: Psychic phenomena, the interest in claims of ESP, precognition, prophecies, psychokinesis, levitation, out-of-body experiences, Seth-ism, reincarnation, Edgar Cayce-ism, etc.

"3: Occult faiths, including exorcisms, devil cults, neo-Oriental religions and psychological interest in Eastern wisdom.

"Kurtz (a philosophy professor at the State University of New York in Buffalo and editor of *The Humanist* magazine) said he does not believe that the born-again movement and the pseudoscientific faiths are entirely separate."

And that was in a time prior to Jim Jones and the Guyana slaughter, a time prior to the power-mad decay of Synanon that turned a once-dynamic force for social improvement into a paranoid nightmare, in a time before the sect calling itself The Church was revealed to be a hype providing rake-off to fund a raquetball factory in mainland China owned by the son of the founder. All examples of following new Messiahs. Born-again, duped again. There're a million suckers born every year.

Chance favors the prepared mind.

And the world is teeming with sharpers who want your mind as clouded with sillystuff as they can shovel into it, so you can be manipulated more easily. In short, they want you as uneducated as possible.

Which leads me to the two terrific items by Isaac Asimov.

The first is Isaac's entertaining and exhaustive treatise titled EXTRATERRESTRIAL CIVILIZATIONS (Crown, $10), which is the very latest thinking on the possibility that there's *someone out there*. For any but the pimplebrained, this book once and for all should shine all the light one ever needs on that fascinating contemplation. I won't go into any lengthier support and praise of Dr. Asimov's closely-reasoned work, save to suggest you get this one, too, along with the ASTROLOGY DISPROVED, as a bulwark against the nuttiness spread by your friends, unscrupulous tricksters, parochial know-nothings and perennial adolescents who want to share their fear of living in the world as we perceive it.

The second item from Isaac goes straight to the heart of how dangerous it is in these times to be ignorant of what's *really* going on, in politics, in the sciences, in cultural and social changes. He wrote it as one of the regular "My Turn" op-ed columns in *Newsweek* (21 January 1980).

Every one of you should read this piece. I'll give you a couple of snippets in a moment, but if you want a Xerox copy of the entire outing, if you send a stamped and self-addressed envelope to me care of *Future Life*, and mark on the outside in *bold print* ASIMOV ESSAY, I'll make sure the editors forward them to me, I'll reproduce them and fire one back to you free. A public service against the Forces of Dumbness.

But just to whet your appetite, and to promulgate further the message of this month's column, here's one paragraph:

"There is a cult of ignorance in the United States, and there always has been. The strain of anti-intellectualism has been a constant thread winding its way through our political and cultural life, nurtured by the false notion that democracy means that 'my ignorance is just as good as your knowledge.'"

It's that old saw that everyone is entitled to his/her opinion. In my own wonderful elitist fashion I've never accepted that for a moment. What I *will* accept is that everyone is entitled to his/her *informed* opinion.

Chance favors the prepared mind.

Knowledge, education, use of reason, constructive cynicism. Those are what keep us from becoming like the man I saw on the news the other night, the item I mentioned earlier.

We're having horrendous busing problems here in Los Angeles. All those hypocritical lip-service Liberals who condemned the Deep South for its racism, for keeping the blacks down, for not integrating, are showing themselves to be a solid part of the racist tradition of this country. As long as de po' nigguhs was over there in Watts and South Central L.A., getting shitty educations (if any at all), everyone out here could be as bold in their speech as they cared to be. But the minute Judge Paul Egley said all them there lily-white urchins had to share schools with darkies...they suddenly went crazy.

And on tv the other night, at a meeting held in one of the San Fernando Valley all-white schools, where a lottery was being held to determine which half of the students would be bused, somebody's father got up, screaming, ran to the podium and threw the baskets of name-slips all over the floor. He was roundly cheered by the rest of the audience, except for the few rational parents who realized in a way that commends their nobility to our attention, that the discomforts and problems of busing are one of the prices we as a nation must bravely pay for hundreds of years of enslavement of a large segment of our people.

That man is a racist.

He doesn't know it.

He can rationalize it any way he chooses—usually on the basis of not wanting to put his kids through any travail—but the core recognition is that he has inherited a racist attitude from the overwhelming weight of American historical practice.

He is uneducated. His mind is unprepared for the tide of history. And he will suffer for it. Worse, he will make his kids suffer, and his

44

community. Multiplied by thousands, he is a living example of the ugliness of the human spirit that prevails when we live with superstition, gossip, myths, corrupt misconceptions about the state of the pragmatic universe.

There's only one danger attendant on such an attitude, of course. And it is that we as a species will drive ourselves right into oblivion.

But then, the cockroaches probably wouldn't invent the equivalent of *The Love Boat, Laverne & Shirley,* or *The 700 Club.*

**INSTALLMENT 6:** 13 November 80
(published 20 January 81
in *Future Life* #25
cover-dated March)

# INTERIM MEMO:

Originally, there were to have been sixty entries for columns in this volume, but actually only fifty-nine pieces included. Not too perplexing, the explanation. Installment number six, during the year *An Edge In My Voice* appeared in *Future Life*, was a 5000-word essay on the NASA Voyager 1 flyby of Saturn, 11 November 1980. It was my thought, when assembling this collection, to exclude that entry as it was previously published in my story-and-essay collection STALKING THE NIGHT-MARE (Phantasia Press, 1982; Berkley Books, 1984). Rationale: from time to time I've heard the distant bitching of a very few of the most picayune collectors of my books, to the effect that I "recycle" stories from book to book. This *kvetching* usually boiled down to their not understanding that ALONE AGAINST TOMORROW (1971) was intended as a retrospective of work I'd done to that date; the inclusion in DEATHBIRD STORIES (1975) of previously-collected stories that completed a cycle of works I'd written on the subject of "new gods"; and no more than half a dozen other of the thousand stories I've written, that were duplicated in a second collection. To mollify the shrikes I've made a conscious effort to remove all duplications from reissues of my books. And so, with the exception of DEATHBIRD STORIES as noted above (ALONE AGAINST TOMORROW has now been rendered out-of-print and I do not intend to allow it to be republished), and a 35-year retrospective titled THE ESSEN-TIAL ELLISON that is forthcoming at this writing, everything appears only once in my published *oeuvre*. Yet despite my determination to pursue this once-only policy,

47

after AN EDGE IN MY VOICE went in to the publisher I was urged by my editor, Kay Reynolds, and others who had read the full manuscript, to replace the Saturn flyby column. I pointed out that the essay had been reprinted in *Astronomy* magazine in August of 1981, and that it was very much in print in STALKING THE NIGHTMARE, and I felt uneasy about including it here. Don't be a bigger jerk that nature intended, I was told, by Kay and Gil and Ed Bryant and Sarah. But mostly by Kay. Why force anyone who is curious about that excluded column to buy *another* book? she said. Because I need the money? I suggested coyly. Not nice, they responded, and hit me with heavy ethical objects. And so, braving the displeasure of the few to win the approbation of the many—thus equipping me with the basic attitude for being a politican—I have replaced Installment 6, and you get every last one of the columns in this cycle. (You also get a late-entry bonus, Installment 61; but that's another story, to be told at the conclusion of this journey.)

## Saturn, November 11th

And we beheld what no human eyes before ours had ever seen.

The world outside was strictly alien. Heavy fog had been slithering across Southern California for two days. Jack the Ripper would have felt right at home. A seventy-car daisy chain crackup on the Golden State Freeway had killed seven people the night before. Creeping through the hills past La Cañada–Flintridge, it was a scene Chesley Bonestell might have painted thirty years ago to illustrate an extrapolative article about the surface of Titan.

The time for patience with artists' renditions was at an end: I was on my way to see the actual surface of Titan. What no human eyes had ever beheld.

Tuesday, November 11th, 1980. The Jet Propulsion Laboratory in Pasadena. NASA's Voyager I was on its way to closest approach with Saturn; with Titan and Tethys; with Mimas and Enceladus and Dione; with Rhea and Hyperion and Iapetus.

In the Von Kármán Center, where the press hordes had begun clogging up since 7 AM, it was hurlyburly and business as usual. The women in the mission photo room were several decibels above hysterical: nothing but hands reaching in over the open top of the Dutch door demanding photo packets.

The press room was chockablock with science editors and stringers and lay reporters fighting to use the Hermes manuals lined up six deep. They were all there: the guys from *Science News* and *Omni*, the women from *Scientific American* and *Time*; heavyweight writers with their own word processors and Japanese correspondents festooned with cameras; ABC and NBC and CBS and Reuters and the AP. The stench of territorial imperative hangs thick in the crowd. I slip behind an empty typewriter and begin writing this column. An enormous shadow blocks my light. I look up over my shoulder at He Who Looms. "That's my typewriter," he says, of a machine placed there by JPL. What he means is that he got to it a little earlier than anyone else and has squatter's rights, as opposed to a sharing configuration. I smile. "Need it right now? Or can I have about ten minutes to get some thoughts down?" He doesn't smile. "I'm Mutual Radio," he says; in his umbrage that is surely explanation enough. My eyes widen with wonder. "Are you indeed? I always wondered what Mutual Radio looked like. And a nice job they did

49

when they turned you out." I pull the paper out of the Hermes and vow tomorrow I'll *schlep* my own machine in.

They were standing in line at the coffee urns.

Everyone looked important.

Everyone was watching to make sure no latest photo slipped past. And the JPL press liaisons were hiding the nifty Saturn buttons.

And everywhere the talk was of the mysterious "spokes" radiating out across Saturn's rings, of the ninety-plus ring discovery, of the inexplicable darkness covering Titan's northern hemisphere.

In the course of human events, far fewer are real than we are led to believe. The staged press conference, the artificial happenings, the protesting crowds that wander somnolently until the television cameras turn on them and they begin chanting, waving their fists. Planned, choreographed, manipulated—to make us believe great things are going down. But they are not. It is sound, it is fury, and as usual it signifies nothing. But occasionally there are genuine moments during which history is being made.

This was written by one of *The New Yorker*'s unsigned editorial hands a number of years ago:

> *This is notoriously a time of crises, most of them false. A crisis is a turning point, and the affairs of the world don't turn as radically or as often as the daily newspapers would have us believe. Every so often, though, we're stopped dead by a crisis that we recognize at once as the genuine article; we recognize it not by its size (false crises can be made to look as big as real ones) but because in the course of it, for a measurable, anguished period—sometimes only minutes, sometimes hours, rarely as much as a day—nothing happens. Truly nothing. It is the moment of stasis between a deed that has been performed and must be responded to and the deed that will respond to it. At a false turning point, we nearly always know, within limits, what will happen next; at a true turning point, we not only know nothing, we know (something much more extraordinary and more terrifying) that nobody knows. Truly nobody.*

There are times when the world collectively holds its breath. The assassination of John Kennedy, the Cuban Missile Crisis, the day the Vietnam War ended, the Manson family murders, the Hungarian uprising in November 1956, Pearl Harbor, Hiroshima and Nagasaki. Real things were happening, the world was changing; the breath paused in our bodies.

And this is one of those timeless moments. Something real,

something urgent, something important is happening.

The human race is fumbling toward the light through outer darkness; and there is a feeling here of movement, of genuine wonder. The sense of isolation dissipates.

The press briefing is held half an hour earlier than expected and the room is jammed to the walls. A full-size replica of the Voyager bird dominates the left side of the briefing auditorium. The television networks have their Martian war-machine cameras ranged across the rear of the seating area behind the press representatives from major news outlets and, seemingly, from every Podunk Gazette in the country. Snatches of conversation in French, German, Japanese. The planet Earth is gathered here to *know!*

The recap of the previous day's findings leaves mouths gaping. They have discovered *something* on Tethys. Is it a crater? No, the albedo indicates it's a hill. The NASA spokesman calls it "a heck of a hill"—hundreds of kilometers across. But only time and greater resolution of the photographs will tell.

Brad Smith, leader of the imaging science team, cannot conceal his amazement as he reports that at least two eccentric rings have been found in the mass of circulars casting their shadow on Saturn's cloud-masses. He says they had no reason to expect such a thing, that it defies all the known laws of ring mechanics. What he doesn't say is that if every Bible Belt fundamentalist who believes we never actually went to the Moon, that we flew over to Glendale and shot all that stuff in a movie studio, could be here, to see what these people are doing, what is being sent back minute by minute over a distance of 930,000,000 miles, they might begin to understand that God was too busy creating esthetics to worry about putting the solar system together.

It is all so complex, so bewilderingly intricate, even the best minds in the room are finding it difficult to keep up with the new discoveries:

The rings, for instance.

A constant revelation. They simply don't know what keeps the rings separated. General knowledge, since the Dutch mathematician Christiaan Huygens discovered the true shape of the rings in 1659, has contended that—at most—there were five. (The state of our knowledge, and the breakneck acceleration in what we've learned, is expressed in this absolutely latest-thinking from THE WORLD WE LIVE IN [1955] edited not only by the staff of *Life* magazine, but by the renowned author of THE UNIVERSE AND DR. EINSTEIN, Lincoln Barnett: "Although Saturn's three concentric rings rotate in a circle 171,000 miles across, they are only a few inches thick. The middle ring, largest and brightest of the three, is 16,000 miles wide and separated from the outer by a 2000-mile gap." That latest-state-of-the-art in 1955 was a caption accompanying a Chesley Bonestell painting of Saturn's three rings.)

As of this November 18th the Voyager team has isolated almost 1000 rings; and the estimates go as high as 10,000. The rings have rings; the rings' rings have rings; and the rings' rings' rings have ringlets.

But what keeps them separated...?

The *NASA News* backgrounder on the mission, dated just October 28th, says this: "At least six rings surround Saturn. From the planet outward they are designated D, C, B, A, F and E. Divisions between the rings are believed to be caused by the three innermost satellites, Mimas, Enceladus and Tethys. The Cassini Division, a space between the B and the A ring, is the only division clearly visible with a small telescope from Earth."

But here it is less than two weeks later and we sit in the morning briefing and hear that the Cassini Division is anything but empty. Rings within rings within rings. And tiny satellites, acting as "sheepdogs" (Jerry Pournelle's wonderful term for them), *seem* to be holding the rings apart, *seem* to be serving as outriders in this complex, astounding system of cosmic detritus.

Science fiction writer Greg Bear asks Smith if he has any random guesses as to how old the rings are, how stable they are, and how long they'll stay in this wonderful sequence. We expect another humorous "well, I can't really say for sure" response, but Smith replies with force, "They're four and a half billion years old, they're very stable, and they'll be there till the sun enters its red giant phase." Everyone is impressed.

No one can even begin to grasp what four and a half billion years means in terms of waiting time at the airport, but it is clearly longer than next Thursday at 4:15 PM.

Humanity is only 1.3 billion miles from the surface of Titan and one of the members of the press corps asks a dumb question. He didn't realize the NASA spokesman was making a subtle joke. An ingroup astronomical joke. His question is answered politely, but everyone in the room thanks God it was not s/he who had asked the dumb question. To look like a schmuck in the same room where Clyde Tombaugh, discoverer of Pluto, sits listening, is to put oneself forever beyond the pale. Five minutes later someone else asks a question to which the response is, "That's a very good question, a very important question," and He Who Asked could, at that moment, be elected President of the World.

I am an eyewitness to history, and I make a mental note to thank Jerry Pournelle for getting me VIP credentials; I am far out of my depth, but I am at the eye of the hurricane and I owe thanks to Jerry.

Slides from images sent back by the Voyager are flashed on the screen. Photos of the Cassini Division separating the A and B rings.

The scientists admit that traditional celestial mechanics cannot account for the phenomenon of their eternal separation from one another. Not even the "sheepdog" satellites can be adequately explained, the way they work, they way they push up and pull down the ice particles, speed them up and slow them down, keep them circling in their intricate cosmic pavane.

But they seem to revel in their lack of explanations. They suppose this, and they postulate that, and they are like kids who have been given a glimpse of a new toy with which they can play for years to come. It is the best part of this extraordinary game that has thrown four hundred million dollars worth of Voyager I and II tinkertoy into eternal darkness. It is the most salutary part of the rigorously analytical intelligence: it loves to have been fooled, it loves to be surprised.

They realize they have made pronouncements of What the Laws of the Universe Are and are being proved wrong minute-by-minute. But they don't defend what they said in error; they admit, they recant, they rush to say no, here's what it is now, and here's what it looks like now, and look at *that*, and look at *that*! One can only love them for it.

They talk a great deal about seeing what's coming in with "Terrestrial eyes" and with "Jovian eyes." What they mean is that we are too ethnocentric, and when Voyager II made its encounter with Jupiter sixteen months ago, they interpreted what was relayed back through eyes and intellects chained to a Terran horizon for millions of years. Now, with bemused embarrassment, they admit to early misinterpretations of visual data because everything was viewed as if it were of the Earth...out there. But Ganymede brought important lessons about seeing with new eyes. Yet it's happening again—with the difference that "Ganymedian eyes" are being added to the viewing of the Saturn system. Nonetheless, how miraculous: seeing with the eyes of aliens. Knowing that what is revealed is only partially real, that much of the "reality" is merely shadow, as seen through human organs not yet completely retooled for new vistas.

These are human beings transcending their limitations, going to a new realm of perception not through the duplicity of drugs and fuzzy sophomoric metaphysics that demean the purity of Zen rigors, but through confrontation with the pragmatic universe, through hard analysis of the laws of that physical universe, no matter how anomalous and labyrinthine they may be.

Angie Dickinson appears in the briefing auditorium and the PIO nabobs begin whirling like dervishes. She is there strictly as an "interested bystander" I'm told, but she gets more attention than Clyde Tombaugh. I sigh deeply.

Voyager has discovered three new satellites: S-13, S-14 and S-15.

53

And they have "undiscovered" one that has been there since 1966.

Quote from the current edition of THE WORLD ALMANAC AND BOOK OF FACTS, 1980 (page 761):

*Saturn has 10 satellites, the 10th having been announced by the French astronomer, Audouin Dollfus, in Dec. 1966. The new satellite is a few thousand miles outside Saturn's ring system, but it is so faint that there is some doubt as to its existence.*

Quick thinking, WORLD ALMANAC! Dollfus's tenth satellite, which he called Janus after the two-faced Roman deity, does not exist. Poor Dollfus. It simply ain't there. Every science fiction story using Janus as its locale is now down the chute. (I gloat. I am not a science fiction writer, no matter how my work is mislabeled by anal-retentive pigeonholers; I have written so few stories that required a scientific education that I have nothing to apologize for. I feel sorry for Hal Clement and Isaac and Poul and Larry Niven. Only Andre Norton can get away with it: her JUDGMENT ON JANUS was written in 1963, before Dollfus's gaffe, and she made her Janus an alien world in another star-system.)

The bird makes its closest approach to Titan, largest satellite in the Solar System and the only one with a discernible atmosphere, at 9:41:12:12 Tuesday night and the final hope that a view through to the naked surface will be possible...vanishes. One of the scientists, who bet a case of cognac that a peep would be possible, loses the wager. And we all lose. Titan is covered with smog. Clouds of liquid nitrogen vapor, but maybe the atmosphere isn't a nitrogen mixture. Hydrogen cyanide is discovered; there may be an ocean of liquid nitrogen down there; if such an ocean exists, the methane icebergs would sink to the bottom.

Much of the human race would not spend four dollars to journey to Los Angeles, blanketed by photochemical smog; but the species *in toto* has traveled one and a half *billion* miles to visit a place with even worse smog.

And on the evening news as I drive home, talk of the Saturn flyby appears at the bottom of the broadcast. Top spot dwells on the war between Iran and Iraq.

I sigh deeply.

Wednesday the 12th of November, 1980. The 10:30 AM briefing on the day of the main events:

2:16 PM Closest approach to Tethys (258,000 miles).

3:45 PM Closest approach to Saturn (77,174 miles above clouds).

3:48 PM Six photos of the new satellite, S-11.

5:42 PM Closest approach to Mimas (55,168 miles).

5:50 PM Closest approach to Enceladus (125,840 miles); Enceladus' radius is 260 kilometers, 162 miles; Earth receive time of the images: 7:15 PM.

7:39 PM Closest approach to Dione (100,122 miles).

9:45 PM Voyager crosses the ring plane on its outbound leg.

10:21 PM Closest approach to Rhea (44,744 miles); Rhea's radius is 750 kilometers, 466 miles.

Quote from *Star & Sky* magazine, November 1980:

> *An object like Saturn's satellite Rhea, which appears as a minute speck in any earthly telescope, can be used to illustrate what the Voyagers are expected to achieve. No surface features on Rhea have ever been seen. The photos from Voyager I will include images of Rhea displaying about 20 percent of its surface to nearly one-mile resolution—equivalent to the best Earth-based telescopic photographs of our own satellite, the moon.*

A quick and infallible test of the imagination quotient of your friends and lovers. Quote the above; if s/he says, "So what?" or "What good is that?" ask for your ring back and walk away fast.

The briefing is even more jammed than yesterday's. I sit with Dick Hoagland of *Star & Sky* so he can explain everything to me. I need to know what albedo means. I'm sure he'll be tickled to explain the ABC's of celestial mechanics to a no-neck scientific illiterate. (At least I don't have to arm-wrestle Mutual Radio for a typewriter. I've brought my own Olympia portable—the one with the Mickey Mouse decal on the case—and I snag a desk formerly occupied by Peter Schroeder of Dutch television and radio. It's a good thing I got there early: Tuesday's smash&grab for mission photos and space to bat out news copy has intensified. One yahoo caught rustling a CBS word processor is lynched before our eyes.)

Opening remarks by Voyager Project Manager for JPL, Ray Heacock, reinforce the sense of wonder. They have been incredibly lucky overnight. During the Titan–Earth occultation period—11:12 to 11:24 P.M.—there has been rain at tracking station 63 in Spain. It started and stopped during a time when, had the spacecraft not been measuring atmospheric properties as the radio signal began to fade, we would have lost masses of valuable data. But it didn't matter during occultation.

More wonder: Heacock says, with an impish grin, that they made an error in timing: because they didn't know precisely where Titan would be (or something like that), the Voyager made the ring plane crossing 49 seconds earlier than expected. Everyone laughs. The bird has been in transit for three years and the biggest miscalculation is 49 seconds. The next time I call the telephone company about a repair and they tell me it can't be done, I will tell them *anything* can be done.

I smile with pride at my lovely species. We ain't so goddam dumb after all.

(Middle of the day Tuesday, a slow time with everybody out to lunch, I went to the astonishing botanical gardens of the Huntington Museum with Jane Mackenzie and Bob Silverberg. We wandered through alien terrain straight out of a 1936 Frank R. Paul cover from *Amazing Stories,* a desert garden of a million kinds of seemingly extraterrestrial cacti. And Bob ruminated. "I was standing next to one of those scientists at the back of the auditorium during briefing," he said, "when he was describing something incredibly arcane; and I looked at him. I was looking at something like 180 I.Q. and I knew that man was smarter than I. Far smarter. And I'm *smart.*")

The briefing goes on. Norman Ness, from the Goddard Space Flight Center, principal investigator on the magnetic field team, explains how the Voyager passed through Saturn's bow shock wave at 4:50 PM when Titan was inside the magnetic field envelope of the planet. He speaks of the solar wind, the flow of ionized gas given off by the sun that hisses through the solar system. There is no poetry in the words...only in the way he speaks of it. Norman Ness barely realizes he has looked on the face of the Almighty.

The photos we're seeing are four times as detailed as what came in over the tv screens real-time. Television's scanning pattern permits only one-quarter of the information contained in the photos sent by the Voyager's imaging systems to reveal itself when we see it on the screen. Even so, the details are remarkable.

But most remarkable of all is the revelation that three components of the F ring seem to defy the laws of pure orbital mechanics: they are braided. Such a thing cannot be, yet we look at the photographs and we see that indeed, the rings do twine. Brad Smith of the University of Arizona is totally at a loss to explain it. He cannot even make a joke. This is the big time, something never encountered before. He looks like a man stunned by the hammer. He says that of all the improbables he might have postulated, even to the inclusion of eccentric rings, which have now been verified, the braiding is so far off the wall he could not even have conceived of it.

We stare at the pictures.

The rings twine around each other. The room falls silent for a moment, we hold our breath; we are living in one of those special moments when *something is happening*, something important.

The celestial engineer has been cutting capers again.

A photo of Mimas taken at 5:05 AM Pacific Standard Time from a range of approximately 400,000 miles shows an impact crater 80 miles in diameter. It shows a rebound peak God only knows how high in the center of the structure. The crater is more than a quarter of the diameter of the whole damned iceball. It may be the largest impact crater, relative to the size of the object struck, in the solar system. What will the shock pattern on the other side of Mimas look like? What will it tell us about how big a projectile can be before it blows something like our moon to smithereens?

*That's* why you asked for your ring back and walked away fast when the feep didn't understand.

During the press conference—between 10:53 and 10:56 AM—the mechanism making search-sweeps for new satellites apparently discovered S-16. Later it turns out to be S-10.

Patrick Moore, he who knows more about our moon than anyone else writing about Luna, asks Smith about a small satellite that might be controlling the inside boundary of the C ring. Smith gets an expression that is the equivalent of crossing one's fingers and responds that he *hopes* it's there...because if it's there it will go a long way to explaining how the rings hold together. He says they will modify the Voyager II search patterns to locate it...if it's there.

It becomes clear that the photos we're being given for publication are merely bullshit PR. That as soon as this circus leaves town the scientists upstairs can employ full computer time to analyze the pictures instead of putting together "pretty pictures" for the press.

And that's exactly what happens.

Within two days, they have analyzed so much of the material that they've revealed a wind on the surface of Saturn that blows at 1100 miles per hour. If that wind were here on Earth it would be blowing in a steady line from Philadelphia to Buenos Aires.

And then comes the explanation for the anomalous "spokes" that were seen radiating out through the rings. It is an explanation so unbelievable that it can only be termed a *Star Wars* special effect.

As the Voyager fell through the ring plane on the 12th, heading for its closest encounter with Saturn, a secondary experiment on board—"The Planetary Radio-Astronomy Receiver"—picked up enormous bursts of energy—static—identical to terrestrial thunderstorm noises...but a million times stronger than anything in the solar system.

The bursts of energy coincided with the mysterious "spokes" seen in the rings.

Putting the results together, the Voyager team has tentatively come up with an awesome mechanism operating within the ring, namely, electrical discharges—lightning—occuring over tens of thousands of kilometers.

The Voyager was literally being shot at by Saturn as it flew past. The "spokes" seem to be—hold your breath—enormous linear particle accelerators!

As best I can explain it to you (and most of this comes from Dick Hoagland), here's what causes this phenomenon that cannot be explained within the parameters of known celestial mechanics.

The density of material in the B, or center, ring is the highest. The highest number of, literally, icebergs per cubic mile. Because of the inevitability of Keplerian mechanics, the bergs closest to Saturn are orbiting faster. Any ice object with an eccentric orbit, even a few meters of eccentricity, will collide with other bergs. Because of the brittleness and cold of this ice they naturally fracture producing, well, producing chips off the old block. Then those fragments collide and chip again and again, getting smaller and smaller. These collisions continue in a never-ending rubble-producing process.

But. When this occurs in Saturn's two-hour shadow, when the fragments sail out into sunlight the smallest particles—micron-size, perhaps—are charged up by interaction with solar ultraviolet light and, because like charges repel as any dummy clearly knows, they literally try to get away from the rings. Producing a levitating cloud of charged ice crystals elevated above the average ring plane who knows how far... several miles to several *thousand* miles.

Grabbed by Saturn's magnetic field (magnetic fields and electrical charges, Hoagland assures me, go hand-in-hand), they are lined up in a linear feature tens of thousands of kilometers long, stretching from the outer edge of B ring in toward Saturn. Straight and narrow as a flashlight beam. These appear in the optical images as "spokes" which rotate anomalously around the planet defying all explanation. At this moment.

Give them a week more.

And so these electrified ice crystals apparently discharge along the length of the spoke creating, in effect, the Solar System's largest radio antenna as well as a natural linear particle accelerator.

Even I, scientific illiterate, aware of the breakthroughs in particle physics that have come from such terrestrial plants as the Batavia, Illinois proton synchrotron, can extrapolate what it would mean to harness that "spoke" mechanism to aid us in discovering precisely of what matter is composed, how it works, how it came to be.

Explain that to the feep who said, "So what?"

I overload. I cannot contain any more new information. I pack it in and lie down and turn on the radio.

The news is all taken up with how high the stock market has jumped with Reagan's latest fiscal pronouncements. And the war between Iraq and Iran. I close my eyes and slap the button off on the radio.

I sigh deeply. Ain't we a wonderful species.

**INSTALLMENT 7:** 1 January 81
(published 10 March 81
in *Future Life* #26
cover-dated May)

# Interim Memo:

A couple of updates of material in this column. The Ennio Morricone FilmScore Society is still in business, at the same address given. Some of the sf newsletters noted herein are now out of business. I'd enumerate those that have gone belly-up, but frankly, Scarlett, I don't give a damn. You shouldn't be reading that crap, anyhow. It'll break you out all over with pimples.

## 7: 1 January 81

Sitting here listening to an absolutely superb recording of Arnold Schoenberg's *String Quartet No. 2 in F-Sharp Minor, Opus 10* (1908), performed by The Sequoia String Quartet on a Nonesuch Digital pressing (D-79005). A miraculous series of musical entities that finally, in the fourth movement, surges into a kind of cosmic atonality. As appropriate for background as anything I might have selected to accompany the task of writing a column that replies to your many letters. I warn you, some of you are veering dangerously near to sanity in your remarks.

As usual, most of you can't follow simple directions. I specifically begged you *not* to write letters, to send postcards with your comments or questions simply and directly stated. So of course hordes of you wrote long and dithyrambic letters in envelopes that were cleverly sliced off when the nameless person at *Future Life* committed a federal offense by opening mail addressed to me with some sort of berserk guillotine machine. In future, chums, I'll only answer postcards. Letters will be heaped immediately on a bonfire and you'll miss out on getting that sick attention you all seem to need.

Thank yous are herewith extended to the several hundred people who wrote in requesting the Asimov essay and followed the directions by enclosing a stamped self-addressed envelope and the words ASIMOV ESSAY on the outside. Those have all gone off. I even returned the 15¢ to the lady who assured me in this life nobody gets nothin' for nothin'. What a cynic. I *told* you it was a public service.

And so to the mail at hand.

Douglas Gray of Johnson City, New York was annoyed by the L-5 Society advertisement in *Future Life* #20, the first issue in which my column appeared. He took umbrage at the Society's solicitation of funds to oppose the Moon Treaty. He made some very sensible observations about the arrogance of the human race in its desire to "colonize" space and compared it to the ethnocentrism of the European nations that "colonized" South America (for instance Spain, that "colonized" whole civilizations out of existence while introducing such cultural necessities as the Inquisition). He believes the Moon Treaty is a rational way to keep the lunar landscape from becoming yet another territorial imperative battlefield for the human race, and he asks my position on this question.

I must confess I know less than I ought about such an important matter. I've tried wading through mountains of L-5 material, sent to me from every corner of the globe, but most of it is so badly written and obtuse that I have never been able to work up the sufficient interest to do my homework. I have a gut feeling that any organization that seriously tries to further the space program is an okay outfit, but in the reading I also get a resonance that I've detected when dealing with Scientologists, members of Mensa, players at Dungeons & Dragons and suchlike role-filling games, and true believers who know with a messianic fervor that science fiction is better than any other kind of literature. It occurs to me that even as mild a querulousness as that will net me hundreds of feverish letters from L-5 proselytizers attempting to "correct my thinking" as born-again types have tried to "correct my thinking." I urge them not to bother. I'm not that firm in my concerns. Just sorta chatting idly about it, friends.

Dozens of you, like Rick Eshbaugh of Greenfield, Wisconsin and Marc Russell of Los Angeles and Pat NoLastName in Minneapolis, have sent me lists of irrationalities to supplement the congeries I entered here several issues ago. I'm saving them all up for a later column.

Dianne Channell of Santa Fe is a terrific human being who has subscribed, she says, because of my column. Her husband is also nifty, because he recommended Richard Hofstader's excellent study ANTI-INTELLECTUALISM IN AMERICAN LIFE, which I commend to you. She also wanted the September through January issues of *Future Life* because her subscription started late and she wanted the columns she'd missed. Well, she's not missing as many as she thought because *Future Life* isn't published monthly, it's published every seven weeks, or eight times a year, so *An Edge in My Voice* appeared in August, September, November, December and February. What this means in terms of what Ms. Channell is missing, I do not know. All I know for sure is that she should write to the subscription and back number fulfillment department where yet another nameless personage will lose her request. This is what we call one of life's little challenges.

Steven Philip Jones of Cedar Rapids, Iowa read a story of mine in another magazine, a story in which a writer tells his heirs to build dorm rooms so struggling young authors can live at his large home after he's dead, where they can write in peace and seclusion. Mr. Jones writes me to ask if the place really exists, if it's here at my house, and how he can take up residence. Mr. Jones seems to have trouble differentiating between fiction and reality. There are such places, of course, and they are called writers' retreats or workshops, but one usually has to pay, or get a grant to live in such an operation. My home ain't one of those. And though I usually have one or another of my writer-friends hanging out here in Ellison Wonderland, the operative word is *friend*. As sincere and talented and wonderful a person as Mr. Jones may be, I assure you that if he were to turn up at my door with a rucksack and a battered Royal portable, I would sic my gargoyles on him. I have spent many years finding *my* sanctuary, and I frankly don't want it festooned with hungry writers.

Peter & Kathleen in Seattle: I didn't write "the taste for Armageddon," whatever it is, and if I ever saw Ray Milland and Jane Wyman in *The Second Time Around* I have forgotten it.

Clarice Dickey of Hartford, Connecticut asks me what music I listen to while writing. She read somewhere that I cannot write without music blaring. She asks if punk or New Wave is conducive to my working situation. First, she's correct. I work to music, as indicated by the reference to Schoenberg at the top of this column. Second, with the exception of Root Boy Slim and the Sex Change Band, the Lamont Cranston Band and a little Elvis Costello, I outgrew rock a long time ago and find most of the shit being listened to today so devoid of craft or message that I would sooner listen to disco, which makes me wanna womit, so that answers *that*. (And again, I'll get a thousand letters from wimps extolling the manifest virtues of the B-52's or The Dead Kennedys or X or Red Crayola or whichever overnight hot flash has you drooling at the moment. And though I've been listening to and enjoying Captain Beefheart for more years than some of you have been extant, that does not mean I confuse the dreck Tower Records has stacked at point of entry with genuine artistry. So you need not write me trying to "correct my thinking." Arthur Byron Cover spends many of his waking—and several of his sleeping— hours trying to get me to listen to groups who run the risk of being electrocuted by their own Fenders when the Clearasil smeared over their paws and faces carries the current. And one *nuhdz* for rock in my life is enough.)

What I *do* listen to is primarily classical; a lot of old jazz heavy into Django Reinhardt, Bob Dorough, Ellington, Monk, all the early sides Miles cut on Prestige, Bird, Prez, Art Tatum; big band stuff from the Thirties and Forties; Moody Blues still holds up, Richie Havens, Return to Forever, Stevie Wonder, Mike Nesmith, Dave Grisman, Hubert Laws, Willie Nelson, Alan Price, Peter Allen; a lot of old Al Kooper stuff and a lot of old Gerry Mulligan cuts; Chick Corea, Dory Previn, Billy Joel, Dick Feller, Howard McGhee, Stephane Grappelli.

But mostly I like classical music. I won't run down the list, I'll just recommend a special nifty album that I managed to luck onto recently that you will go nuts over, if your brains haven't been turned to spackling compound by repeated exposure to The Germs, The Damned, Tortured Puppies or The Plasmatics. (These last four groups I got from Arthur Cover.) (My all-time favorite name for a group stands unchallenged, even with the monstrous inventiveness of the New Wave appellations. It is: JoJo & The Sixteen Screaming Niggers. Now *that's* class!)

The record I urge you to order—by mail is its only current availability—is a most unusual rendering of Bach's *Partita No. 3 in E Major,* Poulenc's *Sonata* and (this is a stunner) Bartok's *Roumanian Folk Dances* (originally written for full orchestra) as performed by Tatsuo Sasaki on xylophone, with Howard Wells at the piano. I am not much one for "novelty" renditions of classical works—Tomita, for instance, bores my ass off—but Mr. Sasaki's interpretation of the Bartok *Dances* is, simply put, astonishing. I have written two new stories to this music already, and if you crave a singular listening experience I cannot recommend highly enough this album (Micro-sonics CG003, $8.00 including postage, available directly from Tatsuo Sasaki, 5842 Henley Drive, San Diego, California 92120). You may use my name when ordering so the gentleman will know whence comes all this attention.

But my *best* working-to music are the film scores of Ennio Mor-ricone. You may know his sound from the Sergio Leone Italian westerns—*A Fistful of Dollars, The Good, The Bad & The Ugly,* etc.—but you probably don't know that he's done almost *five hundred* film scores, songs, albums of background music, television tracks, arrangements, orchestrations, canonical and ecclesiastical works, full orchestra pieces for modern classicism, incidental music and whatall. His "sound" ranges from the dramatic exuberance of, say, *The Big Gundown,* a 1967 Lee Van Cleef oater, to the exquisite loneliness of Terry Malick's film *Days of Heaven,* for which work he was nominated for an Oscar. Morricone is my best companion when I'm deep in the world of what I'm writing.

As long as I'm performing public services, turning you on to esthetic joys you may not have encountered previously, it should be brought to your attention that if you want to sample some Morricone there is now an *Ennio Morricone FilmScore Society* that is doing an heroic job bringing back into print, at reasonable prices, many of The Maestro's best scores. So far they've issued the music from *La Cage Aux Folles, Bluebeard, The Chosen, Tepepa* and *The Divine Nymph.* (You can order direct, it is my understanding. So here's an address: Cerberus Records; PO Box 4591; North Hollywood, CA 91607. Again, since I'm doing the recommending, I suggest you mention my name when ordering; in that way, if you run into any glitches, which are unlikely as this is an outfit I've checked out myself thoroughly, I'll be able to assist you if something gets bollixed.)

Which probably answers Ms. Dickey's question more fully than she might have wanted. But you asked.

George Andrews of Cleveland, Ohio writes to buttress my recom-mendation that you pay no attention to astrology; and he offers the Bible as support. He points out that in the Old Testament God says do not believe in astrologers, soothsayers, necromancers or the like; believe in me only. Which is keen, having God on my side. . .except it seems a bit self-serving on God's part. I mean, if *I* were running for Supreme Deity, I'd say the same thing. Now if God had said don't believe in them and don't believe in me, believe in *yourself*, then I'd feel a lot easier about aligning myself with Him. Or Her. Or It. Or Them. Or None of the Above.

Alma Jo Williams of the James A. Baker Institute for Animal Health at Cornell University in Ithaca, New York picks a semantic tibia with me as follows:

"In. . .your first column you make this statement: 'Those millions go to maintaining the status quo, also known as entropy. I am foursquare for chaos; I am anti-entropy.'

"Status quo is NOT entropy. Entropy, as understood by the physical chemist, etc., is the 2nd Law of Thermodynamics which states that matter and energy can only be changed in one direction, i.e., usable to unusable, available to unavailable, or order to disorder. As one of my Physical Chemistry instructors neatly put it, entropy is a measure of messiness. The opposite is *enthalpy* which is the extracting of useful work from the energy.

"If you are for chaos, you are *pro-entropy*. (It takes energy just to maintain the status quo. As the Red Queen said to Alice, 'You have to run as hard as you can just to stay in one place.') So much for thermodynamics."

Hmpphh!

Definition four; THE RANDOM HOUSE DICTIONARY OF THE ENGLISH LANGUAGE; page 477; column 2:

"Homogeneity, uniformity, or lack of distinction or differentiation: *the tendency of the universe toward entropy.*"

Ms. Williams is, of course, correct.

Further, deponent sayeth not.

Greg Higginbotham of Springfield, Missouri sent along some photos taken of me when I was lecturing there four years ago, and asks how I view the ascendancy of Ronald Reagan to the throne. Apart from the small succor I derive from the knowledge that historically we go to war under Democratic presidents and have extended periods of economic upturn under Republican presidents (and Reagan believes, as did Calvin Coolidge, that "the business of America is Business"), I recall with a shiver Ronnie's instant response to the Free Speech Movement sit-ins at Berkeley in 1964, when he was California's governor and a member of the university's board of regents: he called out the troops and the police, and almost singlehandedly lit the fire that became a conflagration of student–administration confrontations for almost a decade (between January 1st and 15th of 1968 there were 221 major demonstrations involving nearly 39,000 students on 101 American campuses). Yes, it was the times, but doesn't it give *you* a momentary shiver to know that at the initial pressure point Ronald Reagan had the choice of rational negotiation and irrational force. . .and chose the latter?

That, and Reagan's selection of anti-ecologist James G. Watt as Secretary of the Interior (his first utterance upon being named to the post was, "I'm not against ecologists, I'm just against ecological extremists, those who would stand in the way of commercial development of unused lands"), make me shudder at the idea of Bonzo's playmate in the White House. But then, I voted for Carter the first time around (Anderson this time), and I was sorely disappointed; so what the hell do I do now?

Richard Latimer of Dayton, Ohio asks me to do a column on filmmaker Peter Watkins (*The War Game, Privilege, Punishment Park*) or an interview. Well, an interview isn't likely: last I heard, Watkins was in Australia and I have no plans to go tromping off to the bottom of the world unless *Future Life* pays my way, which seems unlikely. But Mr. Latimer enclosed a dandy long quote from Watkins that I want to reprint here, not only to encourage you to look into his films, which are exemplars of social conscience, as well as being damned good cinema, but because it speaks to my intentions with this column. You see, when I first engaged to do these screeds, Kerry O'Quinn, one of the publishers, had some trepidation about what he termed my "frequent pessimism." He was afraid I'd unload a lot of negative vibes on youse folks and that would run sales down the tube. I tried to tell him that I'm actually a cynical optimist and that when I do a smash&grab on some subject it's usually out of a sense of viewing-with-alarm. Well, I'm not sure Kerry is complacent even now that I've been at this for seven installments. I get the feeling that he doesn't know quite how tough or lackadaisical you can be. I have faith in your ability to deny the corrupt state of the world to your own ease of existence, chums; and I know my pitiful rages won't have much effect. But as to this canard of being pessimistic, I offer Peter Watkins's comments, as published in Joseph A. Gomez's biography of the director:

> *"I should have thought that you would have been bloody glad that I didn't come out with a silver tray with answer 475 and say, 'Here you are, darling; go home and take this piece of dogma.' . . .If I were a pessimist, I would have made Laurel and Hardy reruns since 1965. I think our society is totally caught up in the abuse and misuse of these words 'optimistic' and 'pessimistic.' I don't believe that one is pessimistic to look at very real problems that we are involved in. . .I think I am an optimist to talk about these problems in the sense that if I don't talk about them, it would be because I couldn't care less about humanity or*

*the potential of mankind. But I do care very much, which I think is optimistic. I also care enough to make these films. I also care enough about your own sense of responsibility not to do what is done with you every day in your life—in education, in television—which is to force-feed you with directives, force-feed you with answers, force-feed you with directions to move—until you are zapped left, right, up and down. I won't do that to you. I will try and show you a problem as hard and as strongly as I can; but what to do about it, even if I had the answer, which I don't usually, I would never say to you. I would never reveal it. I would chew it over in my own head; because I would leave you to try to develop your own strength to find the answer."*

Liz Wilderson of Leavenworth, Kansas wants me to do a column on the Hugo Awards and asks how fans can vote for the Hugos and how they can obtain the annual list of nominees. Despite my having won 7½ of the large metal things, I am the last guy in the world to chatter about the Achievement Awards of the World Science Fiction Convention. I won't go into any long diatribe about the Hugos and how they're awarded, save to note that Richard Lupoff has just had published through Pocket Books a splendid anthology called WHAT IF? VOL. 1, subtitled *Stories That Should Have Won the Hugo*; a collection that includes as strong and convincing a set of arguments for the revamping of the Hugo-awarding mechanism as any I might cobble up.

The paperback is only $2.50 and I commend it to your attention more for the Lupoff editorials contained therein than for the stories, all of which are gems; which says a lot about how important I think Lupoff's comments are.

As for how to vote, well, all you have to do is become a member of the World Convention each year, and you automatically get a ballot. As to how to join a convention, and how to obtain a list of the nominations as soon as they're released, well, you might care to subscribe to one of the three newsletters of the sf/fantasy world: *Fantasy Review* (monthly, Robert A. Collins, 500 N.W. 20th Street, Boca Raton, FL 33431, single copy $2.75, $20 per year), *Locus* (monthly, Charles N. Brown, P O Box 13305, Oakland, CA 94661, single copy $2.50, $24 per year) or *SF Chronicle* (monthly, Andy Porter, P O Box 4175, New York, NY 10163, single copy $1.95, $21 per year). Each of these publications will give you the address of the current WorldCon convention committee, and will keep you abreast of the selections. Vote for me. I'm greedy.

Lori Bailey of Alton, Illinois suggests that the two books of tv criticism I wrote (THE GLASS TEAT and THE OTHER GLASS

TEAT) were not enough horror for me to suffer and that I should do it, as Count Basie puts it, *one more once!* I suggest she read that one more once written as the introduction to my book STRANGE WINE. It is as much update on the ghastliness of tv as I can muster in these, my declining twilight years.

David A. Green: forget it. Roderick Sprague, Moscow, Idaho: dumb idea, forget it. James J.J. Wilson, Downers Grove, Ill; Cadence Gainey, Hatfield, Penn; Robert Wayne Richardson, Bristol, Tenn; and Christy Ory, Scottsdale, Ariz; thank you thank you thank you. You are each and every one a credit to your species. Chris Summers of Hanover Park, Illinois and Kim Tankus of Dusseldorf, West Germany: don't send me your stories. I don't read stories submitted to me. I've already said why in a past column. Sorry to cut you off, but it ain't me, babe.

Eric Shinn of Columbia, Maryland: yes, I may have written an introduction to a book of stories by Keith Laumer, who was once my friend, but we have not been friends for a long time and the last thing in this life I'd want to do is get involved doing the screenplay for a Laumer book. As far as I'm concerned, Mr. Laumer no longer exists in my world. I'm sure the feeling is mutual. And that's how I want to keep it. Try Paul Schrader or Stirling Silliphant.

Tom Looby of Vergennes, Vermont writes to say he read my apocalyptic introduction to APPROACHING OBLIVION and he's scared about what's happening to the human race, and wants me to tell him what to do. Well, I'll tell you, Tom, it's a long and arduous process, this what-to-do business. Every time we cut off the censors at the pass, some bunch of self-appointed guardians of morality like Jerry Falwell and his Moral Majority rise out of the slime-pits to burn books. Every time someone beats an institutionalized criminal like, say, a movie studio or a tv network for plagiarism in a court of law, a dozen other thugs steal a little more craftily. Eternal vigilance, kiddo. You have to be as smart as you can be, as tough as you can be, and as pragmatic as you can be. Don't believe everything you read or everything they tell you. Keep asking questions. And when you get angry about something that's going down, in your school, your town, your state or the world at large—DO SOMETHING ABOUT IT. Put yourself on the line! Risk a little! And even if you only do a little bit of good, you'll feel like a bloody hero, you'll alter the state of the universe a tot, and you'll get tougher for the *next* time. Here's one to start on now: help get gun control passed in the U.S. Senate. No more Lennons being gunned down senselessly. Don't buy that bullshit about people needing to protect themselves from crooks with guns. Most of the murders every year aren't by crooks or muggers...they're by people getting pissed at people and blowing them away. Or guns in the hands of nutcases like the one who offed Lennon. Gun control, gun elimination *can* help. In a big way. And I say this as a resident of Los Angeles, which in 1980 became #1 Murder City in America—1,042 slayings.

Jim Dawson of Sterling, Virginia wants me to do a column on vasectomies, noting my history of having had one. It's on the way, Mr. Dawson. Most of the time, though, I just sit on top of the silent tv set, smiling at the ceiling; otherwise, it hasn't had a deleterious effect on me. Hmmmmmmmm.

Some of you, like Sharon Norberg of Miami, Florida, wrote me letters that required no answers. Mrs. Norberg wanted to tell me how much she liked the *Star Trek* movie. Others wanted to deliver long panegyrics on topics almost as boring. I have read as much of as many of these letters as I can. (Sometimes I fall asleep.) Before Mrs. Norberg lectures me on how my putting down of dull movies can inhibit tender souls' dreaming of the future, I suggest she do something concrete about getting the Equal Rights Amendment passed in Florida, a matter that has much more immediacy for dreams of the future than her plonking down $5 time after time to see the exploitation of what little love remains for *Star Trek* by its fans.

While we're on the moronic subject of the *Star Trek* movie, back in April a Mrs. Lisa Baker of Castle Rock, Colorado wrote *Starlog* columnist Bjo Trimble asking her to rap my knuckles because I had, in her view, made an error in noting when I reviewed the film—Paramount's contribution to the Ennui Enhancement of life in general—that an ornament on a headband worn by Persis Khambatta hung on the left side in one shot, then over the right on a follow-up. This seeming error in my otherwise flawless reportage of the year's dullest movie apparently drove Mrs. Baker, a grown woman, into paroxysms of anger. Bjo wrote her, quite properly, that her *Starlog* column was intended for other purposes than villifying Ellison and that it was none of her, Bjo's, business and that if Mrs. Baker was that outraged at my assailing her sacred cows, she ought to write me directly. Since I have not heard from Mrs. Baker directly, but since the matter has come up nonetheless via a Xerox copy of her letter, forwarded to me by my editor, Bob Woods, let me just say this:

Mrs. Baker is a pathetic case. A grown woman so distanced from reality that her ire is raised enough to prompt the writing of a letter not about how high her taxes are, not about how much she's paying for gas, not about nuns being shot to death by government troops in El Salvador, not about gun control or abortion (pro or con) or Nestlé selling death-dealing baby formula to underprivileged countries... but about a minor point in an undistinguished movie.

I may well be taken to task for pillorying this woman. What harm is she doing by objecting to my alleged error in a critical article, it may be said. Why kill a gnat with a howitzer? Well, I'll tell ya, gang, it's like this: Mrs. Baker is a classic example of what many of *you* have become. And the name for that is zombie.

Mrs. Baker will no doubt reject this. I'll be apprised in short order that Mrs. Baker has led the fight for equal rights in Colorado, that she cooks meals for shut-ins and old folks every day and then drives them over to the recipients free of charge, that she rescued eleven orphans from a burning building, that she discovered a cure for bone-marrow cancer last week, that she is a serious political cartoonist whose work in the Castle Rock *Blat* has brought dozens of crooked politicians to book, that she is beloved of her family and friends, that she has written the definitive social conscience work on the Dreyfus Case, and that in her spare time she does RN work at the local leprosarium. No doubt I'll be told all of this, to prove how shallow and vicious I am in calling Mrs. Baker a zombie.

But until such time, I judge only by the internal evidence of her letter. A letter that is concerned with silliness, a letter that reveals her dander is gotten up not by what goes on in the real world, not even what goes on in the slapdash world of an imbecilic movie, but what goes on in a piece of criticism of that slapdash movie! I submit Mrs. Baker as an object-lesson to all of you who justify your obsessions with movies whose sole purpose in this life is to *make money for multinational corporations that own movie studios* by lying to yourselves that these movies bear some relation to life, either as we know it today or as it pertains to the future.

I submit that all of the multi-million-dollar monstrosities you've slavered over in the past five years—from *Star Wars* to *Alien*—and I *liked Alien* a lot—that not all of them, taken in totality, equal by one one-millionth the humanity contained in *The Elephant Man* or *The Competition*. Not one of them says as much to us as human beings, instills as much hope in us, speaks as clearly to the human condition, as do *Paths of Glory* or *A Child is Waiting* or *The Deer Hunter*.

Even to *discuss* empty and empty-headed persiflage like the *Star Trek* movie in the same breath with *Oh, God!* or, again, *The Elephant Man* is to elevate transient commercial dreck to the level of serious attention. And for Mrs. Baker to spend even a microsecond of concern on my being right or wrong about such a minor cavil in the first place, even to dignify her concern by suggesting all my critical faculties should be called into question because I didn't perceive—as she suggests—that the second shot of Persis Khambatta was seen *in a mirror*, indicates that Mrs. Baker read the critique and then went back to see the goddammed movie *again*, just to be able to say I was wrong. Now Mrs. Baker may well be correct. That second shot may have been a mirror reflection (though if a viewer sharp enough to see that the ornament was hanging on the opposite side couldn't tell it was a mirror image, that says something about the quality of direction in the film) but I'd have to go see the film a second time to ascertain same. And frankly, if I need a couple of hours sleep I won't pay $5 to Paramount for the privilege, I'll just reread Mrs. Baker's letter and doze off.

I attack not Mrs. Baker herself, but what she has become. A person whose concerns are trivial in a world where triviality and mediocrity are used to keep us diverted, entertained, oblivious to what Tom Looby has begun to suspect, that we are in trouble, that we are becoming ever more helpless because great forces push and bend us, that we must be alert and awake and aware. . .and never permit ourselves to forget that sports and trash movies and dope and God-shouting and all the other toys of the Status Quo, whether called Entropy or something else, are intended to turn our senses and our anger away from the desire to fight back.

Mrs. Baker attacks the wrong foe. Television is her enemy; the venal corporations that put together a bad movie to take her $5 from her are the enemy; the designers of products that fall apart on schedule and for which she cannot get replacement parts are the enemy; stupidity and triviality are her enemies. Our taste in films may differ, Mrs. Baker, but when I walk out of the theater, at least I live in the Real World. God or whoever's in charge only knows where *you* live!

There are more letters. Seventeen more as I sit here. But I've spent too much time on Mrs. Baker and a few others. So I'll have to save them for the next roundup, just a mere six months away. I hope this interlude of sweetness and light has buoyed up your spirits. Feel free to drop me a postcard. Workouts like this merely get me in shape for the serious work to be done.

And have an angry New Year.

**INSTALLMENT 8:** 27 February 81
(published 28 April 81
in *Future Life* #27
cover-dated June)

# INTERIM MEMO:

I got a letter the other day from George. Damned if they aren't discussing this "creation science" bullshit all over again in the pages of the *San Diego Union*. At a lecture I gave in Grand Forks, North Dakota in March of this year, someone asked me how do we finally knock the fools and obscurantists and believers in craziness out of the box once and for all. I told the woman that we can't. Apart from hydrogen, the most common thing in the universe is stupidity. They keep coming up out of the Bandini like stinkweeds, folks. And if they aren't after John T. Scopes's scalp, they're after ours; and their mission is to keep us all as imbecilic as they are. So, no, we never finish fighting them. It's a holding battle. But if they win the foray, books get burned, and we go back to the Flat Earth. So hang in there. I'm getting a little weary, but I'm with you. If I can just get these spikes out of my wrists.

Up to now, I've been playing with kids. Assaulting the nonspecific targets of irrationality and obscurantism in my view. And apart from the deranged mercenary who wrote me today telling me that he had survived the Nam, Angola and Rhodesia wars (ostensibly he gets his kicks opening up with an M-16 at little brown babies) and that I didn't know what honor and patriotism were all about, I haven't had too much angst thrust upon me by these columns. But all that is done. Here and now I take on the big demon. Beginning with this column, my friends, I declare myself at arms against The Moral Majority.

And now we will find out how deeply runs the stream of courage you and I have perceived in the publishing and editorial staff of *Future Life* (and by extension, *Starlog*).

Because *this* demon doesn't pull in its dripping fangs. It will take on television networks, major industries, the organized church and even the United States government. So when the ka-ka hits the colander, we will soon see if the magazine in which these columns can be found is ready to go up against the direct lineal descendants of Torquemada, Cotton Mather, Senator Joseph McCarthy, Josef Goebbels and the House Un-American Activities Committee: those who would censor and legislate and boycott every opinion that doesn't conform with their own repressive, provincial, reactionary and downright antediluvian perceptions of the universe.

All of which they do in the name of Motherhood, Apple Pie, Bleeding Christ and The American Way.

Which makes it hard to fight them. Because as soon as you try, they start screaming Degenerate or Commie or Antichrist or Perverter of the Minds of Children.

I said to someone the other day that if I were to take them on, I'd damned well better pay off the mortgage on my house, because if they choose they can unleash a million letters to my sponsors, saying they'll never again buy this or that product if I'm permitted to go on raging with all this evil and immoral rot, and then I couldn't make a buck, and that would mean I couldn't make the mortgage payments on Ellison Wonderland, and would lose the house and find myself out in the street... as happened to so many people during the blacklist days of the Fifties. I also said I'd have to find sponsors who were beyond the vengeance of The Moral Majority. The few that occurred to me—and you might suggest a few others, friends, one never knows when the hard times will hit—were *Playboy* and the manufacturers of toilet paper. Or the phone company.

But, after all, we *are* writing a column for *Future Life*, not for *The Nation*. And so it should definitely be in genre, don't you think? This frontal assault on those who want to pull CATCHER IN THE RYE from public libraries, it ought to deal with science and the future and like that...right?

Glad you agree, chums.

Because we wish to start the festivities with one lovely aspect of The Moral Majority's crusade against reason. It is called Creationism. As opposed to the theory of Evolution. You remember all that stuff, don't you? The Scopes Monkey Trial and such good jazz. You thought that was all settled in the film *Inherit the Wind*, did you? You thought Spencer Tracy had won the day for Darwin and the descent of species.

Wrong and wrong.

Which leads me to introduce to you, in this corner, a nifty little scrapper for sanity named George Olshevsky; and over there in that corner a small group headed by Duane T. Gish, Gary E. Parker and a shadowy legion of slavering, slope-browed, prognathous-jawed atavists who were apparently bitten by a 35 mm print of *One Million B.C.*, who believe that men and dinosaurs lived at the same time.

But...enough from me. I turn the column over now to a replay of letters and newspaper clippings from last January. I wish you well on this deranged journey, and I'll be back next issue to make some comments.

Oh, and by the way: don't show this column to your local Creationist. It'll only make him/her fwow up his/her cookies.

---

Dear Mr. Ellison:

Last month the San Diego *Evening Tribune* carried an item on creationists which carried statements by one Duane T. Gish, creationist, in response to comments at the recent AAAS symposium held in Toronto. I couldn't take that bullshit being printed in a newspaper without a proper rebuttal, so I duly composed one and sent it off to their editorial page. Lo and behold, they printed it in full and I felt vindicated. Then a week later, they printed a letter from Gary E. Parker, which tries suavely and rather articulately to put down the points I made in my own letter. Unfortunately, Parker is full of it, despite his professorship and Ph.D. (professor at Christian Heritage College?? Give me a break!), but his writing is good enough that the average reader could be swayed into believing that creationsim is actually a defendable hypothesis, and that I, who have studied evolutionary theory for some time and purposely kept things simple and clear in my original letter, actually don't know what I'm talking about. So I wrote a second letter pulling out a few creationist quotations from their own books (actually, a children's book by Gish) for the world to see. I had had enough of evolutionary scientists constantly being forced to defend their work against the irrational onslaught of the creationists and had decided to carry the attack into their own camp a bit.

Well, the damned *Tribune* just sent me a note which reads in full as follows:

"Thank you for your letter to the editor, replying to the reply of Dr. Gary E. Parker to your original letter, which we printed on January 24.

"This is a controversy which is not likely to be settled in our lifetimes, certainly not in the letters column of this newspaper. We do not wish to prolong the dialogue at this extraordinary length. Each side would desire the last word.

"Your letter is so interesting, however, that I have taken the liberty of forwarding it directly to Dr. Parker. I hope this meets with your approval.

"Sincerely, Ralph B. Bennett, Chief Editorial Writer."

First of all, as far as scientists are concerned, there is no controversy and whatever controversy there was was settled back when Huxley and Wilberforce battled it out. The current flap has been raised by fundamentalists for arcane reasons of their own, not because any scientists worth their reputations give credence to creationist ideas. Second, by giving the creationists last word, he makes it Creationists 2, George Olshevsky 1—a clear win in their favor; he could certainly have cut the debate after my second letter. Then we would both have had equal time, if nothing else. Third, forwarding the letter to Parker won't convert him; Parker will just file it. In fact, the creationists could even send a few goons to my place (the address was on the letter—a requirement for publication by the *Tribune*) to throw rocks; those kind are not known for their subtlety of thought. I sent a postcard to Bennett expressing some of these thoughts, but I don't think it will do much good.

My question is, faced with this situation, what would *you* do? You have some experience dealing with these types, and any advice you could offer would be appreciated. I'll even drop the subject entirely, if that's what you recommend.

George Olshevsky
San Diego, CA

*From the San Diego* Evening Tribune, *Saturday, January 10, 1981:*

## Creationist denies fossil's use as proof of evolution

### By ROBERT DI VEROLI
Tribune *Religion Writer*

*Scientists who use the fossil record to say evolution is a fact are like people who think a Model T could change into a Model A, says Dr. Duane T. Gish, director of the Institute for Creation Research in El Cajon. "I can't even imagine a scientist saying a thing like that," says Gish, a biochemist whose organization promotes biblical creationism as a scientific alternative to the theory of evolution.*

*It was Dr. Porter M. Kier, former director of the National Museum of Natural History in Washington, D.C., who said this week that "evolution is a fact," because of "overwhelming and incontrovertible" evidence furnished by the fossil record.*

*"There are more than 100 million fossils in museums over the world, all identified and dated. That's 100 million facts that prove evolution without any doubts whatsoever," Kier told the American Association for the Advancement of Science in Toronto.*

*"The fact is that among all those fossils, not one intermediate or transitional form demanded by the theory of evolution has been found," Gish said in an interview.*

*These transitional forms, or series of missing links between one kind of animal and another, should be lying around everywhere, but in fact are nowhere to be found, Gish added.*

*"All these fossils are just that—records of animals that once existed, but they give no evidence of one kind of animal changing into another as the theory of evolution demands," he said.*

*"It's just like going to a museum where you see a buggy, a Model T Ford, a Model A Ford, a V-8 Ford and a modern Ford. They're all different kinds of Fords. You can assume that one model changed into the other, but there's no intermediate forms to prove it.*

*"The proof of evolution and what evolutionists have looked for ever since Darwin are these intermediate forms between one kind of animal and another. They themselves have said their theory demands them, but they've never found them."*

*Many confirmed evolutionists such as Dr. Stephen Jay Gould of Harvard and Dr. Karl Popper of England are saying they must develop a new theory of evolution precisely because these transitional forms have never been found, Gish said.*

*He said one alternative evolutionists have discussed is the theory that one kind of animal "rather abruptly"—on a geological time scale—*

78

changed into another without going through the intermediate, transitional stages that could show up eons later as fossils.

"In other words, they're admitting there is no evidence in the fossil record for the gradual change of one creature into another demanded by the Darwinian theory of evolution," Gish said.

"That's something we creation scientists have been saying for years. Now some very prominent paleontologists, evolutionists and other scientists are saying precisely the same thing.

"This actually amounts to an abandonment of the Darwinian theory because the Darwinian idea was that change was slow and gradual and due to natural selection. Now evolutionists are saying that's not so."

Gish said that more and more evolutionists are admitting evolution does not fulfill the criteria of a scientific theory, agreeing with Popper that while science rests on observation, the process of evolution cannot be observed.

"No scientist has ever observed the origin of life or the evolution of anything," Gish said. "It's something you accept as a matter of faith, not fact. Actually, the fossil record supports creation, not evolution, but we don't see either one taking place, of course.

"Neither creation nor evolution can be tested in the manner required by a scientific theory. That's why it's unscientific to say evolution is a fact. That's strictly a statement of faith."

Gish said those who accuse creationists of basing their views on religious faith are thus basing their own views on an act of faith, not on fact.

"Neither creationism nor evolutionism is a valid scientific theory," he said. "When they talk about their evolutionary theories on the origin of the universe or the origin of life they are operating outside the limits of empirical science. They are in the realm of metaphysics, not science.

"We just believe in presenting both sides and letting the students decide for themselves."

---

*From the San Diego* Evening Tribune, *Saturday, January 24, 1981:*

## Report from creationist under attack

Editor:

Looking through the stack of *Evening Tribune*s that has accumulated while I was out of town, I came across an item titled, "Creationist denies fossil's use as proof of evolution," by Robert Di Veroli, on page A-7 of the Jan. 10, 1981 issue. Di Veroli reports comments by Dr. Duane T. Gish on the theory of evolution, in response to the assertion by Dr. Porter M. Kier that "evolution is a fact" backed up by "evidence furnished by the fossil record."

As reported therein, Gish's comments are complete garbage. He seems quite ignorant of the entire fields of biology, geology and paleontology. Were it not for the alarming fact that the influence of creationists shows signs of seeping into legitimate science textbooks and classrooms, and thence into the minds of children still too young to distinguish truth from rubbish, I would not waste my time writing. I write in the hope that what I say will at least see print and be presented to the public as a reasoned alternative to Gish's reported statements.

—Gish is reported as saying, "The fact is that among all those fossils, not one intermediate or transitional form demanded by the theory of evolution has been found." This is utterly false. It would be false if even one transitional form were known, but it so happens that practically every fossil ever found can be regarded as intermediate or transitional between earlier and later forms. The details of just what is meant by "intermediate" and "transitional" are subject to proper scientific debate, and it is here that the creationists try to drive their wedge.

As examples of "transitional forms," I can cite the entire fossil records of horses, elephants, rhinoceroses and humans. I can cite Archaeopteryx, a form perfectly transitional between dinosaurs and birds. I can cite Presbyornis, a recently discovered fossil bird transitional between ducks and long-legged shorebirds. And I can refer the reader to numerous texts describing countless others. Gish further is reported as stating, "These transitional forms...should be lying around everywhere, but in fact are nowhere to be found." The transitional forms are lying around everywhere; Gish seems to lack the wit and perception to see them.

—Gish is reported as saying, "Many confirmed evolutionists such as Dr. Stephen Jay Gould of Harvard and Dr. Karl Popper of England are saying they must develop a new theory of evolution precisely because these transitional forms have never been found."

Further, Gish notes, "In other words, they're admitting there is no evidence in the fossil record for the gradual change of one creature into another demanded by the Darwinian theory of evolution." When Darwin published his theory in 1859, the fossil record was still far too sparse for scientists to decide on the details and mechanisms of the causes of evolutionary change.

Now, after 122 years of collecting fossils from all over the world, scientists are in a far better position to determine why species change into other species. Darwin's principal discovery, that species have changed into others over the course of geological time, is the fact of evolution. For various reasons, not all scientific, these changes were thought to have taken place gradually and slowly.

The accumulation of evidence in the fossil record now requires a serious look toward revising this "gradualism" and replacing it with "punctualism." This states that species change quickly and abruptly, not gradually, into other forms.

The idea of evolutionary change itself is not questioned; only the rate of change is being examined. Gish's statements as reported in the article are designed to mislead readers into thinking that scientists want to abandon the theory of evolution for the "theory" of creationism. I cannot think of any assertion that would be further from the truth.

—Gish observes that, "No scientist has ever observed the origin of life or the evolution of anything. It's something you accept as a matter of faith, not fact." I would like to know how Gish can expect scientists to project themselves 3½ billion years into the past to observe a process which took several hundreds of millions of years to occur. Obviously no scientist has ever observed the origin of life! That does not mean that it did not take place, and that certainly doesn't mean that we can never understand the process.

No scientist has ever seen an atomic nucleus, but we nevertheless have atomic bombs. No scientist has ever seen an electromagnetic field, but we nevertheless have radio and television. For that matter, I have never seen Gish, but I think that his existence is a fact, based on the evidence of his photograph in the *Tribune*.

Just because a process is too slow to be perceived over the very short span of recorded history does not mean that we cannot infer its existence in ways that make sense. We are presented with a panorama of life on Earth extending backwards in time to its very beginnings, a panorama presenting science with patterns from which inferences can be made. One inference, biological evolution, is supported by countless data from the natural sciences. It is no longer something to be taken on faith, as it may have been in 1859, but a fact the acknowledgment of which is necessary for further progress in biology, paleontology, biochemistry, biophysics, immunology and medicine to take place.

—Gish is reported as saying, "Neither creation nor evolution can be tested in the manner required by a scientific theory. That's why it's unscientific to say evolution is a fact." Gish is correct when he asserts that creation is not a theory; but he is incorrect when he asserts the same about evolution. A theory is a logical structure built up in a consistent manner by inference from a body of facts. A theory, to have any scientific value, must specify tests of itself, that is, make predictions that can be verified. For example, the theory of evolution predicts that the fossil record will be progressive in time, because species changes build on one another. You cannot have a wing without first having an arm; you cannot have an arm without first having a front foot; and you cannot have a front foot without first having a fin. The theory of evolution predicts that fins will come before feet, feet will come before arms, and arms will come before wings.

This is exactly what is observed in the fossil record when the transitional forms between fishes and birds are lined up in chronological sequence. I have never seen a statement of the "theory" of creationism anywhere—I think because no such thing exists—but the few disconnected scraps I have assimilated lead me to believe that creationism would predict the appearance of species in the fossil record completely at random, with no visible relationship to one another.

Six-legged gzorkles would be just as likely as housecats, and we could have birds in the Devonian period just as easily as we could have them in the Cenozoic. Yet nothing like this exists. The fossil record is orderly and systematic.

Creationism is not the correct description of the way things happen in real life. There is no earthly reason to present creationism as a scientific theory to young people, who have a hard enough time with science already without this added pseudoscientific baggage.

George Olshevsky
Member
Society of Vertebrate Paleontology
Linda Vista

---

*From the San Diego* Evening Tribune, *Saturday, January 31, 1981:*

### Evolution–creation debate in full cry

*Editor:*

In his lengthy letter (VOP, 1-24-81), George Olshevsky attempted to defend evolution against the creationist statements of Dr. Duane T. Gish reported earlier. As one who taught evolution in my college biology classes for several years, I can sympathize with Olshevsky's intentions, but unfortunately, the points he raises are sufficiently out of date and error-laden to embarrass contemporary evolutionists.

As examples of "transitional forms" ("missing links" supposed to show how evolution occurred), Olshevsky cites horses, humans and Archaeopteryx (a "reptile-bird"). These are the same examples I used long ago with my college classes—the same examples that creationists like Dr. Gish have used in winning debates with noted evolutionists at major universities across the country!

*Practically every fossil discovery once hailed as a transition from some animal to man, for example, has been discarded. Neanderthals are now known to be people (Homo sapiens), some of whom suffered bone diseases. Piltdown (Eoanthropus) and Java Man (Homoerectus) are also hoaxes. Nebraska Man (Hesperopithecus) was reconstructed, flesh, hair and family, from a single tooth—the tooth of an extinct pig!*

*Only the African australopithecines, such as "Lucy," remain as possible links to man. But, according to USC's Charles Oxnard, these forms did not walk in the human manner, and human types (e.g., the Kanapoi hominid) precede man in the fossil sequence, which means these forms could not have been man's ancestor.*

*The "reptile-bird," Archaeopteryx, was the "missing link" discovery I preferred to use with my class. It had teeth, claws and a tail like a reptile, yet it had wings and feathers like a bird—"a form perfectly transitional between dinosaurs and birds," Olshevsky says. And that's what I thought, until some astute students pointed out that Archaeopteryx had completely developed feathers and the fully functional furcula ("wishbone") and wings of a strong flyer—and no hint of how scales might have evolved into feathers, or legs into wings. Furthermore, bones of typical birds have been found as far down in the geologic sequence as those of Archaeopteryx, so Archaeopteryx specimens we have obviously could not have been the ancestors of those birds.*

*Conceding that Archaeopteryx is no transitional form, Yale's Ostrom proposes that the real "missing link" between reptiles and birds is "pro-avis," a form supposed to show how scales and arms evolved through a flapping, insect-catching stage before becoming the true feathers and wings of Archaeopteryx (*American Scientist, *Jan./Feb. 1979). However, Ostrom also states quite clearly: "No fossil evidence of any pro-avis exists. It is a purely hypothetical pre-bird, but one which must surely have existed."*

*Now I have to admit to my classes that such a statement is pure faith, "blind faith" at that. Although Ostrom is a first-rate scientist, his view is not scientific; it cannot be inferred from the fossil evidence, since none exists.*

*Olshevsky concedes that evolution may have been taken on faith in 1859. Indeed, Darwin recognized the absence of intermediate varieties and the presence of complex and diverse life forms in the lowest known fossil-bearing rocks as "perhaps the most obvious and serious objection which can be urged against the theory." Olshevsky's assertion that later discoveries gave substance to Darwin's hope is woefully at odds with the evidence, including my own doctoral work in paleontology and extensive fossil collection, and with the cutting edge of contemporary evolutionary thought. As the Field Museum's David Raup puts it:*

*"Well, we are now about 120 years after Darwin, and knowledge of the fossil record has been greatly expanded...ironically, we have even fewer examples of evolutionary transition than we had in Darwin's time.*

*By this I mean that some of the classic cases of Darwinian change in the fossil record, such as the evolution of the horse in North America, have had to be discarded or modified as a result of more detailed information."*

Olshevshky is 100 percent wrong; the accumulation of evidence has made the classic case for evolution more a matter of faith, no less.

Unfortunately, Olshevsky is 100 percent correct in his statement that none of the scientists mentioned above is giving up his belief in evolution and adopting a creationist position. But that very fact puts me in an embarrassing position as a science teacher. I have to tell my students that, in spite of the repeated failures of evolutionary theory, most scientists are bent on forcing the evidence to fit some sort of evolutionary view—even Olshevsky's "punctualism," which Gould calls, "The Return of Hopeful Monsters," a view that is based on genetics that have never been observed and fossils that have never been found.

"Scientific creationists" like Dr. Gish, however, have been presenting their case on the basis of known scientific principles and fossils that have been found. Olshevsky states that he has "never seen a statement of the 'theory' of creationism anywhere," yet there is actually an enormous amount of creation science literature written from elementary to graduate research level, much of it produced right here in San Diego at the internationally recognized Institute for Creation Research (which also houses a creation museum).

Olshevsky is rightly concerned about "the minds of children too young to distinguish truth from rubbish." It's certainly true that students with access to all the evidence regarding human origins, for example, might properly wonder which really is rubbish—evolution or creation. But training in "healthy skepticism" is foundational in true science education, and, open discussion on both sides of the evolution/creation question seems to be an excellent means to a worthy goal.

If evolution is supported better by the evidence than creation, then what do evolutionists have to fear from exploring both sides of the origins question? If creation is better supported, what does science have to lose by pursuing truth to whatever conclusion fits the facts the best? Isn't that what education in science is all about?

Dr. Gary E. Parker
Professor of Biology/Paleontology
Christian Heritage College
El Cajon

---

Sent February 2, 1981 to the Tribune:

Dear Sir:

Thank you for printing my long letter of 1/24/81 in VOP. Unfortunately, it had the side effect of spawning an almost equally lengthy response from the creationists, namely, the letter in VOP for 1/31/81 from Dr. Gary E. Parker, Professor of Biology and Paleontology at Christian Heritage College. He suggests that I have not kept up with the "cutting edge" of evolutionary theory, which is, of course, false. Contrary to his assertion that my points were "out of date" and "in error," the examples cited in my letter were well chosen and beautifully illustrate the fact of evolution. Many of the details can be found in George Gaylord Simpson's book, THE MEANING OF EVOLUTION (revised edition, 1971), which is by no means as dated as Parker might have us believe. Stephen Jay Gould's magnum opus, ONTOGENY AND PHYLOGENY (Belknap Press, Harvard, 1977), develops a highly subtle and original description of the process which engenders new species from old. An excellent recent statement of the thesis of punctuated evolution is Steven M. Stanley's book, MACRO-EVOLUTION: PATTERN AND PROCESS (Freeman, 1979). I suggest Parker return to these volumes to acquire a broader perspective of what evolution is all about. It evidently escaped him the first time around.

No paleobiologist in his right mind would ever point to a specific fossil and declare that it is *the* transitional form between two other specific fossils. Only an incredibly small fraction of all the prehistoric animals that have ever lived occur as fossils, and the odds against finding a complete sequence of transitional forms are inconceivably remote. It should be very clear to Parker that the term "transitional" involves generalization, and I am baffled by his seeming ignorance of this obvious point.

All scientists of evolution acknowledge that the fossil record is imperfect. This fact, being negative evidence, can never by itself invalidate the evolutionary hypothesis. It is, rather, the fact that practically every known fossil shares *some* morphologic characters with other forms that is of major significance to the theory of evolution.

In his discussion of hominids, Parker invokes hoaxes and errors—some of which, such as the Piltdown Man, might actually have been planted by creationists bent on muddying the waters—which are totally irrelevant as documentation of the hominid fossil record. Further, he seems unaware that Neanderthals were quite different from modern man (see "Neanderthal the Hunter," by Valerius Geist, in the January 1981 issue of *Natural History* magazine), and by his own admission acknowledges that australopithecines "remain as possible links to man." The sequence from the monkey-like *Aegyptopithecus* through *Ramapithecus* to *Australopithecus* to *Homo* documents a major trend recognized by virtually every scientist of hominid evolution.

The primary impact of the work of John Ostrom of Yale on *Archaeopteryx* stems from his documentation of over 20 morphologic characters that *Archaeopteryx* shares with dromaeosaurid dinosaurs, and not his clearly labled as hypothetical sequence illustrating his view of the evolution of flight. The most current summary of avian evolution is Alan Feduccia's THE AGE OF BIRDS (Harvard University Press, 1980), in which is unambiguously documented the existence of a functional furcula and primary and secondary flight feathers in *Archaeopteryx*. We do not at this point care how feathers might have evolved from scales, nor how flight feathers and a furcula came to be in a fossil which is otherwise a typical small dinosaur. We do not at this point care whether *Archaeopteryx* is exactly one half bird and one half dinosaur, nor just where this occurs in the fossil record. The single solid inference provided by *Archaeopteryx*—glaringly obvious to any scientist but totally lost on Parker—is that birds and dinosaurs are closely related, because *Archaeopteryx* is indeed, as I asserted previously, a form perfectly transitional between the two groups.

Parker notes that "bones of typical birds have been found as far down in the geologic sequence as those of *Archaeopteryx*." Not yet, they haven't! Not one positively identifiable avian bone has been discovered in the Jurassic or earlier other than *Archaeopteryx*. I have made an extensive survey of the scientific literature in the course of my own work, and have determined that all known putative Jurassic avian fossils—which are extremely rare in any case—not accompanied by feather impressions cannot be reliably distinguished from small dinosaurs or pterosaurs.

Creationists demand that evolutionists supply them with evolutionary links to substantiate their theories. The evolutionists proceed to do so. The creationists then demand links between the links. On occasion, the evolutionists can still supply them. Then the creationists demand links between those links. Eventually, of course, fossil record peters out, at which time the creationists shout, "Aha! The links are still missing! Your theory is wrong!" This is the kind of garbage reasoning that is parroted by Parker when he cites David Raup—totally out of context, incidentally—in his letter.

What, then, do the creationists offer in place of evolution? Is there a coherent theory that can be subjected to scientific scrutiny and debate? How are species formed, if not by evolving from other species? How do creationists account for the systematic nature of the fossil record, or the fact that morphologic phylogenies closely resemble phylogenies developed by protein amino acid sequence analysis, or the observation that ontogeny seems to recapitulate phylogeny, or the remarkable fact that all the living things on Earth down to the level of bacteria use the same genetic code and the same genetic material, DNA? The theory of evolution, incomplete as it may be, provides detailed explanations that make sense. All that the creationists can say is simply, "That's all just some kind of coincidence," or, "That's the way God works, and we'll never understand God." Healthy skepticism is indeed the agent of scientific progress, but I am not so skeptical of the enormous body of evidence for evolution that I would discard it in favor of the total chaos of creationism.

Thus, when I stated in my letter that I had never seen a statement of the "theory" of creationism anywhere, I meant exactly that. I am well aware of the vast propaganda that passes for scientific literature, published by creationists and backed by fundamentalist religious sects trying to turn back the clock to the good old days when the Earth was the center of all creation and religious thought dominated Western culture. Let me quote from a book in my possession, written by the very Duane T. Gish quoted in the *Tribune* on 1/10/81, titled DINOSAURS: THOSE TERRIBLE LIZARDS, published right here in San Diego by our own nest of creationists, and designed for sale to children for $6.95:

"When did these animals become meat-eaters, if indeed they were meat-eaters as most scientists believe? Genesis 1:29–30 indicates that as originally created, man and all animals were to be plant-eaters only. We believe it is very likely that some animals, such as the dinosaurs, lions, tigers, etc., became meat-eaters after sin came into the world." (page 37)

Gish offers the following explanation of the function of the odd skulls of certain herbivorous dinosaurs: "No one has ever been able to figure out what these hollow bony structures were used for .... Maybe this creature could mix some chemicals together similar to those used by the bombardier beetle, and store them in a storage chamber. Then when a meat-eating dinosaur like *Tyrannosaurus* came after him, he could squirt a big charge into his combustion chamber (the hollow structure on top of his head?), add an anti-inhibitor at just the right time, and ZZZZZZZZZZZ! Fire and smoke would come pouring out right in the face of the *Tyrannosaurus*." (page 55, accompanied by a color picture of *Parasaurolophus* blowing away *Tyrannosaurus* with his fiery breath, on pages 50–51)

Indeed! Lack of space prohibits quoting more of these creationist howlers.

Creationists accuse scientists of making up this fantasy of evolution and basing it on faith, not fact. Yet there is not a shred of evidence that sin and carnivores are in any way connected, not a shred of evidence that dinosaurs breathed fire. And why, if *Tyrannosaurus* and *Parasaurolophus* were both originally created as plant-eaters, would the herbivore have been given this fire-breathing apparatus to defend itself in the first place?

Yes, tragically, creationism has an extensive literature. So do astrology, occultism, parapsychology, flying saucers, pyramidology, scientology and any number of other bizarre human endeavors.

Having an extensive literature is no guarantee against folly. Proper scientific debate of the merits of creationism has indeed taken place, but it was so short and swift that most of the creationists—including Dr. Gary E. Parker—missed it completely.

George Olshevsky
Member
Society of Vertebrate Paleontology

**INSTALLMENT 9:** 25 April 81
(published 9 June 81
in *Future Life* #28
cover-dated August)

# INTERIM MEMO:

The Harlan Ellison Record Collection mentioned in this column not only still exists, it has grown like The Blob. There are now over 1500 more-or-less satisfied customers who've bought recordings of yr. humble svt. and in 1983 the HERC recording of "Jeffty is Five" was nominated for a Grammy in the Spoken Word category. I mention all of this in hopes that each of you who have been told, to this point in the book, not to write for free samples of this'n'that, or to express your displeasure with something I've said, will join the HERC. This, as opposed to idle freebies or expressing opinions, is commerce. And as we know, having been told by both Calvin Coolidge and Ronald Reagan, this is important because: "The business of America...is business!" So be a Good American: join the Harlan Ellison Record Collection, send me money, go broke, sell your children or your heritage (whichever come first) for a mess of pottage!

PHOTO: KENT BASH

As I write this—weeks late and my sanity maintained largely through the forebearance of my editor, Bob Woods—the mail has not begun arriving in response to last issue's opening encounter with the Moral Majority, the New Right, the Forces of Reactionary Censorship...call them what you will. I expect the usual apoplectic screeds. And they will, no doubt, be of a piece with the several hundred letters that came in to *Heavy Metal* magazine recently, hard on the heels of an editorial I was pressed into writing on the subject of gun control. The editorial was sparked by the death of John Lennon, but it was foursquarely concerned with the inarticulate conspiracy of which we are all a part...when we don't break our asses to get gun control passed in this ever-more-deranged nation.

Even for those few of you who actually still believe civilians ought to be permitted to own guns, a reading of my mail after the appearance of the editorial would serve, I feel sure, to convince you that we *must* have total gun control as quickly as possible. The letters are ennobled by the word "sick." The realization that there are people out among us who are even capable of *writing* such deranged foulness could not but serve to sway you inexorably to a belief that madness is not manifested solely in the personae of the David Berkowitzes, Mark David Chapmans, Charlie Mansons and John Hinckleys who wander stunned and ready to explode through the feartime night.

This resurgence of widespread lunatic behavior is not, I am convinced, a thing apart from the rise of the Moral Majority. I think it is a manifestation of the same disease in the body politic that has caused the fundamentalists and all their clone-children to assume such prominence on the national scene.

It is not simply coincidence that Berkowitz (Son of Sam) listened to the voice of God who told him to kill; that Chapman had been involved with cults and was a brainwashee of the Jesus Movement;

that Charlie Manson was brought up deeply and rigidly religious, and that he sought a new religion in the overlay of mysticism Sixties' layabouts perceived in Heinlein's STRANGER IN A STRANGE LAND with its Christ-surrogate, Valentine Michael Smith; that Hinckley is a longtime reader of science fiction and adventure fantasy. Look at photos of Berkowitz, Chapman and Hinckley. Lay them side-by-side and look at the somatotype similarity. They look as if their moonstruck faces had been cut by the same cookie stamper.

In my endeavor to confront the maleficence of the Moral Majority—its book burnings, its attempts at legislating morality, its Dark Ages sensibility toward science, its Spanish Inquisition vengefulness—I have begun to sense a linkage between mind-dribble fantasy of the sort typified by films like *Excalibur* and the recent NBC effluvium *Fugitive from the Empire,* and the comeback of born-again fundamentalism in this country. I'll go further: I perceive the linkages between mind-dribble fantasy (I'll define that at greater length perhaps in the next installment) (for the nonce, you can assume I mean that subgenre of fantasy dealing with chattering bunnies, furry-footed denizens of deep forests, dragons, lion-maned barbarian warriors, runic quests in search of the lost scepter or the mystic bloodstone, nerds who say *thee* and *thou* a lot, and call their enemies *varlet*...you know what I mean: the kind of books that have unpronounceable words in the title and pastel vistas painted on the covers) and dat ole time religion currently masquerading as a socio-political revival of ethic as only part of the chain that includes berserker assassins in love with Jodie Foster or Jessica Savitch; the proliferation of nauseating knife-kill flicks in which women are endlessly raped, brutalized, carved up, and rendered nonthreatening to males who cannot cope with a world in which women are their equals, even in *some* things; the insensat rise in anti-Semitism, pseudo-Naziism, the KKK (with military training camps in 27 states) and a hundred different cults—each with its own bush-league messiah—dedicated to keeping its drone members dumb and penniless; and the paranoid need of NRA "sportsmen" to convince themselves that a nigger is just about to break into their home and rape their cellulite-riddled wife.

It is my sure conviction that all of this is linked.

And so last issue I ran a series of letters between a paleontologist named George Olshevsky, and some creationists. I turned over my column to Olshevsky, whom I see as a courageous man, because he had gone as far as he could go. He had put himself on the line against the cabal, and the medium in which the fray was fought, a San Diego newspaper, chose not to serve the ends of rationality and exhaustive discussion; but merely the commercial end of "let's you two fight" until they felt the audience was growing bored. So Olshevsky, frustrated, wrote me (definitely the court of last resort) and asked if he should keep at it. I responded by giving him a much larger forum than formerly.

And I said, last column, that I'd come back this time to make a few parting remarks on the subject. The preceding have been those remarks, buttressed by these:

After the Lennon gun-control essay, I received the kind of mail I expect to get from last issue's refutation of the idiocy of creationism. One of the letters was on embossed Nazi swastika stationery. It was from a man in the U.S. Navy, at the Groton, Connecticut submarine base. I hope he was trying to be funny, using that stationery.

Uh-huh. That's my hope.

But if I get another one from him like that, I think I'll send it on to the Base Commander, who may have been in WWII and who may remember what that crippled cross stands for. Because it seems to me that in these days of trembling crystal, with the glass singing its song of impending shatterment, and lizard men in three-piece ice cream suits promising us salvation in the life of a sheep, there are very few realities whose unarguable truth is not up for grabs. And one of the most firmly secured is that twenty million civilian victims of Nazi brutality, twenty million homeless ghosts, whisper to us night and day that we must ever be on guard against a return of that hurricane insanity that challenged god and man and sanity. For smartass punks who think it's rebellious or hip to make use of the swastika, history is waiting to snatch you away and give you over to the sleepless ghosts.

\* \* \*

I need a break.

So this section of the current installment will be given over to making a buck. Pure self-serving, calculated commercial enticement (of an interesting sort); but if I can't apprise you, my readers, of this...then who the hell *can* I buttonhole?

But...

Like the charming little pack rat that leaves something behind when it steals some bright object, I will give you a dream in exchange for your time and attention. (Actually, this "trade" accredited to pack, or wood, rats is more a matter of Disneyesque anthropomorphism than zoological fact. There is good in the most evil of us, and contrariwise, what seems to be ethic may be only circumstance. To wit: the little fellers can only carry one thing at a time; so if it sees some nifty object near your campfire, and it lusts for it, then it drops what it was carrying. Thus was promulgated the legend of the equitable behavior of pack rats, based almost entirely on a pack rat having carried off a vial of botulism, leaving behind the Koh-i-noor diamond, which was later presented to Queen Victoria after the annexation of the Punjab.)

The dream is this: a dream of mine, but I'll share it.

It was in the late Forties. See now this kid, Harlan, thirteen or fourteen years old, riding in the back seat of his mom and dad's green Plymouth, on a Sunday late afternoon. In those days the family "went for a ride." Nowhere special, just out for a leisurely spin to buy an ice cream cone, to drive into Mentor, Ohio where a certain ice cream parlor carried comic books the kid couldn't get in Painesville. See them, the three of them, Mom and Dad and the kid, driving along a country road in Ohio. . . listening to the radio.

In those days wonders came across the airwaves. I've written about those wonders in "Jeffty Is Five." Adventure with Jack Armstrong and Capt. Midnight and Terry & the Pirates. Comedy with Jack Benny and Easy Aces and Eddie Cantor. Drama with Orson Welles's Mercury Theater, Lux Presents Hollywood and the Molle Mystery Theater where I first heard Robert Bloch's name, and his terrifying story "Yours Truly, Jack the Ripper" that led, years later, to my writing my own Jack the Ripper story, "The Prowler in the City at the Edge of the World."

Wonders that taught me how to think visually.

If it had not been for listening to radio drama, I would never have been able to write motion pictures; and the stories I've written would not be quite so clearly viewable on the screen of your mind. Imagination is served wonderfully by sound. One can create in the theater of thoughts sets and artifacts that it would cost Hollywood billions to actualize. And I was a child of radio dreams.

See then: this kid Harlan and Mom and Dad, driving down Mentor Avenue, on a Sunday afternoon early in the Forties. And the radio spoke:

"Quiet, please." A pause, heavy with expectation. Then, again, "Quiet, please."

The voice of Ernest Chappell. One of the great radio voices. A sound that combined urbanity with storytelling wisdom. And the show was on the Mutual Network; it was, of course, the legendary *Quiet, Please,* created by Wyllis Cooper.

I begged my mother and father to leave it on, not to change over to one of the more popular Sunday comedy shows; and they left the dial where it was, and I heard something that I have never forgotten, something I will share with you now.

Ernest Chappell narrated Wyllis Cooper's scripts. The programs were backed up by sound effects and music (the theme was the 2nd movement of Franck's *Symphony in D Minor,* a work I cannot listen to, even today, without being thrilled to my toenails), but essentially it was Chappell, just speaking softly. Quietly. Terrifyingly.

What I heard that Sunday afternoon, so long ago, that has never left my thoughts for even one week, through all these years, was this:

"There is a place just five miles from where you now stand that no human eye has ever seen. It is. . . five miles *down!*"

94

When I heard that, and even now when I say it at college lectures, even when I simply type it on a page, a chill takes possession of my spine.

And the story was wonderful. (I'm sure if I were to hear it now, forty years later, it might be woefully thin and unworthy of the weight I have put on it...but I've managed to obtain recordings of the five or six shows that are still extant, and they are superb...so memory, this once, probably serves me well.)

It concerned a group of men working in the deepest coal mine in the world. (Coal mine? It's been forty years; it may have been a tin mine, or a diamond mine.) And they break through the floor of the mine and it turns out to be the ceiling, the roof, of the biggest cave in the world. I mean *big!* So gigantic that even the most powerful searchlights can't penetrate the darkness through that hole. Nothing can be seen down there. It just goes down and down. A stone, dropped through the hole, keeps falling...there is no sound of its having landed.

So they rig up something like a bathysphere, and a couple of guys are lowered in it and...they're attacked by pterodactyls before they can reach the bottom!

Now that's all I remember of the plot; but tell me something, troops: how many stories you heard or saw or read fifteen years ago, ten years ago, even *five* years ago...do you remember that clearly today? And I heard "Five Miles Down" at least *forty* years ago. And it's still with me.

Still with me to the extent that very soon now I will be writing a story titled "Down Deep," which will open with Wyllis Cooper's basic idea, and go from there. Still with me to the extent that I have always loved the sound of dramatic readings and have learned my lessons well from Orson Welles and Wyllis Cooper and Ernest Chappell.

Which brings me to the commercial aspect of this part of the column. My public readings started drawing some small attention a number of years ago; and I was approached to put some stories on record. I did so. They sold out. Now, because I love reading my stories, and I cannot be in every middlesex village and farm where someone might like to hear me read a story, I have initiated The Harlan Ellison Record Collection.

This will be real nifty, gang. It is a sorta kinda record club that will publish a regular *Newsletter* with information about my college appearances, upcoming publication of new stories, ongoing reports of the progress of my film work—even the unlikely possibility that *I, Robot* might get made at last—and pieces of unpublished works, inside stuff...be the first on your block to be bored silly!

But the best part, the really snazzy part, is that you will have a chance to buy records as we release them, in signed and numbered editions, at prices lower than the *few* specialty bookstores we'll be using as outlets will be selling them for. The first record is already available, a reissue of the album *Harlan! Ellison Reads Ellison*. This record includes complete versions of "'Repent, Harlequin!' Said the Ticktockman" and "Shatterday." The first edition of this record, long unavailable, is selling through antiquarian book dealers for fifty bucks a shot.

The way to join the Collection is simple. Five bucks gets you a membership and the *Newsletter*. Send the five dollars in check or money order to: The Harlan Ellison Record Collection, 8530 Wilshire Blvd., Suite 309, Beverly Hills, California 90211. If you want a copy of the *Harlan!* record, include an additional $7.95.

And yes, this is a commercial venture, and I don't want to lead you astray by trying to infer that someone else is behind this Collection. It's my money backing it, and I stand behind every record.

But the dream I'll be sharing with those of you who enjoy my work is the dream I got that Sunday afternoon in Mentor, Ohio, when I heard Ernest Chappell say...*five miles down!*

\* \* \*

And next time I'll finish off the current screed against the Moral Majority, and get into the subject of knife-kill movies.

Till that time.

**INSTALLMENT 10:** 5 June 81
(published 21 July 81
in *Future Life* #29
cover-dated September)

# Interim Memo:

Only those who have been so petrified by Nuclear Holocaust Paranoia that they have taken up permanent residence in useless backyard bomb shelters installed by their parents in the Fifities are unaware that since this tenth column was written, the Religious Far Right has expanded its efforts. Like all demagogues from Torquemada to Hitler to Senator Bilbo and Father Coughlin and Joe McCarthy, they have waved the tattered flags of God and patriotism, and their benighted forces now attack on all fronts: political, academic, sociological, scientific. And *People for the American Way,* praised in this column, has fought back. It is still in operation, gathers more support each year as Falwell's Fools overstep the bounds in more and more people's personal lives. I urge your attention to this column, and recommend that you get involved. *People For* needs your support. Like the ACLU and a few other organizations dedicated to the First Amendment, they are all that stand between us and the intellectual Dachaus wherein the tunnel-visioned would have us take up residence; a neighborhood that makes the bomb shelters look cozy by comparison. Oh, and Jimmy Doohan is fully recovered.

So here I am last April 21st, round about midnight, sitting in the studios of radio station WMCA in New York, doing "The Candy Jones Show" with a dude named Richard Viguerie. Jot the name on the slate of your brain. Mr. Viguerie has made millions with a direct-mail operation that circularizes advocates of the aims of The Moral Majority. If your local school board currently sports a couple of whackos who want to pull CATCHER IN THE RYE or ONE FLEW OVER THE CUCKOO'S NEST from the library and you enlist the aid of your senator to put pressure on the rest of the school board not to bow to pressure from the narrowminded and subliterate, all the whackos have to do is get in touch with Mr. Vieguerie's Committee for the Survival of a Free Congress and—as in 1978 when the CSFC spent over $400,000 to help elect 31 conservative candidates in both houses—within mere hours the desk of that hapless senator will be a veritable Sargasso Sea of apoplectic screeds accusing said public servant of being a perverter of the young, a willing handservant of the pornography cabal, a crypto-Commie and an individual who would, no doubt, pimp out his/her children for a few filthy pfennig.

If your senior senator looks on the Human Life Bills sponsored by Senator Jesse Helms as scientifically corrupt, morally reprehensible, criminally irresponsible and just downright unenforcible—Senate Bill 158 and House Resolution 900 will outlaw abortion by amending the 14th Amendment with these words: "Human life shall be deemed to exist from conception, without regard to race, sex, age, health, defect or condition of dependency"—then Dick Viguerie's computers go to work sorting and culling just the right geographic and demographic segment of the New Moral Right to start inundating said senior senator with enough hate mail to repaper his office.

Mr. Viguerie, who has called himself "politically Christian," which seems to me to fudge more than a little with the idea of the separation of Church and State, has grown slick and financially fat by bringing to the arena of political demagoguery a wizardly wiliness with the ways of microcircuitry that makes the special effects of George Lucas look like Edison's earliest experiments with tungsten filaments.

So there I am, sitting behind a microphone on WMCA, with this great gray eminence of the New Anal Retentive Right, and he is crowing about how these conservative activists are something new, something fresh and original.

And I cut in on his self-aggrandizement by saying, "I beg to differ. The New Right isn't original; we've had its like at least once before. Except that time they called it The Spanish Inquisition."

Candy Jones told me, after the program, that WMCA's computerized phone system had logged in over eight thousand calls waiting to be heard; far and away the largest number of call-ins the show had ever experienced.

Bringing me, at last, to my closing remarks (for the time being) about The Moral Majority.

The Moral Majority abhors sex outside of wedlock. But they are solidly behind no gun control. Not to be crude about this, but they want to make sex illegal, yet they don't mind if every self-styled vigilante packs a .357 Magnum.

The Moral Majority wants sex education in schools abolished so the herpes epidemic can go unchecked, yet they want prayers in schools to be reinstituted. Religious training is, to them, a state matter, rather than a parental choice; but sex education is a parental choice but not a state matter. Government intrusion is welcome when it serves their Fundamentalist ends, but verboten when their bluestocking prejudices are challenged.

The Moral Majority really believes God has a political position on the Panama Canal.

The Moral Majority really believes gays and young people are a menace that must be met with stern action. If you fought in Vietnam you're a patriot. . .as long as you don't stage a sit-in on the lawn of the VA hospital and demand to know why you're rotting away or going insane from exposure to Agent Orange. At that point you become a freako troublemaker. If you're a woman who got raped and knocked up and want the fetus aborted, well, that's sad as hell, sister, but your womb has citizenship according to Herod Helms and his senatorial nightriders, so have the kid, even if it's born without a nose. . .and shut your mouth, bitch.

According to Judith Krug, director of the Office of Intellectual Freedom of the American Library Association, attempts to censor books in the nation's libraries have more than *tripled* since last November's election of Reagan. "We have been averaging over the past several years three to five reports of attempted censorship a week," Ms. Krug said in an interview with *Publishers Weekly* (2/20/81). "The first two weeks of November, there were about that number per day."

So if all of this about which I've written for three installments scares the bejeezus out of you; if the fact that over sixteen *million* dollars worth of advertising has been pulled from television shows *rumored* to be on The Moral Majority's forthcoming hit list; if you cannot believe lunacies such as that contained in a letter to *Christian Life* magazine by a woman who wrote ecstatically that her six-year-old daughter was "born again" after hearing Lynda "Wonder Woman" Carter's "testimony of faith" in the March 1980 issue read to her; if you stand dumbfounded when Secretary of the Interior James Watt tells a Senate subcommittee he doesn't feel any guilt about denying future generations all the parklands he wants to pave over and condo-ize because, "We don't know how many future generations there'll be before the coming of the Lord, anyhow"; if you wonder what the hell pinstriped Jerry Falwell is doing out in Louisville, Nebraska, with his thirty-three-member, squeaky-clean "I Love America Singers," putting up the money to back a church school that refuses to comply with the licensure requirements of the Nebraska State Department of Education, and telling his audience, "We're here to stay! You [meaning the government] can't control us"; if all of this seems ominous as a cancer specialist suggesting you stop into his office to discuss your biopsy report...then I urge you to jot another name on the slate of your brain.

The name is Norman Lear.

And he personifies the philosophy that the only reason to become famous and rich and powerful in these parlous times is to use that fame, wealth and power to help make this a slightly better world in which personal freedom as a concept is not perverted to the debased uses of an unholy alliance of tv evangelists, amoral politicos bent on climbing higher, direct-mail hustlers, milk-the-ignorant fund raisers, hate-spewers, gun-lovers and sociosexual repressors. He is a man who very clearly sees the dangers to *all* of us in the twisted coupling of Fundamentalist crackpots and amoral politicians.

Norman Lear has caused to be born an organization that answers the question we all ask: what can *I* do? The organization is a non-profit, tax-exempt entity called PEOPLE FOR THE AMERICAN WAY. It's on line already, it's working, it's in Washington and it's a clearinghouse, fighting-mad organization that is dedicated to taking back the American flag from the direct lineal descendants of Cotton Mather and Father Coughlin and Senator Joe McCarthy.

Here are a few facts that explain *why* People For The American Way *had* to come into existence today:

Religious broadcasters now own over 1400 radio and tv stations outright. In addition, hundreds of hours are purchased weekly by electronic ministries on independent secular stations. They reach over 130,000,000 Americans weekly.

The Religious New Right raised over $150 million last year alone.

They're spending millions not on preaching, but on politics—just one group reports spending $3 million on its political efforts this year, which is why so many liberal and humanistic senators and congresspersons were defeated, to be replaced by the clones of Jesse Helms and James Watt.

In state after state they have taken over state and local political party organizations.

They have organized powerful lobbies in Washington, in State Capitols and City Halls.

They've distributed "moral report cards" telling their followers which politicians are "good" Christians and which are not.

In order to be a "good Christian" and a "good American" you must not differ with their opinions. (Even as conservative a politician as Barry Goldwater has said that they're terrific if they're on your side, but if you cross them...look out!) You *must* believe in increased military spending; *must* support Taiwan; *must* be against the Panama Canal Treaties, the Equal Rights Amendment, abortion, teacher's unions, the Department of Education, and the SALT II treaty.

So if you feel frightened, and you want to do something, the address for People For The American Way is 1015 18th Street, NW; Suite 310; Washington, DC 20036.

Write them for literature and let them know of encroachments on your personal freedom in your area; like the kid from Bridgman, Michigan, Richard Hernandez, who wrote me that his short story in the Bridgman High School's newspaper, *The Beeline,* was banned because he used the words "God" and "damn" in juxtaposition. He didn't write *God damn,* or *goddam,* he only wrote "Oh, God—and damn!" And when he objected to this petty censorship in his capacity as editor of the paper, in a special editorial...the editorial was banned.

It's not just the principal of Bridgman High, it's the frightened, running-scared, Spanish Inquisition tenor of the times. And maybe People For The American Way is the first line of defense for all of us who are not joiners, who feel acutely that we must *do* something, but don't know where to go to do it.

And trust me that you *can* do something. You are not as helpless, as much a pawn, as they would have you believe. Each of us can effect change. (Remind me sometime to tell you how Leonard Nimoy and Carl Sagan and naturalist Arnold Newman and some dedicated men and women and even I saved an entire ridge of paleontological goodies just last week here in Los Angeles.)

You *can* move the world. You *can* be Zorro.

And for the three—out of several hundred—readers of this column who wrote me suggesting that this protracted outtake on the Moral Majority had no place in a magazine called *Future Life,* I tag off with merely these two bits: If it's inappropriate to discuss that which affects the future life of all of us, then perhaps you agree with James Watt that there may not be many more generations before the coming of the Lord.

102

And ultimately, this quote from Ralph Waldo Emerson.

"The religion that is afraid of science dishonors God and commits suicide."

Take *that,* Creationists!

---

SHORT BITS: I *promise* next issue to go into a discussion of knife-kill movies, the one I promised for this time.

I *promise* to go into detail on the subject of "mind-dribble fantasy," issue after next.

Get hold of a copy of A FIELD GUIDE TO THE ATMOSPHERE (Houghton Mifflin, $13.95) and check out the color photos. One in particular shows a cumulus cloud formation that, so help me, is a dead ringer for the flying saucer from *Forbidden Planet.* Show it to those who assure you they saw a saucer. But hide the explanation of what it is under the photo. Let them run amuck at this "proof" of the existence of UFOs...and then whip it on 'em. Heh heh.

Rebecca Ann Brothers writes to alert us to the existence of a new cult. The "Galacticans." Not just fans of that tv show-that-shall-go-unnamed, but people who have constructed a quasi-religious cult based on concepts presented *in* the show. She assures me she's not making this up, that a close friend of hers has been swallowed up in the cult. Terrific. Jonestown claimed the lives of over 900 innocents, duped and led to slaughter by a failed evangelist. Scientology became a church based on the snake-oil psychology of an ex-pulp magazine writer. Half the world burned and died because of the cultish blandishments of an unsuccessful paper-hanger. And now the idiotic ripoff of *Star Wars,* foisted on the tv viewing audience by quickbuck entrepreneurs, becomes the basis for yet another cult. Glen Larson as the Holy Ghost? Gimme a break, willya!

If you haven't yet caught George Romero's new film, *Knightriders,* I commend it to your attention. It has its flaws, as what among us doesn't, but it is a sensitive, intelligent film filled with beautiful images, memorable characters, a fresh and original sensibility, and a determination to treat the audience with respect. Ed Harris, Tom Savini and my friend Cynthia Adler (outstanding in a cast that is, itself, outstanding as ensemble) will remain in your memory for many rich moments of recall. And, blissfully, the film is almost totally free of the violence that has come to be the hallmark of American films.

About the birthday presents you've been sending. Look: it's strictly swell of you, but knock it off, okay? I've got just about everything in the world I could want, and the money to buy the few things that arrive on the scene late. There's no room in the house for most of the things you think I'd like (that I really don't like), so they wind up going to the Salvation Army. Save your money. It's nice of you to think of me, but in the future, don't bother. If you *really* want to send me a birthday greeting, do it in the form of a small donation to the National Coalition to Ban Handguns in Washington, or to People For The American Way, or to the Klanwatch project of the Southern Poverty Law Center in Montgomery, Alabama, or to the campaign to stop the Human Life Amendments, c/o National Organization for Women in Washington. You'll pay me all the compliments I could ever want, and all the respect I'll ever deserve, by committing just a tiny share of your awareness and wherewithal to these important programs.

(But if someone out there happens to have a hardcover copy of Robert Nye's novel FALSTAFF in good condition, I'd take it as a helluva birthday gift if they'd allow me to purchase it.)

It will have happened several months ago as you read this, but as I write it James Doohan of *Star Trek* has had a massive coronary. He seems to be out of danger now, having been taken off the pacer yesterday; and Leonard Nimoy was over to see him and says he looks pretty good; and when he was finally taken out of the intensive care unit and put into a room with a phone he started calling back those of us who had been keeping vigil. First Walter Koenig called to say Jimmy was okay, and about ten minutes later Jimmy himself called. He said they may do a heart bypass, but nothing was certain at the moment. So by the time you read this "Scotty" will no doubt be well on his way to full recovery. He appreciates letters from his fans. So instead of writing a letter to me this month, telling me what a thug I am, drop a note to James Doohan care of the office of Gene Roddenberry at Paramount Pictures in Hollywood.

END OF SHORT BITS. Except to say: apology accepted, Allison Bell.

* * *

A few random remarks about the film *Outland*; not particularly because I was asked for my opinion (though several there have been who did precisely that), but simply because I saw it and the film manages to encapsulate some thoughts I've been wanting to share with you about sf films since I began this series of columns. Thoughts that may explain why I seem to be down on the majority of big-budget special effects movies. All in the spirit of better communication between us, if you get my drift.

On sum, all things given, at base...I rather enjoyed the movie. *But only as long as I was watching it.* Like sex, even if it's bad sex, you *seem* to enjoy it while it's happening.

But as soon as it was over (the film, not the sex, dummy), I began realizing what a stupid piece of shit it was.

I think *that's* the intellectual crucible in which all films of this sort should be tested. How do you feel about it when you're walking away from the theater and discussing it with other intelligent people? Not the kind of fans who applauded during the scenes in which someone's body exploded, not the sort of nonjudicial adolescents (of every age) who can slaver over matte effects and miniature models and bright lights while turning off their critical faculties; but people who genuinely love and *enjoy* good movies (and if you haven't figured out that I'm one of those by this time, well, we simply aren't getting through to each other). People, in short, who resent it when the script does something incredibly, gratuitously stupid that invalidates an otherwise acceptable story and makes you distrust *everything* the makers throw up on the screen thereafter.

Look: One of the basic tenets of *good* science fiction has always been that it has an intellectual content that sets it apart from and above the usual sprint of merely-entertainment diversions. While we'll suspend our disbelief to allow James Bond or Burt Reynolds to jump a car in a way that we know defies gravity and the laws of impact or whiplash, we balk at permitting that kind of mickeymouse stunt in a sf film. Because we know that science fiction deals with the laws of the universe and its accepted physics.

So when the error, the lapse in logic, is a simple one that could have been avoided without slowing or crippling the plot, that need not have set the snail on the blossom of our enjoyment, need not have darkened our feeling that we are safe in the hands of a creator who will reward us for our attention and the price of a ticket, we react more sternly than were it just another *Blues Brothers* or *The Hand,* which are brainless loutish films but from which we expect nothing better.

Reiteration: If you cast back over the reasons why certain sf films disappointed you, chances are a good many of them will be this sort; silly, sophomoric, kindergarten-level scientific illiteracies that defy what even the dullest people know about science and pragmatic reality.

I speak of the kinds of errors—and I'll offer a flagrant one in a moment—that are made by directors (and in this case a director who deludes himself that he can write) who are too arrogant to hire and listen to a knowledgeable consultant. They wouldn't have the gall, the nerve, the temerity, the *chutzpah* to make a film about the Civil War without engaging the services of a savant like Bruce Catton to authenticate detail and history; or a film about quenching an offshore oil-rig fire without getting Red Adair to validate the technique; or a film about Cortez's depredations in Mexico without constant refer- ence to Beral Díaz del Castillo. But they are such self-important spoilers that they blunder into the arena of science fiction with some half-baked derivative idea and they sell it to an even *less* literate studio executive and proceed to make the film without even a passing nod to the possibility that they are cramming their cinematic feet in their cinematic mouths.

The writer and director of *Outland,* one Peter Hyams, is the man responsible for an earlier exercise in stupidity, *Capricorn One.* When I consider Hyams's abilities as a plotter of sf-oriented ideas, I am put in mind of the rhetorical question, "If you nail a duck's foot down, does he walk in circles?"

Lemme give you a f'rinstance that brooks no argument, not even from the most slavishly adoring fan of this film.

There is a scene in *Outland* where Space Marshal O'Niel, played as well as can be expected in a drone scenario like this by Sean Connery (who looks as if he wished he were back making a worthwhile flick like *The Hill*), draws blood from a corpse to ascertain if narcotics are present in the dead man's system. For the moment we'll ignore the implausibility that they have maintained the corpse in a plastic bag rather than simply cremating it in one of the mining colony's furnaces, which would be *de rigueur* in an enclosed life-system such as that portrayed on Io. Since space on shuttles would be at a premium, logic dictates that a clause would have been inserted in every laborer's contract with the mining corporation, Con-Am, that should death occur while on the job, the body could not be shipped back to Earth for burial. So they'd simply blow it out into space or burn it. But I'll even go along with the unexplained (to my satisfaction) plot-device that the body is conveniently left in transit storage for Connery to examine. (Which wouldn't happen, also, because the baddies wouldn't want an autopsy done that would show their dope had been instrumental in killing the guy. See what I mean? The more you examine the story, the more easily it falls apart.)

To get to the point, Connery sticks a needle into the tracheal cavity, ostensibly into the carotid artery, and up bubbles about a quarter of a pint of bright red sloshy blood into the barrel of the hypodermic.

The only trouble with *that,* as any dolt who has ever watched *Quincy* on tv can tell you, is that it ignores the reality of forensic medicine and the reality of lividity. For those of you unfamiliar with the concept, lividity is what draws the blood to the lowest part of the body in a corpse. (Don't try to fudge it by saying, "Yes, well, that's how it is if there's *gravity,*" because even on Io, innermost moon of Jupiter, gravity is on the order of one-twelfth to one-fifteenth Earth g, which would make lividity work the same way, especially after the unstated number of days the body had lain in that plastic bag. And even trying to rationalize the gravity question doesn't work, because we can see that the mining colony has *artificial* gravity. Take *that,* Saracen dog!)

So if Connery stuck that needle into the neck hollow, all he'd bring up would be *air,* because all the blood left in the corpse would

106

have long since drained into the ass! And any first year high school biology student knows that. But not Pete Hyams, who fancies himself a writer of sci-fi movies.

And as if *that* ain't moronic enough, there is also the reality of coagulation. Days after death, you stick a needle into the body *anywhere* and nothing bubbles up like Old Faithful. What you get is clotted brown glop.

Look: I'm getting angrier and angrier, the more I think about this. My editor is waiting for this column, he swears he'll have me defenestrated if I don't get it into the overnight post office express shipment, and this is the second time I've mailed the sucker out. But my summation of the final five hundred idiocies of *Outland* was capsulized; and I really want to lay this monstrosity out at length. So I'm retyping these last two pages and laying over the remaining sections of this analysis till next time, when I'll finish *Outland* and tie it in *somehow*—Falwell willing—with my essay on knife-kill movies.

This is called a cliffhanger. It is intended to bring you back, panting for more, next issue.

And I leave you with this final warning:

You know what you should do if an Irishman throws a pin at you? Run like hell. He has a grenade in his mouth.

**INSTALLMENT 11:** 18 June 81
(published 1 September 81
in *Future Life* #30
cover-dated November)

Look: since this is something like a couple of months beyond my first anniversary at this job, already a year down here in the trenches with you, it occurs to me that maybe there's a thing you ought to know about me. No big deal revelation, just a setting forth of credential that's slipped through the interstices. It is tendered before I get down to the second part of the bloody disembowelment of that hircine chunk of celluloid called *Outland,* begun last issue. And it is this:

I don't just *like* movies; I *love* them.

Your humble columnist sees something like two hundred films a year. What I don't catch at studio and Writers Guild screenings or first-run in theaters, I see on the cable movie channel or on airplanes or in hotel rooms when I'm on the road. Additionally, I have a Beta-cassette library of over two hundred films that I run over and over to study techniques of film writing, or to analyze scenes that stick in my mind. I am, after all, in the business of writing motion pictures; and I take the craft seriously.

What I'm getting at here, is that you're not dealing with just another pretty face. I am hardly a *nouvelle vague* journalist sway-backed 'neath a freightload of academic terminology—I am still bored to tears by *L'Avventura;* Claude Lelouch's films seem to me as empty as Phyllis Schlafly's head or Reagan's rhetoric to the NAACP convention; and I don't give a damn if Spielberg *didn't* explain how Indiana Jones could hang onto that Nazi sub's conning tower for 2000 submerged international nautical miles, because I love *everything* about *Raiders of the Lost Ark.* Like you, I go to movies to be dazzled, enriched, entertained and uplifted; and to give myself over with the trust and innocence of a ten-year-old.

Thus it pains me to have to swat away the foul ball canards of those very few dullwitted among you who contend that merely because I don't accept each slovenly wetbrain of a "sci-fi flick" as the greatest thing since *Crime and Punishment,* that I am an effete snob unfit to sample the wizardly wares of Holly and Wood. So as credential for my overbackwards even-handedness about films, I offer here a short list of movies I've seen in the past four or five months, grouped simply enough as to those I liked (to a greater and lesser degree without minor carps) and those I thought gummed the big one.

AYES: ...*And the Band Played On; Tess; My Bodyguard; Tell Me a Riddle; The Man with Bogart's Face; Twinkle, Twinkle, 'Killer' Kane; Brother, Can You Spare a Dime; The Hunter; Tom Horn; 6th and Main; The Last Metro; Fort Apache, The Bronx; Kagemusha, the Shadow Warrior; La Cage Aux Folles II; Knightriders; Thief; Nighthawks; Altered States; The Four Seasons; Raiders of the Lost Ark; Escape from New York; The Great Muppet Caper* and *For Your Eyes Only.*

NAYS: *Nine to Five; Falling in Love Again; The Howling; Seems Like Old Times; The Mirror Crack'd; Tribute; The Hard Way; Cruising; Bad Timing; The Earthling; Back Roads; Where the Buffalo Roam; Starcrash; The Hand; Outland; Bustin' Loose* and *Superman II.*

I've tried to discern a pattern, but apart from utterly subjective gut-reactions that I came away from these films either positive or negative, the only codifiable statistic is that of the forty films noted above I liked twenty-three and disliked seventeen. I'm not sure that tells us much; except that I go to a film predisposed to enjoy; and only what they throw up on the screen changes my mind.

The foregoing: presented as testament to the innocence and intent-to-enjoy of the critic. Presented: to avoid the non–salutary prejudgment that the critic *wants* to eviscerate moron films such as *Outland.* I don't. But I must. For all of us.

And I think going to see a film as pluperfectly dazzling as *Raiders of the Lost Ark* makes the point so manifestly, all words of further argument can be dispensed with. Sitting there during *Raiders* I kept hearing that voice in my head that all-too-often makes snide remarks about what I'm watching. But this time it kept saying, "Yes! Dammit, *yes!* This is what all the others should have done for me."

*Raiders* is so sensible, so magical, so *dear* a film, that one cannot keep from being dissatisfied with all the others—including *Star Wars*—that promised to take us out of ourselves completely. The film has the power of chronokinetics: it moves a human being through time. I became ten years old again, even as I retained my adult faculties of discrimination and erudition; but my childlike sense of wonder, my perception of place and age were whirled backward. I was a kid again, enjoying a film not just in the prefrontal lobe, but in every micromillimeter of exposed skin and nerve-ending. It was *total;* and becomes the cinematic trope for the word "entertainment."

If you can recapture what *Raiders* does to a filmgoer, and apply that elevated standard of visceral manipulation to all the other films in this genre, then I need never again go to these lengths in gutting such a drooling idiot of a film as *Outland.*

To recap my last column. One cannot help but resent and distrust a film that makes so many gratuitous errors; that fails to demonstrate even a first year high school student's basic understanding of science or medicine or logic; that manipulates plot and characters in such a patently cheapjack manner to the service of a ripoff comic book plot; that denies everything we know about human nature; that is, simply put, so clearly a derivative shuck.

The core of contempt this film congeals in me lies with the basic concept. By admission of the writer/director Peter Hyams in many interviews, he approached the producing entities Warner Bros. and the Ladd Company with a single sentence *précis:* "It's *High Noon* in outer space." And they cut a deal on the spot.

Let me sidetrack for just a moment.

Likely it won't surprise you—what with my ill-deserved rep as a cranky esthete—that I admire critic John Simon with very few reservations. The veneration, in this instance, extends itself to presenting a recent quote from Simon that subsumes as epigram the point this sidetrack makes.

He wrote: "I remember one of my freshman English students at the University of Washington asking with genuine concern, 'But I don't understand, Mr. Simon. What is wrong with being average?' There is nothing much wrong with being average, but there is considerably *less* wrong with being above average, and still less with being outstanding."

To put it another way, this time in the words of John D. MacDonald, "In a half-ass world the real achiever is king."

And if you are a motion picture and only average—or as I submit way *below* average where it counts—is there much point in spending fourteen million dollars, sixteen weeks' production time of uncounted talented artists and technicians who might better spend their time on something outstanding, not to mention the scarce theater booking space and attention of hundreds of thousands of filmgoers who spend millions of dollars for baby sitters, parking, travel costs and the high price of admission, if you are at best only average?

When a manufacturer in this country wants to run a market test on a new product, the city most often selected for the proper demographic sampling, the city considered the most *average,* is Columbus, Ohio. The residents of Columbus don't seem to understand how deeply they are being insulted by this "honor." They don't seem to realize that in the name of having the latest Arby's sandwich or sanitary napkin or fruit juice combo tested on them, they are categorized as *average.* And in these days of trying to please the lowest possible common denominator, average becomes synonymous with *mediocre.* Unexcelling. Middle. Undistinguished. Non-idiosyncratic. Predictable. Malleable. Columbus and all its inhabitants become merely marketing tools, fit for nothing better than consuming useless products. This is not the deification of taste, it is the standardization of no taste whatever.

Now to link average with Hyams's one-liner to the heads of the

Ladd Company and Warner Bros. Sidetrack now concluding.

On a specific date now lost to historians, in 1966, long after I'd given up hope that *Star Trek* would be the realized dream I'd been gulled into believing it would be, but before my own segment had been aired, a writer who had just sold the series a teleplay encountered me at a Writers Guild meeting. My own script for "City on the Edge of Forever" had been circulated to a number of first-time or potential writers shooting for berths on the series, so he knew I was considered to have "a beat" on what they wanted. He desired to let me know he's sold the show, and in some small way, I suppose, sought my approbation.

He said to me, "I just sold them a script. Guess what it is?" I smiled and said I had no idea, why didn't he tell me. And with absolute innocence he said, "I just took the plot of *Flight of the Phoenix* and rewrote it with Spock instead of Jimmy Stewart."

Though personally I have affection for this man, I was unable to keep myself from turning away from him in disgust. I remember the instant with clarity and pain. My lips skinned back over my teeth like a wolf's. I didn't have the reason or the heart to express my loathing of what he had done. He had taken that which had been done better, earlier, as a feature film, and cribbed from his fellow writer. He had debased the craft and his own talent, high or low, and sold derivative material. For a buck, no more than that, he had performed that cliché act best typified by the back cover ad *Galaxy Magazine* ran in its earliest days: he had converted a non-sf story into a kind of witless space opera by changing the equivalent of *cayuses* to *spaceships*.

It perfectly captured for me, in that awful instant, how writers in Hollywood willingly debase and rupture their abilities in the headlong rush to pander to the illiteracy of producers.

I've never mentioned how I felt to that writer, and we are friends. But I will never have respect for him as an artist.

Peter Hyams stood in front of the deal-makers at the Ladd Company and said, "*Outland* is *High Noon* in outer space," and the wee, limited, horizonless mentalities of those whose purses he wished to wallow in, twitched their noses and once again conceived of the audience as *average* and cut him a contract. They subsidized mediocrity.

But *Outland* is not *High Noon*.

The latter is a film of passion and courage, with a clear subtext that speaks to the fog of fear and cowardice that covered Hollywood during the Fifties due to the House Un-American Activities Committee witch-hunts that blacklisted, among others, the scenarist of *High Noon*, Carl Foreman. It is the story of a dedicated man doing his job and not being swayed by the self-serving timidity of his community.

The former is a crippled and dishonest mockery of that noble 1952 effort. And the core of corruption that is *Outland*'s most notable

114

feature is redolent of that slavish mockery. More, it is a screenplay that demonstrates Peter Hyams has the plotting sensitivity of a kamikaze pilot with eighteen missions to his credit.

Wedded to the bone-stupid idée fixe of transposing *High Noon* one for one, without expanding or restructuring the plot to account for alien conditions and a different societal mesh, Hyams made this film an exercise in repeated inconsistencies, illogicalities and contrivances sufficient to give a coprolite a tic.

Let me enumerate.

In *High Noon* we have a prairie community setting with a population of maybe two hundred people, most of whom are farmers and small businessmen and ranchers. They are not gunslingers, they are middle-class burghers and common laborers. It is not surprising, therefore, that Gary Cooper's Marshal would find almost no one to help him. They were people who had relied entirely on the Marshal for peacekeeping, of which there had been no serious necessity in some time as the film begins. It was a slow, slumbering town without danger.

Contrast that with the mining colony of Io, where the toughest, burliest laborers in the Solar System have come to brave incredible adversity to burn titanium out of a hundred-meter deep crater in airless, high-pressure circumstances. Over twenty-one hundred men, the equivalent of oil riggers and high steel workers and gandydancers. Not cowards, but grizzled roughnecks who work hard, drink hard, and whose lives of confinement would produce not—as Hyams contends—passivity, but a tendency to brawl, to seek hardy entertainments, to get involved in the politics and work-problems of their enclosed society.

In *High Noon* the character of the town is so clearly laid out that we have no difficulty in believing the timid mouselike citizens hide behind their shuttered windows. But in the Con-Amalgamated refinery 27 it is impossible to believe that Marshal O'Niel could not find enough mean, sympathetic, tough hands to make up a cadre of deputies. For God's sake, look at yourself! Are *you* a coward? I'm not, I'd join the cause. And so would you. And so would all those lineal descendants of long-haul truckers, anthracite miners and merchant marine deckhands. It is simply impossible to accept that men recruited and signed to time contracts for their burliness and ability to suffer life under such extreme conditions would *all* be sniveling, head-in-the-sand cowards.

But to maintain with blind illogic that trope of *High Noon,* Hyams defies what we all understand of simply human nature.

Futher. Con-Am is government regulated. All through the film O'Niel says they're afraid of losing their franchise, that's why the Earth government has placed Marshals on hand. If the police of any city found they had a serious situation for which they needed more men, they would simply go out and deputize. Conscription. And there are *always* men who sign up for such *posse comitatus*. But not at Con-Am 27 where the moron plot demands that to maintain the *High Noon* parallel, Sean Connery has to go it alone. That is manipulation of reality in deference to the belief that an audience is too stupid to perceive the corruption of real life.

Further. O'Niel acts stupid throughout. If he intercepts the phone conversation between refinery foreman Sheppard—the Peter Boyle villain—and the shadowy criminal cartel from whom he's been buying his narcotics, all he has to do is tape the call and then go arrest Sheppard, lock him up till the next shuttle, and send him back for prosecution. But he doesn't tape the conversation, which is solid evidence.

Further. He *finds* the drugs stashed in the meat locker. What does he do with this valuable evidence that will be needed for a trial? He flushes it down a toilet. Very smart. Show me even the stupidest country hick deputy who would find dope he needed for a bust, who would then flush the evidence.

Further. O'Niel knows two gunmen are coming in on the shuttle. Instead of calling the space station and having authorities there check the luggage of all passengers for weapons, thus stopping them at the start, he allows them to board. Or maybe I'm being too picayune. So then, if he isn't a complete asshole, let him stand with his deputies (even the traitor deputy) at the egress port of the shuttle when it arrives. Let him speak to the onboard personnel and have them send out passengers one at a time, have them drop their pants while their baggage is searched, and catch the two "best professional killers in the Solar System" (as the voice on the space-phone called them) before they gain access to a huge refinery complex where they can set up an ambush. And if your deputies say, "We don't want to get involved," then if you are the topkick of the peacekeeping force you simply say, "Your ass is fired, collect your gear." Try and convince me that all these space cops, career men, obviously, will risk loss of pay and being drummed out of the service, because they're afraid to help O'Niel . . . *which is their job!*

Further. If O'Niel has such certain knowledge that Sheppard is the power behind this scam, and if you don't want to acknowledge that all O'Niel has to do is take the fucker into custody till help arrives, then have him simply go to Sheppard's office—as he does on several occasions—tie the clown up and sit there with his laser rifle trained on the port. Have him wait for these two skillful assassins and when they come to check in with their boss, to find out why they can't find O'Niel, let the Marshal blow them out of their socks.

But that's too logical. Too simple. Too direct. It would deny us the joys of that imbecilic chase through the refinery. A chase that defies its *own* internal consistency, not to mention the simple precepts of logic. Let me point out a few to you.

"These guys are the best," said the mysterious criminal voice on the space-phone, when Sheppard called for help. (And do you perceive another lamebrain manipulation of reality in that Sheppard can call for help whenever he needs it, but O'Niel can't? Or won't. Simply put: *he doesn't,* thereby making him seem even more a dolt, rather than the superior cop we're asked to believe he is.) These heavy duty killers come fully equipped with laser rifles that sport heat-seeking telescopic sights. We are treated to shot after shot of these infrared heat-seeking devices tracking back and forth. But each time they get O'Niel in their sights, with him unaware of the danger, *they miss the first shot!* Every single time. Thereby giving O'Niel a chance to escape, fire back, to pull a diversionary maneuver. What science, what technology, what skilled trackers! What horse cookies!

If these are the two best assassins the crime syndicate and Sheppard can come up with, I'll throw any two of the punchiest button-men in Brooklyn against them and relax.

And for a big finale, for the towering moment of absolute idiocy, Hyams asks us to believe that these killers who are "the best," who apparently have been out in space a long time, who understand the laws of physics (which is more than can be said for Hyams), are simple-minded and/or distracted enough to fire a laserblast at a greenhouse window, thus exploding them out into the vacuum.

The night I saw the film, the audience booed and hissed at this ridiculous climax. I was pleased to see that not even an audience slavering to enjoy one of these "sci-fi flicks" for special effects was prepared to let themselves be so intellectually insulted. I wish Mr. Hyams had been there. And I wish I had the spoiled fruit concession.

I've spent about five thousand words in two columns stripping this gawdawfulness to the rotten core, and I could go on for another five thousand. The phony scare technique of having a cat jump out at Frances Sternhagen. The avoidance of common sense in O'Niel's being able to tap Sheppard's line but in not putting a recorder on the wire so he could find out who the traitor in his midst might be. And the big moral chuck of not having O'Niel simply walk into that dining bay and say, "Okay, you hundred working stiffs, you're all deputized, let's go get the Bad Guys!"

Further. Where is the labor union for these workers? Don't tell me that the United Mine Workers or the Teamsters or the futuristic equivalent of an AFL-CIO wouldn't have shop stewards there protecting the rights of the men. Don't tell me that in that vast body of over two thousand men there wasn't *one* like Victor Riesel, the columnist who had acid thrown in his face for trying to expose union corruption. Don't tell me that there wasn't *one* union man who would see his fellows were being killed by contraband junk proffered by a company man, who wouldn't spread the word and organize other workers. And what kind of schmucks are these 2,000+ workers supposed to be, that they can see others of their number running amuck and dying from some nasty substance, who don't blow the whistle? Even in wholly owned company towns the miners and factory workers stand up for their rights. To ignore that entire aspect of the situation denies the realities of the Labor Movement for the past hundred years. Only in the incomplete, manipulate-as-you-will duplicity of a bad writer can such factors be eschewed.

*High Noon* was about something special. Like Arthur Miller's "The Crucible" it was about being a "good German," about letting the powers of repression and censorship and evil do their dirtywork unhampered. It might be shown today as a warning against the New Puritanism of the Moral Majority.

*Outland* is about nothing. It is simply a cheap filmic device to give the makers of little plastic models a chance to convince you your sense of wonder has atrophied. It is an untalented man's career getting another boost from your innocent desire to see a good science fiction film. It is the bastardization of someone else's original idea, ineptly translated to a genre where it does not work.

In an issue of *Starlog* just about the time the film was released, Frances Sternhagen said in her interview, "This isn't really science fiction. It is set in a science fiction ambiance, but it is more like an old Western. It just happens to be an old Western on a satellite of Jupiter."

And *that* is the most corrupt thing about *Outland*.

Thirty years after *Galaxy Magazine* conceived the perfect example of what sf would look like if it were put in the hands of dabblers, fools and perverters...the template becomes a nasty reality. It is called *Outland*.

Ms. Sternhagen, an intelligent actress who, in this case, has made an incredibly dumb statement, does not seem to perceive the invidiousness of her comparison. I won't comment on how Ms. Sternhagen—most recently on Broadway in Strindberg's "The Father"— would look on such a transposition of the classics. "Oh, it's just 'Miss Julie' rewritten as a superhero comic." "Oh, it's just 'Richard III' as a roller disco comedy." "Oh, it's just 'An Enemy of the People' as an underwater ballet for Esther Williams."

But the inept and inappropriate warping of *High Noon* into a genre where it doesn't work bothers her not in the least.

Such tenebrous thinking from a respected artist only serves to validate for the jimooks who made *Outland* their arrogant stupidity in cobbling up such a piece of duplicity.

Why do I tell you all this?

Because every time you spend your money to swell the box office coffers for monkey-puke like this movie, you encourage the know-nothings at outfits like Warner Bros. and the Ladd Company to listen

118

to babble like "This is *High Noon* in outer space," and to foist off on you again and again the most slovenly, childish, unsatisfying imitations of thoughtful sf they can get away with.

But then, I suppose if you enjoy playing the boob, you'll fight with me over nits in this analysis. . .and queue up for the next dreg a halfwit has sold to other halfwits.

In which case, as Jefferson said in another context, you'll be getting exactly what you deserve.

**INSTALLMENT 12:** 2 July 81
(published 20 October 81
in *Future Life* #31
cover-dated December and
republished in expanded form
15–21 January 1982 in *L.A. Weekly*)

# INTERIM MEMO:

I had nothing to do with it, officer. I have a brass-bound alibi. I was elsewhere when *Future Life* magazine gasped its last. All I know for certain is that the kids who buy the companion magazine, *Starlog,* were more interested in reading sillyass articles about how *Star Trek* phasers make that funny noise than they were about advances in science or how to prevent pollution or what life might be like on the planets circling Proxima Centauri. And so the excellent staff of *Future Life*—Bob Woods, Barbara Krasnoff, Laura O'Brien and a host of others during the year I wrote these first twelve columns—were informed by the publisher that, sadly, uplifting the mentalities of kids drunk on SFX and Hollywood hype was a chore no longer in favor with the rabble. And *Future Life* vanished. The column lay dormant for five months, and then I was solicited to continue it in the *L.A. Weekly* (all of this, in greater detail, in the afterword to this book). For my first column in the *Weekly,* because events subsequent to its having been written the previous July had provided me with additional, contemplative material, I recycled the final *Future Life* column, my twelfth, as two installments, which became $12^2$ and 13. This makes for some small confusion among archivists; but if they didn't like being befuddled they'd have become shoe salesmen or poets. So this is the transitional column.

Once upon a time not too long ago I was married to a young woman whose every waking moment was underlain by a preoccupation with thanatopsis.

Perhaps it was only *Weltschmerz;* but I ruminate about her occasionally, and I'm more and more inclined to believe it was genuine thanatopsis.

I won't make you go to the dictionary. *Weltschmerz* is one of those words that sums up in German what would take paragraphs to illustrate in English. It means sorrow which one feels and accepts as his/her necessary portion in life; sentimental pessimism; literally, world-pain. *Thanatopsis* comes from the Greek personification of death, Thanatos. Like thanatophobia, it is a view or contemplation of death that transcends mere mortal awareness that we all come to an end in darkness.

I lived with her for a year, and was married to her for somewhat less than another year; and on November 20th, 1976 I sent her away and divorced her when I finally realized, for reasons I will not go into here, that I could not trust her. It was a culmination of a chain of events that I number among the most debilitating in my variegated life.

One month earlier, on October 8th, 1976, my mother died, after a long and dehumanizing illness. She had spent too long on the machines that kept her alive in the biological sense, but which could not bring her back from the condition of vegetable *thing* she had become.

She lay in the hospital bed, having become a cyborg.

Half-human, half-machine...extruding tubes...one with the ohm and the kilowatt...without tears or smiles...having no need to brush her teeth in the morning or a magazine to help her sleep at night. I touched her face and she did not know it. I put one of my tears on her cheek and it did not move.

And so finally it came to the end of the story, came to final moments when someone had to make the decision to kick out the plug. Someone made that decision.

Those ashen months of 1976, for these and other reasons, were a terrible time for me. Yet as barren of sunlight and joy as those days were, I never shared the world-pain or the absorption with thanatop-sis my ex-wife had known. She would often say to me, "Why bother? What does it all mean? What's the point of living?" I would wither a little inside, because no argument suffices if the skin and bones don't understand that the answer is: we live to say "No!" to death.

Through all the days and limitlessly longer nights, I never felt my soul in the grip of the fist, never lost the humanism that keeps me warring with the rest of my species. We are one of the universe's noblest experiments; we have a right to be here, I've heard; and if we struggle long enough against the forces of ignorance and mischievous-ness that bedevil us, we will be worthy of that place in the universe. I believed that, continue to believe it, and only *once* during the mon-strous period was my faith in the nobility of the human race shaken.

A month after my marriage became a portion for foxes, two months after my mother finally found the trail opened for her reunion with my father, I experienced the lowest moment I've ever known in my consideration of those with whom I share common heritage. On December 22nd, 1976—for the first and I sincerely hope only time—I was dashed to despair in the sure and certain knowledge that we are an ignoble, utterly vile form of life, unfit to steal space from weeds and slugs and the plankton in the sea.

That moment came in a motion picture theater, and I, who fear almost nothing, was frightened. Not at what was on the screen; at the audience around me. Fellow human beings, a stray and unspecific wad of eyes and open sensory equipment, common flesh and ordinary intellects, so petrified me with horror that I had to hold myself back from screaming and fleeing. I wanted to hide. I can't get over it, even now: *I wanted to hide.* I was more scared than I'd ever been, before or since.

Pause. Deep breath. Quell the memory. Force back the abreac-tion. Stop the shiver as it climbs.

On that Wednesday night, I was escaping my life. I got in the old dirty Camaro and drove into the San Fernando Valley just over the hill from my house. Down there in the Valley is not Hollywood, it is not Brentwood or Westwood, it is barely Los Angeles. In many ways it is a suburb of Columbus, Ohio. As writer Louise Farr has said, it is the edge of the American Dream that bindlestiffs and bus-riders have come to seek where the sidewalks are made of gold. Or at least partially inlaid with bronze stars. But it is Country, in the way Fort Worth will always be Country, no matter how urbane and cosmopoli-tan Dallas becomes. It is tract homes and fast food and the Common Man keeping barefoot and pregnant the Common Woman.

Oh, there are fine shop and big homes—in Woodland Hills and the newer 850-to-million-five estates—there are nonpareil French restaurants like Aux Delices and Mon Grenier; there are pseudo-hip *boîtes* like Yellowfingers and L'Express, but every once in a while they get the French syntax wrong and wind up with names like Le Hot Club. Nonetheless, it ain't all no-necks and polyester crotches. It is just, like where you live, The Valley. As close to the American Dream as Common and *average* may ever hope to get.

I drove out, drove around, could not escape myself. And decided to take in a movie. Any movie. Didn't give a damn what or which.

In Tarzana, out along Ventura Boulevard, near the big tree under which I am told Edgar Rice Burroughs lies buried, in the bedroom community named after his greatest creation, there is a multiple-cinema like the thousands thrown up in every American city these past decades. Cinema I—Cinema II—Cinema III—Cinema IV they call themselves, these windowless, airless cubicles. They are not theaters. Theaters had spacious lobbies and balconies; they had cut glass chandeliers and ushers with flashlights; they had an authoritarian manager in an impeccable tuxedo to whom you could complain when the noisy schmucks behind you wouldn't shut up; they had a candy counter with freshly popped popcorn that got real butter slathered over it, not some artificial crankcase drainage that had never seen the inside of a cow. They were theaters, not these little boxes, which, if they had handles, would be coffins. In Tarzana they have caused to be thrown up a six-box edifice called Theeeeee Movies of Tarzana.

I didn't care what I saw, just as long as I hadn't seen it before. Every screening room had a double feature. I picked the one that had two films I hadn't heard much about. I don't remember what the A film was, but the second movie, the B, was one that had been around for a few months, that I'd missed.

It was called *The Omen*. You may know the film.

It was crowded for a Wednesday night and the lights were up as I wandered down the single aisle to find a seat. *The Omen* would start in a few minutes.

I gauged the audience. I've come to hate seeing films in ordinary theaters since the advent of television. People talk. Not at the screen, an occasional *bon mot* as response to something silly in the plot or a flawed performance, but to each other. Not *sotto voce,* not whispered, not subdued, with the understanding that there is *something going on here,* but at the top of their lungs, as if they were yelling to someone in the kitchen to fetch them a fresh Coors. They are unable to separate reality in a theater from fantasy in their tv-saturated home. They babble continuously, they ask moronic questions of each other, they make it impossible to enjoy a motion picture. It is the great dolt audience, wrenched from the succoring flicker of the glass teat, forced out into this Halfway House between television stupor and the real world: not yet fully awake, merely perambulated into another setting where the alpha state can be reinduced. I looked around at my fellow filmgoers. Not much different from the crowd you last shared a

Saturday Night at the Movies with.

I do not think I malign them too much by characterizing them as eminently average. From their behavior, from the mounds of filth and empty junk food containers I had to kick aside to get to my seat, from the stickiness of my shoes from the spilled sugar-water, from the beetled brows and piglike eyes, the feet up on the backs of seats in front of them, from the oceanic sound of chewing gum, I do not think I demean them much by perceiving them as creeps, meatheads, clods, fruitcakes, nincompoops, amoeba-brains, yoyos, yipyops, kadodies and clodhoppers. But then, the garbage dump smell of bad breath, redolent armpits, decaying skin bacteria and farts mixed with bad grass always gives me a headache and puts me in one of my foulest Elitist humors.

Nonetheless, I was there, the film was to start in a few minutes, and I was trying to escape (in the worst possible situs) the world. So I took a seat next to a young man and his date, a young woman. I gave them the benefit of the doubt: a young *man* and a young *woman*. I was shortly to learn that I had misjudged them. Actually: were-*things* passing for human.

I will describe them physically.

The young woman was vibrating against the membrane of her twenties. Gum moving in the mouth. Shortish. Ordinary in every esthetic consideration. Just a female person, holding the right hand of the young man who sat to my right. What distinguishes her most in memory is that she was with *him*.

Ah. Him.

There is a sort of young man, never older than twenty-five, that I occasionally encounter at college lectures. The somatotype is one that you'll recognize. Large, soft, no straight lines, very rounded. A lover of carbohydrates. Pale. An overgrown Pillsbury doughboy. Weak mouth. Alert. Very sensitive. And I usually have to confront this type when I've done a number on Barbra Streisand, with whom I've had a number of path-crossings in my life, and whom I do not like a lot.

So when I've mentioned Ms. Streisand, and have expressed my opinion of her, one of these great soft things leaps up in the audience and, usually with tears in his eyes, reads me the riot act. "Barbra is *glor*ious! Barbra is a *star!* What do *you* know about *any*thing? You're just jealous of her!" Followed by exeunt trembling.

(God *knows* how much I envy her. She can wear a cloche and wedgies so much *better* than I. Don't shoot the shwans.)

Beside me sat one of those. He looked like Lenny in Steinbeck's OF MICE AND MEN. Probably not all there; several bricks short of a load; only 1.6 oars in the water. Big, soft, holding her hand.

Enough. Let me get directly to the moment.

This film, *The Omen,* is a textbook example of what we mean when we speak of gratuitous violence. That is, violence escalated visually beyond any value to plot advancement or simple good taste. That which makes your stomach lift and your eyes look away. Not the simple ballet of death one accepts in *Straw Dogs* or *The Wild Bunch* or *Alien* or *Bonnie and Clyde:* I've seen death close up a few times. Those films are okay.

No, *The Omen* is another can of worms.

And the moment came like this:

There is a scene in which David Warner gets his head cut off by a sheet of plate glass. We have been set up for this scene in a number of ways, so we will feel trepidation and mounting tension. Warner has evinced that sweaty, doomed attitude we have come to know through years of moviegoing as endemic to those the plot demands get wasted. The whining passengers of the *Poseidon;* the downy-faced aviator on his first recon flight with Gable or Robert Taylor; the PFC who stands up in the Bataan jungle to yell to his rifle squad, "Hey, it's all clear, no more snipers!" Pee-*ing!* Bullet through the brain. We *know* poor David Warner is about to get shitcanned in some earsplitting way.

As the group of which Warner is a member rushes through the street of some Algerian-style city (it's been over five years since I saw the film and detailed specifics of plot are blurred), we get artful intercuts by director Dickie Donner of Warner's sweaty, crazed face ...a truck or wagon or somesuch with a large sheet of plate glass lying flat on the bed, protruding off the rear of the vehicle...Warner rushing...the truck trundling...the glass looking ominously ready ...an impediment in the way of the truck...Warner...glass... ohmiGod! we know what's going to happen because the intercuts are harder, closer together, the music begins to crescendo...the impediment stops the truck...the wheels of the truck smash into it...the truck stops short...the flass wrenches loose and zips off the rear of the truck...Warner seeing the glass coming toward him....

Now we *know* he's going to get hit by the glass.

And because we're trained to drive instantly to the most morbid escalation of the death-equation, we *suspect* he'll be decapitated. And *that's* the point to which violence is at least tolerable, acceptable, required by the plot.

But.

Little Dickie Donner, famed far and wide as the director of the television kiddie show *The Banana Splits* and a movie about a superhero, charming Richard Donner directs the scene like this (remember, you're sitting in a theater all unaware of what's coming at you):

Intercuts. The glass slicing through the air. David Warner's face registering terror as he sees it coming. His eyes starting from his head. His mouth open in an animal scream of horror. The faces of the other actors distorted in ghastly expectation of the impact. Glass! Warner! Screams! Closeup on the glass slicing into Warner's neck. Blood spurts across the glass. The head rolls onto the glass. Glass and body carried backward to smash against a wall. Glass splintering.

Okay, we think, horrible. That's it, though. It's over.

Wrong, and wrong.

Now the head rolls down the glass, draining blood from dangling cords and emptying carotid artery. Blood smears on glass in long slimy streaks.

*Enough!*

The head bounces off the glass, hits the cobblestones, rolls.

*Enough!*

Camera follows the head bouncing down the street.

*Enough! Enough already!*

The head rolls into a corner.

*Enough! God, cut me a break here!*

The head comes to a stop as the camera comes in on the final spurting of blood, the face contorted in horror, the eyelids still flickering...

And here is the ultimate ghastliness of that moment, close to Christmas of 1976. Not on the screen. In the theater.

*The audience was applauding wildly.*

They were, God help them, *laughing!!*

And beside me, that great soft average American boy and girl, fingers twined tightly, were pounding their fists on his knee. From him: moaning bursts of sound, as if he were coming. From her: sharp little expletives of pleasure, as if she were coming.

Rooted, unmoving, my hair tingling at the base of my scalp, memorable fear overwhelming me, I sat there in disbelief and dismay. What kind of lives could these people live? What awful hatred for the rest of the human race did they harbor? What black pools of emotion had been tapped to draw such a response? The character David Warner played was not a villain, so they couldn't be excused or understood on the basis of catharsis...that no-less-bestial but at least explicable release of applause and whistling when the Arch-Fiend or the Renegade White Man or the Psychopathic Terrorist gets blown away. No, this was a high from the violence, from the protracted, adoring closeups of blood and horror.

This was America experiencing "entertainment."

I can't remember the rest of the film. I'm not sure I actually stayed to the end. I know I didn't see the feature film I'd come to see. I may have stumbled up the aisle and into the night, decaying inside from the death of my mother, the breakup of my marriage, loneliness, sorrow...and the evil rite I had just sat through. But now, five years later, I recall that moment as the absolutely lowest point I've ever reached in loathing of my species. I could not even fantasize wiping them off the face of the Earth. That would have been to join with them in their unholy appreciation of the senselessly violent. I just wanted to be away!

Now, five years later, I see the twisted path stretching from that night of monstrous perception to an omnipresent mode in current movies.

In the phrase credited to writer-interviewer Mick Garris, *knife-kill movies.*

How many have you seen?

*Texas Chainsaw Massacre, Prom Night, He Knows You're Alone, Don't Answer the Phone, Dressed to Kill, When a Stranger Calls, Motel Hell, Silent Scream, Blood Beach, My Bloody Valentine, Friday the 13th, The Omen II, Mother's Day, Zombie, Eyes of a Stranger, The Boogey Man, New Year's Evil, Maniac, Terror Train, Humanoids From the Deep* and, yes, I'm sorry to include this for those of you who adored it, *The Howling.*

How many knife-kills have *you* sat through?

More important: ask yourself *why* you went to some of these films, when you knew in advance how twisted, how anti-human, how sexist, how degenerate they promised to be?

Are *you* a great soft average American boy or girl? Did *you* come when the sharp stick gouged out the eyes? Did *you* applaud when the heads were sawed off? Did *you* gasp with pleasure at the special effects when the straight razor sliced and the blood spattered the camera lens?

Are you still deluding yourself that you're sane?

**INSTALLMENT 13:** 2 July 81
(published 20 October 81
in *Future Life* #31
cover-dated December and
republished in expanded form
22–28 January 1982 in *L.A. Weekly*)

# INTERIM MEMO:

By the time I'd broken the twelfth column for *Future Life* into my first two columns for the rejuvenated appearance of these peripatetic observations in the *Weekly* (as explained in the previous Interim Memo), a number of incidents had occurred and new psychological data had surfaced. In this second half of the original column, expanded for its new readership, I made reference to some data published as an editorial in the 15–21 January edition of the *Weekly*. What it said was: "Findings by Neil M. Malamuth, 1981 Visiting Professor at UCLA, and James V.P. Check, published in the *Journal of Research in Personality,* indicate that movies do ineeed *significantly* increase male acceptance of violence against women. They took 272 men and women and divided them into three groups. One group viewed *Swept Away* and *The Getaway,* both of which show violence against women as having justification, while the other two groups—a designated control group and a group of *ad hoc* volunteers—saw *A Man and a Woman* and *Hooper,* which were chosen because they exclude all forms of sexual violence. To prevent predetermination of attitude, the subjects were led to believe they were taking part in a rating system test. After viewing the films, the subjects then had to fill out identical questionnaires that used basic psychological attitude testing methods to determine (1) each subject's general acceptance of interpersonal violence, (2) how much each accepted myths about rape, and (3) each subject's beliefs about the adversarial nature of male–female sexuality.

131

The men who viewed the two violence-prone movies demonstrated a 'significantly' greater acceptance of violence and rape and higher tendency toward adversarial sexual relations than the men who viewed the two non-violent movies. Not surprisingly, they also showed a far greater acceptance of violence than the women with whom they had seen *Swept Away* and *The Getaway*. (Interestingly, *all* the women scored approximately the same, demonstrating non-acceptance of violence no matter which movies they saw.)"

As I was saying. Knife-kill flicks. The subject of a new book titled SPLATTER MOVIES. You like that a lot? Splatter movies. Cute.

Though there are exceptions the apologists will always cite, the bulk of the violence—total, psychopathic, sudden and seemingly the only reason for making these films—is directed against women.

Oh sure, there are a few men who get whacked out in these films; but their deaths are usually sort of *pro forma;* almost as if they were reluctantly added to the script against the advent of just such criticisms as these, so the righteous director (who is usually co-scripter) and the producer can *justify* slaughter by saying, "Well, hell, didn't you see the guys who got snuffed? How can you say we hate women?"

But that's misdirection. Afterthought. It's like George Wallace talking about state's rights when what he really means is *let's keep the niggers in chains.* It's on the moral and ethical level of those who excuse Nixon's criminal acts by saying, "Hell, *everybody* does it!"

No, what we're dealing with in nifty little films like Brian De Palma's *Dressed to Kill* and *Blow Out* is a concerted attack on females.

Females burned alive, hacked to ribbons, staked out and suffocated slowly, their limbs taken off with axes, chainsaws, guillotines, threshing machines, the parts nailed up for display. The deification of the madness Jack the Ripper visited on pathetic tarts in Spitalfields in 1888.

As a man who hit a woman once in his life and swore never to do it again, I reel back from these films where hatred and brutalization of women is the governing force of plot. I'll admit it, I cannot watch these films. I get physically ill.

But they must be drawing an audience. More and more get made each season. Saturation advertising on television pulls you to them. They make money. And money begets money; and the begetting sends even greater numbers of minimally talented filmmakers to the form. They proliferate. And the sickness spreads.

You wonder why the Moral Majority has some coin with otherwise rational Americans? It is because they fasten on festering sores like the spate of knife-kill films and they argue from the solitary to the general: moral decay, rampant violence, rotting social values. Joining with these latter-day Puritans on a single issue, though one may despise what they're *really* trying to do, is the downfall of all liberals.

Even so, their revulsion at these films (which they patronize like crazy) is the healthiest thing about such movies. Everything else, from motivation for making them to artistic values, drips with perversion.

I have a theory, of course. Don't I always.

These are not, to me, films of terror or suspense in the time-honored sense of such genre definitions. *The Thirty-Nine Steps, North by Northwest* and *Gaslight* are classics of suspense. *Frankenstein, The Wolf Man* and *Alien* are classics of terror. The lists are copious. *Rosemary's Baby, Knife in the Water, Repulsion, The Haunting, The Innocents* (from Henry James's TURN OF THE SCREW), *Psycho, The Birds, Dr. Jekyll and Mr. Hyde, Dead of Night.* Add your own. You know which ones they were that scared you, held you helpless in the thrall of fear, gave you memories that chilled not sickened you. From *Snow White and the Seven Dwarfs* to *The Parallax View* and *Carrie.*

It was always the scenes leading *up* to the violence that you remember. You needn't watch the death. . .you had been wrung dry before it ever happened.

What do I consider a terrifying scene? Here, try this:

Chill beneath a cadaverously-gray autumn sky, the tiny New Mexico town. That slate moment in the seasons when everything begins to grow dark. The epileptic scratching of fallen leaves hurled along sidewalks. Mad sounds from the hills. Cold. And something else:

A leopard, escaped, is loose in the town.

Chill beneath a crawling terror of spotted death in the night, the tiny New Mexico town. That thick red moment in the fears of small people when everything explodes in the black flow of blood. A deep-throated growl from a filthy alley. Cold.

A mother, preoccupied with her cooking, tells her small daughter to go down the street to the bakery, get flour for father's dinner bread. The child shows a moment of fear. . .the animal they haven't found yet. . . .

The mother insists, it's only a half block to the bakery. Put on a shawl and go get that flour, your father will be home soon. The child goes. Hurrying back up the street, the sack of flour held close to her, the street empty and filling with darkness, ink presses down the sky, the child looks around, and hurries. A cough, deep in a throat that never formed human sounds.

The child's eyes widen in panic. She begins to hurry. Her footsteps quicken. The sound of padding behind her. Feet begin to run. Focus on darkness and the sound of rapid movement. The child. The rushing.

134

To the wooden door of the house. The door is locked. The child pinned against the night, with the furred sound of agony rushing toward her on the wind.

Inside, the mother, still kitchened, waiting. The sound of the child outside, panic and bubbles of hysteria in the voice, Mommy open the door the leopard is after me!

The mother's face assumes the ages-old expression of harassed parenthood. Hands on hips, she turns to the door, you're always lying, telling fibs, making up stories, how many times have I told you lying will—

Mommy! Open the door!

You'll stay out there till you learn to stop lying!

*Mommy!* Mom—

Something gigantic hits the door with a crash. The door bows inward, and a mist of flour explodes through the cracks, sifts into the room. The mother's eyes grow huge, she stares at the door. A thick black stream, moving very slowly, seeps under the door.

Madness crawls up behind our eyes, the mother's eyes, and we sink into a pit of blind emptiness...

...from which we emerge to examine the nature of terror in the motion picture. Fear as the masters of the film form have showed it to us, and fear as the screen has recently depicted it, with explicit vomitous detail, with perverted murder escalated from awfulness to awfulness. Having seen the deaths of dozens, one is spiraled upward to accept the closeup deaths of hundreds. Knives are not enough, they're old hat. Razors are not enough, that's been done. To death. Meathooks are not enough, that's a cliché. Has anyone squeezed that bag of blood called the human body in a car crusher? Yeah, well, we can't use that. How about a paper pulping machine, a blast furnace, a rubber stamper, a meatgrinder, a Cuisinart? What's more ghastly than the last piece of shit? Acid? Rat poison? If we use acid or rat poison we have to show the victim writhing, vomiting, tearing her own throat out, the burns, the drool. Hey, is there something that'll explode the eyeballs right out of their sockets? Then we can show the raw red pulpy brain behind the empty holes. Now *that's* fresh, new, inventive, state of the art. Maybe we can call it *Scanners.*

Or *Outland.*

The scene just described, a scene shot for the small theater screen, in black and white, with a minimum of production values, with unknown actors, shot with misdirection (in the sense of that word as magicians use it) and subtlety is from a little-remembered 1943 RKO Radio Picture, *The Leopard Man,* based on a brilliant Cornell Woolrich thriller, BLACK ALIBI (1942). I offer it as a fine example of cinema terror in its most natural, unsullied incarnation, from the *oeuvre* of Val Lewton. To students of terror in films, the name

135

Val Lewton will be familiar. Had I wanted to be less precise but more chic, I'd have cited the early Dassin or Hitchcock.

But as a more reliable barometer of the centigrades to which artful horror can chill a filmgoer, I find no equal to what Lewton produced in merely eight films between 1942 and 1946, with budgets so ludicrous, achievements so startling, and studio intentions so base, that they stand as some sort of landmark for anyone venturing into the genre, whether a John Carpenter or a Brian De Palma.

Using the foregoing as yardstick, and comparing the knife-kill flicks against them, I submit what we're getting these days are not films of terror or suspense or even horror. They are (and here's my theory) blatant reactionary responses to the feminist movement in America.

Surely there are no great truths being propounded in these films, no subtext that enriches us with apocryphal insight, no subtle characterizations that illuminate the dark night of the soul, no messages for our times...unless the message is that every other person you pass is a deranged killer waiting for you to turn your back so he or she can cut your throat.

No, I've convinced myself, even if you might have trouble with the theory, that this seemingly endless spate of films in which women are slaughtered *en masse*, in the most disgusting, wrenching ways a diseased mind can conceive, is a pandering to the fear in most men that women are "out to get them."

In a nation where John Wayne remains the symbol of what a *man* is, the idea of strong women having intellectual and sexual lives more vigorous than men's is anathema. I submit the men who go to see these films *enjoy* the idea of women being eviscerated and dismembered in this way. They get off on it. In their nasty little secret heart-of-hearts they're saying, "That'll serve the bitch right!"

The audiences that go to these films, that queue up to wait an hour for their dollop of deadly mayhem, are sociopaths who don't know it. Beyond that, and I have no way to prove it, I think these films serve no purgative, cathartic end. They merely boil the blood in the potential rapist, the potential stomper, the potential knife-killer.

Last week's editorial in these pages proffering clinical substantiation of the theory that splatter movies, knife-kill flicks, raise the tolerance level of men for violence against women merely adds to the already existing body of such evidence that self-interested filmmakers and tunnel-visioned knee-jerk liberals like me have refused to acknowledge.

They are the twisted dreams from the darkest pit in each of us, the stuff against which we fight to maintain ourselves as decent human beings.

I leave it at that. For the moment.

But next week I want to relate what happened when a few responsible people tried to *do* something about these films. It was an adventure among airheads. Knees jerked, hot air filled the land, writers who've spent their whole lives fighting against censorship were pillored as being self-appointed censors...oh, it was spiffy.

And it encapsulates more than we wish to know about the nature of self-blinding fear that produces a moral vacuum, masquerading as courage. Next week I stop being polite.

**INSTALLMENT 14:** 25 January 82

# INTERIM MEMO:

You know, I'm not sure for a moment that anyone reading this book for amusement, intellectual stimulation, arousal of ire or as a short course in becoming a curmudgeon, gives a damn when the columns were published, and what the cover-date of the magazine might be. One tries to pre-guess the complaints a book might draw, before it's published: did it have an index, have the typos been expunged, is the design ducky? But the beefs are always unexpected. So for those who found the listings on the previous thirteen columns, as to origin of publication, a fast pain in the fundament, unlax. From this point forward it was only a matter of three or four days—maximum—between the writing of the columns and their appearance. When *An Edge In My Voice* was being done for a magazine that published eight issues a year, rather than for a weekly, it meant a lag-time between inspiration and execution, and publication, of 2½–3 months. So every-thing was a trifle chilled by the time it was in the hands of the mob, and another three months before their enraged responses saw publication. So what we have from this point forward is almost-instant ignition and conflagration. It made for heavy-breathing immediacy, not to mention threats of fire-bombings and disembowelment, some of which were even made by the readers, rather than me.

The German poet Günter Eich (1907–72) wrote, "Be uncomfortable; be sand, not oil, in the machinery of the world."

I won't say that's the only beat to which I march, but as readers of this column may have already perceived, it is well out front among the ethical commands that motivate me. I do not even attempt to ennoble my troublemaking by assuming the mantle of gadfly. That is too safe an appellation. Like jazz, that came up the river from the whorehouses of New Orleans to find respectability in Kansas City and Chicago and the white-tie legitimacy of big bands like Paul Whiteman's, thereby getting itself almost respectabilized out of existence, I get the feeling that when a commentator on the passing scene begins to be almost endearingly called a "gadfly," he has become acceptable. He has traded his effectiveness as sand in the machinery for the safe status of a loveable curmudgeon.

Thus, I prefer to remain your basic, garden-variety pain in the ass. I do not write what I write, what I observe, to shock. It is done to startle. There *is* a difference; I'm sure you'll grasp that difference.

Nonetheless, in the words of an ancient Japanese aphorism, "The nail that stands too high will be hammered down." That is to say, there are dangers attendant on startling the machine that make life less than a rippling rhythm. For instance, I wrote an op-ed piece for the Los Angeles *Times* recently in which I tried to point out the dangers of worshipping the Common Man (and Woman): you wouldn't believe the nasty letters I got from the most common of men and women about that essay. One can be a Communist, a molester of children, a white-collar organizational embezzler, a reactionary dolt spreading racism and militaristic paranoia, a former butler or housemaid for a movie star selling cheap gossip for bestseller notoriety . . . one can be almost any species of unsavory immoralist and be excused the practice by those who conceive of themselves as common clay. But don't *ever* make a case for Elitism; they'll getcha! You can be as flawed as you wish, gentle readers, as long as you don't make out you're in any way *better* or *nobler* than the groundlings.

This attitude of disingenuous humility on the part of many of our in-print critics—thus permitting them to enjoy the approbation of monkeys—makes it scratchy as hell for those who aspire to higher standards in ethics or Art. Let John Simon point out that Liza Minnelli has based a career in large part on a ghoulish echoing of her mother's tragic life, or that she has a singing voice that could stun a police dog, and he is pilloried for his bestial behavior. That Simon hews to standards of critical appraisal too lofty for the bunion-brains who think of "public embarrassments" (as Richard Schickel termed him in *Time*) like the other Simon, Neil, as America's premier comic playwright, escapes them. Schickel is another example. He is not the first to point out that the emperor has no clothes; that Neil Simon is to dramaturgy as Genghis Khan was to good table manners; but he did it in the open, in flat-out terms; and the common clay that cannot handle Pinter or Stoppard, whose meals of Neil Simon go through them like beets through a baby's backside, tsk-tsk in horror that such an American Institution should be so unceremoniously castigated.

What has all this to do with your charming columnist and the past two weeks' essays inveighing against the monstrousness of knife-kill "splatter" movies in which people, mostly women, are ripped and gutted and impaled and treated like *carnitas* intended for some cinematic charnel house burrito? Well, I'll tell you, gang, it went like this:

Only a short time after I'd written those columns as an essay, shortly after I'd come to the personal position that the use of irresponsible state-of-the-special-effects gratuitous violence in exploitation films was a growing trend that would permit the wimps of the Moral Majority to impose unbearable restrictions on the motion picture industry, I had occasion to experience at first hand the way in which a nail can be hammered down by those whose floating ethics and lack of personal courage moves them only to silence for fear of invoking the wrath of the groundlings.

My adventure through the land of the airheads began at a screening of Brian De Palma's film *Blow Out*. It was a film booked by the Writers Guild Film Society Committee for its members. Now, the WGA Film Society is a *private* membership operation in which 1885 members of the Guild subscribe to a series of 42 films a year at $1.25 per couple. The films are booked into the available slots by a complicated process I'll codify later. They are selected from approximately 300 offered to the Guild by the major studios, by a Film Society Committee comprised of (among others) critic Arthur Knight, Ray Bradbury (one of the founders of the Society, twenty-two years ago), scenarists and teachers Arnold Peyser and William Froug, and me widdle self. More on the Committee itself later.

Let me now reprint a letter I wrote the *WGA* Newsletter following the events pursuant to the screening of *Blow Out*. It will encapsulate the history of this contretemps and will lead into our next thrilling installment in which your intrepid pain in the ass finds himself facing the direct lineal descendants of those who stood by and watched Dreyfus get sent to Devil's Island.

Oh, how I do love to dramatize these encounters.

## Apologizes to Film Society

Unaccustomed as I am to apologizing publicly for my occasional erratic behavior, I must perforce extend just such an apology to most of the audience of the Film Society screening of *Blow Out* at 2:00 on Sat. Aug. 1.

What I despise in unruly audiences, what I have inveighed against more than once in these pages and in our theater...I was guilty of myself.

Three-quarters of the way through that Brian De Palma film, without even realizing I was doing it, I leaped up and began shouting and—at the top of my voice—stalked out of the theater. It was reprehensible behavior, and I am heartily ashamed of myself for it. That I was totally unaware of what I was doing, that I was impelled by my loathing of the brutalization of women that film contains, is no excuse. It was a visceral reaction and I lost control completely. Not until I'd driven home, still trembling with disgust and anger, was my friend Jane able to tell me what I'd been screaming.

I had no recollection of the words. But Jane tells me this is what I shouted:

"Jesus Christ! Another sick De Palma film...I should've known!" (At that point I hit the aisle.)

"The man is sick, the man is twisted." (At that point the audience was laughing.) "Next come the mindless eviscerations and anatomy lessons!" (By that time I was out the door.)

Don Segall (the writer, not the director) followed me out and was justifiably annoyed at my behavior. He upbraided me, saying, "If you don't like the films you ought to resign from the Film Society," to which I responded in a blind fury, "Resign from the Society, fer chrissakes, I'm one of the ones who *picks* these goddam films!"

John Considine and his lady, and a few others, followed my example and came out also. They did it quietly. I'm told that of the several thousand attendees of the various screenings, only 16 walkouts were logged. I guess that distresses me almost as much as my own uncontrolled actions.

My revulsion at *Blow Out* stemmed, in large part, from a carry-over abhorrence of De Palma's previous exercise in woman-hatred, *Dressed to Kill,* which we also screened at the Film Society; and from my growing awareness that these movies are more elegantly mounted examples of what has come to be known as the genre of "knife-kill flicks."

My gorge grew more buoyant as *Blow Out* progressed, pressured by a column I had written just a few days earlier on the knife-kill phenomena.

As a member of the Film Society Committee (and I hope a responsible member), I have brought the matter of these films to the attention of my fellow committeemen. It is my feeling that we must reappraise the manner in which we select films for the members to see. I am dead against censorship *of any kind.* Nonetheless, we do *select* the films for the Society, from those available to us with considerations of play-dates and the other strictures put on us by the studios; and as we would opt not to show a film we knew in advance was a dog, it seems to me well within the bounds of our selection process that we should pay some attention to the advisability of showing films that pander to less than noble instincts in an audience.

Ostensibly, it is the main purpose of the Society to offer to the members those films that will be of benefit in the pursuance of our craft. Even stinko films can serve that end, if only to proffer warning. But as we would not screen a film we knew to be a certified, card-carrying disaster...so, I feel, we should demonstrate restraint in showing films that consciously, gratuitously debase the human spirit.

If members of the Society wish to go to commercial theaters and pay their money to see films of this nature, all well and good. But *we* ought to have higher standards.

As a craftsman who works seriously at the holy chore of screen writing, I think it's time we examined more responsibly the nature of the cheapjack predators prowling through our industry, for whom we have to bear the brunt of censure from the New Puritans, the Moral Majority nuts and the self-styled viewers-with-alarm who want us to pre-censor what we write.

All of us get tarred by the brush, every time another woman gets an icepick in her eye in the course of one of these films.

—**Harlan Ellison**

# INTERIM MEMO:

By 5–11 February, with only three columns published in the *Weekly,* the happy natives were beginning to growl. Letters began appearing. Oh, you'd have loved them. Some were so vile and defamatory that the editor, Phil Tracy, a man of stern substance, forged in the cauldron of *Village Voice* lunacy, was reluctant to use them. Fortunately, there was enough of a need on the part of the publisher to build circulation (using me as cannon-fodder) that a few ripe items saw print. As they've already gone into public domain because of their publication in the *Weekly,* I've included them from this point forward, where they apply. Because occasionally I'd make reference to them in a subsequent column. You'll find these missives following the column that appeared in the same issue of the paper with them. A sense of perversity compels me to drop all the many letters that praised me, called me the savior of humanity, that wanted me put up for canonization, alla that. I'll only be reprinting the ones that screamed for my scalp. One of these days I'm going to do a volume of reminiscences about my weird life. I think I'll title it WORKING WITHOUT A NET.

*Letters reprinted with permission from the* L.A. Weekly

The essay on knife-kill splatter movies was published. Then came the Saturday my gut laid it on the line in terms of *doing something* about such films, not just writing about them from a safe distance. The moment when one had to walk the walk and not just talk the talk. I stormed out of a Writers Guild Film Society screening of De Palma's hideous *Blow Out.* Screaming, having totally lost control, I realized that I had been one of the members of the Film Society Committee who had *booked* the damned film...without having seen it. A repeat of the error we on the Committee—Ray Bradbury, Arthur Knight, Allen Rivkin, William Froug, and Arnold Peyser—had committed when we'd screened De Palma's previous exercise in woman-slaughter, *Dressed to Kill.*

Then here's what happened, very fast. I wrote a letter to the Guild Newsletter apologizing for having disrupted the show, pleading temporary nutso. (Last issue's column.) Then I requested a special meeting of the Film Society Committee to discuss our responsibility in terms of showing films whose chief appeal was a floodtide of gore. Not violence, *per se:* gratuitous, stomach-turning, special-effects slaughter. What I said to the other members of the Committee was that after 12 years of sitting with them selecting films, I had come to a moral position *for myself only,* that if we were to continue booking that kind of stuff, I'd have to motor. To my delight and resuscitation of faith in the Human Race, everyone else felt the same, and it was unanimously decided that we would exercise greater discretion when booking the films for the Society.

We felt so good about having thus taken a stand for life over death, that critic Arthur Knight outlined all the foregoing in his August 21 "Knight at the Movies" column in *The Hollywood Reporter.* The first responses were gratifying. Dozens of people called and wrote to say, "Good for you!" On KNX NewsRadio, August 31, George Nicholaw, v.p. and general manager of the CBS outlet here in Los Angeles, presented an editorial in which he called the action of the Committee "leadership by example" and praised the move as an act of selectivity and not censorship.

On the 22nd, Rip Rense in the Page 2 section of the *Herald Examiner* ran a brief piece about the Committee's action and in a day or so it was picked up by the AP wire. We all felt terrific.

147

Then a staff writer for the *Times* got hold of it and on September 2nd he wrote a "Film Clips" piece that was sufficiently muzzy in tone, lacking sufficient background about how the Film Society Committee worked, to make it appear that Bradbury and Knight and Ellison and Peyser and Froug were setting themselves up as censors. Sure. Believe *that,* and I've got some swell pterodactyl steaks I'll sell you cheap. In case no one remembers, Bradbury's most famous work is FAHRENHEIT 451, one of the most potent stretches of fiction ever written against censorship; and nobody who writes the stuff I write would be stupid enough to believe in even the slightest infringement on the First Amendment.

Nonetheless. Before the day was out, the shitrain had begun to fall. Typified by the following extract from the *Times* article:

> One veteran screenwriter, who asked that his name not be used, said the Committee's action reminded him of the old Hays Office, established by the movie industry in the 1920s to guard against indecency. "I remember the Hays Office and all the other crazy offices that the motion picture industry has put up," he said. "A lot of these young people haven't gone through that. I don't believe in not showing anything to anybody. If our people don't want to see something, they should stay at home."

There was a lot more. Nasty phone calls threatening war to the death, snide remarks from passersby at the next week's screening (which happened to be *Wolfen,* a violent film we booked without moral qualms because it was a good movie *about* something other than titillating bloodletting), and what was for me the most hilarious incident of all:

As I approached the Writers Guild Theater the next weekend, I saw a guy with a clipboard, soliciting signatures on a petition. I walked over, hoping it was another sign-up against James Watt, and saw it was a petition against censorship. "Hey, that's terrific," I said. "Lemme sign." The guy handed me the clipboard and a pen, and I signed right on the line, adding my name in printed form, and my address. He smiled and said thanks, looked down, saw my name, and started to get crazy with me. "But this is a petition against *you!*" I grinned right back and said, "No it ain't, chum. It's against censorship and I'm for that one hundred percent, which, if you weren't an airhead, you'd know." So he started trying to tear off the page and I said, "Ah, ah, ah. If you do *that,* you invalidate the petition." Then I went into the movie.

But not until a meeting of the Board of Directors of the Guild, and a vote of confidence for the Committee's procedures, did the abuse slack off. Letters continued coming in to the Writers Guild *Newsletter* (edited, ironically, by the very same Allen Rivkin who sits on the Committee) where each one, no matter how off-the-point or lame-brained, was duly published. I guess we just don't have this censorship system down pat yet.

Okay, so now we're coming into the homestretch on this subject. *Why,* you ask with good sense, why *isn't* what the Committee did an example of censorship? And what the hell does all this mean beyond the tempest in the teapot?

Look: the Film Society is, first of all, a *private* group, open only to members of the Writers Guild of America and their families. Four or five times a year, the Committee gets together and under very difficult rules manages to select 42 films. That's all the open slots we have. Forty-two. We have to select 42 films from the maybe 300 available to us. Most foreign films we can't get, because the Laemmle chain of theaters controls them and figures, quite correctly I think, that the audience for "art" films is small already, why should they cut out a couple of thousand potential ticket-buyers just to give away films free to a Film Society? So we are limited in that way. Then there's the play-dates allowed to us. We can't show films prior to release, and can only book them for showing up to a month or so *after* they've opened. And since we have to book well in advance, what happens is that we're selecting films that usually aren't even in final editing when we sit down for our meetings.

We're operating semi-blind. But because of the makeup of the Committee, we have access to rough cuts, films in progress, studio scuttlebutt. So we avoided *The Postman Always Rings Twice* even though it seemed to have everything going for it in pre-release hoopla—remake in unexpurgated form of a classic James M. Cain novel, excellent director, top stars, supposedly tough script—because word leaked out that somehow this one was going into the tank, and we picked up on a film that hadn't been sold so heavily before-the-fact because Knight had seen clips from it and thought it was going to be a comedy smash. The film was *Arthur.*

We go on gut instinct and our sources throughout the industry. That's why the members of the Committee have been appointed. *Anybody* in the Guild can serve on the Committee, but with the exception of those who've served for years, most of the summer soldiers who sit with us have no access to films, have no way of cajoling studios into parting with their precious product, and don't like the long hours of hard work and phone calls. So the Film Committee functions in the same way as the editorial board of The Book-of-the-Month Club.

BOMC gets offered several thousand books a year as possible selections. They pick a couple of hundred. Are they censors because they choose to offer this book and not that book? No, they are making

149

informed selections. That's what the Committee has been doing for 22 years.

And here's the airhead part. For 22 years the people who were namecalling have gone to the Guild Theater, and there's always been a film waiting for them. How the hell did they think that film got there? The stork? Santa Claus? Didn't they ever wonder why, on a given Saturday, they wound up watching *Tess,* rather than, say, *Maniac* or *Debbie Does Dallas?*

How did they figure a film booked four months earlier got to the projection booth at the appointed time?

None of that really matters. The system the Film Society uses is, by years of painful trial and error, the only one that can guarantee a steady flow of decent films for the members of the Guild. That's beside the point. What matters is the question of alleged censorship, and the response of uninformed, otherwise intelligent and concerned people to the unsupported *suggestion* of censorship.

The airheads seem to me to be not only doltish in this matter, but cowardly. If they *really* gave a damn about someone telling them what they can see and what they can't, why aren't they out in front of the offices of the Motion Picture Producers Association, picketing against the code that rates films G or PG or R or X? Why aren't they lobbying against outfits like Wildmon and his religious zealots, or Falwell and his vast Moron Majority? Cowards because they accept the rules and regs set down by the television networks that emasculate everything they write for the tube. Cowards because they let movies and books get banned all over the country and never offer their services in an *amicus* way to stop such depredations. Cowards because they are so terrified by the threat of a Moral Majority that they abrogate their responsibility to moral and ethical behavior for fear of looking like the enemy.

My big RANDOM HOUSE DICTIONARY OF THE ENGLISH LANGUAGE tells me that a censor is "any person who supervises the manners or morality of others." In flat-out terms that means keeping someone from seeing or doing something they want to do. But if the films the Committee chooses not to select for screening—remember only 42 out of 300+ can be shown each year—are available to the public in a couple of hundred theaters all over Los Angeles...where the hell does the censoring come in?

Now that makes simple sense. The kind of sense that becomes obvious when one takes the time to examine the question, not just rely on the word of someone shooting off his bazoo, who "asked that his name not be used."

But the foofaraw happened. Men who have spent most of their adult lives *fighting* censorship, who chose to exercise a sense of responsibility, who tried to say there are better films than these dark, ugly charnel house films, got the screaming pack of airheads on their

150

case. Vicious fucker that I am, I suggested to the Committee that we let the airheads have their way. Instead of booking *The French Lieutenant's Woman* and *Absence of Malice,* that we give them six straight weeks of splatter films. *Friday the Thirteenth, Part II* (in which a spear goes through the back of a woman, through the man she's screwing, and impales another guy under the bed), *Night School* (in which decapitated heads wind up in sinks, fish tanks, toilets and a kettle of soup in a restaurant), *Don't Go In The House* (in which women are tied to walls and then cremated by a guy with a flamethrower), *Halloween, Part II* (in which kids bite into apples filled with razor blades), and *Maniac* (in which a man knifes a woman to death, scalps her, puts her scalp on a dummy and then makes love to the dummy).

Gee, I don't know why the Committee looked on that suggestion with horror and revulsion. Can't understand, simply can*not* understand why Ray Bradbury and gentle Arnold Peyser looked sick. Don't know no way to figure *why* Arthur Knight and Bill Froug got green. Why Rivkin withdrew a dinner invitation.

What the hell's the matter with them?

Are they censors?

See you next week.

# LETTERS

*Dear Editor:*

Please edge Mr. Ellison's voice out.

—Ginny Bugay
Santa Barbara

*Dear Editor:*

Harlan Ellison reminds me of a reformed alcoholic. The self-righteous, cutesy, "dramatic" (his words, not mine) little estuaries he drivels on about the brutalization of women got the depth of a dry lake bed.

Wasn't it he who once wrote a story (a great story) about man's best friend getting eaten by man's best friend? (Or was it the other way around?)

Brutalization of women. What is that? Is that what my ex-old lady meant last Tuesday when she told me she was leavin' me for a better piece of mind? Leavin' me 'cause I was too hard to deal with? Don't you see, man, they need to be brutalized! Otherwise they don't have anything to fight for.

Remember Ann Lombardo (back in the days when Harlan was

really writin' some fuckin' inventive, out there, dynamite shit)? That woman could sing, huh? All those notes she hit from her toes, did she get that depth 'cause some writer with a guilty conscience pulled a grandstand play in a box filled with human pencils and pens and blank sheets of paper? No, man, she got that way by being *brutalized* (and reading original stuff, and maybe some drugs).

So Harlan should take it easy, use his imagination...know what I mean? Like how about a sequel to *A Boy and His Dog*? How about something with some juice to it. I mean what happened? Cut the bullshit and give us the real thing. The girls are doin' all right, they'll get along without him. OPPPPssssss...the phone's ringing. Gotta go. Maybe it's my ex-old lady wanting to go a few more rounds. Meanwhile...see ya...I got to feed my dog.

—Randy Holland
Malibu

*Dear Editor:*

Harlan Ellison is a whiner disguising himself as a morally outraged citizen. I hadn't realized until three weeks ago that Alan Alda was so superbly rivaled. Fuck, if he doesn't like knife-kill flicks (I don't), then don't go (I don't). It's the best protest he can register. Of course, it won't get him much attention. And what, pray tell, is the *point* of his articles? He is getting to it, one hopes. I hate to think of seeing his "ever so suave" photo weekly. (Looking forward to some Ginger Varney pix, though. Oh...I'm sorry. Was that sexist?)

If you could turn all that anger of his on to some relevant topic of the real world, like police killings or poverty, you'd have something going. Too much to hope for, I guess. So, since I'm not likely to ever see it, tell me, Harlan, how many times did *Death Valley* make you puke?

—John Blackman
Los Angeles

152

# INTERIM MEMO:

What follows is a selection of published letters from *The Comics Journal* reprint (October 1982) of the knife-kill columns; and a rather spirited response by your faithful columnist to said letters. They are offered in the spirit of further proving the correctness, in another context, of former British prime minister Harold Macmillan's observation: "I have never found, in a long experience of politics, that criticism is ever inhibited by ignorance."

*Letters reprinted with permission from* The Comics Journal

# LETTERS

## Not A Speck of Taste

Though flawed and derivative, Brian De Palma's *Blow Out* is a fascinating and ultimately moving film. The climax, which evokes the profound sadness Poe discussed in his essay on *The Raven,* reaffirms De Palma as one of the greatest and most deeply human figures in popular cinema.

It's not surprising that Harlan Elllison hates the film, since it is well-documented that he has not a speck of taste. But for him to attack it so stridently for its violence, one would at least expect that Ellison's own work is untainted by exploitative bloodletting. But this is not so. Here's a typical example, from "The Prowler in the City at the Edge of the World": "He found a woman bathing, and tied her up with strips of her own garments, and cut off her legs at the knees and left her still sitting up in the swirling crimson bath, screaming as she bled away her life. The legs he took with him." Talk about your concerted attacks on females!

Am I taking this out of context? Of course I am. Was Ellison judging *Blow Out* out of context when he walked out on the film? Of course he was. Fair is fair.

By quoting the above passage, my intention is not to discredit Ellison as an author. I just read "Shatterday," and I absolutely loved it. But as a critic, face it, Ellison is the pits.

Joe Zabel
Youngstown, Ohio

## Anti-Horror Film Rantings

While I agree that many of the spate of horror films released lately have been abominable, I cannot let Harlan Ellison's anti-horror film rantings in *Comics Journal* #76 go unanswered.

Let me make my objections point by point:

(1) Ellison, the self-appointed personification of humanism, describes the audience with whom he shared a viewing of *The Omen* as "creeps, meatheads, clods, fruitcakes, nincompoops, amoeba-brains, yoyos, yipyops, kadodies, and clodhoppers" and then goes on to make snide comments as to their personal hygiene because he doesn't share their appreciation of the film. I personally dislike *The Omen,* but do not feel compelled to viciously attack those who do. I guess that I am not as good a humanist as Ellison.

(2) Ellison, the champion of feminism, attacks a young woman in the audience solely on the grounds that he doesn't like the young man she was with. The young man, in turn, provokes Ellison's contempt

because he reminds him of the "sort" he has had unpleasant run-ins with in the past.

(3) Ellison describes the audience laughter at the ludicrous decapitation scene in *The Omen* as "the lowest point I've ever reached in loathing of my species." Worse than Auschwitz, Harlan? Worse than My Lai or Beirut? You've been out of touch with the real world too long, Ellison. The fact is that *The Omen* is a ridiculous movie that elicits laughter by its ineptitude. The decapitation scene is so poorly done that all but the most self-righteous viewers find it silly.

(4) As for Ellison's snide attack on what he likes to call "knife-kill movies" (an inherently prejudicial term), he is guilty of tarring with the same brush both worthwhile and worthless films.

If *Dressed to Kill* belongs in the "knife-kill" category, doesn't *Taxi Driver* as well? Or *Apocalypse Now*? *Chinatown*? Of course, it is not fashionable to attack Scorcese, Coppola, or Polanski, while it is open season on De Palma.

(5) The charge that appreciation of gory special effects calls one's sanity into question is so outlandish that it needs no rebuttal.

(6) Ellison's blind hatred of Brian De Palma leads him to abandon any semblance of journalistic responsibility. His claim that *Dressed to Kill* and *Blow Out* contains scenes of "Females burned alive, hacked to ribbons, staked out and suffocated slowly, their limbs taken off with axes, chainsaws, guillotines, threshing machines, the parts nailed up for display" is simply false.

(7) Ellison is like a reformed alcoholic who cannot abide the thought of someone else taking a drink. His paranoia of misogyny is so intense that it leads him to abandon any attempt to view the subject of horror films objectively.

(8) Ellison states, deprecatingly, of horror films, "They are the twisted dreams from the darkest pit in each of us." Of course they are, isn't that the point? Doesn't that quote apply to "Dracula," "The Wolfman," or "Dr. Jekyll and Mr. Hyde"?

(9) Ellison's claim that *Halloween II* contains scenes "in which kids bit into apples filled with razor blades" is not true. It is not known to me whether Ellison is lying, or if he is criticizing films he has not seen. Neither is considered worthy of a writer of Ellison's stature.

(10) As I am not a member of the Writer's Guild Film Society it would not be proper for me to comment on its internal affairs. I do feel, however, that Ellison's self-righteous views on censorship are open to criticism. Why is it wrong for Jerry Falwell to attack the morality of those who wish to see films he disapproves of, but it is all right for Ellison to call into question the sanity of those who do not share his aesthetic viewpoint?

By making these attacks on horror films during a period when demands for censorship are mounting, Ellison puts himself in the position of a man pouring gasoline on a fire. While bemoaning the spread of the flames.

Neal Harkness
Roseville, Michigan

### Harlan's Courage

I want to congratulate *The Comics Journal* on its 50th Anniversary, and for its decision to run Harlan Ellison's "An Edge In My Voice." I've missed his thought provoking column since the demise of *Future Life*. His say-it-like-it-is journalism fits nicely into your monthly package and I hope the column has found a new home.

Since the Ellison interview in the *Journal,* I have collected a number of his books and have done a lot of reading on the man himself. I only wish I had the inner courage Harlan possesses to speak my mind and demand notice. I am not so outgoing, so it is nice he is so willing to share his personal adventures and crusades. Perhaps he can inspire us all to demand a better tomorrow.

My first exposure to his work was, coincidentally, in the first issue of *Playboy* I bought in March of 1979. As he states in the introduction to "All the Birds Come Home to Roost," it is one of his finest and most dramatic stories to date. The pain and fear presented affected me deeply at the time I read the story, and still does when I think about his tortured soul.

If his column is in the *Journal* to stay, I would suggest alternating his essays with short stories every few months for variety. I really want to read some of his older works that are now out of print. We need a publication to revive that material.

I am eagerly working to expose uninformed people about Mr. Ellison's writings and have recruited at least one new fan to his legion.

Before I close, may I make a suggestion? I live a long way from a comics shop, so I have to purchase direct sales from my cousin 125 miles away in Denver. It would be very helpful if you could list prices of special items on your checklists, as it is very hard to guess amounts which depend so much on which stock paper the individual publishers decide to print on.

I would be interested in reading a review of the "How-To-Draw Tips from the Top Cartoonists" being advertised in this month's comics. I am a hopeful cartoonist for the future, who is greatly aided by books on comic book art, but my $11 comes hard. Perhaps one of your resident reviewers could shed some light on the book.

Also, how does the advertised "Official 1983 Price Guide to Comic Books" compare with Overstreet's? The price is right if the quality is up to par.

Dean A. Boeff
Sterling, Colorado

## You Are Not Alone

Amid your usual selection of multi-syllabic elitism and breast-beating came an eloquent, touching and enervating text, that being Harlan Ellison's "Face-to-Face With the Beast in a Place With No Windows." His point has been made before, most notably by Gene Siskel and Roger Ebert; yet, in no way has the point of overstatement and wretched excess been reached, and I applaud his reiteration of the problem and his fresh insights on its growth.

I, too, lament the turn a once responsible genre has taken. It is painful to watch directors like Carpenter and De Palma make promising starts and then descend to pits of filth because it's an easier row to hoe. Suspense equals blood and gore is not a correct equation. Suspense is *Jaws,* or *Psycho,* not *Blow Out* or *Tattoo.*

I saw *Tattoo.* I thought it might be a suspenseful battle of wits and of wills between captive and captor. Silly boy! It was just torture, for both the victim and the audience. The film, in a way, was even worse than the slasher films, because the victim would be put through some gruesome torture and then would be deprived of the merciful release of death; they'd just run another torture on her.

And I stayed! I stayed through that whole picture, praying that the director would pull a double-reverse and put something interesting up there. I kept thinking no one could let something this bad go out. As many hands as it had to go through, surely someone should have said no. Even bad films have something going for them, even if it's just their own unique badness. This film had nothing, no reason to live, no excuse to be shown. When the credits finally came, I found myself beat down into my seat, breathing a sigh of relief that I was still reasonably whole.

Do not still your voice, Mr. Ellison. Though this, too, is a cycle in cinema that will one day be consigned to the ghetto of drive-ins where it won't hurt anyone, the day must be hurried in getting here. Just when I think that blessed day has arrived, another works its way out of the woodwork. Just last Thursday I was feeling that confidence. Then Friday came, and with it, *The Sender* and *Halloween III.* Keep plugging, Mr. Ellison. It may seem one against the many, but you are not alone.

Bill C. Kropfhauser
Columbus, Ohio

# HARLAN ELLISON REPLIES:

Harkness should be held aloft in one of those Stri-Dex pimple pad commercials as a classic example of what results from prolonged intellectual self-abuse. Hair is obviously growing all over his brain. (1) I am merely a Humanist, not the personification of same. A subtle difference that escapes Harkness, a sophomoric refutationist who clearly cannot distinguish between the message and the manner of presentation of the message. Whatever self-assertive aspects of my personality he finds threatening—possibly because he envies those qualities—they blind him to the cogency of what is being said. It's a flaw in himself that Harkness should try to deal with, for his own good. He's correct, however, in his assertion that he isn't as good a Humanist as I. (2) Likewise, I am a Feminist, not a champion of Feminism. Feminism (which lad Harkness apparently finds a threatening concept) doesn't need me to champion it. But advocacy of Feminism does not mean blind adulation of all females, even as one's publication in something called *The Comics Journal* need not necessarily signify toleration of muddleheads like Harkness who read it. Observations on the behavior of the young man and woman in question were made solely *on* their behavior. This is accepted procedure in judging lower forms of animal life. (3) One shouldn't have to honor the devalued coin of such *non sequitur* silliness as this by trashing its proponent, but simply in the spirit of attempting to make Harkness's intolerance a tot more pervious, the following common sense: I was not personally in attendance at Auschwitz, at My Lai, or even Beirut. I *was* in attendance at that screening of *The Omen*. And while no doubt the depth of my feeling was subliminally informed by such atrocities—as well as those we know as Babi Yar, Kent State, the Russian Great Purge of 1936–38 and Wounded Knee—surely even someone as disingenuous as Harkness will grant that one doesn't pre-plan *which* moment of anguish at man's inhumanity to man will be the one that triggers the heartfelt wail. (4) Only someone groping desperately to discredit another's emotional/intellectual position drags in irrelevent considerations. Scorsese's films are *about* something, most particularly *Taxi Driver*. The film in nowhichway can be called a knife-kill film. It is deeply, intelligently concerned with close and uncompromising analysis of a social ill, which is why Hinckley is foreshadowed in the film and becomes its self-fulfilling prophecy. De Palma's *oeuvre*, from the first (and excepting *Phantom of the Paradise, Get to Know Your Rabbit,* and *Carrie*) has solely been a vehicle to show the brutalization of women for no nobler purpose than the titillation of ghouls masquerading as innocent filmgoers. Scorsese's *King of Comedy* further develops his scrutiny of the *Taxi Driver* social phenomenon, and like the former film is Art of a high order. It's a shame that, again, Harkness cannot make the imperative distinction. Dragging in Coppola is simply flummery. And I'd happily have included Polanski in the piece; I just didn't think of him. But in any case, what has my *not* addressing these directors' work got to do with those I selected at random to deal with? This is skip-logic at its worst. (5) No comment beyond this: you set your rules, Harkness; and for the sake of discussion I'll set mine. (6) Harkness knows full well I didn't say that De Palma's films contain scenes of "Females burned alive...etc., etc., etc." He knows full well it was a general comment about the genre. Even so, his attempt to discredit falls apart because De Palma's films *do* contain repeated and intense scenes of graphic violence against women using knives, straight razors, ice picks, thugee-style wire loops and other implements whose introduction in the films is solely for the purpose of showing women being hacked to ribbons. (7) Damn straight, Harkness. My abhorrence is *exactly* that strong. And I'm not that crazy about you, either. (8) No. (9) You lose again, Harkness. I'm neither lying nor reporting second hand. The razor-blades-in-the-apples scene occurs early in the film and is reprised when the mother brings the boy with the bloody mouth to the hospital. Either *you're* so desperate to make a case for sick movies or your memory is deteriorating from too much exposure to vileness. It is also possible that the print I saw, in pre-release, was edited by the time it reached your theater. It was a vile and gratuitous bit of evil, and the releasing entity may have had a momentary spasm of good taste and excised it; thereby denying you a moment of pleasure. (10) It was made clear that the action of the Writers Guild Film Society had nothing to do with censorship. Since the films were available in hundreds of theaters throughout the LA area, we were simply making an artistic judgment as to which films we would show to fill the limited slots available for Society screenings. No one told anyone *not* to see the films, or threatened them with any form of retribution or boycott if they did, as Falwell does. Harkness understands the difference, as does anyone who read my essay; and no amount of cupidic rhetoric can fog the issue.

By dealing at length with the simpoleon *kvetching* of Harkness, I don't have to repeat the lesson with Zabel (who ought to know there is a vast qualitative and emotional difference between the printed word and the visual presentation four times life-size of graphic violence). My thanks to Boeff and Kropfhauser. They cannot know how much good their letters do in the struggle to sustain one's passion in the face of such paralogia as Harkness wallows in.

The great danger of thinking(?) such as Harkness's, is that it confuses artistic and esthetic selectivity, and standards for same, with censorship. As one who confronts censorship at ground level every day—as opposed to parvenus like Harkness who talk a good game but do nothing to impede the incursions of the Falwells—I recognize the difficulty of walking the tightrope. Nonetheless, it is a balancing act every intelligent, self-examining and concerned individual should practice, lest we fall into the bog with Harkness.

It is interesting to note, however, as addenda to the essay: in the year since it was published in the *L.A. Weekly,* (according to knife-kill flick *maven* Bill Warren, who is on top of such things, working as he does for the Motion Picture Academy), over 130 of these splatter abominations have been shelved. Though produced and slated for distribution, the outcry against this pollutant has become so great that the theaters and distributors have opted to pull back from further saturation bookings. The downside of the situation, though, is that they will all, no doubt, show up in our livingrooms via cable, as their need for massive product permits of very little selectivity based on good taste or artistic value. But at least, a year later, the voices raised against this shit have had some effect.

# INTERIM MEMO:

Three months after this column was written, the Camaro
bit it, and so, damned-near, did its owner. You can skip
over to Installment 29 if your curiosity is piqued. But
you've gotta come back here after you've read this column
and then #29. And if we pull that off, we can talk over the
Sudetenland.

## Why Everything Is Fucked Up, Since You Asked

Maybe this is the first dangerous step on the path to winding up like Napoleon or Genghis Khan or Ronald Reagan, but I think I've finally figured out the answer to why everything is fucked up.

Why are you fishing around in the closet for a jacket with straps in 36 short? This is serious, fer godsake. I've got the answer. It has to do with my car.

Lemme tell you about my car. I drive this 1967 Chevy Camaro I bought for cash new. It's the upper-6 and it's got more than 160,000 miles on it. Actually, it's probably closer to 165,000 but for three years my speedometer was way off so by the time I got it fixed I'd lost a true total. But even at 160,000 miles in fifteen years, it's a swell vehicle. What I'm talking here is a car that gives me between 31 and 40 miles to the gallon in the city. And last year, for instance, I put in about two hundred dollars' worth of repairs. And it can beat a Mercedes away from the light if the need arises.

It's dirty. I've got to tell you it is really grungy. On the outside. Inside, it's clean, where people sit. But I haven't washed it in eight years, as best I recall. (In 1974 a woman I was dating sneaked it off and had it washed and waxed because the dirt was so thick that friends of mine who would see the car parked outside a movie theater were leaving messages on the doors and trunk: ELLISON WASH THIS DISGRACE! DON BUDAY. But that was an overstepping of our relationship and a big mistake. Car didn't run well for six months thereafter, till it built up a protective coating of shmootz again. Wonder whatever happened to that woman?) My car has a bumper sticker that says A CLEAN CAR IS A SIGN OF A SICK MIND. It's not a crusade with me; it's just my belief that if God, or Whoever's-In-Charge, had wanted my car to be clean, God, or Whoever's-In-Charge wouldn't have filled the world with dirt.

I'm digressing. The point is, I have a fifteen-year-old car that runs like a sonofabitch, and even when a California Highway Patrol officer pulled me over on the Ventura Freeway because he wanted to buy the car—"It's a classic," he said, "the first year they made a Camaro, I'll give you a thousand for it"—and I said no thanks and he

165

gave me a ticket just to be a prick, even then I wouldn't sell it. No amount of hassling by my well-meaning friends will make me part with that nifty vehicle in order to purchase some shiny new box-on-box Detroit iron or one of the sporty little Oriental runabouts with no trunk space and you ride with your knees tucked up under your chin. If I could afford a well-preserved 1949 Packard, well, maybe I'd consider it. But exchange my dear Camaro for some 1982 issue sop to the failing economy? No thank you.

That car is a gem. It starts when I turn the key; and it runs like Sugar Ray Leonard after a hard fourteen rounds. Maybe you have a car that has served you terrifically for a long time and you know what I'm talking about. There is no anthropomorphism about this, I don't call my car by some pet name, I don't deify it or get crazy when some schlub scrapes the fender; it's just *car* and it does what it's supposed to do. I feel no need to change it every three years just so I "look good" on the street. A car is a thing to get one from here to there with the minimum of fuss. An overhead-cam outfit is no substitute in a rational universe for a mistress, despite all the sociological tomes equating one with the other in the minds of macho American males.

The radio in my car is also an integral part of my having found the answer to why everything is fucked up. It is a Blaupunkt. I had it installed in an old Austin–Healy I owned in 1965. Bought it for cash new. Never gave me a moment's aggravation it was built so well. And when I bought the Camaro in '67 I pulled it and had it transferred. Not until November of last year did it begin acting up. So I tried to get it repaired. First half a dozen radio repair joints made faces and said, "Aw, hell, this is an old piece of shit; no point in trying to repair it. Cost you as much to repair it as to buy a new one. Now look at this dandy EarBuster Royale we have over here, it's only two hundred and...."

So we took it to a Blaupunkt agency here in town and got more of the same. No parts. Old radio. Forget it. Buy a new one. As if we were asking them to perform some hideous sexual obscenity unpracticed since the time of the Druids.

My assistant, Ms. Marty Clark, a sensible woman of vast positive qualities and inordinate intelligence, upbraided me for wasting so much time on this project. "Things are made to fall apart," she said. "The center cannot hold. Let go of the past. Buy the new and let me get back to *important* work, you loon!"

I persisted. My argument was this: we have become a nation of marks, a country of fast trick johns. Kadodies. Jamooks. Country bumpkins being fleeced every day for every farthing in our bib overalls. Planned obsolescence, a concept that Americans as recently as forty years ago would have found anathema, has become a shrug-the-shoulders-and-accept-it way of life. We *expect* the toaster to go on the fritz in thirteen months, just after the warranty expires. We *expect* the digital watch we bought at The Akron to begin running backwards, widdershins like the White Rabbit's timepiece, after a year of faithful service. We *expect* the screws to come loose in the lawn chair after one summer in the sun. We *expect* the roof to leak even though the reshingling company swore it was watertight and charged us half our yearly income.

No, I said, determined to fight this to the last bastion, this is a quality piece of goods, this Blaupunkt. The company is known for making sturdy product and to hell with these lazy bastards who are too featherbedded to do a proper repair when they can high-ball us into buying some *new* piece of crap that'll conk out in six months. I want *this* radio repaired, I said, stamping me widdle foot in pique.

So we wrote directly to Blaupunkt and laid all this on them. Will you stand behind your reputation or won't you? And we managed to reach someone in that organization who felt as I did, and they took the radio and repaired it. Cost: $22 plus another $14 to have it pulled and reinstalled.

Are you getting my drift here? A seventeen-year-old radio that never screeched or went out on me was repaired for a pittance. It was, and is, quality goods.

I've read statistics that proved most young married women between the ages of 20 and 35 don't want to buy furniture that will last fifty years. They want what is called in the stick trade "borax." Color-coded junk that falls apart in three to five years so they can garage sale it and buy all new flotsam that won't last beyond the time it takes the kapok in it to get digested by the smog.

Used to watch an old man who made luggage. Used to go to his shop in Evanston, Illinois and watch him work. He was a sad old man. He recalled having made fitted luggage for Galli-Curci and Caruso. Intricate, beautiful goods with cases that fitted inside cases, with hand-tooling and the finest leathers. He pointed to the plastic imitation-leather wrapups his shop now sold, and he sighed. "No room for craftsmen now," he said, his old eyes seeing past glories. "Nobody wants to spend good money for luggage they'll dropkick out of the airplanes." We *expect* the pithecanthropoids at the airport to bash up our luggage.

And that, at last, is what has everything fucked up.

How the hell can we be surprised that American car makers are going down the tubes? The Japanese make better cars. How can we strut around still believing in American Know-How, when all the VCR gear comes from over there? How much pride in craft can an average laborer in an automobile plant take in ten thousand un-painted door panels that swing by him each month to get one rivet driven into them? How can workers feel anything but distanced from purpose in their lives when they never see that something they've

167

built with their hands has turned out solid and professional and useable?

The guy who built the lovely art deco dining nook that Carol Barkin designed for me comes back again and again to look at it with pleasure. When they had it on the cover of *Designers West* he took as much pride in it as Carol or I. His name is Leon Opseth, and he's a painstaking craftsman who is forced to throw up the usual wallboard-and-stucco boxes we've come to accept as "okay," just to stay in business. But he hates that shit. He comes back here to my house to look at the Art Deco Dining Pavilion (as we call it) because it took him the better part of a year to build to order. It is as much his as mine or Carol's.

They built my dear old Camaro to last in 1967, and they built my Blaupunkt to last in 1965, and Leon built the Pavilion to last in 1980.

And the typewriter I use is an old Olympia office machine that has typed millions of words and only the ! and the L key are giving me any trouble. And there's a little French bootmaker in the Valley who charges only fifteen bucks to put new soles and heels on my thirteen-year-old boots, instead of the $25 everybody else charges for doing a slovenly job.

What has everything fucked up is that the idea of doing a superlative job with pride and craft, for a reasonable price, has fallen on sour days. Most of us want the fast buck, and we don't want to stand behind what we did if, in fact, we ever felt any responsibility for that single rivet.

But if that's the way we believe the world has to work, if we accept being jamooks hustled by three-card monte hustlers in multinational mufti, then one day a hundred million years from now when the human race has succumbed to planned obsolescence, and the cockroaches have taken over, and they excavate the ruins of my house, they will still find a chair I've got downstairs that is 50 years old and is in top condition.

And they will look at the chair and be able to deduce just how our body was bent and what we looked like. Because that chair was built to do one job: to be a *chair*. And to keep doing that job forever.

And maybe I'm ready for that 36 short straightjacket, but I suspect the time has come as Recession and Depression and Stagflation strangle us, to begin insisting that what we make and what we buy last as long and work as well as my crummy old Camaro.

168

**INSTALLMENT 17:** 16 February 82

# Interim Memo:

Yes, I know I repeated the quote from Günter Eich in this column. Chalk it up to cataphasia. Also, the penultimate paragraph makes a reference to one of the letters you found at the end of Installment 15. Never let it be said an Ellison forgets.

# How to Make Life Interesting

The subject is boredom. The sepulchral malaise of our aeon, induced by great gobbets of leisure time afforded to all, without the concomitant rise in group or individual imagination that would provide innovative ways to *spend* that free time.

Boredom. Tedium, ennui, lassitude. World-weariness and jaded appetites. The day begun with a yawn and ended with fog. Lives safe from the stalking sabertooth or the Black Plague, yes indeed; but rich, filled with various excitements, new endeavors and random adventures? Pshaw! An after-dinner colloquy on the merits and demerits of supply-side economics can hardly be equated with the thrill of stalking the Minotaur through his maze. Enhanced computer photos of Mars come back to us from NASA and reveal that the surface of the Red Planet bears no resemblance to Bradbury's wonderland of beer-can-filled canals and spiderweb crystal cities. Mars looks like Nevada's Fairchild Desert, only not as lively. Primetime television actually allocates hours to Merv, Mike Douglas, Donny & Marie and Jerry Falwell. Athos, Porthos and Aramis, yes, to be sure: but Jerry *Falwell?* Oh my. Boredom, tedium, ennui and ho as well as hum.

What ever became of the exciting life as lived by the Cro-Magnons we envy in the new film *Quest for Fire?* Sleeping out in the thundering rainfall, slaying great beasts with pointy sticks, ripping steaming entrails from the prey and savoring a gourmet meal hunkered down among one's hairy peers? As one with Edwin Arlington Robinson's Miniver Cheevy—who "wept that he was ever born ...loved the days of old when swords were bright and steeds were prancing...he dreamed of Thebes and Camelot—Miniver Cheevy, born too late, coughed and called it fate, and kept on drinking"—as one with Miniver we lament the highflown adventurous excesses of times before we came to this place of sighs.

The frontiers, we are told, have been condominiumized. The golden horizons merely reflect the lights from the Golden Arches. New dimensions do not exist. The best we can hope for by way of stimulation is a full expansion to 60 channels of cable television.

171

Forgive my temerity, but what we're talking here is not Prometheus stealing fire from the gods.

So what, you ask me, is our alternative?

Well, imagine my delight that you should inquire.

Creative activities in the area of cursory interpersonal relationships, I reply. Random encounters. Casual contretemps guaranteeing a smack rush of adrenaline. I speak here not of zipless fucks or tawdry goodbarism in Santa Monica bars. What I commend to your attention is the carefully-orchestrated play-action situation in which danger, action and adventure manifest themselves throughout the humdrum of your everyday life.

Lemme give you a f'rinstance.

Last week, about Thursday, I had a dental appointment out in Pacific Palisades. After Bob Knoll was done with me, I made my usual hegira to Mort's Deli, a place where they know how to make a cheeseburger well-done without it tastes like the ashes of Nineveh.

I'm sitting there at a table eating, when I chance to overhear the conversation at the next table. Call me an eavesdropper if you will; call me madcap; call me a pisher . . . but even as you and you and you, I have this terrific peripheral hearing that picks up the sound of tectonic plates deep in the Earth, crunching as they turn in their seismic sleep. *Not* hearing the conversation at the next table, *that* would be a trick.

The focus of the conversation was a sleek young woman of the sort that I, in my irrational bigotry, perceive as scion of wealthy Beverly Hills parents: a shimmering creature with legs waxed and floating soft lenses in turquoise. She was wearing either a Capezio leotard by Rudi Gernreich or one of those Jane Fonda Workout cotton leotards from a boutique on Robertson. My familiarity with specifics in this area is not letter-perfect. It was a black leotard. Over it she wore Ralph Lauren shorts in a horizontal stripe pattern of magenta and cerulean blue, and a Bonwit Teller blouse. Her sweatband was by Head. Her sneakers were by Adidas. Ralph Lauren again for the leg warmers. She had not been jogging. She did not sweat, neither did she perspire nor glow. And of this I am certain: she toiled not, neither did she spin.

This creature of idle hours, chatting and Fresca-sipping in the late afternoon when all her more responsible sistren [sic] were slaving in windowless offices under the lash of insensitive sexist junior executives, was skimming across the shallow surface of what passed for conversation with a pair of young men in their early twenties who resembled, in my twisted view, Via Veneto pimps. Truly such could not be the case, as they spoke something resembling English (though the recurrent phrase "fer-*shooor*" seemed alien argot), and they were clearly of the same social set as She-Who-Must-Be-Pampered.

Though I surely denigrate them unjustly by suggesting their

hands had never been sullied by exposure to common labor—the boys no doubt make substantial livings selling *Grit* and the young woman probably has expertise running a McCormick thresher—the substance (if one conceives of tapioca as having substance) of their conversation was as follows:

"How's the powder at Aspen?"

"I went crazy and bought these new *après*-ski boots at Abercrombie & Fitch."

"Fran said Big Bear was heaven last week."

"Where were you when Dot and Ferdie got up the party for Snow Summit?"

You get the idea. Subjects of pith and moment.

Now, as I listen in to this scintillant rodomontade, my face falling forward into my carrot-and-raisin salad every time I nod off from the sheer excitement of it all, one of the guys calls her by her first name—I'll call her Denise so they can't get me for defamation of character even though the best defense, Henry Holmes tells me, is the truth—and the other guy soon thereafter calls her by her last name, "Hey, Kauffman," another alias.

So now I know Guido and Enzo are talking to Denise Kauffman and I continue listening. Why am I listening to such banalities, you ask? Perversity? Snoopiness? No, in thunder! Boredom. How excited can one get about carrot-and-raisin salad? I am big-B bored, so I listen to what comes next, never intended for the ears of such as I.

Denise: I'm going up to Big Bear this weekend.

Guido: Oh yeah? Who with?

Denise: David.

Enzo: Is that the guy we met, the car rental guy?

Denise: No, he's the dentist. You know, with the mustache.

(I hasten to add this is not a description that later we will discover to be that of *my* dentist, the enormously-skilled and highly ethical Robert P. Knoll, wizard of plaque-removal. This was another dentist entirely. They breed.)

Guido: Where you staying?

Denise: He's got a really terrific cabin up there, a chalet like, you know.

Enzo: I thought he was married.

Denise: He is. His wife doesn't know.

The conversation moved on apace. But I was caught in the thrall of an opening for play-action danger and adventure. An opportunity to breathe vigor into an otherwise tepid afternoon.

And so, when I finished my food and had tapped the corners of my mouth with one of Mort's Deli's antimacassar napkins, I stood up and stepped sidewise to their table. Looming over her, but looking out the front window of the Deli; addressing the cosmos, as it were, I said in the sort of voice and manner made legend by Dan Duryea in dozens of episodes of *China Smith* and half a hundred "B" films, "Denise. As of now, David's wife *does* know."

And then, very quickly, I motored.

As I crossed the sidewalk in front of the Deli window, where inside they sat, I was rewarded by a scene of such utter panic and bugfuck terror that it made the rush of the lemmings to the cliff seem like close-order drill in a KKK nursery school.

In a moment I was gone.

Leaving behind a social butterfly whose ski-wax had congealed, who would be on the phone to David, D.D.S., in a nanosecond, screaming, "David! David! Your wife's put a private detective on us! She knows, David! OhMiGod, *Daaaavid,* what'll we do!?!" This is a true story.

You say you're bored? You say you need excitement? You say you need escape from the closed-in four walls of your drab existence? I commend to your attention the words of the German poet Günter Eich (1907–72) who wrote, "Be uncomfortable; be sand, not oil, in the machinery of the world."

On the other hand, this advice and apocalyptic little tale will no doubt convince the woman who wrote in to this newspaper's letter column recently, "Please edge Mr. Ellison's voice out," that I am even more of an unsavory scut than she expected. But then—

Life is full of unexpected surprises, have you noticed?

# LETTERS

*Dear Editor:*

What if we like to watch little bunny rabbits being crushed and eaten by big snakes? Are we okay then?

—Jed (the) Fish Gould

**INSTALLMENT 18:** 21 February 82

# INTERIM MEMO:

The pebble goes into the Pond of Life, and the ripples of Chance go out and out. This one's gonna be a trifle tricky, so stay with me.

This was one of the most widely-circulated of all the columns; it was picked up as referent by a number of newspapers, and a few syndicated columnists mentioned it *en passant*. It was reprinted as "Night of the Long Knives" in *The Comics Journal,* issue #90 (May/June 1984).

But in March 1983, in issue #80, *The Comics Journal* reprinted a chronologically-later column which you will find entered here as Installment 30. Both of these columns dealt with Edward Asner—though Installment 30 only mentions Asner in passing. Are we together on this, so far? The later column was reprinted earlier, and the earlier column was reprinted later.

The later column, Installment 30, was reprinted under the title "Hysterical Paralogia, Part 1", and drew its share of comments from the readers of *The Comics Journal*; but some of them are, uh, how shall I put this delicately, slow readers. Possibly due to overdosing on issues of *The Amazing Spider-Man* and *Dazzler* comics. Thus it was, in late August of 1984, after this entire book was completed and was being set in type for publication, that I received from Tom Heintjes, news editor of *The Comics Journal,* the text of a letter from one Brian Smith of Marshalltown, Iowa. This letter was scheduled for publication in issue #93 (September 1984) and it was in response to Installment 18 (reprinted, if you are still with me, in issue #90) and Installment 30 (reprinted more than a year earlier). Heintjes solicited my response to the letter, which is a doozy, and I sat down on August 21 to write a brief paragraph of auctorial rebuttal to Mr. Smith's doozy of a letter.

2600 words later I had written an unexpected 61st installment of *An Edge In My Voice.* Twenty months after I'd typed my last column, the fires leapt up and nothing had changed: I was back on the barricades. *The Comics Journal* published the reply to Mr. Smith as an original installment of the column in issue #93 under the title "So Why Aren't We Laughing?"

You will find that final, unexpected essay as the final, unplanned Installment 61 of this collection. I make reference to it here—and will again at Installment 30—because chronologically this is where it all started, so you'll remember where it came from when you get to Mr. Smith's letter and the 61st *Edge* at the big ride-out finish of this book.

Ed Asner was on the news the other night: the cameras caught him in the parking lot of the Beverly Glen Centre. He had a bodyguard with him. What a punch under the heart of *déjà vu* I had. All I could think of were recalled images of right-wingers picketing Jane Fonda. And the scroll of memory unwound further and I was in front of the Century Plaza on a night during Lyndon Johnson's administration, when LBJ was addressing the moneyed Beverly Hills constituency, and we were picketing against the war in Vietnam, trying to get LBJ's attention, and the late John Wayne came storming out of the hotel, having attended the megabuck-per-plate banquet, and he waded into the protesters, who were at a decent remove from the front doors. And I conjured up the memory of the way it was treated on the video news. Hondo Wayne, the very personification of American *macho,* in an heroic stand against the unwashed tools of Communist Duplicity.

(The fact that those protesters were mostly school teachers and pregnant mothers and students and office workers, not lackeys of the Dreaded Red Menace...or that their cause was a concerned and just one...made no difference. Rooster Cogburn was being pluperfectly Amurrican, showing what stern stuff we frontier defenders of the faith were made of.)

Ed Asner is a public figure. He is the star of one of the three or four series currently on television that is worth one's viewing time, as opposed to such deifications of imbecility as *The Dukes of Hazzard* or *The Las Vegas Battle of the Showgirls.* As Lou Grant—all the way back to *The Mary Tyler Moore Show,* where he created the character— Asner has been a model of rectitude and humanism for a nation desperately seeking heroes.

Now, he is also the President of the Screen Actors Guild.

And he is a private citizen concerned about this nation's place in specific foreign involvements.

In all three capacities, he is speaking out. And we are being told there is some sort of sleazy impropriety in his doing so.

We are being told by ex-actor Ronald Reagan (out of the mouth of his chum Charlton Heston) that Ed Asner is misusing his position as head of a labor union when he "dabbles in politics." Amazing. No one bothers to note that Mr. Reagan, when *he* was President of the very same union, used his position to build a base for his subsequent political career. No one has done a tv commentary recalling Mr. Reagan's public statement in 1947 that SAG "will not be a party to a blacklist" but under his aegis banned Communists and noncooperative witnesses who appeared before the House Un-American Activities Committee.

We are being told by ex-actor Ronald Reagan (via the recipient of the Ten Commandments) that Ed Asner is misusing his popularity as an onscreen personality when he makes public statements about our involvement in El Salvador. Amazing. No one seems to remember that Mr. Reagan, when he was doing *General Electric Theater,* tried to coerce writers into adding to a script a scene in which a Communist mother slaps her child because she catches him praying. There have been no CBS editorial rebuttals to the impropriety accusations dumped on Mr. Asner, in which it is pointed out that Mr. Reagan, in every political campaign he has waged, has offered as his credential for "understanding the common laborer" the fact that he headed up a union.

One need not comment too ironically that being the President of SAG bears little relation to ramrodding unions whose members toil in mineshafts or sweep city streets. But that's just picking a nit off one already heavily festooned with the critters.

We are repeatedly bludgeoned with the specious logic, "What does an actor know, anyhow? He may be a crusading newspaper editor on television, but he's just playing the part." It is to giggle, friends. If actors don't know shit about the Real World, then what do we make of ex-Senator George Murphy, ex-U.N. Ambassador Shirley Temple Black, Ambassador to Mexico John Gavin and, er, uh, dare I think the unthinkable, the old Gipper hisself?

I realize this is a concept that may jangle the nervous system of those who think all actors have the intellectual capacity of, say, the characters Billie Burke used to play, but I would trust the judgment of Ed Asner or Robert Culp or Katharine Hepburn or Jane Fonda a lot further than that of Justin Dart, an industrialist, William Bradford Shockley, a physicist, or Jerry Falwell, a fund-raiser for censorship. Dart believes "home-rule" means bigger and more soulless multinational corporations; Shockley can "prove" through his theory of dysgenics that blacks are inferior to whites; and Falwell knows for certain that anyone in favor of the Equal Rights Amendment is going straight to Hell. Tell me that these three dabblers in politics are any wiser than Ed Asner and I'll tell you your head ought to be rented out for the National Hot Air Balloon Races.

It appears the only opinions that have merit, the only ethical stands one can take, are those that agree with the administration in power. Equal time provisos are not served by Big Brother having primetime access to all three networks while insurgent opinions get a

178

soapbox on the corner. Only the most naive among us still believe that the CIA had no part in the overthrow of the Allende government in Chile. Evidence to the contrary is so blatantly overwhelming that only those protecting the exchequers of the 3000 U.S. firms doing business with the junta down there could make such a duplicitous assertion. Yet last week Reagan's front men made a public denial of U.S. involvement in Chile in response to the Costas-Gavras film, *Missing*.

And the front men are establishing a pattern of intended destruction toward Asner. It all began when SAG joined with Norman Lear's People For The American Way in opposition to the Moral Majority. Charlton Heston and Robert Conrad and the rest of that sanctimonious lynch mob were irate. When the Humanitarian Award SAG proffers to a well-known actor every year was denied Mr. Reagan—by an 86 to 12 vote of the SAG Board of Directors—the front men for the White House went looney. Last Sunday a rump meeting was called by these undemocratic forces, to recall Asner and to get SAG Public Relations Director Kim Fellner canned. It's all a pattern, and we've seen its like before. It manifests itself in such vile ways as being confronted at the top of the escalators at LAX by a nitwit wearing a sandwich board that reads NUCLEAR PLANTS ARE BUILT BETTER THAN JANE FONDA.

We live in a time in which cowardice is garbed in moral outrage. Procter & Gamble bows to the whims of self-styled regulators of public morality like the Rev. Wildmon. School boards ban CATCHER IN THE RYE and CANNERY ROW because one or two semiliterate parents drop into Cheyne-Stokes breathing at the sight of the word fuck on a printed page. Deaths by handgun in 1980 in Sweden were 21, in Canada 52, in Japan 48 and in Great Britain 8: they have strict handgun control. In 1980 the handgun body count in the United States was 10,728. But no one will buck the Gun Lobby and the National Rifle Association.

And Ed Asner had to hire a bodyguard because the airheads have threatened his life. Because he has had the temerity to point out that the ugliness in El Salvador has the makings of another Vietnam for us. And while we may not care too much for Fidel Castro, I wonder what Cuba and our relations with Cuba might be like today if we hadn't supported the Batista regime to protect U.S. business interests.

Men like Ed Asner understand that the responsibility that attaches to becoming famous in their special line of work, whether as artist, actor, writer or scientist, is a serious requirement that they use that power for betterment of our days and nights. Is a perception that bucking the front men and the dark philosophies they serve can only bring disaster down on them. Jane Fonda knew it. Arthur Miller knew it. Lillian Hellman knew it. Cliff Robertson knew it. Shirley MacLaine and Marlon Brando knew it. And now Ed Asner is on the line.

I met Asner once. We talked for maybe a minute and a half. I do not see him as Simon Bolivar or Jomo Kenyatta or George Washington. He is simply a man with convictions and a good head on his shoulders. But he is on the line at this moment...as visible target and, God forbid, as scapegoat.

What he is bucking, in the greater sense, is the climate of fear that is so reminiscent of the Forties and Fifties. Mr. Heston (who may see himself as Moses or El Cid, which outpoints a mere crusading newspaper editor in any sweepstakes) seems determined to do Mr. Reagan's dirtywork in terms of scaring the bejeezus out of us, thereby further deepening the miasma of suspicion and paralyzing terror that permits unlimited arms buildup and greater control of our thoughts through Big Brotherdom. Asner is to be the sacrifice.

Ed Asner is no hero. He is the essence of the Common Man who, in the words of Henry David Thoreau, serves the State best by opposing the State most.

I wonder how many of us can be courageous enough to make our voices heard in his defense. What he says and what he does may be sanctified or muddleheaded, but damn it to hell it's his *right* to make his position known. And using his clout as a television personality or as an official of a union is no more meretricious than an industrialist, a Nobel Prize-winning physicist or a tv evangelist using *their* special clout to achieve *their* ends.

Ed Asner speaks for many of us. By hard work and excellence of craft he has been put in the position of being heard. That he does it, instead of laying back as so many of us do, is a demonstration of that which is most enduring in the national spirit.

We are *all* speaking. Ed Asner merely has the mouth.

Let's not let them put a gag in it.

**INSTALLMENT 19:** 1 March 82

# INTERIM MEMO:

By March, a number of newspapers in other parts of the country had begun picking up the columns for reprint. It wasn't as nice as syndication (which, in a world of Erma Bombeck and Heloise columns, is unthinkable), particularly because they weren't paying me for the usage. In the rarefied world of the Fourth Estate we have a high-tech term for this: *rip-off.* Nonetheless, these little screeds were being viewed beyond the county limits of Los Angeles (I was soon to find out just *how* far outside) and my co-defendant in the improbable Fleisher Lawsuit (about which nothing will be said in this book), Gary Groth, publisher of a magazine called *The Comics Journal*, in a vainglorious gesture toward sophistication, began reprinting *An Edge.* Actually, he didn't begin reprinting till October of 1982, but the first few columns were older ones, of which this item was the second. For that reappearance, Groth kept mewling till I came up with a "title." I called it

*Gobbledygook on Olympus*

I mention this purely in a spirit of keeping nothing from you, nothing! You have a bit of spinach caught between your two front teeth. You are adopted. Your mother and I are getting a divorce. There is no Easter Bunny.

# Gobbledygook on Olympus

As one with Jacques Barzun, Willard Espy, Edwin Newman and John Simon, long have I confessed to this obsessive love affair with the English language. Fer sure, I rilly love it a whole lot! Long have I inveighed against the incorrect use of "hopefully" and the cretinous "at this point in time." Oh, wow, I'm rilly into it! Jangling to my delicate nervous system is the pronounciation of *noo-cue-lerr.*

Molly Haskell, one of the film critics for the New York *Times,* has written, "Language: the one tool that enables us to grasp hold of our lives and transcend our fate by understanding it." Hey, I'll go for that. Fer sure.

Well, given all of that, you can just imagine my surprise when I was hit by a falling buzzword the other day. It came out of nowhere; and like a deadly dum-dum, it had my name on it.

And what it was, was this:

A representative of a large talent agency called a tv network executive, and when he got the man's secretary on the line he asked her (direct quote), "Is he speakable?"

Let us pause for an instant. What is creeping toward us will not be deterred by an instant's pause. When we get back to it in the next paragraph, it'll still be slithering ahead. Trust me. But do pause with me for this excerpt from a little book called LANGUAGE IN AMERICA: "Let us define a semantic environment as any human situation in which language plays a critical role. This means that the constituents of the environment are (1) people, (2) their purposes, and (3) the language they use to help them achieve their purposes. Because there are many different human purposes, there are, of course, many different kinds of semantic environments. Science is a semantic environment. So is politics; commerce; war; love-making; praying; reporting; law-making; etc. Each of these situations is a context in which people want to do something to, for, with, or against other people, and in which the communication of meaning (language) plays a decisive role. *A healthy semantic environment is one in which language effectively serves the purposes of the particular context in which it is used....* The semantic environment is polluted when language obscures from people what they are doing and why they are doing it."

Is he *speakable*!?! No, you chimpanzee, he's *unspeakable*!

What slithers toward us is the miasma of semantic pollution, that creeps in on little cat feet, takes a shit, and creeps on. The context is the film/tv industry. The language is ever increasingly more oppressive obscurantism, euphemisms, buzzwords, jingoism and looneytune psychobabble.

God (or Whoever's in charge) knows it's hard enough carrying on an intelligible conversation with producers, studio executives, agents, network vice-presidents and those who call themselves "packagers" (whatever the hell *that* means) when, for the most part, and despite their cloak of arrogance, they haven't the vaguest idea what they're talking about. Add to the unassailable perception that far too many of these paladins of power have the intellectual capacity of an artichoke, and their determination to speak in a tongue best described as Functional Imbecilic...and you find yourself in a world of verbiage that would stun even Lenny, the slow-wit of Steinbeck's OF MICE AND MEN.

As self-appointed mad dog yapping at the heels of the verbally underprivileged, I have solicited samples of current Show Biz Talk from a dozen different sources in The Industry. None of whom wish to be named.

Here's a beauty. Two agents walking into the Academy Theater the other night. The first one says, "I'll be damned if I know *what* Paramount's buying these days." The second one replies, "Well, fer sure, they don't want anything soft." And the first one concurs. "Yeah, they want hard center."

Translation, as best I can piece it together after long analysis with philologists, is this: "soft" originally meant any motion picture that was a story about people. Such films as *Resurrection, Kramer vs. Kramer,* or *My Bodyguard.* Small films. Personal stories. But the term has come to be a denigrative in these times of "hard center" films such as *Raiders of the Lost Ark, Smokey and the Bandit,* or *Animal House* that clean up at the box office. In a "hard center" film, I'm given to understand, development of character goes by the wayside and what becomes dominant is—and here's the another one—*the plunge.* Meaning: throw it at 'em fast and hard and chew on their eyeballs.

Offshoot of "hard center" in television is "high concept" as in the phrase uttered by an ABC programmer recently, "Don't try to sail anything by me that isn't high concept."

What means this? As associate producer of tv mini-series told me the perfect example of a "high concept" series is *The Dukes of Hazzard.*

"You've got to be pulling my *gotkes,*" I said. "That series is as empty of thought as Phyllis Schlafly's social conscience."

"Wrong," she replied. "It's high concept because there's nothing else like it. No imitators." (Allah be praised, I murmured.) What "high concept" means, in the word of gibberish, is non-replicable. Done once, and impossible to imitate.

Further. In The Industry people are either "hot" or "not hot." No in-between. You get hired or not hired that simply.

These days a "producer" does many things, but producing a film ain't one of them. For that, you need a "line producer." By classtime tomorrow, students, write down a list of what it is that a "producer" *does* do these days. See if you can fill one side of a postage stamp.

"Let's cut a deal," they say. They also say, "We cut the film together." I think they mean they edited it. *Cut* and *together* are mutually contradictory. At least where I come from. "Let's take a meeting," they say. "Great," I reply. "Where shall we take it? And will we have to carry it portage overland or can we simply send it Federal Express?"

"What's this character's franchise?" That's a new one. It is a phrase spoken by network executives on the buying end of a hustle from some independent producing entity. (I love that "entity" business. I always picture something like the creature from *Alien,* all drool and mad staring eyes.) What means this word "franchise"? It meaneth, I'm told, what is the character's occupation, and is it an occupation that allows for unlimited stories in a continuing series? Newspaper reporters have the same. Lady private eyes, wryly witty doctors, airline stewardesses, cross-country truckers—we're talking here highly plungeable franchises. Optometrists, certified public accountants, shoe salesmen and ornithologists are definitely "not hot."

"Is he talkable?"

"Let me put a phone call in your stead."

"This deal is a highly seductive situation."

"It's a deal-breaker."

Then there's the concept of the "rolling break," a creation of the late David Begelman, a model for us all not only of rectitude and high-profile hard-center ethical behavior, but of astonishing mutations in the spoken word. The "rolling break" (which I am given to understand is a creature of myth much like the unicorn, elves, gnomes, leprechauns and Ronald Reagan's concern for the poor) is an element of a deal whereby at certain levels of profit by the producing entity, the party entitled to a "rolling break" gets certain amounts of profit-participation. I've always wanted to participate in a profit; orgies have become so enervating.

The semantic environment is polluted when language obscures from people what they are doing and why they are doing it.

When the Press Secretary for the President of the United States says, on Monday, "We have no intention of sending troops into any foreign country," and on Tuesday says, "Yesterday's statements are inoperative," and we don't rise up in our wrath to defenestrate the sonofabitch, what we are doing is letting him say, "What I told you yesterday was a flat-out, bald-faced lie and today I'm saying just the opposite."

And when a minion of some producing entity suggests we take an "if-come deal" and we don't leap across the desk to strangle him or her with her or her own Cardin ascot, we are letting him or her say, "We'll take your talent for free, and we'll blue-sky it, and if someone at the web leaps up to bite it, and we cut a deal, we'll give you a full card as 'creator' and your Tony Bills and your Michael Douglases and your Norman Lears will all know that you're hot!"

To which we can all reply, hopefully, at that point in time, "Fer *sure!*"

Bearing in mind that we are dealing with creatures all drool and mad staring eyes, for whom human speech is not their natural tongue.

# INTERIM MEMO:

There were people who did not realize I was using hyperbole. They still show up at Shain's in Sherman Oaks, California—where I still eat with alarming regularity—looking for the bullet holes.

## Dining as Action-Adventure

Had I not been there when it happened, you would very likely be reading this restaurant review as rendered by the *Weekly*'s indefatigable gourmet critic, Stanley Ralph Ross. But I *was* there when the two guys came in, took Uzzi machine guns from cabretta-grain attaché cases, opened fire, and blew away the one-eyed man sitting at the double beside the window that looks out on the patio.

The restaurant is *Shain's,* at 14016 Ventura Boulevard, in palatial Sherman Oaks. The owner is an old friend of mine, Don Shain; and I had no intention of doing a restaurant review this early in my column's life. But how can one resist talking about such a den of mythology when it has become, in only twenty months, not only a first-rank eatery...but one of the focus points of the universe where time and space converge to produce the sort of mystical episodes that quickly become legend?

I was eating lunch at Shain's last Thursday when the two pistoleros came in. They looked like a couple of home computer salesmen from Apple. Sincere suits, earnest ties, sensible shoes. They were seated at table 16 by the afternoon hostess, Irene, who took their drink order. I was at my usual table, number 3, at the rear of the large dining room between the bar and the patio. I didn't like their looks. They had the chalky complexion of improperly-fired Limoges china. Beady little eyes like marmosets.

They sat over their drinks speaking in hushed tones but occasionally glancing at the one-eyed man at the double, table 6. He was an old man in a loud Hawaiian shirt, with one of those plastic inserts in the pocket that held half a dozen ballpoint pens in different colors. They eyepatch was paisley. It was on his left side, the blind side closest to the guys at table 16.

As I ate, I kept an eye on the scene. Over the best bowl of French onion soup gratinée this side of the Pleasure Dome of Kublai Khan—enough thick mozzarella to refloat the *Titanic*—I saw them lift their attaché cases to the table, knocking over the drinks but paying no attention to the mess. I knew something was happening, but I couldn't catch the eye of Shain, who was up front at the reception desk. (I later learned he was taking a call from his close friend, David Stockman, Reagan's Director of the OMB, who's looking for a new job.)

As Barbara and Luana, two of Shain's staggeringly sensual and efficient lunch-time waitresses, brought my entrée, the remarkable broiled lamb chops a la Toussaint, thick prime cut chops marinated in soy sauce with the faintest angel's touch of garlic, I tried to say, "Something ugly's going down over at table 16."

But Barbara and Luana, who only work the lunch crowd, and who moonlight every evening as mud wrestlers at Chippendale's, were discussing the relative merits of the thunderlock over the flying mare, and they weren't paying attention. At that moment I saw the two assassins close the lids of their cases, behind which they had been unfolding the stocks of the Uzzis, and before I could yell a warning they opened fire.

They blew the guy out through the window and onto the patio.

You know how good a restaurant Shain's is? Not even Jose, the busboy, broke stride. He continued filling the crystal water goblets; Shain continued smiling in his very best host manner; Barbara and Luana refilled coffee cups and delivered the ebullient half pineapple stuffed with fresh fruit and cottage cheese. As for me, well, I suppose this sudden and brutal taking of a life would have nonplussed me, had I not been carried away in the transports of delight by chef Toussaint Moallic's lamb chops with their precisely crisped surfaces.

But the two Federal agents seated at table 18 laid aside their crepe veronique and the justly-lauded poached salmon in puff pastry and had the pair of thugs in custody before I'd even had a chance to order Shain's most outstanding dessert, the Key West lime pie, available—as far as I know in this city—*only* at Shain's. The remarkable thing is that they got to the killers only instants before the day bartender, Kay Cole, leaped the bar with her .357 Magnum in hand, and drew down on them as the Feds were cuffing them.

It was just another standard lunch at Shain's.

At dinnertime one can *really* count on excitement. The Sunday hostess, who doubles as waitress at nights, Barbara Andrews (who murdered her first husband trying to gain control of his steamship line), has mastered the astonishing feat of being able to throw an enormous *margarita* goblet filled with gaspacho the length of the dining room, to land right-side-up in front of him or her who ordered it...without spilling a drop as it sails over the heads of delighted diners.

How, I hear you asking, can all this wonderfulness be? How, you inquire, could what seems to be merely an elegant and secluded dinner club of the most urbane sort, also contain a setting for unforgettable experiences of the most bizarre species?

Perhaps it is because Shain, who for fourteen years before

190

kicking the filthy habit and getting into an honest line of work as a restaurateur, was a well-known A&R man for such record companies as Capitol, MCA, Pickwick and his own CBS custom label, Great Western Gramophone. Perhaps it is because chef Toussaint, who used to cook for Prince Sihanouk of Cambodia, has learned all the arcane secrets of black, white and dove-gray magic including the ability to cloud men's minds so they cannot see him (which is handy when the waitresses mix up the orders and the vegetarians at table 2 get New York steak boursin). Perhaps it is because Shain's was, for many years, the personal watering hole of Bud Abbott, who called it the Back Stage.

But more likely it is just that the ghost of Don Buday haunts the restaurant. Buday, a colorful gypsy figure of Hollywood's most glamorous era, was found comatose in the ladies' room of the restaurant in 1953 when it was called the Ventura Inn. Rumors flew at the time, and the names Kim Novak, Evelyn Ankers and Marie Windsor were bruited about. But nothing was ever proved, and the Grand Jury refused to bring in a true bill. Buday never regained consciousness to tell what horrors had befallen him in the women's potty. And warm summer nights as the patrons laugh and sup stylishly on the patio or inside the warm and friendly dining room, savoring the crispiest duck a l'orange you've ever let melt in your face, the ghost of Don Buday can he heard singing offkey in a strange foreign language high in the wine loft.

Perhaps it is all of these memorable qualities that make Shain's precisely the kind of fine dining experience you're seeking. Or perhaps it is that I can be found there eighteen out of every twenty-four hours, seven days a week. (Shain's is one of those rarities, a restaurant that *is* open seven days a week. Lunch 11:00 to 3:00 Monday through Friday; Sunday brunch 11 to 3; dinner 6 to 11 Monday through Saturday; Sunday dinner 5 to 10; closed Saturday lunch; all major credit cards accepted.)

And if you want to hear about the giant komodo dragon Shain keeps tethered in the small dark room behind the kitchen...and if you want to hear about the night Jimmy Carter made a pass at Shelley Winters...and if you want to hear about the night a matron from Highland Park found a black pearl in her Greek peasant salad...just drop in for dinner and I'll make myself available to chat. Or call for a reservation at 986-5510. If Irene answers, don't mention my name. She's still upset about the baby.

Incidentally. Quite a lot of this column is true.

**INSTALLMENT 21:** 10 March 82

# INTERIM MEMO:

Around this time the obscene and threatening phone calls began. Fortunately, they all came in to the *Weekly*. My friend and editor, Phil Tracy, began looking wan and chivvied. I had to take him out for BBQ ribs at Diamond's and Dr. Hogly Wogly's Tyler Texas Pit Barbeque at least once a week. In journalese we call that reparations.

One do get mail. And, as promised, a valiant attempt will be made by your faithful columnist to answer as much of it as seems rational. As I noted in an early installment of this column when I was doing it for *Future Life* magazine, the mail I receive in response to wry observations of the world I set down in these little outings is ennobled by the word *weird*. Some of you veer dangerously close to sanity.

But I must confess that I have come to love you as an audience. There are far fewer of the whackos writing me from the *Weekly*'s readership than I used to draw from those who bought *Future Life*. Don't ask me why. Most of you heeded the appeal only to write postcards, so I was spared elongated screeds. And nine out of ten of you during the first nine weeks have been extremely kind in your remarks. Several of you have not. The *Weekly* has published some of those. Each of the correspondents who wrote snotty letters has been visited in the dead of night. The grief-stricken families ask that flowers not be sent; contributions to the Home for Unwed Writers should be sent in memoriam.

As a ground rule, I won't be replying in these pages to kind and gracious folks who wrote to say I am a credit to my species and a wonderful fellah who speaks out against the evils of our times. I accept the compliments with toe appropriately scuffing the dust, but it ain't truly the sort of thing that deserves comment beyond a deep bow and a sincere thankyou.

The complaints are, of course, another matter.

They are usually deranged and I will do my best to present said material in as unflattering a light as possible, thereby affording me the opportunity to ridicule my critics without permitting them a proper forum to reply. This is called Democracy. I learned the technique from Spiro Agnew and Richard Whats-His-Face—you know, the one whose upper lip always sweated when he was lying.

Take for instance an unsigned letter I got from a woman the week following my column about how I preferred my dirty 1967 Camaro to one of those incredibly expensive "sporty little Oriental runabouts in which one rides with knees tucked up under one's chin." The letter (with the plethora of typos and illiteracies and misspellings corrected) read as follows:

"Hey, Ellison, a 'sporty little Oriental' etcetera etcetera must be *awfully* small if even *your* knees are tucked up under your chin. I guess you can tell that my opinion of you is pretty small, too. Signed, Not a Fan."

The allusion is made, one supposes, to my height. I am 5′5″ tall, which seems to me a perfectly acceptable height for a human being. Or a caterpillar. Heightist remarks of this inane sort are one of the last conversational bastions of the intellectually deprived, to be sure, but we must go *beyond* the content of the denigrative to pierce the true motives of one who takes time out of her day just to cast a random insult at a stranger. When we slog our way through the psychotic morass we find that surely this is no casual brickbat, but the need of a seriously inadequate person to draw attention to herself while hiding behind the anonymity of an unsigned letter.

We all know the syndrome. It is a classic symptom of arrested adolescence. The kid in the schoolyard who throws a stone when the object has his or her back turned.

But being an essentially loving and concerned guy, I could not let this cry in the wilderness go unheeded. Attention was what the correspondent sought and, in a spirit of Christian charity, not un-known to us of a Semitic persuasion, I determined to locate the letter-writer and give her some of the attention she so desperately sought.

It wasn't all that difficult. Like most people who do an unsavory act and want to be punished for it, she left all manner of clues behind. The most important was that while she had not signed her letter, she *had* used a business envelope stolen from her previous employer. As I knew some people in that firm, I called them and asked them to check around, to see what possibilities for identification they might find. In an hour or so I received a phone call advising me that the woman my contacts had suspected was the writer, who had been fired from the firm some time earlier, was now working for another company in Los Angeles, a record promotion company or suchlike.

I was told that she went by the name "Spock" and that she was quite a fatty. I was given the phone number and address of the company for which she now worked as receptionist. All in the spirit of helping her overcome her feelings of unworthiness, I called the company and asked for "Spock."

"This is Spock," said the woman who had answered the phone.

"Ah," I said. "Well, it seems to me that if you're going to insult people, you ought not to be in a position to get found out. And while I may have to ride around in even a tiny car with my knees tucked up under my chin, at least I'm not such a grotesque overweight blimp that I can't *get into* the car."

There was a horrified silence at the other end of the line.

"Who is this?" A tremor of panic in the voice.

"You know who it is, Spock," I said. "I'm watching you. My agents clock your every move. You can't sneak a Twinkie without my killer minions letting me know."

There was a discernible *gulp* at the other end. I knew the therapy, generated out of compassion, was already having salutary effect. "What are you going to do?" she asked.

"Do? Do?" I responded. "Why, Spock, dear old tugboat, I'm not going to do *any*thing." And I added, "I guess."

"Bye-bye," I said, and went my way, knowing that another good deed, like bread upon the waters, had been cast out into the lonely darkness of the world.

Beyond that exchange, the most interesting of the several hundred I've received in nine weeks, only three postcards seem to need responses this time.

The first was from Nancy Buchanan, who applauded the stand this column took against knife-kill splatter movies in which women were endlessly brutalized, but who suggested I dote for a moment on films that were *child*-hating. She noted the existence of a number of films reprising the sentiments of *The Bad Seed* in which children were portrayed as the spawn of the devil, or as harbingers of evil: *The Omen, The Exorcist,* et al. And she asked, "Do Americans really hate kids?"

To which I respond, of course Americans hate kids. Older Americans, that is. And kids hate older Americans. It is called the generation gap. And there is provocation on both sides. But I don't think films such as *The Exorcist* are manifestations of that distrust and hatred. I think such films seek to enhance the terror and evil of the plot by taking the symbol of innocence, a child, and using it as a vessel of ghoulish malevolence. It is an artistic construct, not having much to do with sociology.

Richard Morse asked, "Given the horrors you've written of so far, how do you preserve your outlandishly high opinion of humanity?"

Easy, kiddo. I believe to my shoe-tips that the human race is the noblest experiment ever attempted by the uncaring universe, and any species capable of painting the Sistine Chapel ceiling, of writing MOBY DICK, and of putting a man on the surface of the moon, is a species worth giving a damn about. It is when representatives of that noble experiment settle for McDonald's toadburgers, Judith Krantz novels and *The Dukes of Hazzard* that my love affair with the human race becomes polluted, and I rail not against what we can be in our noblest moments, but what we settle for. I wrote an op-ed piece in the L.A. *Times* to that effect, shortly after New Year's, speaking out against The Common Man . . . saying that it was the *Un*common Man who moved society forward, brought about social change that bettered people's lives, and made us proud to be human beings. Like

197

the "man in the water" at the Washington, D.C. crash of Air Florida's flight 90 back in January, the man who passed the rescue ring from the helicopter to five other survivors while waiting in the freezing water until they had been saved. And who drowned for his act of humanity. He has been painted as an example of "the common man," but I see him as an Extraordinary Man.

With recurring examples of nobility such as that, how can one hate our kind totally?

And the final card was from one Kent Beyda who sought to invalidate my criticism of splatter movies by saying he had sat behind me at a press screening of *The Howling,* a film he said he "would defend to the death," as a wonderful example of film making. Well, my carp about that movie was less with what was on the screen than the ghoulish manner of the audience. Mr. Beyda swears I screamed my objections out loud and made it difficult for him to hear the full richness of sound as the werewolves ate their victims. If such was the case, and I suggest Mr. Beyda is full of horse puckey right up to his eyeballs, I apologize for getting in the way of his full enjoyment of the gore he so clearly needs to sustain him in his otherwise tragically boring life. But as I have checked with the others who sat in the row on both sides of me, to ascertain if I was, in fact, so rude...and as they have informed me that I sat there like a little gentleman throughout the film save for the one time I turned around and said to the guy behind me that his fetid breath was wilting my shirt collar, I must believe that Mr. Beyda is perhaps fudging the truth just a tot.

Beyond these specific responses, I thank all of you—too numerous to thank individually—for your support and kind words. I trust next time we sweep up the mail, in about six weeks, there will be more scintillant examples of run-amuck thinking and verbal mayhem.

Until next week, I take my leave. Incidentally, as you read this column, know that it was written in a motel in Florida where I pound out these words while getting ready to go out to do yet another public speaking engagement in behalf of the Equal Rights Amendment. We have less than four months, friends. And if you have it in your power to add some thrust to the final days of this noble effort, it behooves you to get off your complacent asses and *do it now.*

**INSTALLMENT 22:** 19 March 82

# Why the ERA Won't Go Away

I'm back from sunny Florida. Hardly a vacation. I do quite a lot of college lecturing. Always did a brisk business with institutions of higher learning in Southern states. But when the National Organization for Women slapped a boycott on the eleven remaining states that hadn't ratified the Equal Rights Amendment, I honored the blockade by turning down all speaking engagements in non-ERA states *unless.* The "unless" was that if they wanted me to appear badly enough, they had to sponsor a concurrent ERA fund-raiser, or a seminar, or whatever form of Pro-ERA chivari the local NOW/ERA branch thought would serve the commonweal best. That's been the MO for about six years.

Most of the universities gave that option a pass. "We don't want to get involved in politics," they usually said. (I always restrained myself from pointing out that if they didn't want to get involved in politics—what an unthinkable concept for a college, alleged to be a "marketplace of ideas"—they ought to eschew the government contracts for new war toys that help fund their campuses.)

But Tulane in New Orleans and U. of Chicago in Illinois went for it, and I did what I could. Two weeks ago I went to Tampa to speak at a futurism seminar, and the U. of Tampa was sensational in establishing liaison with the Tampa NOW office and its president, Pat Rowentree.

The time for ratification for the ERA runs out in less than four months, and everywhere I go I get a distinct feeling of desolation and betrayal by men and women alike, those who have put their time and their hope into this desperately-important Amendment to the Constitution. They see the years and the effort going down the drain. So in Tampa and St. Pete and Boca Raton where I had interview after interview, night and day for eight days, I kept saying, "It's not over. Do not despair. We just have to start all over again."

The ERA will not go away. Women have been trying to get similar human rights laws passed since 1923! And as dismal as the situation may seem now, every reliable poll tells us that 65–68% of the American people *want* an ERA. Consider that figure and then ask *why* the opposition to something so direct and uncomplicated as the 25 words that comprise the core of the Amendment. (For those who may never have seen those 25 words, they are: "Equality of rights under the law shall not be denied or abridged by the United States or by any State on account of sex.")

Since the Amendment doesn't even *mention* women, it becomes obvious to all but those blinded by the flapdoodle of a self-serving termagant like Phyllis Schlafly that it is not a *women's* Amendment. . . it's a *people's* Amendment. So why the strident voices of the anti-ERA forces, and who the hell *are* these 32–35% who are keeping the majority of us from bringing the United States fully into the 20th century?

Well, there are the Mormons, of course, whose religious view of women is that they are inferior and are best kept in the role of little homemaker; allegedly to preserve "the family unit," that nuclear family they constantly tell us is the cornerstone of civilization. But the census informs us that though twenty years ago only 1 out of every 10 households was a single-person household, today only 1 out of every 4 is a traditional family unit, thereby demonstrating that our culture is rapidly heading toward a set where the individual dominates and controls his or her own life, as opposed to the traditional template of Mom-Pop-&-the-Kids all snuggled under one roof.

And the biggest financial backing for Schlafly and other anti-ERA operations is Big Business. Millions have been funneled into anti-ERA coffers by the multinationals. Why? But the last large pool of cheap labor in this country is not Blacks or Hispanics or Paraplegics or Midgets. It is women. Consider what the controllers of major corporations think about women being at parity with men when it comes to salaries.

I do not offer the above remarks as surmise. Recently, in Florida, one of the Miami newspapers uncovered the fact that $40,000 had been channeled into Florida by a major corporation to buy the two votes necessary to keep the ERA from passing the State Senate.

All of this is four months away from being irrelevant.

When I said this on a radio call-in show in St. Petersburg, a woman phoned in to ask what I said to men who opposed the ERA. I replied that I seldom have to say anything to men about the ERA. Not that many men don't oppose it, but that men can keep quiet because they have misguided women doing their work for them as Fifth Columnists. These are women held in the stingy paw of the mischievous Schlafly and her breed, who are, themselves, pawns. Why should men get out there and look like chauvinist assholes when they can gull women into taking the front lines and sucking up the philosophical bullets? Even Schlafly is tool, mere figurehead. With her to hate, we have no need to go behind her to see the dark masters she serves like the good little handmaiden she is.

202

It is a classic example of avoiding having to look at the corrupt nature of some of our most cherished institutions by pillorying the women who serve those institutions. It is one more example of prejudice against women as manipulated decoys of the real power-masters.

But the ERA will not go away. As more and more women are bruised by society, as more and more cases of sexual harassment on the job surface, as more and more women find their legal rights abridged, as they find they cannot get loans for cars, or credit, or the bank blessing to start their own business. . .as they understand that a husband in Utah can sue a hit-and-run driver for striking a child, but the wife and mother cannot. . .as they find out that a widow pays inheritance tax in Nebraska but a widower does not. . .as they perceive that if a wife dies the husband would not automatically keep receiving Social Security. . .as they learn that in Illinois a man and a woman working for the same publicly-funded clinic, who are the same age and earned the same money and retired after the same number of years, would receive pension checks of which the woman's would be much smaller. . .when they are astonished to discover that by Alabama state law a boy can have a summer paper route but a girl cannot. . .when more women tragically join the ranks of the denied and bruised and frustrated. . .the ranks of the angry will swell.

And the ERA will not go away. Because the way we've set up the game, women will lose more often than they'll win. And even the most misguided, even the ones who actually believe that an ERA will mean their golden-tressed daughters will have to fight in foxholes and that unisex toilets will make perverts of us all—even those women will have the scales ripped from their eyes. And they will join the men and women who resent the hell out of those remaining eleven porkchop-politics states that have denied us a better country and a better condition of life for male and female alike.

At which point, the liberal-conservative revolution of the Sixties and Seventies in this country will come to seem to us merely a Sunday outing. Because like it or not, women are as capable of fighting back as men; and when *that* revolution breaks out, gentle readers, which side you were on in 1982 will mean about as much as a lone white face in the middle of a crazed ghetto-burning.

Thoughts like that make me look on an early retirement in Bora-Bora with great delight.

Less than four months. If you haven't done something yet, get your ass in gear. By July it'll be too late.

# INTERIM MEMO:

When *The Comics Journal* reprinted this installment, I titled it A HERO FOR OUR TIMES. I believed it then, I believe it now, and when interviewers ask me who my "heroes" are, I name Hank Aaron, Willie Joe Namath, Ralph Nader, Gloria Allred, Christine Craft and most notably, Norman Lear. What a sad, fuckin' place this world would be for all of us, even you dips who support Falwell, without Norman Lear in it.

I move to the rear of the bus for no one in my admiration for Norman Lear. During a recent radio interview, the host asked me who my "heroes" were, and though I was hard-pressed to expand the living list much beyond Ralph Nader, John Simon, Joe Namath, Gloria Allred and Francis Ford Coppola, the first name that popped out of my mouth was "Norman Lear."

To me, he represents in great measure what I respect in terms of decency, rectitude, human concern and application of talent. But more, he is as close to a model of how to handle and put to proper use the benefits of fame, power and success as anyone currently in the public arena. I have observed his career closely since March of 1969 when I attended the taping of a situation comedy then called *Those Were The Days,* a proposed series which ABC (in its infinite wisdom) turned down. It was not until two years later that CBS picked up the show, which has enjoyed what might conservatively be called ebullient success for the last eleven years. The Lear-generated series, of course, was *All In the Family* (currently metamorphosed as *Archie Bunker's Place*).

On that evening in 1969 I perceived Norman Lear as a man of courage and high goals, and over the years I have had no reason to alter my opinion, even when conglomeration made him an industry and the quality of some of the product his Tandem Productions proffered was less than iridescent. Tandem/Embassy is big business now, and while Lear may have turned over much of the day-to-day workings of his creative mill to the worshippers of the bottom line, simply because one man cannot reasonably be expected to ride all horses at once and still get a decent night's sleep, any sane estimation of the situation will agree that though business is definitely business, by doing bigger business a man like Lear can employ the clout it accrues in service of the commonweal. Which is, in large part, what he has done. But now comes the *but*:

But two Sundays ago Norman Lear's two-hour special on ABC, *I Love Liberty,* billed by the network against Lear's objections as "a star-studded entertainment salute to the freedoms that make our country great!" manifested itself as a horrifying example of the well of good intentions being poisoned by television's First Commandment: "Blandness in the defense of offending no one to preserve ratings is no vice" (paraphrasing a famous quotation we will deliver in its original form later in this column).

In the name of "looking good," this massive outlay of talent, effort, megabucks and primetime succeeded only in demonstrating that it serves no worthwhile end to slip a Trojan Horse into the enemy camp if the strategist in charge fails to unlock the trapdoor so the warriors hidden within can descend on their adversaries.

At Chavez Ravine they call that losing sight of the ball.

*I Love Liberty* was, for two hours, nothing but a panegyric of tub-thumping, self-deluding, flag-waving self-congratulation in the time-honored tradition of America's bad taste bad habit of hollow posturing that we are "the last best hope of the Earth."

This columnist's ambivalence while writing these words is nothing less than Olympian. I have written elsewhere of my unbridled adoration of Norman Lear for his having set on-line the anti-Falwell organization called People For The American Way. To find myself now trashing the first major public demonstration of that group's credo, gives me what Delia Salvi called "your basic *agita*." Had my expectations for *I Love Liberty* not been so high, I might not have had them so crushed.

And in what I perceive as the total failure of the tv special to do what it set out to do, what so desperately *needs* doing, I think we may glean several important realities about television, about bucking the system, and about the nature of compromise.

Near the burning core of what *I Love Liberty* was conceived to do, lies the reality that Lear has become one of the most prominent targets of the Reverend Jerry Falwell and his Moral Majority. Lear has been the specific subject of virulent attacks that parallel in tone and intensity the White House-backed attacks on Ed Asner by (among other mouthpieces) Charlton Heston. If you recall, I did a piece on *that* running-dog embroglio several weeks ago.

Both campaigns have less to do with the actuality of Lear or Asner than that they have spoken out. Neither Reagan nor Falwell can take much heat, and so they set their demon legions on whoever dares challenge their brainwashing programs of the American people. When Lear was instrumental in creating People For The American Way, Falwell stepped up his outrages. Though *I Love Liberty* as a concept was planned far in advance of the major Falwell assault, on October 3rd, 1981, the good Reverend signed and sent out a mass mailing headed WHO IS THE #1 ENEMY OF THE AMERICAN FAMILY IN OUR GENERATION?

The letter read, in part, "Dear Friend, This man has been slandering and discrediting me and the Moral Majority for several months now. And if he has his way, I will tell you what will happen. . .everything you and I have fought so hard for—will go right

208

down the drain! Here's the man's name: NORMAN LEAR! Many people believe he is the man who has successfully brought filth and sexual perversion into our living rooms and led the way to today's gutter programming."

The letter then went on to pillory Lear for story lines used in the long-defunct *Mary Hartman, Mary Hartman* series, extolling the virtues of the Moral Majority and Wildmon's ill-named Coalition For Better Television, and begging for contributions to fight this snake called Lear, in exchange for which contributions Falwell promised to send a "Confidential Report" on Lear "so you can decide for yourself what his motives might really be."

If one were foolish enough to be gulled by this meretricious appeal to narrowmindedness and paranoia, and to respond to the ominous tone of what Lear's "motives might really be," and one parted with money better spent on buying a book or milk for a child endangered by "gutter programming" (none of which seems to come in on *my* set, dammit), by return mail one received a single undocumented sheet marked CONFIDENTIAL. This *eyes only* revelation was, how shall I put it, somewhat underwhelming.

The heavyweight indictments include such awfulness as the alleged fact that People For The American Way "is nothing more than a stalking horse for Massachusetts Senator Edward Kennedy," that PAW's offices were in a building adjacent to the offices of Parker/Dodd and Associates, national fund raisers for Kennedy, and that Richard Parker, a principal in the firm, was the national fund raiser for that other evil snake, Cesar Chavez and the United Farm Workers. Wow! Imagine my surprise! That's enough, right there, to lynch the motherfucker.

But there was more. (Never let it be said Jerry-Boy gives less than value for his tithes.) It seems that the PAW office in Washington is under the direction of one Anthony Podesta, whose terrorist credentials are laid out in the "Confidential Report" as follows: "a young, liberal attorney and staunch union activist." I'm not sure if the objection to Podesta, that which is supposed to fill us with trepidation at the thought of his paws at the helm of PAW, is that he is young, liberal, an attorney, staunch, or a union activist. But taken on sum the charges are enough to have Podesta schlepped out of his office and remanded instantly to the thumbscrew-and-iron-maiden authorities. Cardinal Fang, the comfy chair and the soft pillow!

But the two best sections of the report are these:

"PAW's supporters include militant homosexuals, labor factions, TV and film producers, feminists, environmentalists, anti-nuclear groups and radical activists." I don't know about you, gentle reader, but I score only three out of seven. Take this little test and see if *you* can survive the JERRY'S WATCHING OVER US QUIZ.

"Not surprisingly," the report concludes, "nearly all of Parker/

Dodd's clients are organizations which represent the above groups. They include Ted Kennedy, Greenpeace, Alliance for Survival, the Kennedy Fund, Congressman Ronald Dellums (a liberal black from Oakland who did everything in his power to legalize sodomy, bestiality, etc., in our nation's capitol), Western Sun, International Food and Development Policy and, at one time, George McGovern."

For a final fillip, the report came stapled to an advertisement for RENDEZVOUS WITH DESTINY, a collection of speeches by Ronald Reagan, with a "tribute" by (surprise!) Charlton Heston. Only fifteen dollars tendered as a "gift" to the Moral Majority.

So here is Norman Lear in October, planning *I Love Liberty,* finding himself an even bigger bullseye, with Unca' Jerry coming on like Gerald L. K. Smith. (Understand: where you or I would find this "Confidental Report" boondoggle so transparently lamebrained that we would roundfile it with the other junk mail, for a Georgia farmer with limited access to the rest of the world, to an uptight Mormon in Utah, to a soured and cynical racist in North Carolina who believes the rest of America is sinking in sin and degradation, this kind of flapdoodle is scary as hell. I do not think Norman Lear was insensitive to all of the foregoing.)

And so, in an effort to look upstanding and clean-cut, to cut off at the pass the Moral Midgets who see Norman Lear as the AntiChrist, *I Love Liberty* was bent over backward and inside-out to be rigorously *American*. But hardly *pragmatically* American. Not the America that continues to lie to itself that it has never lost a war, though we've lost the last two and a half. Not the America that continues to delude itself that equal opportunity exists when it treats its senior citizens, its minorities, its women as if they are useless fodder fit for nothing better than to be consumers. Not the America where we must take arms daily against the messiahs of obscurantism and illogic, whether they be called Father Coughlin, Sen. Joseph McCarthy, Jerry Falwell, Wildmon or Schlafly. But the America of manifest destiny, of John Wayne phony patriotism, of the Moral Majority dream-image from sea to shining sea, without passion, without warts, without a clear view.

It was a sanitized show.

While the intent of the message passim the script may be 180° from Falwell's, the *presentation,* what was on the screen, could as easily have been generated by the Reverend as by Lear. (What the hell all that pre-screening hollering by the Moral Majority was about, I have no idea. There couldn't have been much in the finally-aired show that upset God's Own Pillsbury Doughboy.)

Norman Lear tells me the show did exactly what he wanted it to do. He says I should not lay the blame for what I see as an empty exercise on the burdened shoulders of such ABC executives as Tony Thomopoulos, president of ABC Entertainment. He advises me that this was the *best* network experience he has ever had, in terms of getting what he wanted.

But in conversations with my highly-placed sources at ABC (and bamboo slivers under the fingernails could not drag from me their names), I am given to understand that the script went through an "upbeating process." Anything that seemed dark or downbeat, anything that said we are something less than the last, best hope of the Earth, was "suggested" as material for revision.

And so we had Senator Barry Goldwater, good old "Nuke 'Em Till They Glow" Goldwater, who in 1964 said, "Extremism in the defense of liberty is no vice! And...moderation in the pursuit of justice is no virtue!" up there with endless high school bands playing *The Stars and Stripes Forever.*

Which is not to say that Goldwater doesn't look scrumptious to us today, in the light of Nixon and Reagan. His act is much cleaned up, his ameliorations and mellowings seem honestly motivated, and I wish to God he were in the Oval Office instead of Pruneface. (Which goes to show what a sad pass we've come to, I suppose; but that's another topic for another sleepless night.) Notwithstanding the more humanist image of the new Barry, his presence up there was purely to disarm the Far Right critics. I would have been more impressed had he worked the spot arm-in-arm with Lear's secret master, Teddy Kennedy, about whom I'm not that wild, either, but he's the best we've got from that spectrum of political thought. (Which goes to show what a sad pass, etcetera, etcetera, another sleepless night.)

Virtually everything in the show was *safe.* From the "angry minorities" sketch to Streisand singing *America, the Beautiful.* (I find it interesting that in a show trumpeting freedom and equality, the producers could not find a big name who would play the role of the homosexual minority.) The angry minorities sketch and the presence of the handicapped Geri Jewell, Judd Hirsch as a Jewish immigrant (with the lousiest Yiddish accent this side of John Davidson's) and Mary Tyler Moore representing the beleaguered WASP constituency, all brought me in mind of Lenny Bruce's old takeoff routine on the 1940s war films in which the dogface squad pinned down by enemy fire was always composed of one (1) Italian, one (1) Jew, one (1) guy from Brooklyn and one (1) person of a mocha-skinned Negro persuasion. As Lenny put it, "Rosenthal over there's a Jew; and DiGrazie here's an Eye-talian; and Washington over there's a black dude; but we're *all* Americans! And we gotta stick together...to beat up the Puerto Ricans!"

It was safe. It was above reproach.

So how could it have been done to placate cockeyed critics like me, if anybody gives a damn?

The angry minorities could have had their say about how they are sinned against, with perhaps a bit more passion than Michael

Horse or Rod Steiger wrested from their lines, and with decent, white, middle-class Dick Van Patten getting a lot more exercised at them, to mirror the *real* feelings of the group he was supposed to represent. . . and as they finish their rondelay have a KKK wizard in white sheet, an American Nazi with swastika armband, and a book-banning Baptist cut directly from Torquemada cloth come onstage holding aloft an American flag. And have all the minorities stand as one, and say, "That belongs to us, too!" and have them take it back. And have Van Patten slowly rise and join them.

If the intent, as the producers told us before the fact, was to "take back the American flag" for all of us. . .that would have said it.

But the show didn't say that. Not to me, at any rate; and I was ready to hear it loud and clear.

Which brings me to the bottom line. I have given up on the
Which brings me to the bottom line. I have given up on the conceit that structures like television can be changed "from the inside." Such monoliths have an inexorable way of co-opting even the most dedicated. Hell, I'm a deserter from that war, myself. When you get into a position where you can do something for the mass audience, you begin to lie to yourself and say, "Well, I'll soften it and candy-coat it and they'll get the message subtly. People don't like to be lectured to." And that's dead on. The problem was that the thirty million people who saw *I Love Liberty* are currently watching six and three-quarters hours of television per household every day of the year, and their ability to perceive nuances may well have been bludgeoned out of existence by *The Dukes of Hazzard* and reruns of *Family Feud*. So what they see up there on the screen is precisely and exactly what was offered: mindless self-adulation for patriotism without any danger or specifics about *what to do* to take back the flag from Falwell.

The good intentions were there. But in an effort to get it *on* television, the message got lost. We must not offend anyone. We must look good.

Sadly, the opposition doesn't play as politely.

The only way to defang fools who say the Holocaust never happened is not to tell them quietly and sadly of how you lost half your family in the ovens of Auschwitz; show them Nazi newsreel footage of the bone-piles!

Jerry Falwell is on the air damned near 24 hours a day. And if it isn't him, it's one of his clones in an ice cream suit taking the Lord's name in vain. Falwell doesn't tippy-toe. He calls Norman Lear the #1 enemy of the American family. He raises hundreds of thousands of dollars for propaganda. He sells creationism and book-banning and mindless fear to the millions every hour of the day. Maybe he *doesn't* get thirty million in one shot, but his message is a helluva lot clearer; and like all good lies, if told over and over again, soon it becomes reality:

Norman Lear is, in the truest sense of the word, a *good* man. He cares deeply about this country and its people. But his failing is that of most humanists. He cares too deeply ever to make a fist. He believes, with James Madison, that if you give people the facts, they will make the right choices.

I am torn. I believe that, too. I also believe that those same people supported the war in Vietnam for a deadly stretch of time, that they have stood by as men and women were lynched, that they have turned their backs as SLAUGHTERHOUSE FIVE was pulled from library shelves and tossed on the pyre.

Like Norman Lear, I believe that being an American can be an important thing. But Falwell understands better than Lear that subtleties are wasted on those whose limited perception of the universe leads them to accept the platitudes and bugaboos of Moral Majority philosophy.

I believe to my shoe-tops that being an American means struggling on a day-to-day basis against the demon legions, the ones who would send us back to the Scopes Monkey Trial and the Palmer Raids and HUAC and ignorance. They are ever with us; they reach up out of their graves with moldering claws to infect each new generation. And by proferring drum-beating, flag-waving patriotism devoid of any rueful representation of the dark side of the American character, we only buttress their belief that "doing something" to change America means, quite simply, let's join Falwell in his fight to return America to decency and godliness.

I'm told *I Love Liberty* has people talking, and hundreds of letters have poured in to Tandem saying the correspondents have been awakened to fight for their rights.

It is my fervent hope that's the reality. Because men like Norman Lear are too precious to be allowed to be be dragged down by adversaries who value winning at any cost over looking good and being polite. But looking good and being polite is what television is all about, so I suppose the compromise was in at the git-go and I was foolish to think *I Love Liberty* might slam a door on the Moral Majority.

Which is why Norman Lear is a far better, and a far more significant, Force for Good in our time than your columnist. Somehow, miraculously, he has not grown bitter in the face of battlefront opposition to the demon legions.

I wish I could say the same for myself; and I wish I could have loved *I Love Liberty*.

# INTERIM MEMO:

Long after this column appeared, a young man came up to
me at a college lecture appearance and told me he was Bill
Starr's long-lost son. They made reconnection because the
kid had read this column. And you thought I was just
Another Pretty Face.

# The Saga of Bill Starr, Part I

Because we all understand the invidiousness of believing the myth that the grass is greener on the other side of the fence, let me this week hold the strands of barbed wire down and assist you in stepping over into a seemingly greener pasture, where we will meet a man named Bill Starr, a novelist who recently took a very innovative and courageous action in aid of demonstrating just how weed-choked is the terrain where contemporary writers live and try to earn a living.

One supposes it is in large part due to the huge successes of—at best—a dozen works of fiction each publishing season, that the conceit persists among the laity that writers all live existences of grandeur, glamour and freedom from such fiscal angst as that shared by plumbers, farmworkers, cab drivers and secretaries. Would that it were so. Sadly, it ain't.

As one who has earned his living behind a typewriter for going on twenty-seven years, I can assure you that with very few exceptions most writers eke out barely a subsistence living. It is, to apply a remark by Bogart in a different context, a mug's game. Even the best writers still struggle like crazy to make a decent income. We will, of course, exclude from these comments people like Harold Robbins, Judith Krantz, Sidney Sheldon and Rosemary Rogers who, in my view, are not writers: they are creative typists.

For the mass of laborers in the literary vineyards, even getting a book accepted for publication, even having it produced by a reputable house, even having it released to the nation's bookstores and news-stands, does not guarantee that it will make a cent beyond the advance monies paid, for the scrivener who labored to set down those words.

The reality of book distribution and promotion and display is a doleful one. (For purposes of this essay only, I will restrict myself to the vagaries of paperback publishing, saving for another time the horrors of hardcover realities.)

At the moment I write this, which is today, according to the statistical bible of the publishing industry, LITERARY MARKET

217

PLACE, there are approximately forty major paperback houses. This is a wholly inaccurate figure, of course. I've probably missed a batch. I plucked out only those names I recognized as releasing titles on a regular basis. But each of those firms issues titles under a myriad of imprints. And those are just the mass-market houses. Additionally, there are all the specialized presses, the university presses, the trade edition publishers and the hardcover houses with trade or mass-market editions of titles they've already marketed in hardcover.

Of the dozen-to-forty major paperback houses, the release schedule includes between six and fifteen titles each month. The estimate (conservative, I wager) of total paperback titles flooding the racks each month is between 125 and 175. Two hundred seems to be a not-impossible figure. Newsstands get new shipments of titles twice a week.

And here's the staggering reality: the average shelf-life of an average paperback is between 5 days and two weeks.

What I'm relaying here is the simple fact that if my latest book gets to your nearest 7-Eleven spinner rack today, by this time next week...it's gone. And that doesn't even mean it was sold. What it means is that it had front-cover display for about five days, and then when the new batch of books came in it was put at the back of the pocket (where most people won't look for it, because they think all five of the pb's in that pocket are the same), and then—if I'm lucky and the clerk at the 7-Eleven knows my name—it gets shunted down to the back of a pocket at the base of the spinner rack (where no one looks because they don't want to bend over that far), and ten days to two weeks later it is pulled and is "stripped" for return credit. (Stripping is the procedure whereby the front cover is ripped off and returned, and the book itself is supposed to be pulped. In fact, this frequently does not happen. In fact, the stripped books are bootlegged to a second hand shop or some other knockoff joint. But that's yet another bit of illegal tomfoolery that circumvents the intention to make it easy for the pb retailer so s/he doesn't have to ship back an entire load of postage-heavy product.)

The system works in variants of what I've delineated above. B. Dalton and Waldenbooks and independently-owned bookstores have their methods; drug stores, magazine shops, newsstands have theirs. But it all works along those lines.

So given the foregoing, which books get the push from the publisher? Well, Bantam Books will put massive promotional efforts behind something like PRINCESS DAISY because they shelled out 3.2 *million* dollars to the hardcover publisher, Crown, for the paperback rights. They will not, obviously, get quite so frenetic about promoting a mystery or science fiction or western novel picked up for $3000, or an original book commissioned "in-house" for an advance of even $10,000. When you sink or swim on the sales of a single title, you attach the life preserver of publicity and tv commercials to the Big One and, while it may be chill to put it this way, the rest of the list can dog-paddle for survival.

Yet until recently, virtually every book contract contained the following phrase: "Publisher will expend best efforts in marketing the title."

"Best efforts" is a catchy phrase. While a poet or an academic might find that a Spartan circumlocution, those of us whose brains don't dribble out of our ears would take it to mean *best efforts*. And that purely presents itself, say in relation to PRINCESS DAISY, as two hundred and fifty thousand dollars' worth of newspaper, magazine, television and radio ads, huge dump-bins at point-of-purchase, die-cut book covers in three or four assorted styles, wide-ranging promotional tour for the author to babble on tv talk shows...the whole range and depth of possible ways to get you, the potential buyer, to rush off for a copy. That, by me, is *best efforts*. Because if a dreary item like that Judith Krantz novel can draw down such loving attention from a publisher, then it's obvious the publisher is *capable* of such efforts; *ergo,* that becomes the definition of "best efforts" for *that* publisher.

But as we can see from the fact that anything much below the fiduciary-interest level of a Krantz or Robbins or Rogers book gets, at best, cursory promotion (gone in 5 days to two weeks), we are dealing here with hyperbole. Best efforts if you have written a book for which the paperback house went neck-deep into debt; but dog-paddle if they paid for the book out of petty cash.

But what if a writer who squoze his guts out writing a book he cared about deeply, who sold it to a paperback house believing he had at least a *shot* at promotional parity, found the 5 day/two weeks reality unbearable? What if such a writer, seeing his labors stripped and pulped before they had a chance to reach what he (in his arrogance) believed was a reading public hungering for his creation, decided to fight back? What if that writer, so naive in the ways of the slicker world, did not understand that it's a shell game with the odds hung against his ever making a dollar in royalties, and he decided to take on the Status Quo? What then?

Well, gang, since you're here with me on the other side of the barbed wire, in here with the weeds and the mesquite that looked like green grass from over there outside...since I've got you over here and have explained the *terra incognita* you needed to understand before I could whip on you the saga of Bill Starr...I guess you will forgive me if I break this construct in half and come back next week to demonstrate that if you care enough, if you get mad enough, you *can* whup ass on City Hall. Or, in this case, Pinnacle Books.

Return, if you will, next week at this exact location, here in the weed-choked pastures of publishing, for the story of Bill Starr and a book called CHANCE FORTUNE.

You say you've never heard of that book?

How interesting.

You'll hear about it next time. I promise you.

**INSTALLMENT 25:** 19 April 82

*Letters reprinted with permission from the* L.A. Weekly

# The Saga of Bill Starr, Part II

Continuing the story of Bill Starr and how he took on one of the lesser publishing monoliths, Pinnacle Books, and beat them (pretty much); thereby setting a fascinating precedent for every writer whose literary labors have not been merchandised with an eye to providing fair access to the marketplace.

If you need your memory refreshed anent the background data that comprised the last installment, go find the copy you squirreled away in expectation of this week's denouement. Hurry up, now. I'll wait.

(While they're out of the room, for those of you who were clever enough to retain all that good stuff from last week, here is some bio data on Bill Starr. Just don't look guilty when they come back, or they'll think we've been talking about them behind their backs, the poor devils.

(Bill Starr is one year shy of being fifty years old. He was born in 1933 in Phoenix, Arizona. Served three years in the Marine Corps during World War 2.3: Korea. Honorable discharge. College at Cal-State Long Beach, an Education Major. Having prepared himself for a teaching career, he discovered it was the last thing he wanted to spend his life doing. The sale of a short story to *Caper,* a men's magazine, right around that time, led him into the delusion that he could support himself and a family through free lance writing. Over the years he's been able to do just that, miraculously, with an occasional gig in the construction trades.

(A pair of marriages that didn't work out—a familiar occupational hazard to those of us who make their living behind a free lance typewriter—and a now-grown son who has a steady scam as a computer programmer. What Starr calls a "delayed-adolescent Hemingway/Kerouac period of knocking around the world" after his first marriage went pfut! resulted in some interesting experiences such as an unsuccessful Caribbean treasure hunt and training a small cadre of anti-Castro Cuban freedom fighters (Starr's terminology) who decided, after the Bay of Pigs dustup, that they'd rather go for the Yankee Dollar as businessmen.

(Over the years Starr has written and sold between 350–400 stories, articles, poems, op-eds, greeting card verse, and five books. The most recent of the five was CHANCE FORTUNE, an historical novel about early Los Angeles, and well, hello, welcome back to the column. No, nothing happened while you were out of the room, honest to God. I don't know *why* those other readers have such silly grins on their kissers.)

I was just saying CHANCE FORTUNE was Bill Starr's fifth novel. He sold it through the Los Angeles editorial offices of a New York-based paperback publisher name of Pinnacle Books in December of 1979. It was to be approximately 75,000 words in length, and he had a deadline of June 1st, 1980. He was paid a total of $5500 as advance, in two installments: $2750 on signing of the contract, and the same on delivery and acceptance of the manuscript. His royalty for books sold was to be 8% of the retail price per copy on the first 150,000 copies, and 10% for every copy sold thereafter.

Bear that $5500 in mind. It is pretty close to the kind of money that was being paid for 60,000 word original paperback novels in 1955 when I broke into the field. But this was 1980 we're talking about, and a loaf of bread ain't 13¢ no more, as it was in 1955. Also bear in mind what I told you last time about Judith Krantz getting 3.2 *million* for the paperback rights to that sterling example of classic literature, PRINCESS DAISY. It has everything to do with what happened to Bill Starr.

CHANCE FORTUNE was published in September of 1981. The initial print run was 65,000 copies. It has not been back to press. Say bye-bye to that mythical 10% of the retail price ($2.75) for every copy over 150,000 sold. In fact, with the marketplace as I described it last week, say bye-bye to making even a dollar more than the $5500 Pinnacle paid as an advance.

Now you'd think Starr, a free lancer for many years, would have long-since scuppered the sort of silly amateur naivete that non-writers wallow in when they accept the myth that anyone who gets a book published proceeds therefrom to a life of indolence and frequent sojourns to the Cote d'Azur. But Bill Starr is one of those charming old-style Americans who actually believes a lot of silly mythology (most of it right-wing reactionary bullshit, but I won't get into that here; after all, I'm trying to paint this man as a hero, even if we're at opposite extremes of the political spectrum; I mention this only in aid of your understanding that Starr and I have no buddy system in operation). And one of the myths Bill Starr believes is that if you write a book well, and you get it out there, and if you push it a little, it'll reach an audience that will enjoy reading it and who need to learn what is within its pages.

The word for Bill Starr is naive. But that ain't a felony.

Nonetheless, as an editor at Pinnacle Books told me, "No one tells a guy to quit his job when he writes a book. I swear I'm going to have all our contracts headed up with the words *don't quit your job*. Even though it isn't *my* job as an editor to educate a writer to the realities of publishing, as a past official of the Women's National Book Association I've tried to get this kind of information out to writers and the general public."

But Bill Starr didn't quit a job to write CHANCE FORTUNE. Writing *is* his job, and given the lamentable condition of cheap hustle and talk-show persiflage that has become part of the life of writers who ought to be at home working, but who have to pitch their wares in public like fishmongers, his *job* was selling the book. So, naive sweetie that he is, Bill Starr sent a copy of the book to Ronald Reagan. Because it was about old Los Angeles, because he thought Reagan would like to read it, because he voted for Reagan and admired him and...miracles never cease: Ronald and Nancy Reagan wrote back the following:

"Dear Mr. Starr: Thank you so much for sending us an autographed copy of CHANCE FORTUNE, your novel about early Los Angeles.

"Being avid readers and fans of California history, we were much impressed by your storytelling skill and the fascinating things we learned about our state. It is easy to visualize this fine book as a highly entertaining motion picture. We almost wish we were still acting, so we could audition for roles in it.

"Sincerely, Nancy and Ronald Reagan."

Pause a moment, gentle readers.

Do you have any idea what that kind of endorsement is worth, properly publicized? Well, let me give you an idea.

When Franklin D. Roosevelt let it be known that his favorite leisure time reading was detective novels, it caused the boom in 'tec fiction and was, in large part, responsible for the Golden Age of mystery writing that produced Hammett, Chandler, John Stephen Strange, John D. MacDonald and the Mystery Writers of America. When FDR legitimatized thrillers, the publishing industry leaped for the genre.

In the mid-Fifties an obscure series of spy thrillers that had been kicking around for years, whose author was virtually unknown, was idly mentioned by John F. Kennedy as his off-hours reading passion. The books suddenly came back into print, were bought for films, and became the biggest moneymaking continuing series of bonus-budget motion pictures in the history of cinema. The books were about an English spy named James Bond, and the author—who became a millionaire as a direct result of that offhand endorsement by the President of the United States—was Ian Fleming.

The letter of January 5th, 1982 from the President of the United States and his wife, extolling the virtues of Bill Starr's book, contained a quality and potency of potential publicity that $100,000 worth of advertising could not have bought.

Sweetly naive Bill Starr had innocently struck the mother lode, and his future was assured. Right?

Wrong.

Because Pinnacle Books, in one of the most astonishingly cavalier gaffes in recent publishing history, chose to do virtually nothing with it. Though the West Coast Editor for Pinnacle, Carole Garland, sent out a few minor press releases (which were universally ignored in the tidal wave of PR releases received each week by newspapers like the L.A. *Times*, the *Herald-Examiner* and the very paper in which this column appears, the *L.A. Weekly*, none of which even bothered to review Starr's book), the publisher chose not to expend a farthing to promote the golden egg their Starr had laid at their feet.

Even more appalling was the knowledge Starr received when he rushed to Pinnacle with the Reagans' letter, that the book was no longer available. Three months after publication, CHANCE FORTUNE could not be purchased in your neighborhood 7-Eleven or Crown Books or B. Dalton outlet. It was gone as if it had never existed. Bill Starr, whose felony was that he trusted and believed that he had sold his work to a publisher who gave a damn about promoting and selling his creative efforts, got one helluva dose of Reality.

A soul-crushing Reality that even those of us who live very comfortably from our writing have learned to live with:

Most publishers—not just Pinnacle—don't know what the fuck they're doing. And they always have a hundred thousand dumb reasons to rationalize why it all goes sour. Most of which blame the writer. The miracle is that *any* books ever get noticed. As one former Pinnacle executive told me, after publication of the first part of this Starr chamber proceeding, "It's a shame you focus this problem on Pinnacle, instead of Bantam or Dell or one of the other larger paperback houses, because they're all the same. Pinnacle's an easy target because they're just more openly stupid about their errors, they're just less graceful than the others. But it's the same throughout the industry. The #1 and *sometimes* the #2 book on the list get all the advertising and promotion, budget and attention; and the rest of the titles published that month—between 12 and 15 at Pinnacle, for instance—are simply printed and distributed. They're like baby turtles abandoned out on the desert, left to find their way to the sea."

In the face of this corrosive Reality, lesser human beings such as you and I would either capitulate and continue to labor six months for $5500, knowing we had learned our lesson under the lash of commercial callousness—or give up entirely the dream that being a writer has any greater nobility of purpose than, say, hustling used cars on late night television. Either way, it would have been the death of the spirit.

But here's the swell part.

Sweet, naive Bill Starr, even in the face of an institutional ineptitude that could stun a mountain, fought back. I have spoken in these pages many times about the power each of us contains to move the world, power enough to immobilize a *tsunami.* Too often I've spoken of it in the abstract, like some est seminar mantra, full of hollow passion, untranslatable in real-time emergencies. This time I speak of it in the specific.

Bill Starr took Pinnacle to court.

Oh, not the way Judith Krantz or Irving Wallace, with vast financial resources behind them, would have taken their publishers to court: hundred and fifty dollar an hour attorneys jousting on a darkling plain of interrogatories, motions, depositions, casebook law and inevitable Darrowinian declamations in Federal District Court. No, Bill Starr made only $5500 for six months' work, and so he sweetly and naively did what none of us would have had the simple tenacious wit to do: he sued Pinnacle Books in Small Claims Court.

California law limits damages in Small Claims to $1500; but not only does one defend oneself, thereby saving the cost of an attorney, the plaintiff can sue *anyone* in, say, a great corporation. From the President, Chairman of the Board or Controller on down. And they have to appear in person, in the three-piece skin themselves, unrepresented by counsel...or lose on a default.

Small Claims Court is one of the few wonders of our current judicial system. Confronted with the reality of a major operating officer—bringing down a six-figure annual salary—having to fly in from New York; putting up at the Beverly-Wilshire because a big *macher* like that can't be expected to truck on in to a TraveLodge; getting up at 6:00 AM to *schlep* over to West L.A. Division; sitting and cooling his or her high-priced anatomy thigh-to-thigh with electricians seeking payment of their bills, retirees trying to get restitution from the high school kid who crumpled their bumper, and homeowners suing for the replanting costs of rose bushes dug up by the neighbor's dog; and then having to defend the case without Henry Holmes or Judy Shapiro or Jerry Kushnik to plead eloquently...the great corporation would settle out of court or let it go on default. $1500 doesn't seem like so much money in the face of that kind of aggravation and expense.

And all for a filing fee of six dollars.

So on February 18th of this year, Bill Starr filed against Pinnacle Books. Power.

The case was scheduled to be heard in front of a Judge Pro-Tem at 1:15 PM on Monday, March 22nd in room 123 of the West L.A. Municipal Court Building at 1633 Purdue Avenue.

Starr's intent was obviously less involved with making money than it was with obtaining a semblance of justice. As Starr wrote in a press release of February 25th (also ignored by every major news outlet in the city):

"I hope the case will save the book from sinking into oblivion before the readers for whom it was intended even learn it exists; provide writers who can't afford the expense of regular lawsuits a less costly way of settling disputes with publishers; help publishers understand that books are special products that deserve special marketing consideration; and persuade publishers who do insist on treating books like ordinary merchandise to accept the obligation of ordinary merchants to give consumers their choice of products."

Striking through all the snarled mass of obstructionism that terrifies those of us with just claims, Starr correctly perceived that "except for a few bestselling authors, writers have always been economically at the mercy of publishers, who are rich enough to hire high-powered lawyers to fight their legal battles for them." He also noted that the 1981 Columbia University Survey of American Authors, funded by The Authors Guild, revealed that 80% of America's writers earn less than $5000 per year from their writing.

And guess what? On March 22nd Bill Starr made history. He won.

In the West L.A. Division of the Municipal Small Claims Court, before Judge Pro-Tem Marvin Gevurtz, Bill Starr pled his case as most of us would (though he was "pretty low-keyed and tongue-tied for a writer" according to one observer in the courtroom). Appearing for the defense was Pinnacle West Coast Editor Carole Garland, who expressed no objection when Judge Gevurtz said, "It is clear that no good faith effort has been demonstrated on the part of the publisher in marketing and promoting this book."

(In fact, when I called Ms. Garland for a statement, on March 25th, three days after the trial, she admitted, "His was a book that did not get publicity or promotion." In fairness I note that when I called Ms. Garland after publication of the first installment of this matter, and advised her I was planning to use this direct quote, which I felt was particularly damning and which she had not said was "off the record," as other remarks she'd made were labeled, she told me she hadn't said it. She said what she'd *really* said was that Starr's book hadn't gotten "blockbuster promotion." In fairness I enter this disclaimer. Also in fairness, I must advise you that I wrote down Ms. Garland's words during that first phone call precisely and exactly as she spoke them.)

Ms. Garland said she sent copies of the Reagan letter and the book to all L.A. newspapers, who ignored them. But since the book wasn't even well-distributed to bookstores in the L.A.–Southern California area, where its subject matter was most likely to reach interested readers; since it was not available; it naturally produced reactions from the media such as that expressed by Art Seidenbaum, editor of the L.A. *Times* Book Review, who explained, "We do not review books not in the marketplace." So much for good intentions, backing-and-filling, and the vagaries of telephonic communication.

The downside of the trial is that Bill Starr did not win a monetary judgment of one red cent. He was awarded $35 in court costs and nothing in terms of the potential $1500 recovery permitted by Small Claims Court. More on that in a moment.

Starr had this to say after he won: "This case, as minor as it is in itself, sets an important precedent for those of us who rely on our creative talent for survival. By using the Small Claims Courts, we can face-off the powerful corporations that try to exploit us, as equals before the law, and demand that they treat us with a little respect. That's a big step forward, even if we don't make any money out of it."

No, he didn't make even that piddling $1500 as restitution for seeing six months' worth of creative energy pulled off sale within ninety days of its publication, for the anguish of seeing the main chance go down the drain to oblivion.

It was the same naivete that led Bill Starr to find a way to win the day for himself and all writers laboring in this weed-choked field, that cost him the final measure of vindication. As the man said, he snatched defeat from the jaws of victory.

Instead of simply suing Pinnacle Books, *per se,* Bill Starr should have named in his complaint Stanley L. Reisner, President and Publisher of Pinnacle Books in New York; Patrick O'Connor, Editorial Director; Ira G. Corn, Jr., the Chairman of the Board of Michigan General Corporation, of which Pinnacle is an affiliate firm; Vice President and National Sales Director Jim Reddam; and Pinnacle's Chief Financial Officer, Larry Ostrow.

Can you picture how quickly a check for $1500 would have come winging out of New York into Bill Starr's deserving hands when each and every one of those high officials was served with notice to appear in piddling little West L.A. Small Claims Court? Instead, Pinnacle dumped the onus on Carole Garland. After all, in the schema of corporate arrogance, an Editor is only a vassal (and what does that make the writer?) and losing her from the office for half a day didn't upset anyone very much. (Besides, in the minds of most publishers, editors have too much loyalty and sympathy for those goddamned writers already.)

But even if Pinnacle *had* toughed it out, and sent in their three-piece suiters, Starr could have won damages had he been smart enough to prepare some documentation. Had he assembled royalty statements on other books, had he gotten witnesses from the community of writers whose books *had* been properly pushed, who had made big bucks from conscientious marketing and promotion, had he taken the Reagan letter to an attorney-agent like Jerry Kushnik or a film/tv agent like Marty Shapiro and asked them to give testimony as to the potential of a book like CHANCE FORTUNE for motion picture purchase...he could have won full damages.

How do I know this? Because Judge Gevurtz told me, "If Starr had had *any* verification, I'd have been inclined to award him damages."

Now it's too late. The case cannot be retried in Small Claims on the same allegations. The principle is *res adjudicata,* "that which has already been adjudicated," in effect double jeopardy.

But Bill Starr has learned from his innocence. He is considering alternate charges, and considering suing in *pro per.* When I learned this, I spoke to Pinnacle's Editoral Director in New York, Patrick O'Connor. We discussed the case and the startling precedent it sets for redress by *any* author, and I suggested maybe Pinnacle, out of the goodness of its heart, ought to send Bill Starr a check for $1500, a mere bagatelle, just to demonstate good faith. He opined that was not a bad idea, that he'd take it up with the great gray masters for whom he worked. He said he'd get back to me.

Later that day he did get back to me. The great gray masters had, in effect, said *why bother.* They still had not learned. To them, Bill Starr was still a pisher, farting into the wind.

But Bill Starr, like such other Pinnacle authors as Don Pendleton and Bob Slatzer who are currently engaged in having the publisher's books audited for nonpayment of royalties, has tasted the power that he possesses as a creator and as a private citizen who is mad as hell and ain't gonna take it no more. Pennywise and poundfoolish en-nobles the thinking of the great gray masters.

They may find themselves being outfoxed as they were most recently by one of their successful authors, Marc Savin, author of A MAN CALLED COYOTE, who beat them at their own game. But that's another, also fascinating, story.

Bill Starr is fighting the conglomerate mentality of publishers who run a profit&loss estimate on a proposed book—cobbling up fan-tasy rationales why they should work their asses off for a title that cost them 3.2 million while consigning to the dust heaps a manuscript they picked up for a crummy $5500—he is fighting the thinking of wholesalers who don't give a damn what's between the covers and ask the publisher, "What'll you do for the book by way of promo, how much will you spend?" He is fighting the entire encysted, unworkable, mickeymouse system of Bottom Line ethics and merchandising that has turned the once-laudable publishing industry into merely another writeoff tax-deduction for parking lot owners, shoe store entre-preneurs and multinationals that make their big bucks from turning kids into video game zombies.

Bill Starr fights and speaks for all of us pulling weeds in this field. And he fights and speaks for you, who have the right to go into a bookstore and find something more uplifting and meaningful than just another Garfield non-book.

Bill Starr has set a precedent for writers all over this country, and if they ignore it, they do so at their—and your—peril.

# LETTERS

## Pen Power

*Dear Editor:*

Congratulations on running Harlan Ellison's ballsy expose of the paperback jungle, featuring my Small Claims Court joust with Pinnacle Books over their improper marketing of my novel CHANCE FORTUNE (April 23–29). I can't speak for Ellison's other sources, but it looks to me like he got all the facts straight.

While modesty forces me to decline the heroic image Ellison so flatteringly painted of me, I do agree with his conclusion that only writers, and readers, can save American literature from the degradation inflicted on it by the growing conglomerate takeover of the publishing industry. Whether my book—or any book—is as great as its author thinks it is doesn't matter very much in this conflict. The important question is: Will the readers be able to find the kind of books they desire, or will they be force-fed a bland diet of "generic books" that will be hacked out by computers? (If that's not already happening.)

Our chances of escaping that fate seem pretty slim, with the conglomerates possessing so much wealth and power and the ruthlessness to crush anyone who interferes with their greed for *more* wealth and power. But, like David zonking Goliath, we have a secret weapon—our creative imaginations. If we use that weapon wisely, we can sling our stones through loopholes in ironclad publishing contracts and other means of oppressing writers.

My creative imagination enabled me to think of Small Claims Court as an affordable way underpaid writers can seek justice. Ellison's creative imagination enabled him to spot the news value in my story, while the Establishment media greeted it with overwhelming indifference. What can *your* creative imaginations contribute?

It has been said, with some truth, that writers are too widely scattered geographically and too stubbornly independent to form an effective union. But at least we can communicate with each other and share ideas on how we can resist being screwed out of existence by conglomerate greed and stupidity.

—Bill Starr
Arleta, CA

231

# INSTALLMENT 26: 26 April 82

# Women Without Men

I have about as much of a chance that this column won't get me in trouble as a cobra at a mongoose rally.

Nonetheless, bewilderment and lack of certain answers to what has emerged as one of the imponderable mysteries of the universe goad me to set out what happened, in hopes some of you wiser heads can provide much-needed insight.

Let me hasten to enter this disclaimer: misogyny does not form the basis of this essay. Confusion and the need to know do. If I stumble and commit gaffes, please credit it to innocent sojourns through the unmarked minefield of male–female relations.

A long-time female friend, a woman in her late thirties, successful in her career, by any normal esthetic standards extremely attractive and well turned-out, intelligent and witty and educated, recently voiced a view of life that nonplused me to the degree that I began inquiring of other women I know—*is this the way it is?*

What prompted her remarks was a television interview with a prominent female psychiatrist based in New York. (I believe it was a Dr. Russianoff. We were both part of a dinner group at someone else's home and I wasn't watching the show, only paid attention when my friend—with whom I've had a long, rewarding, non-sexual liaison— urged me to listen to what Dr. Whatshername was saying.) And what she was saying was that a prevailing attitude among American women, especially that group over thirty and unmarried, is summed up in the title of her new book, which is something like WHY DO I THINK I'M NOTHING WITHOUT A MAN?

Dr. Whooziwhat then proceeded to say that the situation in New York anent "finding acceptable men" was execrable. There are, she said, a million more women than men in the Big Apple, and that meant, she said, that men could have their pick of any woman they wanted, while all these estimable women were rotting on the vine or making do with "unacceptable" men. Or something.

And my friend said, "See, I'm not the only one who can't find a decent man." Her phrase: *decent* man.

235

I must have said something offhand, not realizing I'd walked into a buzzsaw, because she then buttressed her argument that it is murder for eligible women trying to find "decent men" by recounting a sight she'd seen the preceding Saturday night at Canter's Delicatessen.

There, seated in a booth, were four extremely well-known and attractive actresses, without men, having a late night snack. "If *they* can't get men," my friend opined, "what chance do I have?"

My remark was then far from offhand. "That's fucking crazy!" I yelled. "How do you know they hadn't all gone to a movie together, or just come from performing in some stage production, or maybe they were gay, or maybe they just wanted a night out with friends, without male companionship? You're viewing the world in the most monocular way possible."

"But it was *Saturday* night!" she yelled back. "If they'd had men with whom they were involved, they'd have been with them." I felt myself reeling from exposure to the concept.

But another woman in the dinner party, a talented and personable executive secretary for a large corporation, chimed in, saying, "I went to a movie by myself last Saturday night, and everyone stared at me with such pity, I felt like a worm. And when I go to a restaurant for dinner alone on a Friday or Saturday night, I'll be damned if the waitress doesn't *ignore* me in favor of all the couples."

At that point I was genuinely horrified and awash with confusion. So I started asking around, and these views have now been verified by at least half a dozen well-oriented and exemplary females of my acquaintance.

And what it comes down to, as best I can parse it through my dizzying bewilderment, is that vast sections of the eligible female population of this country truly believe (as they did in 1911 or thereabouts) that they can *only* have a full, satisfying personal life if they are involved with a man whose company can "go somewhere" (their phrase, repeated by each of these ladies at least once in our conversations). The *somewhere* these liaisons are supposed to go, of course, is a pair-bonding situation in which someone moves his or her clothes into the other's closet.

I've begun to suspect that I'm living in Cloud Coo Coo Land, believing that things had changed sufficiently over the past thirty years so that women in large numbers had come to realize that their worth should not be measured in terms of their acceptability to members of the opposite sex.

(We will, for the nonce, exclude homosexual relationships, because they don't apply to the problem at hand.)

It all seems deranged to me. Take for example that highly dubious statistic of a million more women than men in New York. How many of those women are pre–pubescent? How many are gay

236

and would *prefer* to be with other women? How many are at an advanced stage of life where their interest isn't in getting married or hooked-up with some guy? And what of the concept of the floating population, those who move from relationship to relationship so they aren't always *in* the dating pool?

Okay. Ignore all of that. Let's say there *are* a million more women than men in New York. All of them beautiful and rich and talented and fulfilled in their professional lives. They are considered "excess" *only* if one accepts the argument that it is a one-woman-for-one-man world.

But isn't that the kind of concretized, tunnel-visioned thinking more applicable to, say, Kansas City in 1911 than to the realities of life in New York or Los Angeles?

Or am I nuts? Is it a sight one should pity when one sees four attractive women dining "alone" on a Saturday night instead of paired with men? Or should one merely think—if one thinks about it at all—that here is a woman, or four women, who *chose* to be sans male companion?

Is it not possible for a man to be "decent" if he is good company and has no intention of *going somewhere*? Does all of this apply if there is no sexual implication? Should it be considered rational and healthy for a woman attending a movie alone—on Friday, Saturday, or *any* day—to think of herself as a pariah?

Or have we begin running backward on the treadmill of self-esteem? I ask all of this wanting to know. Observations and opinions and statistical data, experiences and little-known universal truths are solicited.

Because, friends, as far as I can tell, something is *very* twisted here.

**INSTALLMENT 27:** 1 May 82

# INTERIM MEMO:

A letter follows this column. It has nothing to do with this column. It has to do with Installment 14. So why do I reprint it here? Because this was the issue in which it appeared, and I make reference to it in Installment 30, coming up.

"Madge, is this guy anal retentive, or what?"

"Don't ask me. Does he have to tell us *every*thing?"

"I didn't need to hear there's no Easter Bunny."

*Letters reprinted with permission from the* L.A. Weekly

Once more into the mailbag, dear friends.

Bearing in mind two quotes that keynote what this is about each week. The first, from Voltaire, who said, "My trade is to say what I think." The second, from William Blake: "Always speak your mind and base men will avoid you."

But before we get to the current batch of screeds and missives, a message from the author.

Fair is fair, and right is right. Those who have read my columns over the years, in a variety of printed media, know that while I frequently display a nauseating sanctimoniousness, when I later discover that I have been in error, I do a *mea culpa* that would put to shame a former Nazi prison guard trying to escape an Israeli firing squad. Thus, once again, as it falls to all of us made of mere mortal clay, I have been apprised of incorrect statements I made on the basis of inadequate information.

In my column of March 19–25, wherein I answered the first batch of mail directed to this forum, I took to task a young woman who goes by the name of "Spock," who had sent an anonymous letter of random testiness. In the course of replying, I operated off misinformation imparted by a source that bamboo slivers under my fingernails will not get me to reveal. Notwithstanding the "privileged communication" aspect of this exchange, I was given erroneous data, and I said "Spock" had (a) been fired from an unnamed firm here in Los Angeles and (b) had swiped an envelope from that firm to send me the anonymous letter. I was wrong. In fact, she could not have been fired from said firm . . . because she never worked for said firm; and she did not swipe the envelope, because it was available in the office of the firm for which she now *does* work.

This is an apology. It emerges not from fear of reprisal, legal or otherwise, but out of a sense of rectitude. Fair is fair, and right is right. I was in error, and I want anyone who read that column, who might have believed those misstatements were true, to know that I was flying blind. I will work harder to ensure errors do not again appear in this peripatetic congeries of casual, personal observations.

Later this week I will divest myself of the shirt of thorns I presently wear.

One *caveat* to all of you out there, the foregoing as a prologue: except for the occasional instances when space or forgetfulness lobby against its inclusion, each of these columns concludes with a statement that approximately every six weeks I will publicly answer mail received. That notice, in law, is an instrument serving the doctrine of "Fair Comment." It is a First Amendment defense of opinion that speaks to the agreement we enter into when you write and I respond. It says you do so, whether anonymously or with signature, with full awareness that your words can and may appear in print. The legal precedent usually cited in this respect is the instance in which the political cartoonist Paul Conrad did a drawing of ex-Mayor Sam Yorty in a straitjacket, and Yorty sued. And lost.

So understand that if you toss me a question, a comment, some praise or a brickbat, you're fair game for publication. The only exception to that is if you clearly indicate in your letter that what you've written is, as we say, DNQ. Do not quote. I will protect your desire in this respect as ruthlessly as I will attempt to track down those who send scurrilous notes without a signature, an act I consider extremely cowardly. A week or so ago, I received an excellent letter from a local writer, commenting on the paperback publishing columns I wrote; a letter filled with useful data. But the writer asked politely that I not reprint the letter or reveal from what source I'd gotten my information. I like that writer for the trust demonstrated; and the confidence is sacrosanct. If you tell me something off the record, it stays that way. If you want to tip this column off to someone or something that ought to have its covers yanked, the source stops here. You are protected.

Now to the mail.

Skip Press of Los Angeles wrote, "In response to [the two articles on Bill Starr and the lack of promotion his book CHANCE FORTUNE received at the hands of Pinnacle Books], I think if a writer's book isn't being promo'd enough to suit him, he should *schlep* it himself, a la Wayne Dyer and YOUR ERRONEOUS ZONES. Period. P.S. I'm a writer."

You may be a writer, but you're certainly not a pragmatist. Nor, obviously, have you ever tried to get yourself on a talk show with a straight novel. As far as the bookers for these shows are concerned, they don't want the garden-variety writers who will hype their work. They want someone like Charles Higham, who will hawk a piece of sleaze such as his meretricious *exposé* of Errol Flynn that advances the theory that Flynn was a Nazi spy. They want peddlers of sensationalism or fad diets, purveyors of Hollywood gossip or theorists who swear the world is ending next week. They want freaks and authors of non-books. They do not care to discuss Freudian symbolism in THE WHITE HOTEL with D. M. Thomas; instead they prefer a little sexual titillation by way of Alexandra Penney and her HOW TO

MAKE LOVE TO A MAN.

Further, most writers are not good talkers. They are not trained talk show fodder, prepared to put on a dog&pony act for the likes of those who think tv chat formats are "the rebirth of salon conversation." Hell, I did more interviews with Snyder on the NBC *Tomorrow Show* (I was once told) than anyone else...and it was murder trying to get on simply to promote my latest book. There always had to be a "hook."

So when you make a seemingly uninformed declaration that if a writer who got $5500 for a novel isn't getting it hyped by his/her publisher, s/he ought to spend $10,000 taking it from town to town across the United States, hoping s/he can get airtime, *doing what the publisher is supposed to be doing,* you reveal a total lack of perception of the realities that obtain.

F. A. "Tony" Bird of N. Hollywood sent me a postcard on which he printed, "Dear, poor, merry Harlan, Ye waxeth raspy. If you live on the second floor or higher, why don't you drop that typewriter on something hard? Then go surfin'. It's a fine world out there, somewhere—I've seen it."

To Tony, and all the others who seem to believe that I enjoy this condition of perpetual anger from which emerge the words I write, who somehow manage to stumble through the noons and midnights of their lives without accepting any responsibility for the human chain of which they are nominally a part, who don't wanna be brought down, like, and who would advise the rest of us who have to clean up their mess that we shouldn't be such Gloomy Guses and to go surfin', I offer by way of explanation the following famous quote from Pastor Martin Niemöller:

"In Germany they first came for the Communists and I didn't speak up because I wasn't a Communist. They they came for the Jews, and I didn't speak up because I wasn't a Jew. Then they came for the trade unionists, and I didn't speak up because I wasn't a trade unionist. Then they came for the Catholics, and I didn't speak up because I was a Protestant. Then they came for me—and by that time no one was left to speak up."

Going to bed angry and getting up angrier every morning is a filthy way to live, Tony old bird; and while I might not find my joy in surfin' or gettin' loaded, I can think of half a hundred other ways of letting light into my life that would enrich my spirit better than posing here each week with my gardyloos and look-outs about pernicious maggots like Jerry Falwell and John Schmitz and Brian De Palma and Phyllis Schlafly. But, as it has been said, it's a grungy job...and someone has to do it. Those of us who are prisoners of our ethics have no choice. As release, occasionally, I'll write a lightweight, funny column. Just to stay sane. But if *you'd* take some of this crap on your suntanned shoulders, Tone m'man, then maybe I could take a month off and go climb Kilimanjaro.

But as long as you keep doggin' it, dear curl-rider, I have to pack my load...*and* yours. Further, deponent saith not.

Peter Hankoff of Hollywood sent along a snippet of movie review from the L.A. *Times* of April 16th in which film reviewer Linda Gross, while commenting on a film titled *Battletruck,* went into left field to say, "The unpleasant brave new world conveyed is Harlan Ellison sci-fi." Peter was not the only one to bring my attention to Ms. Gross's reference to me. Since I am not now, nor have I ever been a writer of "sci-fi" (whatever the fuck *that* is), despite persistent mythology to that effect, I was forced to presume Ms. Gross was making allusion to my story "A Boy and His Dog"—or more likely, the film of the same name, which was the splendid work of Writer-Director L. Q. Jones. As Ms. Gross clearly did not know what it was I *did* write, I took this opportunity to send her several of my books. She said she'd read them at her convenience and get back to me. As of this date I have not heard from her.

But while I'm at it, I'd like to point out to my readers that while the philological construct "sci-fi" is in wide and common use, mostly for the convenience of city desk headline writers who save space with the five letters and hyphen, instead of the fourteen letters and mid-space of "science fiction," this is a label that many of those who work in the genre despise. They compare it to calling a woman a "broad," a black man a "nigger," a Latino a "spick" and a Jew a "kike." Use it at your peril. And, hi, Forry!

Thankyous to Fran Alstrom, Cynthia Zamperini, Grayson Jordan, Kevin Brennan, Richard Paschal, Christopher Herron Lee (who I'd like to get in touch with me so I can renew an old acquaintance), Jeff Miller and Janice Guffan—all of whom sent informational cards with nice words of praise. As for Joseph Bleckman, your most recent note was as filled with swamp gas as an earlier communique, but the stamp hadn't been canceled, so thanks for the 20¢ postage, thereby proving good *can* come from evil.

There's more, but I guess I'll save it till next time. Gee, I wish I had a terrific punchline.

# LETTERS

## Nobody Is Worth Watching

*Dear Editor:*

Allow me to congratulate you for having the sensational taste to include a weekly column by Harlan Ellison. I followed his column regularly when it was being published in *Future Life,* which was almost the only reason I ever bought the magazine, and I was rather upset when I couldn't find it on the stands anymore. Naturally I was delighted when I discovered that the only L.A. paper worth reading anyway had added even one more excellent reason for roaming the city on Thursday evenings trying to find a copy.

Now allow me to explain why I feel Mr. Ellison has succeeded in making a complete ass of himself. It centers around his feelings toward the films of Brian De Palma. Now, I will be the first to admit that Mr. De Palma has a rather perverse sense of humor and his films may be rather violent at times, but to put *Blow Out* in the same class as *Friday the Thirteenth* and *The Omen* is going a bit too far.

A few years back one of the most cynical and insulting movies I have ever seen was voted "Most Outstanding Motion Picture of the Year." I speak of *The French Connection.* The reason I detest this movie so much is not that it is poorly made, or that it is gory, or that it is violent. The movie is actually quite an impressive piece of film craftsmanship; the editing is excellent, the staging of the action scenes is very well done, and so on. No, I hate this film because the film-makers have presented us with a world in which nobody is capable of recognizing the individual humanity of other people. In short, nobody cares.

At one point the hero steals the  car of a bystander by force (I won't say an innocent bystander, because in this movie, innocent people simply don't exist) and drives through the city, chasing after the villain, crashing into other cars, and judging from the severity of some of the crashes, possibly killing people along the way. Furthermore, this man is not presented as the exception to the rule, he is presented as a rather typical human being. To borrow a phrase from Harlan Ellison, the human species presented in this story would not be capable of painting the ceiling of the Sistine Chapel, or of putting a man on the moon. The world presented in this film is a world in which nobody, and I mean Nobody is worth anything.

What kind of world does Brian De Palma create in such films as *Blow Out?* I'll agree it is a somewhat cynical vision, a world where innocent people are attacked and killed without reason or warning, a world where nobody is safe from a ruthless murderer, a world that

245

would have tested the patience of Job. The difference between this world and the world presented in *The French Connection* is that the characters are capable of recognizing tragedy when they see it. Even in *Dressed to Kill,* a film which is much harder to defend, the look on Nancy Allen's face when she discovers the body of Angie Dickinson told me that she saw beyond the blood to the body of a human being whose life had just been taken. Unlike Popeye in *The French Connection,* she saw the tragedy of senseless murder, as did John Travolta when he discovered Nancy Allen's body at the end of *Blow Out.*

Harlan Ellison defended the showing of an occasionally gory movie, *Wolfen,* at the Writer's Guild screening because the film was "about something," and, having seen it recently, I'll agree with him completely, but I must protest that *Blow Out* is also "about something." It is about the pasteurized America presented to us by the media, and about the real America hidden underneath. Harlan Ellison doesn't know that, because he is so blind to De Palma's films that he walked out early and missed the movie's most important scenes.

And while we are discussing storytellers and their visions of humanity, what kind of world view does Harlan Ellison present in such stories as "A Boy and His Dog" and "I Have No Mouth, and I Must Scream"? I'll leave that for you readers to decide.

—Miguel Munoz-Perou
L.A.

# INTERIM MEMO:

Things started getting scary. Back in February of that year I'd done a column on the attacks being leveled against Ed Asner by Reagan's White House through the gawping yapper of Charlton Heston (Installment 18). By May, the *Lou Grant* show had been summarily dumped and there was abroad in the land—in the words of Tennessee Williams's Big Daddy—"a pow'ful stench of *men*-dacity" as CBS gibbered and babbled how un-co-opted they were. I was outraged and, in one of those calls-to-the-bastions that went out of style in the mid-Seventies, I pleaded for warm bodies to picket. To my amazement, over two thousand readers and members of the ACLU showed up. Things started getting scary. Far-famed as I am for my puckish wit and disingenuous humility, I beg you to believe that this response, the first touch of actual naked *power* I ever experienced, scared the crap outta me. I had a taste of what it must have felt like for presidents, dictators, evangelists and rabble-rousers. And I was delighted to feel an utter abhorrence for such power. I shied back from it as from the pox. And realized that there were actually people out there paying attention to what I was writing; and thus I could not simply run amuck and indulge myself without considering the responsibility. It became a strain: thinking things out before I wrote them. Presenting sides of arguments I loathed but had to consider openly. Trying not to smartass when logic was needed. But things got scarier, as you will see in the next installment, if Uncle Wiggily doesn't get it on with Mrs. Bow-Wow, contract herpes, stave in her head with an andiron, and get twenty-to-life up at Q.

Last week I told some dude who wrote in telling me to go surfin' and not to let the bad old nasty world get to me, that if *he* would accept just a smidge of the burden of the world, that I could knock off and have a vacation. The subtext, my blossoms, was that a teensy demonstration of courageous commitment would help detoxify my overweening need to get involved in so many "causes." Courage and commitment are topical threads that run through these columns, have you noticed that?

Well, this week I offer you a painless way to put your suntanned carcasses on the line without danger. All it'll take is two hours of your time next Monday night. Monday nights are dead, anyhow.

I won't ask you to hike down through 120° heat to the Mexican border to support Cesar Chavez's farmworkers. I won't ask you to brave National Guard rifles legging it from Selma to Montgomery. I won't ask you to mass in front of the Century Plaza Hotel to protest Johnson's war in the Nam and risk getting a 'tac squad baton up your nose, like we did back in 1967.

All I'll ask is that you join with hundreds—maybe thousands—of us who will be picketing in front of CBS Television City on the corner of Fairfax and Beverly in Hollywood, between 9:00 and 11:00 at night, this coming Monday the 17th, to protest CBS's cowardly cancellation of the *Lou Grant* series.

This protest is being jointly sponsored by Americans for Democratic Action and the American Civil Liberties Union.

You will be in good company.

The company of those of us who understand that the ratings on *Lou Grant* were not the reason CBS canned what is, unarguably, one of the finest and most relevant shows ever to emerge from that charnel house of ashen cowardice and enbalmed ideas known as the television industry. You will be in the company of those who can sweep away all the Uriah Heep disingenuousness of the spineless network executives who bowed to Falwell's Moral Malignity and Wildmon's pernicious Coalition for Redneck Television, and Reagan's all-star hit squad of Chuck "El Cid" Heston and little Bobby Conrad, the town bully. You will be at one with those who are determined not to let the shadow legions take from us everything we prize by way of freedom of thought and speech, without one helluva fight.

Monday night the 17th. Nine o'clock to eleven, smack in the middle of that primetime window when we usually can rely on Asner and his co-stars to give us something to think about, as a brief respite from the profundities of those other, renewed, CBS winners—*The Dukes of Hazzard, Magnum, P.I., Dallas, Simon & Simon* and *Knots Landing.* Forget having your cat spayed; give a pass to washing your hair; shine on getting laid; definitely eschew a night of Coors and teevee. Be there or be square. You're needed! All of you: the two-car split-level layabouts, the San Pedro bikers, the Hollywood Hills dilettantes, the Reseda shift-workers, the barrio hideaways, the Fairfax ghetto septuagenarians, the three-piece Beverly Hills gourmets, the UCLA frat rats and Powell Library bookworms, the Orange County crypto-liberals and all of you who bore the ass of your kaffee klatsch partners deploring the encroachment of the book-burners in our daily lives. *All of you!*

You're so goddamned adroit at finding rat-hole rationalizations for not laying it on the line. This time there's no out.

It's not the loss of a television show that matters! It's the reasons they *did it!* Kimberly–Clark pulls its spot ads from *Lou Grant,* Wildmon targets the show as evil, the White House sends out its yapping mouthpieces, and we are one step closer to the pit. Be there or be in peril of losing your mortal soul. Do I overdramatize? Sue me. But be there!

They were picketing at Fairfax and Beverly last Monday night, the 10th; there was a protest march in San Francisco; thousands have already begun deluging the President of Kimberly–Clark (whose products include Kleenex nose-wipe, Delsey ass-wipe, Kotex, New Freedom and Light Days feminine hygiene products, Huggies baby-bottom wrappers and various other paper products from table napkins to cigarette papers employing the Kleenex trademark), Mr. Robert C. Ernest, with outraged postcards and letters advising him that Kimberly–Clark's cowardly decision to abandon *Lou Grant* in the face of an idle boycott threat by the Falwell–Wildmon forces has infuriated them to the extent that they are refusing to buy Kleenex products.

An idle threat it is. Only the most fervid subscriber to Ronald Reagan's oft-stated quote from Calvin Coolidge that "the business of America...is Business" is blind to the timidity and floating ethics of many great American corporations. (When Wildmon's Coalition for Better Television linked up with the Falwell horde, and began threatening sponsor boycotts of shows the Fundamentalists considered "saturated with sex, violence and profanity," such pillars of corporate mettle as Gillette, General Foods and Procter & Gamble caved in and ran scared before Wildmon had even released a list of targeted shows.) But an ABC-TV poll conducted last year produced the heartening

250

statistic that as little as 1.3% of the total population would actually support boycotts of advertisers on shows they watched.

One would think that such monoliths of industry would just tell The Reverend Wildmon of Tupelo, Mississippi to go get stuffed. But they didn't. They caved in and pulled their support from an array of series on all three networks. But they never copped to the reason they'd done it. It was always dissembling: "We feel our advertising dollars can be better spent elsewhere," or "The ratings did not indicate we were reaching the desired demographic audience for our products."

But Kimberly–Clark is the most flagrant case yet. They assault us night and day to buy their paper goods, but they won't demonstrate any scrupulousness in the area of social conscience. They are forever taking out institutional ads advising us what models of probity they are, but they won't even hang in there, in the face of empty threats from the fundaments called Fundamentalists, to support the First Amendment.

Why not join with the thousands already letting the Kleenex Krowd know you despise their craven behavior? Why not pause in the reading of this column to dash off a postcard or brief letter to Mr. Robert C. Ernest, President; Kimberly–Clark Corporation; North Lake Street; Neenah, Wisconsin 54956, to let him know that pulling his spot ads from *Lou Grant* permitted CBS to rationalize its cancellation of a show whose star had the courage to speak out against Administration policy. Why not do that, right now. It'll take you three minutes.

I'll tell you what. I'll make a deal with you. If you'll put down this column for three minutes to send such a telegram, or write such a postcard or letter, I'll tell you a new joke I heard. It's a terrific joke. How could anything be fairer?

Okay. Go do it. When you come back, I'll be here humming to myself, and I'll tell you a joke that'll brighten your day.

Hmmm. Hmmm. Hmmm-dee-dee. Hmmm.

That was swell of you. Thank you. (I was humming Bizet's *L'Arlésienne* Suite No. 1 while you were away.) Here's the joke.

God is taking a constitutional through Central Park in New York City, see. Just kind of a late evening stroll checking out the mugger population, and S/He passes this statue of Adam and Eve they have in Central Park. And S/He stops for a second, and looks at the statue thoughtfully, and S/He murmurs, "Why not?"

So God snaps the fingers and the statue comes to life.

"Look," God says to the now flesh-and-blood Adam and Eve, "I'm going to give you an hour of life, since before everybody else was, you were, and now you ain't but they are. You've got an hour, free and clear, to do what you want."

So Adam, stark naked, looks at Eve, also starkers, and they both

251

get all flustered and embarrassed and red in the face, and Adam says, very shyly, "Uh, er, you want to, uh, maybe go in the bushes and uh er . . . ?"

And Eve, blushing furiously, says, "Uh-huh. That would be terrific." So they rush off into the bushes and God stands there bemusedly, and in a moment S/He hears a thrashing and crashing and flailing of branches and uproar of such exertion that S/He smiles.

Half an hour later out come Adam and Eve, drenched in sweat, pink all over from their activities, grinning sheepishly and holding hands. So God looks at the Cosmic Digital S/He has on Her/His wrist, and S/He says, "But that was only half an hour. You've still got another thirty minutes to do anything you want."

So naked Adam looks at naked Eve and he says, "You, uh, wanna go back and do it again?"

And Eve grins broadly and says, "Yeah, sure. Except this time *you* hold down the pigeons and *I'll* piss on 'em!"

And on that note of jubilant pragmatism, I take my leave for another seven days and we will part smiling, and not be in contact again for another week unless you want to take a stand against the shadow legions and join me at 9:00 this Monday night, on the corner of Fairfax and Beverly Boulevard, in front of CBS, to carry a picket sign and let the spineless masters of tv's fattest network know we think they suck runny eggs.

You can come up and say hi, if you like. You can't miss me. I'll be the angry guy wearing the Harlan Ellison cap, looking to see if the guy who told me to go surfin' got back from Malibu in time to join us out there.

# INTERIM MEMO:

Back in Installment 16 I did a rap on my then-car, my dear '67 Camaro. You'll read what happened to it in *this* installment; and the update is that I heard from one of my readers, who sold me a gorgeous 1950 Packard, which (I'm told) after only two years in the refurbishing shop, will soon be schlepping my bones around Los Angeles. Very deco. Cream and ocher.

The day after this column appeared, things got terminally scary when Installments 18, 28 and 29 beat out entries from the New York *Times,* the Los Angeles *Times* and the Washington *Post* to win the prestigious Silver Pen award of the international journalism society, P.E.N. It was my first journalism award, and the plaque commends the work in the name of "protecting freedom of expression and opposing censorship, dishonesty, discrimination, or any other threat to a free and responsible press." P.E.N. Los Angeles Center awarded me an actual, real-life Silver Pen, a replica of a 1920 Lalique implement. I use it constantly. But it was scary. These little pisher commentaries of mine were being seriously considered. Oh, sure, it was heady and made my ego swell up ever larger; but it was also *très* scary. A. J. Liebling I ain't. E. B. White I ain't. Jimmy Cannon I ain't. I find humility exceedingly unnerving.

Photo by Gary Leonard

Shoulderblade deep in ruminations about mortality, this week's installment comes to you from very near the scythe-edge of the Hereafter.

Today, Thursday 27 May 82, is my birthday. I'm 48. Happy happy the usual bullshit.

*Last* Thursday, I had my closest dance with the Faceless One who lives in the Boneyard. If you were on the San Diego 405 Freeway at about 2:45 in the afternoon, you saw my beloved 1967 Camaro, about which I've written in this column, overturned and spilling gas across four lanes southbound this side of the Venice off-ramp. Close, dear friends, too fuckin close. When the driver ahead of you in the #1 lane suddenly hits her brakes for no discernible reason when the traffic has suddenly clogged up, and you're doing fifty, and suddenly she's doing thirty, either you decide in that instant simply to pray that your karma account is in the plus column and keep on driving up her tailpipe and out her front windshield, or you get *very* responsible and decide to let her reach a ripe old age by cutting into the median pulloff lane. Remind me never again to think like a humanitarian.

The swing into the pulloff lane was fine. Had she slowed down to let me pass on the left, had she speeded up to get the hell out of there, nothing would have happened. But as I zipped past her thirty, doing fifty and slowing, I saw her face—a white balloon with a terrified expression on it—staring at me through the window. She stayed right abreast of us. God bless you, lady. The back end started to slew. We were going to broadside her, centerpunch her into the other three jammed lanes of traffic. You'd have heard about it on the 5:00 news.

So I cut back toward the divider.

The wheels went up onto the curved surface designed to flip you so you don't go straight over into the oncoming lanes. We started to turn over.

255

(They tell no lie. Time *does* elongate. You don't get your life flashing before your eyes...thank God...I wouldn't want to have to go through all *that* again...but the nanosecond of what's happening *at that instant* slows down to a crawl. The mind carefully and leisurely considers everything. My assistant, Marty, was riding shotgun. If we flip once and land on the right side, please let it only be one roll, then I'll fall on her and crack her spine. What about the cab flattening? What about sliding?)

I wedged my foot under the brake pedal, hung onto the steering wheel, jammed my ass into the corner of the seat...and we went over. We landed on the right side, slid about six feet and came to a stop. The woman in the car beside us went blissfully on her way, leaving destruction behind without thought to stopping. But the guys behind us saw what was going down and they slowed and stopped. Marty was rattling around in the bottom of the car like a ping-pong ball. I was hanging above her like a Carlsbad bat.

Then I smelled the gas. The tank was dumping all over the car. Suddenly there was a face at the window over my head. The guys from the cars behind us were screaming, "Gas! Get out of there, it's gonna blow!" But they couldn't pry open the door overhead. It had sprung, and the weight was at a bad angle. I yelled back to them to press in the door button on the outside, and I swung around and used my legs to jack open the door. Then I crawled out, grabbed Marty, yanked her up, dropped her into the arms of the good citizen, and dove back inside.

My typewriter was in there.

I went back a second time for my suitcase with the manuscript of the film I've been writing—the *only* copy—and as I was rooting around trying to pry it loose, a cop appeared overhead.

"Get the hell out of there!" he screamed. "Not till I get my stuff," I yelled back. "Get the hell out of there, I'll arrest you if you don't get out of there!"

"Before or *after* it blows up?" I said.

He ran.

I got the suitcase, threw myself out of the car with it, and there we waited as gas drenched the San Diego Freeway till the fire truck came.

At 6:00 I was on a plane to Anchorage, Alaska, to deliver a lecture. "Wear the grease-stained pants for the lecture," Marty said. "Scars of battle. It'll be impressive."

So much for you, Faceless One! I'm gonna live *forever!*

A couple of Mondays ago, the 17th of May, a great many of you who read this column came out to picket at CBS, to protest the political censorship that resulted in the *Lou Grant* show being cancelled. There were two thousand of you out there, including the surfer. There were a few actors—Nick and Trish Mancuso, Paul

Kreppel who played the cocktail pianist Sonny on *Making a Living,* and a few others—not many, though. You'd have expected more of them—it is, after all, their fight, too. You'd have been disappointed. They weren't out there. Not many students, either. Some. Not many. I didn't see any directors. A few writers. Not many, a few. Mostly what I saw was *people.* No stars, no media faces you'd recognize, nobody very prominent. Just you two thousand dynamite citizens concerned about the erosion of your rights. A lot of members from the ACLU who understand that freedom has to be safeguarded endlessly, without surcease, without catching a well-deserved nap. And *people.*

I came down wearing the Harlan Ellison cap I said I'd wear so you could stroll up and say hello. I also came down with my Joe Morgan little league Louisville Slugger just in case any Mark David Chapman John Hinckley Sirhan Sirhans wanted to get physical in reference to something offensive in my writings. Not to use it, merely to use it as a walking stick deterrent against the unexpected. Pasteur said: "Change favors the prepared mind."*

A lot of you came up and said, "You brought us out here." I always said the same thing in response. "No. *You* brought you out here!" One kinda sad-eyed guy said he'd been laying back since the late Sixties early Seventies. He said coming out and walking with us made him feel good about himself for the first time in longer than he cared to remember. I liked him a lot.

It was a high, gentle readers. It probably didn't do one scintilla of good toward getting CBS to reconsider its cowardly actions, but it was the *doing of it* that was worthy.

There was a sense of being at the right place for the right reason; of being correct in our actions. A sense of community. The three hundred Spartans standing off Xerxes' multitudes at the Hot Gates of Thermopylae. The SNCC marchers going against Alabama mad dogs and cattle prods. Children in the streets of Budapest flinging Molotov cocktails at invading Russian tanks.

Yes, yes, I know. I overdramatize. Sue me. *You* shoulda been there. A chill up the spine, friends. Something real happening, life happening, and most of all: *people.*

I have come to care for some of you very deeply.

Today is my birthday. Don't send candy, I'm overweight already. Flowers grow in my backyard. I can use any of the non–L. Frank Baum *Oz* books written after 1921, or a nice pipe from the Cigar Warehouse or...most of all...a solid lead where I can buy a spiffy clean, well-running Packard circa 1951.

Other than that, send no gifts. But if you know where there's a Packard, let me know. My poor dear Camaro is in the Rheuban Motors impound yard, and they tell me it's dead. That motheruncher

---

*See 42

the Faceless One is squatting on the corpse. He didn't get me or Marty, but he finally caught up with Camaro.

A 1951 Packard could ease the pain.

Happy birthday to all of you. We're *all* gonna live forever!

# INTERIM MEMO:

I actually put a title on this column and its follow-up. I called them THE SPAWN OF ANNENBERG, Part 1 and Part 2. For me, these two columns were what the whole thing was about, the columns of personal observation. I'd like to take a forked stick to the *TV Guide* mentality.

When they were reprinted in *The Comics Journal* (issues #80 and #81, March and May 1983 respectively) they were retitled "Hysterical Paralogia" and if you recall my Interim Memo on Installment 18, this column and that earlier one inspired a late entry in the *Edge* sweepstakes, the final installment of this collection, item 61. If you've forgotten that reference, I urge you to return to that glorious Interim Memo of yesteryear and to the thundering hoofbeats of the great horse Silver.

# The Spawn of Annenberg, Part I

Memories of being on Death Row at San Quentin twelve years ago rush back to me this week as I read *TV Guide*.

My then-attorney, pre-Henry Holmes, was Barry Bernstein. We were, and are, friends. He had smuggled me into Q in the guise of a law clerk. He thought I might like to write a column about a man whose appeal he was handling, who had been convicted of beating to death his common-law wife's five-year-old son. I was fascinated; but I did not like it. Not a moment of it. That was in 1970. In 1973, for another newspaper than this one, I wrote two columns about that day in the joint. Between the visit and the writing of the columns, the judgment of Murder One was reversed; and in October of 1979 the man fulfilled the final requirements of his parole and, today, when I had these thoughts I will impart in a moment, I called Sacramento to find out from the state Parole Board what had happened to the man with whom I had visited on Death Row, before the Death Penalty had been outlawed. I was told the man was now totally free of jurisdiction of the Parole Board, that he had been fully rehabilitated, that he had paid his debt to society, and they had no idea where he was. I am not using his name. I don't have the right to muck about with his new life.

Yet the memory of him there in that tiny interview cubicle, that day in September of 1970, of what he revealed of himself, still frightens me. I sat and listened to a creature human in form, but utterly alien in nature. I hope to God he *has* been thoroughly rehabilitated—as I am told the wife who now appears on television speaking out against child abuse has been rehabilitated—but the clear memory of him persists, and knowing he is out there somewhere. . . still frightens me.

Most frightening, most non-human, was the moment when he manifested what penologists and psychiatrists refer to as Ganser's Syndrome.

I said to him (it's been twelve years and I have to approximate this), "The trial record says you kicked the boy to death. Is that

261

true?" And he replied, "I always wear tennis shoes. They're not hard shoes, you know."

Ganser's Syndrome (first described by the German psychiatrist Sigbert Ganser [1853–1931]) is a relatively rare reaction pattern also known as "the syndrome of approximate answers." It occurs primarily in prisoners awaiting criminal trial, and secondarily in patients under examination for commitment to mental institutions. The answers these individuals give are always related to the question, but at the same time are absurd or beside the point. Authorities disagree as to whether Ganser's Syndrome is a psychosis, a psychoneurosis, or the result of low mentality. That it has a psychotic flavor cannot be denied, and some investigators suggest that the loss of rationality is an unconscious attempt to reject the total self and its life history.

Ganser's Syndrome is a variety of what is overally termed paralogia. False, illogical thinking, found particularly in schizophrenic reactions. That conversation on Death Row came back to me as I read *TV Guide*'s June 5–11 issue. Paralogia. We go step-by-step. Follow me, if you will.

I quote from THE ENCYCLOPEDIA OF HUMAN BEHAVIOR: "Paralogical thinking may take many forms. A subject who is preoccupied with his own subjective thoughts and fantasies may give answers that reflect his interests and attention narrowed to a point where his thinking becomes restricted and unrealistic. Some subjects draw false inferences to protect themselves from the truth. In one case a schizophrenic patient learned that his girl friend, with whom he had never had intercourse, had become pregnant. He immediately concluded that the conception was immaculate, that the girl was the Virgin Mary, and that he himself was God. Paralogia may also take the form of distorting reality to conform to personal desires or delusional ideas. If a nurse smiles at a schizophrenic patient it may be enough to convince him that she is his mistress. If a paranoid sees two people looking his way while conversing, he is apt to conclude that they are talking about him, to his detriment. Paralogical thinking is sometimes described as prelogical or paleological thinking, since the thought processes are similar to those found in children and primitive man."

Accepting this theory, paralogia represents a regression to the stage in human development when the mind was dominated by feeling and perception rather than by logic and reasoning.

Remember that. By the end of all this it will tie in with the horrors of the Me Decade, est and Lifespring and transactional analysis and Scientology and Skinnerian behavior modification. But most of all with Walter Annenberg, Ronald Reagan, anti-intellectualism and the insidious, omnipresent, socially corrosive indoctrinaire power of *TV Guide* in aid of reactionary attitudes for the past

262

thirty years.

What we have this installment is an attempt at rational thought, as opposed to hysterical screed, in which the latter, some of you have suggested, I indulge too frequently. Let's see how well you respond to painstaking ratiocination.

Back to paralogia. As exemplified by a letter from one of this column's readers, who pilloried me for my attack on Brian De Palma's films, featuring gratuitous and graphic brutality against women, on the grounds that *The French Connection* was a film filled with violence, where a cop commandeers a car from an innocent motorist, chases a criminal through the streets of New York, smashes other cars en route, almost runs down a plethora of pedestrians, and then wrecks the guy's car. Paralogia. What the one film has to do with the others, I do not know. There is no approval (or even *mention*) of *The French Connection* in my essays; the appropriation of a car in the heat of pursuit bears no relation to sticking an icepick in a woman; paralogical thinking strikes again.

A similar reordering of reality manifested itself in *TV Guide* June 5–11. On page A-2 of the Los Angeles Metropolitan edition we find the usual editorial "As We See It." While it was very likely not written by the President of Triangle Publications, Inc., publishers of *TV Guide,* the honorable Walter H. Annenberg, it damned well straight reflects his thinking, and has done so for three decades. Let me quote, in part, from that editorial.

"Ed Asner, the outspoken actor who stars as tough-talking editor Lou Grant, recently denounced, with soapbox bombast, CBS's cancellation of his series. '...I find it shallow that the network wouldn't have exerted itself on behalf of the show, especially so that the yahoos of the world couldn't claim another victory in their attempt to abridge free speech.' Whoa, let's back up there a minute, Ed...*Lou Grant,* good as it once was...in 45th place is where you were likely to find Asner's series....As for the 'yahoos,' Asner obviously meant those poor, misguided souls who had the temerity to object to, among other things, his pledge to raise $1 million to buy medical supplies for leftist guerrillas in El Salvador.

"More recently, Asner has even accused the White House of putting political pressure on CBS to cancel his series. Asner must be suffering delusions of grandeur if he thinks this Nation's leaders have no more important matters to worry about than a foundering series or its egotistical star. ....This, Ed, makes you the biggest yahoo of them all."

Before I take you to the *very next page* of that issue of *TV Guide,* to tie the paralogical knot, let us examine the suppositions presented as fact in that little snippet of editorial. First, the yahoos of whom Asner spoke are clearly and obviously the minions of Falwell, Wildmon and the other cadres of the Repressive Fundamentalist

263

Right. The Moral Majority yahoos who've been so busy attenuating freedom of speech all across the board, from pushing creationism to pulling books from public libraries to having schoolteachers fired for dissenting views. Second, the souls who objected to Asner's humanitarian efforts are neither poor nor misguided. They are powerful corporations like Kimberly–Clark, the Kleenex sponsor that withdrew its spots from *Lou Grant,* one can properly conjecture, because it operates a large factory in El Salvador. And third, how outrageously paranoid is it for stupid, uninformed, egotistical Ed Asner to suspect that "this Nation's leaders" spend their spare time harassing those who speak out. How foolish of him to think that the chivvying of Jane Fonda, Shirley MacLaine, Arthur Miller, Lillian Hellman or Marlon Brando might preshadow what's happened to him. How egomaniacal of him to think that the government's smear campaign of Jean Seberg, that drove her to suicide, might indicate a capacity for malice on the part of this Nation's leaders. How self-centered of him to remember all the people blacklisted during the HUAC and Joe McCarthy eras. How shallow of him to think that this Nation's leaders, knowing of J. Edgar Hoover's endless harassment of Martin Luther King, no doubt creating a climate in which the likes of a James Earl Ray would pull the trigger, and doing nothing to stop it, might suggest a Nation's leaders who are capable of sic-ing the dogs on an actor who has the temerity to exercise his First Amendment right to speak out.

Yeah, what a paranoid, ego-crazed yahoo Ed Asner is.

And what a horrifying example to the rest of us. We smaller fish are supposed to be scared shitless. If they can wound someone as securely positioned as an Asner, what the hell chance have we minnows got? The chance of a snail in a bucket of salt. The chance of a snowball in a cyclotron. That is called terrorization by example.

And the example is brought home to us forcibly by *TV Guide,* Mr. Annenberg's mouthpiece with a circulation of 17 million weekly, the largest selling magazine in America... where paralogia rears its cockeyed head on page A-3, chockablock with the editorial telling Ed Asner that he's a yahoo because he thinks his show was cancelled by this Nation's leaders, when it is obvious that the show was cancelled because it was in 45th place out of 108 programs in the Nielsen ratings.

On page A-3 the New York bureau chief of *TV Guide,* Neil Hickey, trumpets as follows: "*Taxi* lives! The Emmy-award-winning series that ABC recently cancelled has been retrieved from the ash heap by NBC, dusted off and will grace that network's lineup with freshly minted segments sometime next season... *Taxi*'s fans were desolate when ABC dumped the series, which has generally gotten high marks from critics as one of prime-time television's less banal offerings. But its numbers slumped to 26 percent of the audience last

264

season, and the show ended up in 53rd place...."

Do you perceive the manifestation of paralogical thinking? On the left-hand page *Lou Grant* was cancelled because it was in 45th place, and it serves the dumb CommieSymp Asner right for shooting off his big bazoo...and on the right-hand page *Taxi* has been "retrieved from the ash heap," "dusted off," and "will grace" with "freshly minted segments" next season's primetime viewing. But *Taxi* was in 53rd place!

Now I think *Taxi* deserves to be saved, as well as does *Lou Grant*. Both are series of merit. I make no quibble with the good sense of NBC in restoring it to the air, though NBC's decision not to pick up *Lou Grant* may also say something about the overall situation.

You see, *TV Guide* on the right-hand page goes into panegyrics about how Emmy-winning has been *Taxi*'s history, but on the left-hand page they ignore *Lou Grant*'s honors in that area.

The simple fact is that each of the shows has won exactly the same number of Emmys. Twelve each.

And *TV Guide* doesn't exactly tell the truth when it says "45th place is where you were likely to find Asner's series." Here are some Nielsen ratings. Beginning with the week of 6 January, and ending with the week of 23 May, the Nielsen standings of *Lou Grant* were as follows: 17/43/53/36/53/21/56/58/53/41/37/41/42/39/31/48. What you may not know, however, though these standings are about on a par with what *Taxi* was doing, and noticeably better most weeks of that period, is that *Lou Grant* does spectacularly well in the rerun months, ending up last year at something like 17th out of 108.

So hurray for *Taxi* at 53, but fuck you Asner with *Lou Grant* at 45. I couldn't have stomped that kid to death: I wear tennis shoes.

So why, we might well ask ourselves, dealing rationally and not emotionally, does *TV Guide* go out of its way to fudge the facts to make Ed Asner look like what it is the White House has been telling us he is, a dangerous subversive who should not be afforded a public platform from which to spout his "soapbox bombast"?

Well, when I continue this long and step-logical series of observations next week, I will suggest some answers. Dealing with Mr. Annenberg and his chum Mr. Reagan, dealing with those of us who have survived the Me Decade, dealing with intellect as opposed to emotion, and dealing with *TV Guide* as a tool of the anti-intellectual worshippers of the Common Man in their heroic and unceasing crusade to keep us stupid and malleable.

But I promise I won't get all hysterical about it.

[To Be Continued]

# INTERIM MEMO:

Forked stick fury, part 2.

A little more than two years later, in the April 1984 issue of *Mother Jones,* Eric Nadler wrote an article titled "Guiding TV to the Right," in which virtually everything I said in these two columns, and more, was restated. I do wish he'd mentioned that an enemy of the people had said it years before he noticed. But in the event you didn't catch it, in the 6–12 October 84 edition of *TV Guide,* Ronnie's chum Walter Annenberg takes three lugubriously written pages to make "The Case for President Reagan" and in the *News Update* section on the flipside of the last page of Annenberg's editorial we have a reprise of the endless song *TV Guide* sings about how unfair the networks are to Reagan in their coverage of his messages. Walter wails and moans for utter impartiality from the networks, and uses his magazine, one of the most widely-read and powerful implements for the dissemination of a political position while nobody's aware of the hype, to promote his own favorite horse. If the damned magazine didn't run photos of Morgan Fairchild as frequently as they do, I swear I'd cancel my subscription.

# The Spawn of Annenberg, Part II

Snake-oil salesmen, used car dealers and television hellfire ministers understand, with a clarity that approaches satori, that wearing the cloak of innocent Good Ole Boy is a charade guaranteed to win the hearts of the easily-misled. This aw-shucks presentation, toe scuffing the dirt, cannot win the *minds* of the easily-misled, because for the most part the mind has been put into neutral. Pretending to an innocence that would make Rebecca of Sunnybrook Farm seem like a ripe candidate for a *Hustler* centerspread, the dealers in deception out-Gary the late Cooper. In the hype industry it's called *disingenuousness*.

I've never yet seen a City Slicker who couldn't be fleeced, greased and decreased by some yokel-*manqué* from Chittling Switch, Iowa stammering his way through an elegant scam with all the bumpkin hayseed *savoir-faire* of the primally rapacious.

For the last thirty years that "Good Ole Boy," Walter H. Annenberg—former U.S. ambassador to Great Britain and Northern Ireland, President of the Annenberg Foundation, Founder and President of Annenberg School of Communications, trustee and advisory board member of more prestigious institutions than you could shake a trickle-down theory at, husband of the former ambassador to the Court of St. James's—who is also President of Triangle Publications, Inc., of Philadelphia and Radnor, Pennsylvania, publishers of *Seventeen* magazine and *The Daily Racing Form*—has been the publisher and Guiding Philosophical Intelligence behind *TV Guide*. At seventeen million copies sold per week, *TV Guide* is the largest-selling magazine in America.

*TV Guide:* the *Partisan Review* for pimplebrains.

Every week, like crabgrass, mildew and the sign-off Sermonette, *TV Guide* comes to millions of American homes. It is invited in with squeals of childlike delight, cosseted and cuddled like a tribble, scrutinized and well-thumbed for the multifarious joys it proffers.

Pre-Universal Pictures rules about the powers possessed by vampires make it clear that a *vorwalaka* must be willingly invited into a home before he can attack his victims.

Every week for thirty years, like the *vorwalaka*, the spawn of Annenberg has been invited into American homes where quietly, unostentatiously, toe scuffing the dirt, it has practiced its bloodsucking abilities on the intellect and good common sense of 17,000,000 × God Knows How Many unsuspecting victims.

For three decades *TV Guide* has been in the forefront of anti-intellectualism; it has fostered paranoia among the easily-misled about any newscaster, performer or writer who has had the bad sense to speak out against those reactionary "old time values" so dear to the charred cinder Jerry Falwell calls a heart; it has consistently painted those involved with the television medium as venal, cocaine-besotted, unpatriotic corrupters; it has lobbied against the emergence of American women with a sense of their personal manifest destiny; it has belittled social movements and those who have laid their future on the line to further those movements.

Perhaps I see dust-devils under the bed when I suggest this unfaltering editorial tone of reactionism is directly attributable to the mind of Walter Annenberg. Surely Andrew Mills and Neil Hickey and Roger Youman and the other editors of *TV Guide* would deny it, would rail against the image of themselves as ideologues of Annenberg, would swear an oath that their views are their own. Perhaps. Yet one does not espouse contrary opinions to those held by one's employer, at risk of finding oneself out dancing for dimes on Wilshire Boulevard.

But if this *is* mere conspiracy paranoia on my part, how do we rationalize a desire to believe these *TV Guide* writers and editors are free to think as they choose, write as they choose, with the endless examples of soft-sell reactionism passim almost every issue of the magazine?

Take a look at just the last four months' worth of *TV Guide*. In the February 20 issue they ran an article ostensibly pillorying television for perpetuating the stereotype of blonde women as being brainless, big-busted instruments of male pleasure. But in the April 17 issue they ran a seemingly lightweight article by Jeff Greenfield bemoaning the demise of traditional marriage as a prototype in primetime. The piece lays heavily on the twisted relationships of *Dallas, Dynasty, Flamingo Road,* et al., and whimpers for a return to the days of Ozzie and Harriet, of Beaver Cleaver's family, of *Father Knows Best.* That families of such seamless wonderment existed, for the most part, only in the minds of those bitten early in life by Judge Hardy's clan, makes no difference. Let us not have stereotyped dumb blondes, on the one hand. . .and let us return to the never-never land of untroubled nuclear families on the other.

Paralogia. Illogical thinking. Contravening viewpoints.

Further, in the May 8 and May 15 issues of *TV Guide* were to be found the two parts of a twisted polemic by Benjamin Stein in which

270

self-determining females—such as the female reporter played by Linda Kelsey on *Lou Grant*—are called "desperate and angry role models." The two articles make a not-too-subtle, often hysterical plea for women to return to those tried-and-true role models we grew up with: woman as wife, mother and lover. Forget the *angst,* you broads!

As if this dichotomous thinking were not enough, in the June 12 issue, just last week, Frank Swertlow of the Hollywood bureau ran a "news item" that Meg Foster was to be dropped from the renewed CBS series *Cagney and Lacey* because "two women who worked in a male-dominated profession [cops] could be perceived as being gay." Swertlow reported the astonishingly idiotic remarks of series producer Richard Rosenbloom—"There were some scenes in which they seemed to be more man than the men"—and the remarks of an unnamed CBS programmer—"They were too harshly women's lib. . . . The American public doesn't respond to the bra burners, the fighters, the women who insist on calling manhole covers people-hole covers. . . . We perceived them as dykes"—without a scintilla of editorial concern.

Paralogia. On one hand let us not stereotype dumb blondes presented as dumb blondes. . .on the other hand let us flee in cowardice from strong women presented on an even footing with men. The key here is that nobody *really* gets upset in the name of those who use Miss Clairol, so it's okay to offer this as a real issue. But *TV Guide* says nary a word about such a flagrant and reactionary view of strong women in the work-force.

But if *TV Guide* is a reflection of Annenberg's view of Life in These United States—given that his view is that shared by Jesse Helms and Ronald Reagan—and as Annenberg is a deeply entrenched member of Reagan's "shadow cabinet" along with such other pillars of Big Business as Joseph Coors, Holmes Tuttle, Leonard Firestone, Charles Z. Wick, Justin Dart, Henry Salvatori, Asa Call and Norman Chandler of the L.A. *Times* we can, I think, handily assume the world-view matches up—then such paralogical thinking parses.

Further examples from recent issues:

June 12: *Why American TV is So Vulnerable to Foreign Disinformation.*

May 29: *Anatomy of a Smear: How CBS News Broke the Rules and "Got" Gen. Westmoreland.*

February 27: *How Accurate is the Network News?*

April 3: *Tales of a New York Reporter: Stealing Stories, Hoodwinking Sources, Sensation-Mongering.*

March 20: *President Reagan* (in an exclusive interview) *talks about Leaks, Boycotts, News Bias.*

And, of course, last year's big dust-up over *TV Guide*'s "expose" of cocaine use in Hollywood. I don't recall the dates, sorry.

But the ones that prompted your columnist to write last week's part one, and this followup, were the heavyhanded attacks on Ed Asner in the June 5 issue about which I commented at length last time, and an article in the same issue by (of all people) John Leonard of the New York *Times,* ridiculing intellectuals who say they don't watch television. This latter screed, rife with paralogical thinking and as self-hating as a Jewish anti-Semite talking about kikes, is only the latest in an almost cornucopial flow of anti-intellectual pieces *TV Guide* has offered as a staple of its "think-pieces" since its inception.

I have admired Leonard in the past, and I must conclude that his writing of this vicious little polemic is yet another example of *TV Guide* cajoling—for reasons I dare not consider—good people into doing bad things.

I hope you saved that June 5 issue. I choose not to go into exhaustive quotes from its length. Reading it twice was enough to make my gorge become buoyant.

But it falls right into line with the paralogia dished up every week by *TV Guide* in aid of belittling rational thought in favor of "gut-feelings."

We have emerged from what was called the Me Decade. A time when everyone was urged not to think too deeply, not to reason things out too carefully. Better to *feel* it, to get in touch with your emotions, to let it all hang out no matter *what* you felt. The country of the mind was portrayed as a cold, empty, hidden place from which no true emotions could flow; an uptight, anal-retentive way of living that cut one off from "real relationships."

This totemization of naked emotion, this stigmatization of reason, led to hundreds of thousands of people being bullied into a condition of shame at their ability to examine problems or life questions or political questions or complex societal trends. It led lemminglike rushes into mysticism, illogical beliefs, obscurantism, Scientology, est, Lifespring, an almost total takeover of Skinnerian behavior modification as the way to teach college-level psychology, deification of the raging boob as an exemplar of The Common Man.

"I'd like to share my feelings with you," became the mating cry of the American Pop-Eyed Galoot.

It put Sherlock Holmes in the toilet and made a god of Raskolnikov.

And it flowed to, and from, that Reagan-mouthpiece of subtle, innocent-seeming, toe scuffing the dirt anti-intellectualism, *TV Guide.* The weekly vampire that hides behind serious examinations of *The Love Boat* in order to slip into your home and your head the "old time values" that women should be back in the mold of Beaver's mother, that Ed Asner is a yahoo because he doesn't like the White House manipulating the cancellation of *Lou Grant,* that intellectuals are all fuzzy-minded eggheads who don't know which end of the nail to drive into the wall, that writers are all drunken dope fiends more concerned about their swimming pools than maintaining American Values, that when one of the networks manages to say something accurate about Reagan's love of Big Business at the expense of poor people that they are duplicitous and unAmerican.

Sigmund Freud once observed that sometimes a cigar is just a cigar. Contrariwise, sometimes an innocent-seeming journal that tells you how wonderful it is for Joanie to love Chachi is seen, in the light of day, to be a bloodsucking vampire whose unstated purpose in life is to turn you into one of the Undead who lives entirely at the edge of the skin with no recourse to cool reason.

Because if you merely *feel,* and never *think,* then you'll never suspect that life might be better, out from under the merciless thumb of Reagan and his "shadow cabinet."

And have a nice one, Mr. Annenberg.

**INSTALLMENT 32:** 24 June 82

Today the Equal Rights Amendment's lease on life ran out. Some weeks ago I wrote that the movement for equality-before-the-law, regardless of sexual considerations, would not die; that it has struggled for breath since 1921 in this nation; and even if the Amendment were stalled by the legions of divisiveness till today's terrible day dawned . . . we would draw a weary sigh and start all over again.

But I think it cannot hurt you to know the ignominious nature of the people who lied, colluded, extorted and cheated to make this day as dark as it is. I speak this week of perfidy, and through the good offices of one of my secret informants in a high place I relate a bit of history you'll never get from the Los Angeles *Times.*

At the final heartbeat, there were fifteen states that had not ratified the ERA. You should know which ones. Perhaps, like me, you harbor grudges. (In fifteen years, since marching with Cesar Chavez in the Coachella Valley, I have not once shopped in a Safeway market. Viva Huelga, mothuhfukkahs!)

Alabama, Arizona, Arkansas, Florida, Georgia, Illinois, Louisiana, Mississippi, Nevada, North and South Carolinas, Oklahoma, Utah and Virginia.

With one exception, they're all either Deep South states where the oxygen runs thin to the brain, or Mormon-controlled Southwestern duchies. The sole exception is Illinois, where dirty politics in defiance of the will of the people has been *de rigueur* since long before Al Capone rotted away from tertiary syphilis.

In Illinois, where the ERA was a runaway hit with the people, by the proof of endless opinion polls, there was an easy majority win in the state legislature. So they proceeded to gerrymander a rules change, for the first time in the history of the state, whereby a three-fifths vote had to be achieved. And before those votes could be accrued, enough money was poured into Illinois by Big Business to provide Phyllis Schlafly with the bucks to buy off the necessary Quislings.

Yet even with the game's rules switched in mid-play, as recently as three weeks ago it seemed Illinois was still a possible target focus for passage. On June 6th thousands of ERA supporters marched in Springfield, the state capital. House Speaker George Ryan, a rabid

ERA opponent, was quoted in the Washington *Post,* when asked about this action by his constituents, "Why should I want to watch those idiots?"

It was Ryan who singlehandedly blocked every attempt to get the Amendment before the House. Each time it seemed the strong and clever pro-ERA elements would get it on the agenda, Ryan would close down the session. And on the 9th of June, when circumventing action would have changed the House Rules back to simple majority rather than a three-fifths plurality, when it seemed like the day might be carried because Governor James Thompson (who had spoken out in favor of the ERA) was lobbying for the Rules change, Ryan called in all his favors and the change was defeated by a 4–97 vote. More on Thompson in a moment.

In a last-ditch effort to get ratification before the June 30th deadline, hundreds of thousands marched on Springfield, mounted a $30,000 tv advertising campaign, chained themselves outside the State Senate, unfurled a giant American flag in the Senate chambers, and picketed Thompson's mansion.

But the height of human courage and the depth of human depravity was manifested most clearly by seven women who, from May 18th, fasted for thirty-seven days under the great dome in the crowded Capitol rotunda, and those who came to stand before them, to jeer, to curse, to set up banquet tables and eat; as the fasters, dressed in white with purple sashes, fainted from low blood pressure and exhaustion.

From time to time in the course of writing this column, I have tried to answer the two most-frequently asked questions: Why do you hate the human race so much? and How can you continue to have such Pollyanna faith in the human race? In that one image of seven dedicated women putting their lives on the line—not merely making a gesture of protest but actually and literally endangering their lives—I see the very apotheosis of *homo sapiens* as God. And in the horrifying, vicious insensitivity of other women standing before the fasters, slowly tearing the wrappers off Milky Way bars, carefully biting off chunks and methodically chewing the goodies as they hold up placards reading DEATH TO THE ERA SLUTS and IF YOU WANT TO KILL YOURSELF, IT'S A FREE COUNTRY, I find more than enough reason to despise my species as unworthy of continued existence.

In just the 21st day of the fast, the seven women had collectively lost 200 pounds. One of them was a nun. One was a grandmother. One was gay. One was blind in one eye. One of them, Sonia Johnson, the 46-year-old woman who was excommunicated from the Mormon Church and whose husband divorced her because of her pro-ERA stand, dwindled from 123 pounds to 99 pounds, collapsed repeatedly, and had to be taken to the hospital a number of times. Yet until June 23rd, the day after Florida voted down the ERA for the final time, when Speaker Ryan and Schlafly and the Mormon Church triumphed and Illinois said no to over half the population of the United States, denying *us* what we needed and wanted, Sonia Johnson sat hollow-eyed and whisper-voiced in her wheelchair in the Illinois Capitol rotunda, telling us by her sacrifice that the spark of nobility *does* continue to glow in the human spirit. Telling us that we must not let what happened in this country after the Vietnam war happen again. Telling us that years of militant activity can sap our strength and weary us, but that just because a Watergate removes one thug from our view, that we must not be lulled into inactivity by the lure of too long a rest. When Nixon went, a soft GeraldFordlike hum, of the machine put into idle, settled over the land. And we rested too long, and kids today have no idea what all the *angst* of the Sixties and Seventies was about. And Nixon and Agnew finally had their way with us, even though they are off somewhere still getting fat and making a buck: they had their way with us because their clone-child Ronald Reagan rules the roost. Because we said, "I'm tired. I've been fighting for ten years. I need a break." And we went to our beds. And in the night they took the country from us.

Reagan and Schlafly and Falwell and Haig and Watt and Walter Annenberg (more about whom next week) took it away from us, and everything we fought for, and some died for, during those years of upheaval...seems about to slip away unnoticed.

And so that you won't think *they* ever sleep, so you won't live in the security-blanket warmth of the delusion that there is ever a lack of troops available for the legions of divisiveness, remember that Rules Change in Illinois, and consider this bit of secret history, imparted through one of my secret sources in high places:

In addition to Illinois, a prime target state for ERA passage was North Carolina. On June 4th in Raleigh, the Senate voted 27–23 on a procedural motion to table the Amendment till after the June 30th deadline, thereby effectively killing any chances for ratification.

But North Carolina seemed a likely state. How did it miss by such a tiny margin?

Secret history. On Wedneday, June 2nd, late in the afternoon in the chapel of the State Legislative Building in Raleigh, a secret meeting of twenty-seven N.C. senators was held. They gathered to raise their right hands and reaffirm their "gentleman's agreement" that they would not allow the ERA to pass, nor would they allow it to be considered on its merits. They swore there would be *no vote at all*. This despite a Louis Harris poll showing North Carolinians favored the ERA statewide by an astonishing 61–31% margin. This despite the heavy lobbying in favor of the ERA by Governor James B. Hunt, Jr., ostensibly a strong supporter of the Amendment. But...

On the previous weekend Governor Hunt, in company with Governors Bob Graham of Florida, Thompson of Illinois (remember him? I promised he'd reappear) and George Nigh of Oklahoma—all four being target states of The National Organization of Women as possible ratification sites—met in Durham, North Carolina at a Southern Governors Conference, to find out what others were planning to do, so they wouldn't step on each other's toes, to get their stories straight, and in general to cover their asses. As they say in political circles, an accommodation was reached.

So the N.C. senators, those 27 gathered a few days later in the chapel, knew they had nothing to fear from Hunt. He might publicly decry the tabling of the consideration of ERA—which he did in a statement issued after the death vote—but he was already on line with Florida and Illinois, where the power brokers had long-since decided that the United States would *not* have an ERA in their lifetime.

And here's the little fillip that adds a human note to an historical event.

Hunt had assigned a state lobbyist named Betty McKane, who is a former member of the N.C. Women's Commission, to lobby for the ERA on his behalf. Somehow she got wind of the klan meeting and, in company with other women, she showed up at the chapel. She watched them go in, counting twenty-seven. She watched them emerge, hiding their faces behind hats and papers. Only twenty-six.

She went inside and saw no one. She began searching the chapel. Hiding under a pew she found number twenty-seven, Democratic Senator Jim Speed. He tried to scuttle away. She followed him as he did his crab imitation on all fours. When she reached him he looked up with consternation. She said, very quietly, "You can get up now, Senator; I know who you are."

Then she slapped him very lightly in the face and added, "You've done all the damage you can do."

That noble legislator has been dubbed Jim "Under the Pew" Speed. Fastest sellout in the South.

For now, the ERA is defeated. Defeated but not dead. Since 1921, like Lazarus, it has come back from the grave. The ERA first passed in a state legislature in 1972. Work on it began in 1966 when NOW was organized. Sonia Johnson will recover, and she has announced she will run for the Presidency of the National Organization for Women. Her 37-day ordeal on our behalf will not be forgotten.

But the important lesson that has been learned in the ten year struggle culminating on this dark day is that Rules will be changed when the rats are cornered, that "gentlemen's agreements" will continue to flourish in darkened chapels, and that good manners will not carry the day.

Women have learned that spending ten years fighting under the Marquis of Queensbury rules is fruitless when the opponent rabbit-punches.

280

The ERA is not dead and those who treasure what it means for this country have sadly, reluctantly, but determinedly come to understand that no matter how courageous are the individual Sonia Johnsons of the world, that odious as it may seem, we must learn to fight as dirty as those who come to the talent by nature.

No one dies alone and unnoticed under the stars. We draw a sad, weary breath...and we start again.

**INSTALLMENT 33:** 2 July 82

# INTERIM MEMO:

This column was published in the *Weekly* the week of 9–15 July. The column speaks for itself, nothing very unusual. But. In the letter column we get our first glimpse of someone who signed himself "Jon Douglas West" of Burbank. You'll read the letter immediately following this column. Something about it piqued my curiosity. It wasn't the ordinary bugfuck pseudo-punk posturing of the plastic pinheads who responded to my manner but seldom to what I was talking about. "Jon Douglas West" interested me peculiarly. I did a little checking, mostly because he said he was in the phone book and suggested I come to Burbank to kick his ass. Well....No such person was in the phone book. Not in Burbank, not in Pasadena, not in any of the Valley directories, in Hollywood or L.A. proper. Um-hm, I thought. A li'l duplicity here. So I did some checking. DMV, tax records, utility records, real estate title deeds...I went the route. No Jon Douglas West. Then, when later I mentioned Mr. West, a number of letters began appearing in the *Weekly,* all written on the same typewriter, but with different names, some of them female. Curioser and curioser. So I took it as one of my little projects to locate the entity who was hiding behind the nom-de-plume Jon Douglas West. More on this later.

283

Photo by Richard Todd

How shitty is it, this day on which I sit down to write my column? Let me tell you how shitty it is. You know the Gobi Desert? You know all the millions and billions of grains of sand in the Gobi Desert? If each of those millions of billions of grains of sand in the Gobi Desert were divided into a million billion fragments, and each of *those* million billion fragments were broken into a million billion fragments, and if on each of those million billion fragments of the million billion larger fragments of each of those millions of billions of grains of sand in the Gobi Desert the word SHITTY were carved a million billion times, it would not equal by one one-billionth the utter shittiness of this day as I sit down to write my column.

Don't ask.

Changing the subject so that I do not go mad, I will do my best to tie up a lot of loose ends from recent columns, as well as tip you off to a few good things that may enrich your lives.

But first, if I may, I'd like to complain about the lack of response to what *I* thought were inordinately subtle hints in exceeding good taste about what I wanted for my birthday last May 27th. Not *one* of you went to The Cigar Warehouse's two locations and bought me one of those spiffy $100–$300 Radice (pronounced rah-*dee*-chee) pipes I casually mentioned. Perhaps those of you who continue to write postcards to the *Weeky* saying what a credit I am to the Human Race did not understand that I sit here smoking my pipe as I write, and that for a piddling $100–$300 outlay you could provide me with endless hours of wonder-filled relaxation, thus enabling me to better entertain you. Perhaps you didn't understand that.

Not to mention that my winsome request for any of the Oz books written post–L. Frank Baum brought an embarrassing silence. One guy called and said he'd loan me a few of his copies to read. Now *he* understood the nature of insane possessiveness.

Look, folks, let's understand something. What the hell is the point of having free access to the unlimited power of the Press if one cannot use that power for one's personal greed and aggrandizement? Clearly, most of you do not perceive the point of *having* power. It is a pain in the ass to amass such power; it takes time and annoys total strangers; it entails grinding the faces of the poor and dispensing favors in a thoroughly nepotic manner. Surely no one would waste his/her life in such a wretched pursuit unless there were a payoff. So if you're going to play this game correctly, you're going to have to shape up.

I can be bought. No, let me revise that. I can't be bought, but I can be rented. A nice Greek plateau briar or a copy of KABUMPO IN OZ can put you right there in the fat part of the Spoils System feed trough. Don't make me have to mention this again. It verges on self-serving.

Sharon Gilbert wrote asking why, if I mentioned in my first ERA column that a major corporation had funneled $40,000 into Florida's anti-ERA campaign, I didn't name the corporation? Because I forgot the name of the corporation. It was in the Miami *Herald,* in a major exposé last year. If I can locate the item, I'll drop it into a future column.

I'd like to recommend a quartet of good books. After my columns about Bill Starr and the anguish of being a freelance writer, I received a number of notes asking me if there is a good book on the economics of being a writer. There are, of course, hundreds of books ranging from the useful to moronic on "being" a writer, but until now there hasn't been a comprehensive text concerning itself with THE BUSINESS OF BEING A WRITER. The book is called THE BUSINESS OF BEING A WRITER (what a goddam coincidence), and it's written by Stephen Goldin and Kathleen Sky, both of whom make their living at doing the job. It is published by Harper & Row, will cost you something like 14 bucks, and was published early in June. It covers virtually all of the ground necessary to making the running of your one-person cottage industry behind a typewriter something other than *terra incognita*. I've read the book and, while I may have a few minor carps about this'n'that, mostly because my experiences are different than those of Goldin & Sky, they are charmingly pragmatic and exhaustive in their approach to this labyrinth of royalty statements and intransigent publishers. You will not go wrong if you hie yourself to a place where you can buy this tome. It may not make you a *better* writer, but it will sure as hell keep you from being a *poorer* writer.

286

Though I am only mentioned once, and then *en passant,* I would be a pisher in pique if I didn't recommend a new book on 1950s science fiction movies titled KEEP WATCHING THE SKIES! It was written by a friend of mine, Bill Warren (you see what I mean about the Spoils System and the uses of the corruption of power?). It costs the staggering sum of $39.95—and they have the audacity to demand an additional $1.25 for postage and handling—from a small publisher (McFarland & Company, Inc.; Box 611; Jefferson, North Carolina 28640) but it is simply delightful. Warren has an idiosyncratic eye and a nasty sense of humor that permits him both to totemize and revile most of the monstrosities from 1950 through 1957 with equal aplomb. The difference between KEEP WATCHING THE SKIES! and the usual microcephalic flying saucer movie books, is that Warren is possessed of a special derangement: he loves *all* these awful movies, even the ones about giant maggots from Mars that eat Duluth. There is an innocence, a charm, in Warren's approach that permits the reader to accept the irrational concept that there is even a scintilla of merit in such ghastlies as *Carolina Cannonball* (1955) starring Judy Canova. He goes on at hefty length, telling you almost more than you may wish to know, about something in excess of 160 films; there are cast&credit appendices; an appendix that lists the films in order of release; one on announced but not released films; and a final appendix on the SF serials of the Fifties; also a good Index; and the book is board-bound like a good library edition. It is humungously expensive, but if you like to chortle over the pecadilloes of your parents when they were teens, this is a superb job of writing.

I am a freak for dinosaurs. Anyone save the prematurely adult will cop to a similar fascination. Two new books have crossed my palm that deal with saurians in a spectacular fashion. The first is DINOSAURS, MAMMOTHS AND CAVEMEN: The Art of Charles R. Knight by Sylvia Massey Czerkas & Donald F. Glut (Dutton, $14.95). Ms. Czerkas is, by my way of thinking, the world's finest sculptor of dinosaurs. Her work can be seen at both the Page Museum and the Natural History Museum here in L.A., and it will bring a shine into the eyes of any kid you take to stand before it. Don Glut wrote both THE DINOSAUR DICTIONARY and THE DINOSAUR SCRAP-BOOK (though he made more money writing the novelization of *The Empire Strikes Back*) and what he doesn't know about the beasties, Sylvia does. They have teamed up here to produce an awesome retrospective of the paintings of prehistoric eras done by the late Charles Robert Knight, whose imagination and sure sense of paleontological reproduction combined to bring forth exquisite art at the highest level combining scientific accuracy (at that time) with the wonder one finds in the finest natural history paintings. The quality of the reproductions is better than good, the subject matter is exhaustive, and one flips page after page with one's mouth hanging open.

This is a special treasure, and I commend it to your attention.

The other dinosaur book is William Stout and William Service's THE DINOSAURS, edited by Byron Preiss (Bantam, $12.95). The damned thing is already a trade paperback bestseller, so you probably don't need me to rhapsodize over it, but in the unlikely event you missed hearing about it, this is the very latest we know about dinosaurs, presented in mind-croggling paintings by the multi-talented Stout and in delicious, innovative text by Service. Like the Knight book, this is one of those cornerstone volumes that you will be the poorer for having let slip past. I cannot urge you to it strongly enough. Particularly pages titled *The Shadow, In the Jungle,* and *Hot Weather. The Nose* ain't too dusty, neither.

I was asked to take note of the recent death of Philip K. Dick. That is not an easy thing for me to do. We were close friends once. We fell out. We had not talked civilly to each other in a number of years. I learned, shortly before the two strokes that took him, that he regretted the distance between us and wanted to get together. Time and circumstances and probably pigheadedness on my part prevented that. Now he is gone and, like many of you, I never got to say to someone who mattered, how much he mattered. So I am not the proper person to speak of this enormously talented, tormented man. I am not entitled to eulogize him as so many others have. Only this, as one who came out at the finish line too far behind to make his presence known, is open to me: nowhere in all the highflown testimonials to Phil and his singular writings, has anyone noted that there were greedy and amoral fuckers who used him badly, who kept him paranoid and poor and delusional with nightmares of life that served their own commercial ends. As one denied the right to praise him, I am permitted, I suppose, to suggest that each and every one of those scum who fed off his life-force be condemned to live out the rest of their days under the miasma of anguish and paranoia they visited on him.

A number of you asked why, in my pieces on Walter Annenberg and *TV Guide,* I didn't mention Annenberg's essay, "The Fourth Branch of Government," in the May 15th issue of that publication. I simply forgot it. But it was *L'Eminence Grise* hisself, coming out from behind his editors and hired guns to help Uncle Ronnie attack the tv newscasters who have had the temerity to suggest Reagan may not be sanctified. It was one more salvo in the war against opposition reportage that the Reagan White House has been waging since his ill-deserved popularity began slipping so severely. He said, in the piece, "Our argument is with adversary journalism and advocacy journalism, which are by their very nature biased. We believe there is no place on television news programs for such journalism, that it serves only to confuse the public and weaken the Nation. More than ratings are at stake here; it is the effectiveness of the Presidency

288

itself."

This disingenuous twaddle might make some sense if the automatic weight of The Presidency were not a fact of life. As Reagan and his cohorts have the power of Being There going for them, without strong advocacy and adversary examination of their actions to advise us, we would be totally at the mercy of what they proffer as The Right Way Things Should Be Done.

Annenberg and *TV Guide,* in a fistful of articles—as noted in my columns by date and title—repeatedly bring into question the right and credentials of those who take exception to administration policy. I'm sorry I forgot to do a ride-out on this naked statement by Uncle Ron's most powerful mouthpiece.

But this oversight has been corrected. Thanks Alan, for reminding me.

And next week I think I'll strip the hide off Paul Schrader and John Carpenter, and say a few loving words about *E.T.,* which I urge you to go stand on line to see this very minute.

As for today, if it comes back again, I'm going to throw myself into a Cuisinart.

# LETTERS

### An Open Letter To Harlan Ellison

*Dear Harlan:*

"When the going gets weird, the weird turn pro..."

Armchair psychiatrist? Dubious. Constitutional backseat lawyer? Hardly. Competent political analyst? Amateurish. An excellent writer at one point in time? I am beginning to wonder.

Come on, Harlan, relax, lay out for a few months. The bogey-man of the "far right" will still be there when you feel better. Ed will cool off and this caper should ensure his departure from television to film as it should have.

I too am vocal about the insipid behavior of the "Machiavelli-like" Moralists or anyone of the left, right or center who proposes my tastes. However, we all have one common and most precious bond: that being the First Amendment. As human creatures we all tend to be subjective on issues which inflame our concerns and passions. Most of us are convinced of our positions as being the moral (i.e., "right") one. Just as you have the right to search out paranoid network conspiracies and reactionaries in print, so too do Kimberly-Clark, Walter H. & Company and CBS possess that same right by means of the purse, the pen and the camera. Face it, Harlan, you, me and the rest—we are all stuck with it. Free enterprise and free speech are born of the same mother.

Ed will be okay and make tons of hard, hard earned money. El Salvador will be sadly forgotten for more fashionable pursuits. And Hugh Beaumont is gone forever. If you really need a channel for your energies, both you and Ed could get an effort going for the very victimized Lebanese and Palestinians. (Civilian dead now over 10,000?) Of course, you and Ed and I know who signs the checks.

I'm in the phone book if you would like to come to Burbank and kick my ass. You can turn out the closet lights now....

—Jon Douglas West
Burbank

**INSTALLMENT 34:** 12 July 82

Michelangelo is reported to have said, "Where I steal an idea, I leave my knife."

Were it possible to locate that knife, I would suggest those words be carved into the foreheads of such filmmakers as Paul Schrader, Dino De Laurentiis and John Carpenter.

And while we're at it, though I suspect the low brows of at least two of those gentlemen would not provide ample space, we might add the words of novelist Meyer Levin: "Three evils plague the writer's world: suppression, plagiarism and falsification."

Motion pictures are the damned-near eternal product of an industry that Pauline Kael has lamented as "an art-form controlled by businessmen." When that product transcends it essentially surface-dominated limitations, we find our meager store of permanent memories enriched by *Casablanca, Singin' In The Rain, The Pawnbroker, Lonely Are The Brave, The Wizard of Oz, King Kong, Atlantic City, La Strada* and *E.T.*

When the worship of the marketplace above all other considerations holds sway, we are disgusted, disappointed, gulled and ultimately repelled by remakes of *Cat People, King Kong* and *The Thing.*

Sequels are chancy at best. Anyone puerile enough to plonk down ticket money earned by sweat for such mimetic efforts has no right nattering about what a dreary hundred and five minutes was spent there in the darkness with *Grease 2, Jaws III, Rocky IX* or *Smokey and the Bandit XVII.* But every once in a great while a *Godfather II* or a *Butch & Sundance: The Early Days* proffers riches as worthy, or worthier, than the parent film, and so the denigration of the sequel cannot be wholehearted.

But the egregious *chutzpah* of such brutes as Schrader, De Laurentiis and (I'm pained to say it) Carpenter in thinking they have the ability to remake films already created as close to perfection as the materials permitted, is a demonstration of hubris and venality that compels Olympian scorn.

Whatever flaws may be found in the original versions of *Cat People, King Kong,* or *The Thing* upon the hundredth reviewing, it is clear they were originals, gifts of imagination that were muscular, talents that were first rate, and intentions not wholly dedicated to placating Mammon. Val Lewton, Jacques Tourneur, Cooper & Schoedsack, Willis O'Brien, Charles Lederer, Howard Hawks, Christian Nyby...these were men who worked within a restrictive system, with budgets that wouldn't have paid for one patch of *Tron*'s computer graphics or a side street in the world of *Blade Runner,* but who could not be contained by the comic book plots they put on celluloid, who transcended petty considerations and fleshed out immortal fantasies for generations to come.

Such imagination, such talent, is absent in Schrader, Dino and Carpenter. With the exception of Carpenter, who once, briefly, held out promise of being a director worth watching, these men are nothing better than graverobbers. They bring nothing new to the screen, and worse, they defile that which they have no right to touch.

The original version of *Cat People,* which I ran again the other night for the umpteenth time since I first saw it as an eight-year-old in the Utopia Theater in Painesville, Ohio, has not grown stale with age. One can wince at moments in *Watch on the Rhine* or *Wild In the Streets,* but Lewton's conception of metamorphosis, brilliantly scripted by DeWitt Bodeen and photographed in misty eeriness by Tourneur, maintains its mystical hold on our intellects and emotions.

Even forty years after its initial release, *Cat People* is adult, inventive, artful and, most important, as effective as the first day it played as a "B" accompaniment to an "A" feature now totally forgotten. It is a classic because it adheres to the stringent rules governing *any* kind of Art, and because it has withstood the ravages of time and fad.

By contrast, Schrader's twisted vision of *Cat People* is an exercise in depravity. An unsuccessful exercise in blood and warped eugenics. He has performed an autopsy on a dear thing that was not dead. He has drained out the gentleness, the caring, the characterization, the magic and the mystery and pumped it full of the currently fashionable formaldehyde of special effects brutality, gratuitous carnage, embarrassing nudity, moronic storyline and a full measure of his own crepuscular view of humanity.

Mr. Schrader is a deeply disturbed person. What seemed to be eye-opening insight into the human condition as manifested in the persona of *Taxi Driver*'s Travis Bickle, now presents itself as valid only because of the artistry of De Niro and Scorsese. We have seen what Mr. Schrader thinks of the rest of us inhabiting this vale of tears in *Hardcore, Rolling Thunder, American Gigolo* and *Obsession.* He does not like us. He does not, I think, like himself very much. His Dutch Calvinist upbringing is constantly being raised as apologia for the humorless, unrelenting revenant that stalks films with which he has been associated. That's too easy.

None of us escaped the thumb of God pressed into our temple in childhood by such True Believers as Mommy, Daddy, Preacher,

Teacher and Door-to-Door Bible Thumpers. Nonetheless, most of us do not see women as whores or virgins, do not conceive of Father as avenging angel, do not slough hip-deep through a murky world of sin and punishment.

Yet even if Schrader's baroque image of the darkling world were universal, by what immense stretch of temerity does he presume to say (in the May–June 82 issue of *Cinefantastique* magazine), "Val Lewton's *Cat People* isn't that brilliant. It's a very good B-movie with one or two brilliant sequences. I mean, we're not talking about a real classic."

One or two brilliant sequences that he swiped for his vile ripoff; sequences noted by virtually every reviewer as having been perverted and sophomorically reinterpreted.

One cannot lumber Schrader too much for bringing forth bad films like *American Gigolo* or *Hardcore*. They are, at least, his own original visions. But for this parvenu, lumped in with the other Wise Guy Directors, to presume to retell the films of his betters is an act of consummate gall that deserves nothing better than a forehead lightly carved with Michelangelo's words.

The same goes for Carpenter, who showed some stuff with *Halloween* and then did a swan-dive into the potty with *The Fog, Escape from New York* and now the remake of the Hawks–Nyby *The Thing*...which depredation he attempts to validate by saying he wanted to pull out of the original John W. Campbell story those treasures undiscovered by the original creators.

*The Thing,* if you have not caught it (and how I envy you if you exist in that numinous state), is a picture about which this must be said: one should not eat *before* seeing it...and one *cannot* eat *after* having seen it.

If the treasures Carpenter sought to unearth are contained in the special effects lunacy of mannequins made to look like men, splitting open to disgorge sentient lasagna that slaughters for no conceivable reason, then John Carpenter is a raider of the lost ark of Art who ought to be sentenced to a lifetime of watching Neil Simon plays and films.

*The Thing* did not need to be remade, if the best this fearfully limited director could bring forth was a ripoff of *Alien* in the frozen tundra, this pointless, dehumanized freeway smashup of grisly special effects *dreck,* flensed of all characterization, philosophy, subtext or rationality.

Of De Laurentiis and his aborted remake of *King Kong,* we need not even wait for the judgment of history. Like *The Thing* and *Cat People,* it is deservedly a boxoffice disaster.

But flushing these pustules is not enough.

They were *made.* The sensibility behind their creation is the canker on the rose, the worm in the apple. It is the same debasement that will bring us a television remake of *Casablanca* with poor David Soul in the Bogart role. (I say "poor" David Soul because I know and I admire and I like David Soul. He is a talented man. More talented than he has had the opportunity to demonstrate. I came to this knowledge slowly but with dead certainty.) And now poor David Soul will be pilloried for demonstrating the same sort of towering hubris that drenched Schrader and Carpenter and De Laurentiis: the delusion that he could do better than what has already been done properly best.

I wish I'd been able to say this to him before he accepted the role of Rick. I hope he survives the firestorm that will fall.

I hope others reading this column will have the sense, when they are presented with the opportunity to remake *Gone With the Wind* or *Hud* or *Viva Zapata,* to say to the hypocritical conceptualizers devoid of originality but ass-deep in megabucks, "This is a stupid idea. Get out of my face before I puke on your shoes."

Or, I suppose, they could get rude about it.

**INSTALLMENT 35:** 19 July 82

# INTERIM MEMO:

"Jon Douglas West" stirred considerable controversy. Several dozen letters defending good ole Harlan came in to the *Weekly* in the backwash of his attack. There was something about his manner that was easily as offensive as my own; and those who had now, after approximately twenty-six weeks of reading these little forays into rumination, developed a taste for them—I like to think of myself as the steak tartare or sushi of Letters, it takes a while to acquire the ability to keep me down once I've been swallowed—went after "West." You'll read one of those letters at the end of this installment. But it had been two weeks since I'd started trying to locate Mr. West; and as far as I could tell, exhausting every tool of tracing the skip-tracers use... Jon Douglas West did not exist. He had no bank account, no telephone, no automobile (unthinkable in Southern California), paid no taxes, owned no property, had no military or police record, possessed no charge accounts, did not vote, and had never been married. I can usually track down almost anyone I want to find, anywhere in the States, and on several occasions have done so, merely to board a plane and visit said individuals who have thought they could give me a bad time anonymously. But "Jon Douglas West" had stymied me. So I hired a private detective I'd once used to locate "Terry Dixon." The plot thickens, fans.

*Letters reprinted with permission from the* L.A. Weekly

Insofar as these weekly outings are concerned, I am one with Voltaire, who said, "My trade is to say what I think."

This is a commitment that brings me both praise and hate mail. Neither, really, is deserved. Voicing one's informed opinion is a responsibility gladly shouldered by any concerned citizen. The operative word, of course, is *informed.*

The old saw that "everyone is entitled to his/her opinion" is, in my informed view, horse puckey. These days, information is easy enough to come by, if one merely seeks it out. Thus, no one is *entitled* to a stupid, uninformed or irrational opinion.

Oh, surely enough, they can *hold* such opinions...no one ever said each of us wasn't entitled to be as dippy as we wish to be...and they can even *express* those dippy opinions...no one ever said we weren't entitled to look like a schmuck...but as for being *entitled* to a wrongheaded, uninformed opinion...well, I say nay. We're *entitled* to being as intelligent and clever and up-on-things as we can make ourselves. That's why book-banning is something we must resist with all our might. Access to the source material cannot be protected too forcefully. In the words of Dr. Johnson, "Knowledge is of two kinds. We know a subject ourselves, or we know where we can find information."

(Yes, Virginia, it would be a much duller world in which everyone knew what s/he was talking about; but then, compensatorially, it would also be a less violent world.)

I am forever dismayed at the sort of pedestrians collared by radio stations like KHJ and KNX when they do their respective "Street Beat" and "Voice of the People" features. It seems almost a pathological compulsion on the part of the interviewer to select and air the opinions of the most uninformed passersby. I suppose it's a desire to select "average" people, to get the general free-floating consensus on a contemporaneous question, that promotes such parameters of selection. Yet I question the unstated bias of that "average," if by *average* we believe the general mass to be insensitive, illiterate, filled with misinformation or *no* information, and so tunnel-visioned as to be arrogantly self-serving.

Accepting the mythology that the Common Man/Common

Woman is a dolt, and airing oafish opinions on these programs only serves to deify the numbskull. Yet one seldom hears a thoughtful, considered, closely-reasoned position when the walker in the street is buttonholed. It is as if the reporters select from among the (one presumes) multifarious statements made out there at curbside, only those as simplistic as possible. Are there truly no intellectual thinkers emerging from Fedco or bustling along in front of the County Court-house? One would get that impression by clocking the voices heard day in and day out on KNX or KHJ.

The stricture against voicing uninformed opinions goes for me as well as for the rest of you. It may sometimes seem I take a lofty position in that respect, but I assure you such is not the case. I do as I say, when I do as I do. Permit me to prove it to you, drawing on two recent responses to this column.

The first is a note from a regular reader, Joanne Gutreimen, who wrote on July 8th, "Also you haven't said a word about Israel/ Lebanon. Not like you to stay off a hot issue. Why?"

Well, the reason is *not* that I'm a Jew and am appalled at what's going on in the Mid-East. The reason is simply that I don't know enough about it to make a particularly original or informed statement on the subject. I have chosen to keep my mouth shut on this "hot issue." Similarly, I haven't said anything about the efficacy of the insanity plea, the flat rate income tax proposal, the Prop. 8 "victim's bill of rights," or the Constitutional Amendment for a balanced Federal budget.

This reticence should be greeted with huzzahs of approval from the correspondents to this column who seem to have no special animus toward my weekly pronunciamentos, save that I make them. One such—and this is the second mailbag item—was an open-letter-of-sorts addressed to me by one Jon Douglas West of Burbank, and published in the 9–15 July issue of this very newspaper.

Mr. West, whose letter verged on the imponderable with phrases like "You can turn out the closet lights now . . .," "And Hugh Beau-mont is gone forever," and "I'm in the phone book if you would like to come to Burbank and kick my ass," *seemed* to think these Joycean stream-of-consciousness lines had meaning for others than himself. I don't know about the rest of you, but they were bibble-bibble to me.

What was *not* bibble-bibble in Mr. West's letter, and jumped out at me (which may explain the peculiarity of the *Weekly*'s letter section editor even running such a pointless communique) was the following extract:

> If you really need a channel for your energies, both you and Ed [Asner] could get an effort going for the very victimized Lebanese and Palestinians. (Civilian dead now over 10,000?) Of course, you and Ed and I know who signs the checks.

Unless I misread wonkily, Mr. West is a closet anti-Semite with the closed door very much ajar. No, Mr. West, I don't know who signs the checks, which is why I keep my mouth shut on the subject; but I gather you are making yet another in the unending series of references to The Great International Zionist Jewish Communist Money Conspiracy that secretly runs the world.

(Which, if it actually exists, annoys the hell out of me. Somewhere out there is a kike with twice his/her allotment, because I sure as shit ain't got mine yet. I work much too hard to make ends meet, like the rest of you, and if the Great IZJCM Conspiracy do, in fact, exist, I'd appreciate the Comptroller getting in touch with me so we can straighten out this egregrious oversight.)

Mr. West, unless I misjudge his secret heart of hearts, is a laid-back bigot who understands that spicks, kikes, wops, niggers, gooks and Papists are an everpresent menace, but who is also hip to the reality that use of such words does not get one invited back for dinner. There is no less racism or bigotry in America today than in years past; the only difference is that it's gauche to voice such opinions openly. I take this as a positive thing. If it isn't heard abroad, then the kids don't pick it up as easily, and over a few generations it recedes in the general social atmosphere. One can only hope that with the final passing of those who think they know who signs the checks, these irrational and idiotic prejudices will also vanish down the hole, the bad interred with their bones.

Mr. West cloaks his unsavory opinion, and I don't voice mine at all. Were I to say something about the imbroglio in Lebanon, I would say that Begin is a thug, and always has been. He is not displaying his true colors for the first time. For those who remember history, Mr. Begin was a member of the ultramilitarist Irgun, a terrorist offshoot of the Haganah. He was a bomb-thrower and a merciless advocate of violence no saner and no more compassionate than Meyer Kahane and his Jewish Defense League, whom I despise with as much fervor as I do the assassins of the PLO.

Begin and Sharon are to be condemned for what they are doing in Lebanon. Yet one understands the madness that drives them to such horrors. The PLO has been at it for far too long. Like all True Believers they will not cease until they have been slaughtered to the last infant in its crib...or have converted the last unwilling adversary to their belief. Neither extreme demonstrates rationality or humanity. What am I expected to say of a Holy War being fought in 1982? That it is laudable in any way? That it is nobler by any measure than the *other* Holy Wars being irrationally waged by Protestants and Catholics in Northern Ireland, by Turks and Armenians over a massacre that happened in 1915, by Cambodians and Vietnamese in search of redress for nastiness a thousand years old?

The situation in the Mid-East goes back before the dawn of

recorded history, one presumes. It is at least as old and as raw a wound as the Balfour Declaration and the British White Paper of 1939. Yes, I'm conversant with all that Palestinian history, but it still doesn't unravel the skein. Were I to voice an opinion, it would be too flippant for all those in the PLO and the JDL who will no doubt take these words as inflammatory: I would say that the Jews and Arabs should join forces. With the Israeli genius for warfare, farming, economics and art, with the Arab genius for mathematics, tenacity, devotion and oil manipulation, the dumb fuckers could rule the world in fifteen minutes.

But they won't. They'll continue to slaughter one another. This time it's for a homeland for the Palestinian refugees. But no one seems to suggest that if the Arabs are so damned concerned about these homeless peoples getting situated, why don't they just give them a chunk of *their* vast lands. They are, after all, as they continue to tell us, all brothers.

If we're talking about solving the problem, of finding a home for innocent people, and not just keeping alive ancient antagonisms, why do the PLO's Arab brothers turn their backs on these doomed few and continue to goad them into trying to cop land that the Jews saved from the desert and turned into a garden? There's enough land out there for everyone, but not even Lebanon chose to allow the PLO to annex a chunk for its national homeland. They chose instead to permit a warrior cadre to exist in their backyard, permitted that cadre to make forays against the Israelis until even the dullest-witted could see that a monster like Begin would one day say, "Enough!" and would move against the harboring nation.

Though I am a Jew, I find it impossible to side with the Israelis in this terrible conflict. It has gone too far. Even if one accepts that Israel was driven to this madness by the PLO depredations, it is an unconscionable escalation of genocide by a people who were decimated within memory by just such an organized program of slaughter.

Ms. Gutreimen asks why I've been silent on this matter. Silent, because I don't know enough. Silent, because I see both sides. Silent, because I despise both sides. Silent, because as an American Jew I am ashamed, and proud, and rent with dismay at the lunacy of the human race. I can understand why Jews, who have been chivvied and driven for thousands of years, by naked swords and veiled remarks such as Mr. West's, have at last gone completely mad in what they perceive to be defense of their survival. I can understand it, but I cannot condone it. I am sickened by it, as are all decent human beings.

But I have no answer, save a flippant one. And that won't do. It won't do for Arafat, nor for Begin, nor for some misguided supporters of one side or the other who will read this column and, in a paroxysm of the same insanity that has leveled Beirut, seek vengeance against this columnist.

302

With the Jon Douglas Wests of the world still making themselves known, is it any wonder that paranoia leading to slaughter continues to be the order of the day? And if some of us choose to keep silent on these "hot issues," Ms. Gutreimen, it is only because we know that nothing we can say can put cool water on the brow of a feverish Holy War.

Like Voltaire, it is my trade to say what I think; but even for a run-on like me, there are times and topics that must, in the name of rationality, go uncommented-upon.

The check is in the mail, Mr. West.

# LETTERS

## Fight The Right

*Dear Editor:*

I have just finished reading Jon Douglas West's "Open Letter to Harlan Ellison" [July 9–15]. Actually, I've read it twice so far, having found it impossible to believe—on the basis of one reading—that *anyone* could, in all good conscience, put pen to paper and draft such a letter. Such naivete is soul-numbing, paralyzing in the extreme.

"Come on...relax, lay out for a few months," he advises. "The bogey-man of the 'far right' will still be there when you feel better." He then goes on to condone the actions of Kimberly–Clark, Walter Annenberg and the rest of the neo-fascist lot by invoking the First Amendment in an attitude of Hey, like, they've got a right to their opinion, too, y'know.

Perhaps it's time that someone straightened Mr. West out as to exactly *what* free speech is. Free speech is when I and The Other Guy take to our soapboxes and air our views. It's *not* free speech when I walk over and stuff a sock in The Other Guy's mouth so he'll stop contradicting me, or when I put my views on television or in a magazine before millions of people, while not only denying The Other Guy access to the same exposure, but stealing his soapbox to boot.

And that is *precisely* what the New Right is attempting to do. When Ed Asner is stifled, when Walter Annenberg's *TV Guide* praises the mindless sitcoms that divert us while attacking the news programs that call into question The Established Order of Things, when the President of the United States decides for himself what the people who elected him need to know about the way he runs *our* government, when books are burned and public school teachers are forced to teach mythology disguised as pseudo-science, then free speech has been nailed bleeding to a wall.

There is a difference, Mr. West, between free speech and propaganda. If you control the flow of information, you control the nation. Every power-crazed public official and dictator has understood this. The Torquemadas, the McCarthys, the Hitlers—*especially* the Hitlers—have long recognized this law. The placarded mandate of the late '30s is now becoming the very real threat of the '80s, although the names have been changed to protect the far-from-innocent: *"Henceforward it shall be deemed a crime against the state, punishable by law, to make any criticisms whatever of Reichschancellor Hitler."*

You say that because of the First Amendment, we should all "lay out" and forget about things, 'cause it's a drag. But it's precisly for that reason that we *can't* lay out. There is a very definite threat to free speech in the works today. I'm not saying its a conspiracy. "Conspiracy" implies a *coordinated* action toward a definite goal. Rather, I think we have a *concerted* action, in which different groups, working more or less separately, are all pursuing the same goal at the same time. Individually, they would not amount to much. But collectively, they wield a great potential for suppression. To ignore them is to invite grief. Maybe writers are more sensitive to the situation because they're confronted by it more often. Maybe that's the way it should be.

But don't let us distract you as you lay out and relax, Mr. West. Maybe *that's* the way it should be also. There's a lot of precedent for it. Like the people who, 50 years ago, sat in a cafe on the *Wilhelmstrasse,* drinking warm beer, remarking, "What, the Nazis? Ah, you needn't worry about them. In a few years, they'll be gone, and no one would have noticed. No need to get upset." And they went on smiling benignly as books were burned, newspapers were monitored, jackboots fell at the front door and, somewhere, the choicest hellflame was readied for transport to places with names like Auschwitz, Treblinka and Dachau.

And the benign smilers were in attendance 20 years later, when Joe McCarthy's refurbished brand of Nazis held sway in the halls of government and commerce. "Blacklist? What blacklist? Oh, it doesn't matter. So they'll go and write books instead, or act on the stage; either way, it doesn't matter. No need to get upset." Meanwhile, careers were destroyed, lives shattered, and marriages went out the same ten-story window as an occasional, but not *really* important artist.

So go on smiling benignly, Mr. West. Lie out in the sun, relax, shine it on, m'man. You've found your niche in life, and it's a rare man who can say that what he was meant to do, he does well. Meanwhile, the rest of us will go on doing our job. Just remember: when the hammer falls, it *always* hits the unwary first.

Just thought you might like to know.

Have a nice once, Mr. West.

—J. Michael Straczynski
Contributing Editor
*Writer's Digest Magazine*

# Interim Memo:

As fitting aural accompaniment to the reading of this—and part of the next—column, be advised that Anatar Records (PO Box 27579; San Francisco, California 94127) has released a swell album of songs written and sung by the subject of columns 36 and 37, Susan Rabin. Ten tracks, as punchy and sweet as you might desire. $8.00 a shot includes postage and handling. Those who jammed the club to hear her work will be anxious to add this album to their collections; for those of you who haven't heard Susie sing, just put your head very close to the page and listen. In the event you don't hear the music, you have no doubt, unfortunately, purchased a warped or otherwise defective copy of this book, and I urge you to write the publisher for a replacement. And not to be upset when the attendants from the Home for the Terminally Weird come to your address to invite you to take up residence at the Chipmunk Factory. (Incidentally, in April of 1984, Susan Rabin graduated from law school and began studying for the California bar.)

Photo by Loni Spector

This week, if you'll give me a hand, I can keep a promise I made twenty-two years ago.

Lemme me tell you a story.

Once upon a time in Chicago there was this cabbie named Louie Rabin, who moonlighted parking cars at the Chez Paree. He married Eva, who was the hatcheck girl at Fritzel's when the stage shows were posh at State & Lake. They lived in the Jane Addams housing projects, not too terrific, exchequer-wise, but they had three daughters, anyhow. In them days folks didn't have tv, they had kids. The middle one was Susie. She used to put on teeny playlets in the ·neighborhood; and she rollerskated a lot. At least till she was three, when she got polio.

Susie recovered, but to this day she thinks she's got lousy legs. Too skinny, she says. She's wrong, but what the hell.

Little Susie Rabin went to Northwestern and got a degree in theater in 1962. She also got married. He wanted to be an eye surgeon, the big bucks in ophthalmologoy, so Susie taught high school English and drama, and supported him for the next four years. By the time he had become Dr. Eyeball, there were two daughters and Susie had gotten an MA in broadcasting. But she wasn't doing much in professional singing.

Did I mention she sang? Yeah, she sang. She also wrote plays. She also hung out the wash and used Dutch Cleanser in the sink. But after a while there wasn't too much time for singing. And later, Dr. Eyeball wanted her around the house, so the offers to gig were refused.

Don't anticipate where I'm going with this. A storyteller's supposed to keep you waiting.

Flip them calendar pages. We're talking twenty years of wedded bliss. Bringing us to eight months ago, October 24, when Dr. Eyeball said to his little wife, words to the effect of, "I don't think it's going to work with us, kid."

That was in Mill Valley, up north where they tell me San Francisco still stands waiting for the apocalypse.

Pause a moment. Go back to 1960. I was working in Chicago. That part isn't important. I used to hang out at a joint called The Hut in Evanston. Northwestern students used to eat there all the time. Heard my first Ray Charles sides in The Hut. That part isn't important, either. The connection is that I met Susan Rabin in The Hut. She didn't know from ophthalmology at that point.

I heard her sing, and jeezus she sang like an angel. Said I, to her, in one of the few unselfish moments of my life, "You sing like an angel. I'm gonna make you a star, toots."

So I got her some dynamite Chicago jazzmen, including Eddie Higgins, and she cut a tape. Nothing happened with it. I cut out for New York, to get away from a shit scene, a marriage memory that left rat tracks on my shadow, and never heard of Susan Rabin again.

Two months ago I got a tape in the mail. And a letter. From Susan Rabin. She was coming to L.A. between her first and second years of law school, to try to push music, try to learn how to write screenplays, try to learn entertainment law. I didn't even remember the name Susan Rabin.

But I put on the tape.

I'm listening to it now, as I write this.

Jeezus, she sings like an angel.

Tell me something, gentle readers, what're you doing this Sunday night, August 1? The last time I suggested you take the evening air, to take a stroll with me, two thousand of you turned up outside CBS. And that wasn't to get your esthetic stroked, merely to balm your souls.

This time I'd like to invite you to come hear an angel sing.

Susan Rabin is in Los Angeles, and if I have a hand from you, why don't we make her a star. And I can pay off on a promise I made over two decades ago.

To be fair about it, the eye doctor wasn't a villain. He paid for the demo tapes through the years, but he hated the idea of show biz. "Who makes it in the music business?" he said, with ineluctable logic. No villain, for sure. Nothing wrong with a hard-working husband wanting his wife to be spared the heartbreak, even though she sang to hot reviews at Caesar's Palace and The Troubador and The Ice House and Sweetwater. Nothing wrong with that.

(I'm loading the gun. Not fair. He did more than just pay for a few demo tapes. When she went to Vegas to sing, he took care of the kids. He wouldn't have been anything less than pleased if she'd decided to

310

become a lawyer, or to try for a career in broadcasting, during those twenty years. Truth of the matter is that *she* kept herself from making it, all those years. She bought the okeydoke: home, husband, 2.6 kids and happily ever after. Like so many of you. But sand runs down through the hourglass and castles built in there just fall apart. And October 24 comes to a lot of us who deserve better.)

Now Susie Rabin is on her own. Like a lot of you. And she's going to be singing the songs she wrote like "Sweet Conductor Man" and "Listen to Your Dreams" and "Happy Ever After" and "Chicago Women" at a Santa Monica restaurant called At My Place this Sunday night at 8:00 PM. One show.

Who do you know in the music biz, gentle readers? Why don't you buy them dinner this Sunday night?

Every week in this column we talk about saving the universe. We want to stop Watt from paving us over, we want to put a cap on the bomb, we want them to stop burning books, and each time I give a wail of anguish you say, yeah, ain't it the truth, but what the hell can I do, I'm just one person. Well, maybe it comes down to one person helping one other person.

Here's a dream twenty years old waiting to get fulfilled. I wouldn't steer you wrong. This woman is sensational. A voice somewhere in the neighborhood of Chris Connors and Blossom Dearie and Melissa Manchester.

No cover, a sorta kinda one-drink sitting fee, a custom-designed sound system, a good food menu from quiche (which real men can't even *spell,* much less eat) to steaks, with terrific homemade desserts. Go have dinner At My Place Sunday night. The address is 1026 Wilshire in Santa Monica. Call for a reservation at 451-8597 and ask for the owner, Matt Kramer. Tell him *specifically* you're coming in to eat because you want to hear Susan Rabin.

There's even an open jazz jam after Susan Rabin and her band knock your socks off.

What the hell, you weren't doing anything that wonderful Sunday night, were you? Come on, be a pal. Like the last time we got together, I'll be there grinning and listening. Say hello. But mostly, let this songwriting, playwriting, lawyering, ex-housewife mommy-of-two have a shot at the Diamond As Big As The Ritz. I wouldn't steer you wrong.

This kid sings like an angel.

Louie will thank you. Eva will thank you. Dr. Eyeball will thank you. Matt Kramer will sure as hell thank you if you tell him Susan Rabin brought you in.

And *I'll* thank you.

Sometimes in this life you need to call on your friends to help you keep your promises. I've waited twenty-two years to be a *mensch.* Kindly do not make me look like a schmuck, you know what I mean?

**INSTALLMENT 37:** 2 August 82

*Letters reprinted with permission from the* L.A. Weekly

PHOTO: MARK SHEPARD

*Portrait of the Columnist as "old fogey."*

Once again, dear friends, into Darkest Mailbag with gun and camera. For most of the world it's a case of live and let live; in terms of answering my mail, it's live and let loose.

First: over two hundred of you turned up out in Santa Monica to hear Susie Rabin sing last Sunday. She did a new song about unrequited love for Al Pacino, played her ukelele, took a bunch of encores, blew out the sound system and blew away the audience. If sidebar thanks to your faithful columnist is any gauge of how good she was, be advised I sat there and bathed in the undeserved approbation as many of you came up and said what a keen evening you'd had. For those of you who ordered dinner, I apologize. At My Place is not Ma Maison. It ain't even Dr. Hogly Wogly's Tyler Texas Pit BBQ (on Sepulveda near Roscoe...highly recommended, particularly the Texas hot links). But the good news is that Susan Rabin returns to At My Place on September 12th. And if they have any sense the owners will (a) pay her for performing next time and (b) have her do more than one set.

Second: Sondra Ormsby of Toluca Lake wrote recently saying she'd heard I had a new book coming out, and where could she get it. The new collection of stories is called STALKING THE NIGHTMARE, and publication date, synchronistacally, is today, Thursday the 5th. The book is published by Phantasia Press and can be obtained—for sure—at A Change of Hobbit in Santa Monica on the LA side of the hill, and at Dangerous Visions in Sherman Oaks on the Valley side. I will be doing an autograph party at DV on Saturday the 21st, from 2–5:00, and I'll remind you of that as the date nears. This has been a solicited announcement, for those of you who are curious as to what I write for a living. (You didn't think I was buying that Packard with my paycheck from this column, did you?) Which brings me to:

Third: a reader to whom I am eternally grateful but, shamefully, whose name I've misplaced, turned me on to a swell guy out in Los Alamitos named Greg Busenkell, who sold me a 1950 Packard to replace my poor dead Camaro. The behemoth is, at present, in the shop at John Wilkes Automotive out in Reseda, and I'm assured by John (who is simply put, the most honest, best mechanic in the entire

315

fucking city) that refurbishment will be completed in another three months. You're gonna love it, folks. I'll run some photos of the restoration process in a while. It is heaven! Four door touring sedan, inside running boards, deco dash panel, a back seat on which four people can stretch their legs as if they were languishing on a livingroom sofa. In a few months, when you see this automotive dream in cream and ocher with the HE license plates, moving in a stately fashion through the streets of this magical Baghdad (since the accident I've sworn off driving as if I'm trying to make up laps at Sebring) (actually, since the accident, I've been that rarest of creatures, barefoot in L.A., without wheels for two months) (actually, I rented a teeny vehicle from Budget Rent-A-Car and they stiffed me something way over $750 for two weeks, which leads me to urge you to avoid dealing with these people), honk if you think Merv Griffin is a *yotz*. It'll be me flaunting it, baby, flaunting it!

Fourth: I was truly amazed at the number of you who took me seriously when I blatantly demanded a $300 Radice (pronounced rah-*dee*-chee) pipe for my birthday. One guy called and said if I'd write him two limericks and provide him with a replacement dust wrapper for the first edition hardcover of DANGEROUS VISIONS he'd bought, he'd make me a gift of just such a pipe. Well, I've never written a line of poetry in my life—for which W. S. Merwin, Robert Creeley, Galway Kinnell and the ghost of Randall Jarrell give daily thanks—but I'm nothing if not flexuous, one might even say anfractuous. Not to mention avaricious. And so, for the first time ever since Atlantis sank beneath the waves, O Prince, I present herewith two limericks for that guy who was deranged enough to make the offer (but who hasn't called back, probably because the keepers with the white wraparound jacket located him before he could hurt himself). I make no apologies.

### LIMERICK THE FIRST
A fan of "An Edge In My Voice"
Called the writer to say, "Hey, rejoice!
     "Radice is thine
     "If you'll just incline
"To cobble me some poems with some poise."

Y'like the way I Ogden Nashed *rejoice* with *poise*? Yeah, well, the same to you y'goddam pedant. Go please purists.

### LIMERICK THE SECOND
Of scansion I know not one whit,
My poetry's strictly from shit.
     Obtaining this pipe,
     Needs lines of a stripe,
From a verser who's more than a twit.

The signed originals of these two sterling efforts await claim from the *rara avis* whose insane offer defies belief. I will keep you advised. New horrors! New horrors!

Fifth: Kenneth Echeveral of Westwood got testy with me about that piece on the nobility of being an intellectual. He stood with arms akimbo, stamping his little foot, in the letter, and demanded I give him my definition of an intellectual. I can conceive none better than this cutie from Camus: "An intellectual is someone whose mind watches itself. I am happy to be both halves, the watcher and the watched."

Sixth: I wrote by column on Israel versus Lebanon-based PLO with considerable trepidation. Didn't want to get into that. Said I didn't know enough. Was openly asked about it, so I did a long ramble on the subject, mostly uninformed bullshit. Many people then wrote asking, "If you said you weren't going to say anything about it, why did you then go on and have a lot to say about it?" Well, folks, the medium was the message. It was a column about "everybody is entitled to his/her opinon" even if they don't know from sour owl poop. It was supposed to be a demonstration of how long an idiot can go on about something with no real information. The point was apparently lost on some of you. Lost to the extent that Mayer Brenner sent me a startling piece from the current issue of the *New Republic,* (Martin Peretz in the 2 August issue) which I commend to your attention, intended to inform my opinion. I'm glad *I* knew I was babbling, even if you didn't catch it, because that article is an eye-opener which contains a great deal of solid data about those much-bruited 10,000 civilian casualty figures.

Seventh: the same reverse-logic was used when I wrote the column about women sans men. Dozens of women wrote, surprised at what they termed my *naïveté.* "Of *course* that's the way it is with us," they wrote. "How could you be so innocent of the situation?" Honestly, folks, I am sometimes startled at your lack of faith in me. Of *course* I know that's the way it is...that women continue to identify themselves as being worthy in terms of whether or not they've got a man. I wrote in a calculatedly disingenuous fashion, to make the point, to raise the issue, to get the juices started. Well, gloryosky kids, I received so much troubled mail from you-all that I'll be doing a follow-up column soon, and will even initiate another Public Service aspect of this column: I'm at present assembling a list of six or seven "decent men" to offer to you needy female persons. These men will all be what you term "possibles." I'll run dossiers, personal observations, photos, and then we'll start trying to farm them out to you. This is not a dating service, Great Expectations does a perfectly fine job of that. This will be an experiment to prove that there are still a few good male entities around, and you shouldn't lose hope. Watch for this outstandingly tacky undertaking in the near future.

Eighth: Senator John Schmitz will not be on the list.

Ninth: About two of my personal "heroes," listed in the 1 April column. Gloria Allred, the feminist attorney, and John Simon, the critic. I heard from a number of grousers that neither of these estimable paragons deserved to be admired. I was planning to do a long piece on Gloria, but there's just such an article in the current (August) issue of *Los Angeles* magazine, by Michael Leahy. I'd suggest you read it, in lieu of my intended profile on this remarkable legal Zorro, but unfortunately Leahy's takeout is one of those smarmy juice-jobs that doesn't openly axe the subject, yet uses loaded, slanted and colored verbs and adjectives (such as constantly referring to Ms. Allred's perfectly ordinary and well-formed mouth as "tight and small") to reinforce a warped, negative portrait. It reads to me like the sort of wolf-in-sheep's-haberdashery effort that results when a journalist comes on friendly with the subject to get close, to elicit the subject's cooperation, and then turns out to be singing the song of the Quisling. It's a stinko piece of work, and Leahy ought to be ashamed of himself; so I'll be getting to my own Allred portrait sooner than I'd thought.

As for John Simon, my admiration for him is unbounded, if for no other reason than that he uses the language superlatively and he has critical standards that he refuses to compromise. But Joanne Gutreimen (who consistently sends in thought-provoking postcards) said Simon was a beast because he sometimes attacks the physical appearance of actors and actresses. She noted in particular Simon's now-famous trashing of Liza Minnelli, a dead-on evisceration of that lady with which I concurred wholeheartedly. She singled Simon out as a practitioner of that sort of analysis with the denigrative observation that when a critic has to "stoop" to vilification on grounds of appearance that he was being sexist. She opined that Simon would never pillory a male thespian on those grounds. Well, she's wrong, of course. Simon has often reported on the inappropriate physical appearance of men cast improperly. But further, since actors and actresses are selling their *look,* as well as their acting ability, it seems perfectly correct to take exception to those who simply don't convince in the role they're playing, on either appearance or acting grounds.

And if Ms. Gutreimen thinks John Simon is the only critic who so evaluates, I quote for her—and your—benefit from Richard Schickel in *Time* for 5 April. Referring to that vile Paul Schrader version of *Cat People,* Schickel writes:

"...in the new version, which stars [Nastassia] Kinski, flat of voice, spirit and chest..." and "...the cheerful and lovely Annette O'Toole...."

If it were not that a major selling point of the film was the promise of seeing Ms. Kinski in the buff, such observations might be gratuitous, but as we were unhappily gifted with more of the lady's epidermis than most of us needed or wanted, it becomes fair game for comment. By the way, strictly as an esthetic observation, why John

Heard in that film would even look twice at Kinski when O'Toole, who is a knockout, was faunching for him, is an illogicity impossible to rationalize.

I stand by my admiration of Simon. Sorry, Ms. Gutreimen.

That ties up at least *some* of the unattended minutiae, and next week, unless Uncle Wiggily slips in the gooseberry jam and slides down the coal chute and mucks up the central heating, I will get back to something serious: I will reveal to all of you out there who are simply panting to know about it, the inner workings and Machiavellian maneuvering that we in the know refer to as The Great International Hydrox/Oreo Cookie Conspiracy.

Don't miss it. Empires will totter.


# LETTERS

### The Important *Thing?*

*Dear Editor:*

In order to explain the ravings of Harlan Ellison on the subject of film remakes one should first consider the effects of nostalgia on this romantic and sensitive man.

The tendency of critics to sanctify works through which they received their first communion is not new, particularly important works like *King Kong* and *The Thing,* in which the critic even believes the genre was first defined. But those of us whose early impressions of sci-fi were not supplied by *King Kong, Cat People* or *The Thing* see no such sanctity in these films and can only be dazzled by the broader bandwidth and superior technique of their remakes.

Mr. Ellison also cut loose with a barrage of vitriol for John Carpenter, not only for daring to violate the sacred preserve of his beloved film *The Thing,* but for conceiving of a space monster whose dining habits turned his stomach.

Someone should explain to Mr. Ellison that extra-terrestrial life forms may not conform to his romantic notions of appearance and behavior. Everyone would, of course, like for the first extra-terrestrial to be cuddly, but we shouldn't berate filmmakers whose speculative visions disappoint us.

The notions of extra-terrestrials regarding Earthlings as just so much protein is not new. There are many life forms here on Earth which kill their prey in a horrible and painful manner. Harlan Ellison himself belongs to a life form which kills other creatures in a grotesque fashion.

Just what was it that put off Mr. Ellison? Was it the autopsy scene? Hasn't Harlan Ellison ever cleaned a fish? Was it the doctor getting his arms bitten off? Hasn't Harlan Ellison ever seen an animal in a trap? In spite of its ugliness, the "thing" is biologically far more interesting than James Arness in a rubber suit ever was.

*The Thing* is an important film because it has culled the phonies and old fogeys, like Harlan Ellison, from sci fi fandom. John Carpenter and the creator of his special effects are manning the border stations of science fiction art and they are telling us that the days of the actor in a rubber suit are over.

—Hal Taylor
Los Angeles


## PLO Not Driven

*Dear Editor:*

Mr. Harlan Ellison [July 23–29] demonstrates with fine articulateness the liberal's dilemma in the Middle East. Perhaps you'll allow me to comment on one aspect of propaganda, which is another word for lies, currently prevalent in the U.S.

Being British and Gentile, nonetheless I find myself puzzled by a lack of history or perhaps willful ignorance concerning Israel. The general line of anti-Israel thinking repeatedly contends that the Palestinians were "driven" from their homeland.

The facts are that in 1948 the Palestinian Arabs were urged, by the outgoing British government and the new Israelis jointly, to remain and live peaceably side by side with the Jews. Evidently such a gesture was partly a political discretion, and also perhaps attributable to the magnanimity so often extended by the Jews in general, even in the face of threat. At the time, Mr. Levi, the Mayor of Haifa, made an impassioned speech to the Arab Council to use their influence in encouraging the Palestinians to stay. However, out of 60,000 Arabs in Haifa, only about 6,000 remained, the Arab governments maintaining that they wished to clear the way for a massive assault on Israel by the Arab armies. That being the case, it should be realized that the Arab nations had ample funds to re-house the Palestinians had they so desired.

However, the tragic, and intended, result was that the refugees were forced by their own brother-peoples to remain festering in transient camps on Israel's borders as a political and practical weapon. In a further ironic tragedy, Lebanon—part of the Biblical Land of Canaan and historically precious to Jew and Arab alike—is today decimated by war due to Israel's mounting frustration and consequent desire to crush once and for all the incessant murderous attacks on her people by the PLO.

There are on both sides, as Mr. Ellison forcefully tells, equal moral arguments. It appears, however, that anti-Israel feeling in America is often fostered by those who, deliberately or otherwise, remain steadfastly unaware of the historical realities.

—Drummond Riddell
Hollywood

# INTERIM MEMO:

Column speaks for itself. But the letters following the column are interesting. Jon Douglas West surfaces again, in response to a previous letter from one of my readers. Also, a "Lucy McNulty" opens her mouth, praising the hell out of Mr. West for his efforts against the Ellisonian AntiChrist. The really interesting part of all this is that comparison of the letters showed they were typed on the same machine. So either "Lucy McNulty" was "Jon Douglas West" in drag, or it was Mr. West's girl friend. Different signature, but that doesn't mean much. Anyone as determined as "West" to hide his true identity wouldn't have much difficulty asking a friend to sign a bogus name. Nothing from the private eye I'd hired to locate this guy. Which got the man upset. He'd never been stymied before, swore he'd find out who this clown was, and I just smiled. This was fun fun fun underneath the California sun.

*Letters reprinted with permission from the* L.A. Weekly

# The Great Hydrox/Oreo Cookie Conspiracy

Here in this dank sub-basement, with the flickering light of the single candle casting its wan glow across our conspiratorial faces, I can now reveal to you the insidious particulars of the Great Hydrox/ Oreo Cookie Conspiracy. I know you'll forgive me the melodramatic circumstances of this, our first cell meeting. *They* are ruthless, as I'll outline in a moment, and were *They* aware that we've gathered here like this, as an underground effort to expose *Them,* our chances of surviving the day would be no better than that of an unsplit infinitive in a Judith Krantz novel, a kindly thought toward women in a Brian De Palma movie, a can of pork scrapple at a Chassidic rabbinical student picnic, a sentence sans the word "man" in the mouths of Cheech and Chong. Oh, how I do go on.

I hope you all came here by devious routes, confided in no one either your purpose or your destination, and that even in the absence of a blood-oath you are prepared to take on vast, merciless and inimical forces. I would not involve you, common citizens unused to ·guerilla warfare, had not the sitution grown too large for a single Zorro action. Thank you for coming.

I've long been aware that *They* are using our national dining habits as one more route to the total bastardization of our taste, yet another front on which they wage war against High Art and the Better Things in Life. Why, well may you ask, do *They* seek to do this to us? Because, I respond with barely any prompting, a nation surfeited with the trivial will never question why Real Art (which Susan Sontag tells us "has the capacity to make us nervous"), which has the quality of asking embarrassing questions and examining the dark corners, is being driven out.

As bad money drives out good, so trivial overwhelms and washes away High Art.

Sidney Sheldon sells millions of copies and no one reads Borges. The Human League and Soft Cell fly off the racks while Pergolesi and Jean-Michel Jarre languish. *The Paper Chase* can't pull the Nielsen numbers but *The Dukes of Hazzard* gets renewed even without its stars. Wendy's choke-and-puke becomes standard fare for a generation of kids who cannot get with the taste of clams casino or gnocchi. And anyone who thinks the films of John Landis or John Carpenter are not the highest level of New Art is labeled an old fogey by the jamooks and yipyops who work for *Them*.

For the most part it is the inarticulate conspiracy of those who have been stunned by the hammer.

But *They* have gone too far, have grown suicidally flagrant when they attempt to bludgeon us into accepting the devolution of superior junk food. As an old fogey revealed to one and all by a communicant to the letter column of the *Weekly* in the previous number, I remember with pleasure when Hostess Cupcakes were not filled with that glucose glop that looks like elephant cum and tastes like mucilage. I remember when a Clark Bar was made of genuine chocolate and for a nickel you had enough to sustain you through two quarters of a game played on real grass.

And I knew the difference between Hydrox and Oreo.

Oh, yes, my fellow conspirators, there *is* a difference. A big difference. It is the difference all enlightened junkoids perceive in the admonition to keep one's eye on the doughnut and not on the hole.

Insofar as Oreos and Hydroces are concerned, keep your taste buds on the cookie and not on the filling.

Since my youth I knew the thrill of the ebony chocolate cookie. Chilled in the fridge. Snapping fresh and mysterious, a cookie that spoke of dark times before the written word, the wind blowing across the top of the pyramids, savored 'neath the Hanging Gardens of Babylon. The Hydrox cookie; the Stabat Mater of junk food, the Dusenberg of packaged dreck, the Lou Gehrig of supermarket flotsam. Shelley would have written odes to the Hydrox. Woollcott would have tossed off a dozen *bon mots* to its grandeur. Helen would have given Paris the air and the glorious Hydrox would have ensorceled the topless towers of Ilium.

What we're talking here is one senfuckingsational taste treat. And—despite last issue's letter-writer's belief that my youth was spent chiefly in standing off the raids of Visigoths in some primitive age—the blasphemous Oreo existed even then. Yes, I confess, oh my listeners, I sampled the dreaded Nabisco offering. (One must! How else, then, are we to know good from evil? Even Falwell would be out of a job if we were all flensed of the dark desires.) But one bite was sufficient. I spat it out, washed my mouth with 20 Mule Team Borax, dropped to my knees before the altar of Sunshine Hydrox and swore that lips that touch Oreo would never touch mine. (Okay, okay, no one's perfect. I've made a few exceptions. A guy can't be *entirely* celibate.)

And so, secure in my weakness for this one deadly vice, I have come down through the centuries in late night sugar-shock orgies of Twain, Conrad, Dickens, Borges and a package of cold Hydrox with non-fat milk. Like you, I lie to myself that by drinking non-fat, I will offset the ravages done to my metabolism by the heavenly Hydrox.

Then, merely by chance, some years ago I began to realize there was A HIDEOUS CONSPIRACY AFOOT! First, I saw the tv ads in which hydrocephalic children were uged to learn how to give the Oreo vileness a half-twist so the cookie could be removed without sullying the corpse-white adhesive inside. No, no, I railed, keep your eye on the cookie and not on that bird doo-doo! But *They* had already glommed onto the weakness of the young. (Sure, you assholes, protect kids from sex, but urge them on to the pornography of white creme filling!) And as time went on, I saw the horror double and treble itself.

Oreo came out with Oreo with *Double Stuf*.

Twice as much of that loathsome diabetes-inducing spackling compound. Farther and farther away from the *point* of the treat they were being led. Look, I urge you, my friends, *look* at the ingredient lists on comparable packages of Hydrox and Oreo. By law the ingredient with the greatest percentage of content must be listed first. On the Sunshine Hydrox package the first ingredient is Enriched Flour. Ah, the sweetness of the words! But, hark, look at the Nabisco Oreo package. Do you see that word, first on the list? The five terrible letters that spell out s-u-g-a-r?!

It costs nothing to make ivory glop. The more of it you can con people into thinking they want, the less quality you have to put into the cookie, which is the *raison d'être* of the chocolate sandwich cookie.

Consider the Oreo cookie. Mealy. Chocolate only in the same way that an H-bomb blast-effect is a suntan. Mendacious, meretricious, monstrously mouth-clotting. . .it is anti-cookie, the baked good personification of the AntiChrist.

But *They* are determined to have their way with your ability to perceive quality. If *They* can convince you that shit is caviar, then dog droppings and parakeet poo-poo will be sold in six-paks. And in pursuit of their nefarious conspiracy they have intimidated grocery stores, job lot buyers, food suppliers and even Mom & Pop deli owners. Make the acid test: go to a Ralphs, go to a Hughes, go to a Gelson's (don't go to a Safeway, they tried to break the grape boycott). Look down the rows of packaged cookies. There, endless flotillas of Oreos. Oreos in the 1 lb. 4 oz. package. Oreos in the 15 oz. package. Oreos with enough vile white sugar creme filling to give Cthulhu a diabetic spasm. Oreos with Double Stuf. A veritable Sargasso of poisonous Oreos. And where are the Hydroces? Look. . .look everywhere. Perhaps, if the grocer is a brave fellow, you'll find one teeny section of Hydrox, no doubt smuggled in during the dead of night when the vigilantbands of dark-hooded Oreo thugs aren't watching.

You think I jest, oh my faithful? But no! There was one small grocery in the poorest section of this city, a section where the most redolent cuts of meat were fobbed off on the citizenry, where neon lights had not yet been introduced, where the Hydrox cookies could still be found. I used to slip out past midnight, garbed all in black, and make my secret hegira to that grocery. And there I could purchase Hydrox without fear of the roaming press gangs of Oreo pistoleros coshing me over the head and selling me onto a slave boat bound for Garden Grove.

Last week, when I went for my Hydrox supply, I found that grocery burned to the ground, the owner and his family vanished. Then I knew the time had come to take a stand against the Oreo Conspiracy. *They* had gone too far.

I call on you, those gathered here in this sub-basement...to join with me. Take up sling and sickle, pitchfork and arbolest, let us move against the purveyors of Oreo awfulness. Restore to our down-trodden brethren and sistren that simple joy in tasting the sanctified dark chocolate cookie. For only in Hydrox is there salvation! Only in Hydrox will we...

What's that? Didn't you hear it? There, at the cellar door. It's...it's...*Them!* One of you is a turncoat, one of you is a secret Oreo lover. Oh, God! They're coming for us!

They'll never take me alive!

I know what they do. They send you to Garden Grove and put you in a cell and for weeks on end they brainwash you, make you eat Ding Dongs and Twinkies and Zweiback! Till an Oreo seems like heaven!

But they'll never get me...never...never...!

...mama....


# LETTERS

## More On Ellison/West

*Dear Editor:*

Let me first compliment Mr. Ellison on his skill at evading an issue and suggest that he might try a career in politics. Let me then admonish Mr. Ellison for letting his emotions override his intellect. I am referring to Mr. Ellison's column in the *L.A. Weekly* [July 9–15] in which Mr. Ellison gives a juvenile response to one letter written by a Mr. Jon Douglas West. It is my opinion that Mr. Ellison is guilty of a vast oversight in understanding the theme of J. D. West's letter: that being, the fundamental right of all people to Freedom of Speech.

Freedom of Press implies the freedom of any person or group of persons to publish and distribute their viewpoint to the public. It does not allow for libelous name calling. If Mr. West can afford the time and money most lawsuits require, he would surely have a clear cut libel suit against Mr. Ellison.

I applaud the editors of *L.A. Weekly* for printing Mr. West's letter and compliment them on putting the First Amendment into practice. A true journalistic tabloid presents two sides of an issue and *ideally* (I say, "ideally," because each news tabloid favors a particular viewpoint) allows the reader to make up his or her own mind. Perhaps the *Weekly* staff might consider devoting more space for an "open forum" of opposing viewpoints.

—Lucy McNulty


*Dear Editor:*

I am quite flattered by all the recent attention drawn to my letter [July 9–15] by Harlan and a Mr. M. J. Straczynski, a.k.a. Contributing Editor, *Writer's Digest.*

Am I anti-Semitic because I am outraged by the senseless slaughter of children, men and women for a half-assed political solution? Apparently, the PLO and the Israeli regime have carefully orchestrated the warfare, as Mr. Arafat seems to walk the streets of Beirut without fear of being killed by I.D.F. shelling. Of course, non-aligned citizens have always been relatively expendable, haven't they? Am I anti-Semitic because I am repulsed by the sight of our governor hob-nobbing with the High Society Zionists at a Beverly Hills fundraiser for the Lebanon Invasion?

I'm condoning the destruction and repression of written or electronic materials of information? Did this come to you in some arcane-like vision? I think your political ideology is showing, M.J. All these murky accusations and comparisons to America a.k.a. Nazi Germany, but nothing for our friends in the East. Stalin, Mao and Kim are certainly no newcomers to the techniques of repression, death and destruction to pursue a goal. The Khemer [sic] Rouge had a solution for the problem of book-burning in Cambodia—they simply eliminated the readers.

Are things getting so repressive, so socialized, so right-wing in America that our survival is in question? Should I charter a boat and start shuttling people to the islands? Is Ronnie listening? Are Tom and Jane listening?

—Jon Douglas West
Burbank

# INSTALLMENT 39: 16 August 82

This week I come to you in stereo.

The voice in prose—as you will discover—no less clever, conspiratorial, confessional than the voice as spoken. This week, voyage to a far place with me. The planet Quaymet, vast neon technopolis, smoldering with vice and violence beneath its two pocked moons. Quaymet: extra-temporal, extra-galactic, other-dimensional Casablanca of soiled souls and treachery by the visceral kilometer. Alien Quaymet from the ghetto of desolation at the dead end of Bluemont Boulevard to the soggy underbelly of the Neon Bowery. Quaymet: murderous, bizarre, unfathomable: where stalker and stalked change roles in the flickergasp of a moment...a moment in which the assassin fires his spinal deliquidizer, draining all fluid from the victim's spinal column...a moment in which the cornered victim turns rabid rat and strikes back using a deadly Cymblian octalizer...a moment whose full significance can be codified only in the advanced brain of Quaymet's most famous detective, the electronics wizard, futuristic shamus of a world that never knew the names Hammett and Chandler and Cain, the shadowy sleuth named Emille Song.

Come with me on Friday night, between the hours of ten o'clock and midnight, without leaving the safety and sanctity of your homes. Roll back into the past when *Lights Out* and *I Love A Mystery* and *Inner Sanctum* held you in thrall...and simultaneously roll forward into the future where golden age radio waits to be born again, free of the blight of Top 40 botulism.

Ever solicitous of your intellectual and entertainment needs, fully cognizant that you suffer blackened fingers turning the pages of this newspaper each week just to keep *au courant*, I have broadcast my net far and wide in search of new wonders to lubricate your mind's labia. And, yay, there in far St. Petersburg, Florida, last March, doing some work for the embattled Equal Rights Amendment, I found Robert Cannon and Marc Rose, 48 years divided evenly between them. "Found" them only in the sense that Columbus "found" the Amerinds on the beach. (Dateline Hispaniola, 12 October 1492: "We didn't know we were lost," a spokesman for an obscure Bahamian sect said today. "This pale as a slug dude come wadin' in off the bright blue ocean, really overdressed for the neighborhood, y'know what I mean, and he plants this truly vulgar flag right in the middle of a strictly nifty piece of top quality beachfront property, and starts yellin' he's found us, he's found us, all inna name of some broad Isabella. So we said, 'Day-O, day-O, daylight come and you better go home.' Found us, my ass. We wasn't nowhichway *lost,* sucker!")

So there I was in Florida, not my favorite place in the universe, and doing a lot of interviews and television *nuhdzing,* when my liaison gets this request for us to motor across the Causeway from Tampa for what I *thought* was going to be an interview on the ERA by these two young guys who broadcast on WMNF-FM. Well, imagine my surprise when I get to this spiffy house on 84th Avenue NE and discover that Cannon and Rose are the creators of a radio drama series, a science fiction detective series, a wonderfully clever radio drama science fiction detective series called *Dry Smoke and Whispers* that puts me in mind of Firesign Theatre and days on my belly in front of our cathedral-shaped Philco standard band radio, drinking in the aural wonders of Captain Midnight, Hop Harrigan, *The Land of the Lost* and *Quiet, Please.*

They don't want to interview me, they want me to listen to this goddam *radio show* they've been doing for a couple of years. *Dry Smoke and Whispers.*

They've turned the house on 84th Avenue NE into a studio. It's ass-deep in dubbing equipment, musical instruments, rogue sitars and freaky percussion implements, electronic recording matrices, reel-to-reel serpentry, ceramic models of Emille Song's world, paintings of Quaymet...and right in the middle of it...and them...is Alice Rose. Marc's mother; what we call in the jet set a nifty lady. Elegant, gracious, well-spoken, and utterly devoted to these two whackbats with their cobbled-up visions of Lemincott Syrup Dragons, blotus fish, Troid rock groups and radioactive werewolves.

I am seduced by her affection for them. They play a demo tape. I'm amused and captivated at the professional quality and the depth of imagination. Emille Song and his Watsonlike sidekick, Professor Henchard the weapons expert, come to life for me. I understand why this offbeat labor of love has become a South Florida underground sensation. Rose tells me he's done over 145 different voices for the show; he writes all the music; every bit of the sound effects and editing is done right here. As Alice beams with love.

And then they play me a section of another show, *QBS Today,* and it turns out to be a marvelously inventive news broadcast from the mythical Quaymet. And next they're planning to do a radio series called *Anomaly Calling,* little 25 minute fantasy stories in the vein of *Inner Sanctum* or *Escape.*

Boy oh boy, I say to them, this is what the people of Los Angeles need to hear. This stuff is cleverer than hell and fresh and imaginative and why the dickens don't I *schlep* some of these tapes back home

334

with me and see if I can con someone at a radio station in Elay into running them one night, and I'll do a column on them, and maybe people will listen in, and maybe if they like this stuff as much as I do they'll get the station to contract with you for regular broadcast rights.

And they said whoopdedoo like the guy in the Sparkletts commercial, and we all joined hands and danced around in a ring. As Alice Rose beamed.

So I brought the tapes back and I called Mike Hodel, who has been hosting *Hour 25* for the last ten years over KPFK-FM (90.7 MegaHerz on your FM dial), and I said, "Michael, I have got for you a deal the like of which you ain't gonna believe," and he replied with a testament to the friendship we've ripened over a decade, "Piss off, Ellison, no more moron ideas from you. I'm still paying off on the penguin ranch and the chocolate-covered-pickle-on-a-stick-with-whipped-cream-in-the-warts investment."

It took all my efforts of unleased charisma, plus half a dozen prints in extremely clear focus of a recent scene at the Bide-A-Wee Rent-By-The-Minute Motel on Cahuenga, between a nameless gentleman who wears very thick-lensed glasses and a small but intense group comprised of four little ladies wearing swim fins, mukluks, day-of-the-week panties and rubber gloves, a Hollywood High School basketball player bearing a marked resemblance to the late Montgomery Clift, a short Latino gentleman in clocked socks and brandishing a goldfish bowl, two chickens, a member of the LAPD narco squad in garter belt and Carmen Miranda earrings, three San Pedro Hell's Angels, and a parsnip in a pear tree, addressed to a woman named Nancy (no last names please), before Michael Hodel decided that, yes, it would be in the interests of giving young talent a break to devote an evening of *Hour 25* to *Dry Smoke and Whispers.*

I'm holding on to the negatives.

And that is why, oh my faithful, that tomorrow night, Friday the 20th of August, at 10:00 PM on KPFK-FM (90.7 on your dial), you can hear your obedient servant, introducing you to the brainchildren of Marc Rose and Bob Cannon, as *Hour 25* takes you to Quaymet, to walk those mysterious, foggy streets where detective Emille Song has unraveled the puzzle of "The Blaydenbrook Horror," solved the "Murder on the Huddleston Ferry," survived the "Night of the Eclipsoid Man," and brought to book both "The East-End Reaper" and "The Assassins of Hadragule." For two hours (unless we run over), this column will come to you in stereo. Read the column, see the movie! No, hold it, that's not right. Read the column, hear the radio!

Tune in for *Dry Smoke and Whispers,* for *Anomaly Calling,* and for details of the autograph party this Saturday at Dangerous Visions in the Valley. Yes, of course, we all want to help young talent like Bob and Marc (keep beaming, Alice), but old fogeys like Ellison have to live, too; and what with STALKING THE NIGHTMARE available for the first time at Lydia Marano's Dangerous Visions bookstore, with your humble servant plonking his ass there from 2–5:00, signing anything that doesn't try to run away from the pen, why it's just a feast of reason for the readers of this column this weekend.

And they say Los Angeles is a cultural wasteland.

## INSTALLMENT 40: 20 August 82

# INTERIM MEMO:

By the beginning of September 1982, when this installment was published, my private eye—frustrated to the
point where he had become obsessed by "Jon Douglas
West"—had thrown in the towel. He assured me that if
there was such a creature as was known by the name Jon
Douglas West, he was a miracle of contemporary camou-
flage. There were no records, there was no trace, there be
no trail. It was clear at this point that I'd been correct in
my assumption that "West" (and probably some of the
"supporters" of West in letters to the *Weekly*) were
pseudonyms. And then, suddenly, one night I received a
phone call from a woman who would not give me her
name. I like to think of her as Glinda, the Good Witch of
the North. What she told me prompted the last fillip of this
40th installment. And in the Afterword to this volume I'll
tell you what happened. That is, if the snow man doesn't
come in our house and sit by the gas stove until he melts
into a puddle of molasses, I'll tell you about Uncle Wiggily
and the Dreaded Jon Douglas West.

Gee, it's lonely at the top.

And if you believe that one, I've got some slivers off the True Cross to sell you, real cheap.

The problem is, it *ain't* lonely at the top. It's so damned crowded one can hardly turn over in bed at night without half a dozen total strangers complaining you've stolen the blanket.

What prompts these thoughts is a remark by some pencil-necked geek dropped in a letter to *Rolling Stone* or some other magazine (I forget which, but it doesn't matter) soon after John Lennon was murdered. This jerk—what Mike Hodel would have called a "zero-charisma"—opined that yeah, it was sorry sad that Lennon was dead, but after all, it *was* his own fault...if he hadn't wanted to get killed he wouldn't 've gotten famous, would he?

Now before you shake your head and mumble, "What a bean-brain!" stop and consider how many times *you've* had the same quality and kind of rumination. How many times have you heard a story about some movie star whose house was robbed, whose jewels or irreplaceable *objet d'art* got boosted, and you shrugged and said, "Serves'm right. If s/he didn't want to get robbed s/he shouldn't have been living in that mansion; obvious target for a burglar." Similarly, when you were at LAX and you saw Richard Dreyfuss eating a hamburger in one of those gawdawful Host passenger puke restaurants, and you dashed up with a pencil and a chunk torn off a brown paper bag, and loomed over his shoulder and demanded, "Hey, ain't you Dustin Hoffman? Sign this for my retarded seven-year-old, will ya? She likes your movies. I've never seen one of course, I'm more partial to Burt Reynolds, but she'd get a big kick outta this. Here, just sign any old thing, and say somethin' cute to Bernice Anne Lothskiller, so she'll know I'm not makin' this up," and Richard looks up with a piece of flaccid onion hanging out of the corner of his mouth, and he says (a lot more politely than you deserve), "Not now, please. I'm eating," being kind enough not to mention that nowhere in your demand did the word *please* manifest itself, how many times did you tell your family and friend(s), and all the guys and dolls at the plant what a stuckup, rude, insensitive bastard Dreyfuss was (or Hoffman was)? Who the hell does he think he is? We pay to see his goddam movies; the least he coulda done was stop his life, miss his plane, bolt his food, let me impose on him, invade his privacy, insult him without even being smart enough to know I was doing it, and sign that greasy paper bag for my kid!

And then, so you don't look totally like a *schmuck,* you proceed to do a little Jungian analysis: "This guy's forgot his roots. He's gotten too big for his britches. He's like alla them movie stars and hoity-toity jet setters. Thinks his spoor don't stink. Forgot all the little people who made him what he is today. Sonofabitch just can't handle success. Prob'ly coked out of his brain on some expensive shit anyhow."

Lonely at the top? Not on your tintype, kiddo.

With the plague proliferation of gossip glossies like *People* and the continuing sale of those tabloids you reach for at the supermarket check-out counter, all packed to the gunwales with useless trivia guaranteed to make you think anyone who achieves even low-energy-level notoriety is a dope fiend, a profligate slut, a Nazi spy in hiding, a drunken bum who runs down schoolkids or a crazed psychopath, the monkeymass now believes it is its *right* to know everything about these men and women whose only sin is that they have achieved success.

No one bothers to tell you, when you're poor and hungry to make it, that fame—of even the smallest sort—brings with it a discon-cordant horde of moochers, self-seekers, time-wasters, dynamiting hype artists, emotionally starved groupies and just plain clipsters. One tries to be polite, but after a few years, after a few million incursions, after a ceaseless barrage of requests, demands, hard-luck stories and assorted annoyances that in and of themselves are minor but taken on sum drive you bugfuck, one looks up with flaccid onion hanging out of one's mouth and says, as sweetly as possible. "Get the hell out of my face, you spittoon; can't you see I'm trying to eat? Have a little common courtesy and a little respect for someone's privacy."

You wouldn't have the temerity to walk up to a total stranger and do it, why do you think you have the right to shoehorn yourself into the presence of an *equally* total stranger, just because you caught him or her on The Late Show?

The warped concept we're dealing with here, beyond bad taste and lousy manners, is the concomitant of the Cult of Personality. It is the sense that one is entitled to anything beyond the *work* the artist proffers. It is all *Johnny Carson Show* time. An actor performs in a screenplay, and what he or she does in that film is the gift. Beyond that, the audience is entitled to nothing. A writer commits a book; it is published. *That* is the outer limit of what the reader is entitled to.

Over the past three weeks a woman has called me repeatedly from Detroit. She phumfuh'd and stammered and couldn't speak the first couple of times. When she asked for me by name, and I said it was Ellison speaking, she got so flustered she mumbled, "Oh. Uh. . .*oh*! I wasn't prepared to speak to you." I asked her who she *thought* she'd get if she rang my number? Winston Churchill? Jonas Salk? She hung up instantly. I felt sorry for her, but I forgot it. She kept calling back. Bugging my secretary. Finally, at 2:00 AM (which is 5:00 in the morning in Detroit), she roused me out of a dead sleep, finally to make her wishes known. She'd read one of my books and didn't understand one of the stories. She wanted me to explain it to her. At two in the morning.

Why I was polite, I have no idea. I suppose it was because I recognized her voice and knew the poor thing had been trying to summon up the ego-strength to make this contact. So I tried to explain it to her. Tried. Didn't succeed. Either she was being purposely dense, or she just wanted to chat with this faceless character who'd written a book that touched her.

Finally, when it became obvious that I could not aid her in whatever her secret need was, I told her to forget it. "I've written over a thousand stories, lady. Let it go. You understand 999 of them...try to live with the knowledge that *this* one is beyond you." And she started to get very upset with me. "I didn't expect you to be rude," she said. "I've been speaking with you for fifteen minutes, and you woke me for what is, after all, lady, a matter of no concern to me. I've been polite in not telling you to fuck off. And a lot more courteous than some guy you hassled at this hour for a wrong number would be."

So she started screaming at me that I was a terrible person and she certainly never expected anyone who could write such sensitive books to be so awful to poor little her. And she vowed never again to buy one of my wretched tomes.

I said, "Thank you ever so much. It was wonderful hearing from you. Thank your mother for the chicken soup," and I hung up. For a rotten person, I sleep wonderfully well, and fall off instantly.

John Lennon gets shot by a love–hate fan, Jessica Savitch is trapped at gunpoint in her office by a viewer who fantasizes he is having an affair with her even though he's seen her only on the tube. An actor of my acquaintance is sued for paternity by a woman who lives (and has never been out of) a small Texas town...a town the actor has never even heard of. Three times in the last six months I've had my garbage stolen. For what purpose, I have no idea. Don't ask. I just hope they eat hearty.

Lonely at the top?

You should live so long.

It is so bloody crowded here in the *middle,* that life at the top for Richard Dreyfuss and John Irving and Itzhak Perlman and Jackie Onassis must be like an invasion of the *marabunta* army ants. And before you shrug and say, "Well, it's his own damned fault; if he didn't want to be bothered he wouldn't've gotten famous," remember that no one told any of us precisely how much a lot of you have been warped by *People* magazine.

Oh, and by the way...this column will be giving that world-famous letter-writer, Mr. Jon Douglas West of Burbank, a little touch of notoriety very shortly—not next time—but soon. All in aid of proving that it need not be lonely at the bottom, either.

Fun 'n' games is comin', folks. Don't get lost.

A little more about how lonely it *ain't,* at the top.

Part two the last: picking up checks and "good causes." Having less to do with social conscience and responsibility than it does with whipping guilt on someone. Also, to borrow the title of a remarkable book first published in 1841, it has much to do with "extraordinary popular delusions and the madness of crowds." (Now available in paperback, I cannot commend this astonishing study of mass movements strongly enough.)

Having been—like most of you—scuffling for a buck all of my life, having run away from home at age thirteen and having earned my living since that age (and never having been trained for any acceptable trade I have often noted that I am a self-made man...thereby demonstrating the horrors of unskilled labor), the nuances of Living High escaped me till I came to Hollywood and Struck It Rich. F'rinstance, when one is poor, and one dines out with chums and buddies, one never thinks much about who'll take the check. Automatically it gets divvied up. Okay, who had the tuna on white and the little nut cup? David, that'll be another thirty cents for you; they charged extra for the dijon mustard. We need another thirteen cents all around to make 15% for the tip.

Goes without saying.

But after about five years of my having made enough decent money that I could actually ask a few friends to go out to dinner, on me, I began to notice something that troubled me profoundly. I'd get a call from people I'd known intimately for years, and they'd say let's get together for dinner Tuesday, and I'd say terrific, and come Tuesday a bunch of us would assemble, me with a date, them with dates, and we'd score some Szechuan or Magyar, and when the check came it would automatically wind up in my pocket.

Went without saying.

Now, apart from my tendency to grab for checks anyhow—one tries to be a *mensch*—and apart from occasions where it was very clear I was hosting the feed, I began to notice that it was *assumed* I was paying. No one even made a move. At first I sorta kinda shrugged it off on the grounds that I was working and some of them weren't, or I was making more than some of them, so it seemed reasonable: it's what friends do: the one who has, puts it out for them as hasn't. Goes without saying.

But it went on for years, and I started to get cranky about it. It was being taken for granted: Ellison will pick up the tab. (Now let me hasten to add that this didn't obtain for *all* my friends. Arthur and Lydia always chipped in or reciprocated in other ways; Walter Koenig and the Barkins never mooched; Silverberg and I alternated unless one of us could bamboozle the other into thinking it was his turn; many others I don't recall right now were upstanding in this respect.) But after a while it became obvious to me that I was *expected* to extend this largesse.

I didn't mind doing it enough to call a halt, but in my gut I resented that *no one made the move.*

The same thing has started happening with this column.

Because these weekly outings seem to have reached many of you in a way that made you want to *do* something about whatever contretemps or inequity I shared with you, it is now perceived as a vehicle for mass movement. On a small scale, surely; but nonetheless a great many of you flex and move. (And at this point in the writing, I will start saying *we* rather than *I*. In the purest sense of a gestalt, we are partners in this column. One does not cast out words into a vacuum. If Helen Keller falls in the forest, is there a sound? Without exchange and abreaction it is merely idle chatter unheard on the wind. That's why I answer your mail every six weeks and why Jon Douglas West interests me so.)

What has begun to happen is that we are being deluged with appeals for attention. We are being asked to devote whole columns to endless "good causes." They range from public presentations such as a Jackie Wilson memorial concert, promotion of which is of slight interest to me...through apparently urgent matters such as the campaign to save Mono Lake, about which I know less than I need to know to compel your attention...to crusades in which I believe fervently, such as NARAL's fight to defeat the anti-abortion Helms Bill and Hatch Constitutional Amendment in the U.S. Senate. (Don't worry about this last one, gang; your letters and phone calls have already been conveyed to Cranston and Hayakawa; and I understand through NARAL's Washington offices that phone calls and mail to Senators is running 200 to 1 against Helms/Hatch.)

Is it lonely at the top? Hell, it's so belly-to-butt up there that one imagines the few courageous souls like Alan Alda and Jane Fonda and Ed Asner and Vanessa Redgrave and Elmo Zumwalt, who are not easily intimidated by ridicule or hate mail, whose names can be found signed to encyclicals intended to enlist your support in aid of "good causes," being unable to go out for dinner without the arm being put on them.

The problem is that none of us can be in more than four places at once. If you are concerned about nuclear proliferation, the anti-nuke forces can keep you busy seven days a week stuffing envelopes and soliciting funds. If you think combatting the Moral Majority is the burning issue of our times then you can fall into your bed exhausted every night after having fought them on the fronts of creationism, censorship, political pressure, school prayer, women's rights or a dozen other brushfire areas...and you'll find you had no time during the day to take in your dry cleaning, write that college application, see your lover, or put gas in the car. If it's working for citizen review boards of cops who use the choke-hold too freely, campaigning for an assemblyperson dedicated to stopping the construction of condos in the hills, banning handguns, supporting anti-Klan groups or funding arts programs in deprived neighborhoods...you can never do enough. There is an infinitude of pain and unfairness in the world, and one never knows where to begin. Nor do those pressures on our social conscience ever give us a moment's peace. One can never do enough, not even if we devote our waking hours *in toto*. As for Toto, he regrets ever having returned from Oz, where the biggest problem is an occasional Wicked Witch.

It goes further. Not just the sincere and imploring letters asking for publicity in support of Dr. Stanley W. Jacob, who has been indicted for the alleged bribing of an FDA official in conjunction with his having prescribed the unregulated drug DMSO; not just the urgent call for donations and writings in support of Handgun Control, Inc. against the stepped-up advertising of the National Rifle Association; not just the appeal to promote and speak at the NOW rally in Westwood. It goes much further.

It proceeds past these heartfelt gardyloos in aid of solutions to complex and important social problems; it gets into the area of who picks up the check, and how they whip guilt on you if you choose *not* to pick up the check.

In the past few weeks, I suppose because so many of you came out to CBS to picket against the removal of the *Lou Grant* series and so many of you came out to fill At My Place in Santa Monica when Susan Rabin sang (she'll be back there on September 12th for those of you who missed her first time around), we've been hustled by friends and acquaintances to run columns puffing restaurants, to sell gimcrack novelties, to rhapsodize over this or that young rock group, to serve— in short—a particular narrow interest.

I'm dismayed at the friends and casual acquaintances who are taking a new-found interest in seeking our fellowship. It is dismaying because it's transparent. They want us to pick up their checks. And I've had to say no to them. If I've managed to engender any trust with these essays, then I have the responsibility of not permitting you to be manipulated.

I've lost a friend of some years' standing because I told him no, I wouldn't hype for him in these pages. What he wanted you to get excited about was bogus, and would only serve to make him a few bucks. That isn't why we're here. He is fit; he can earn his own living; we have to; so can he.

We can only do so much. Each of us has a built-in survival mechanism, and it is a given that we will spend ninety percent of our day making sure we hobble on into tomorrow. But we are not sloths, we are not members of the Sleeping Wad, and ten percent of our day is available to "good causes."

As long as we dedicate that ten percent every day, and occasionally get so fired up we expend sixty percent of our energies for a brief spurt...we have nothing to be ashamed of. Nor should we permit those who apply the pressure to whip guilt on us if we say, no, I'm sorry, I can't Save The Goshawk or Defeat Litterbuggery, because I'm busy at the moment auctioneering for the ACLU and preparing a public presentation for the recently torched Hollywood Library.

Yeah, we want you to stay awake, stay alert, and give a shit about the rest of the human race; but you're entitled to a good night's sleep and some lighthearted moments, too.

Don't forget: free-floating guilt is society's way of saying you'll be drained to the husk if you don't operate in moderation. This warning comes to you through the good offices of the Surgeon General and a very very weary columnist who said, last week, when a check was presented: "I think this one's yours."

# Interim Memo:

Mention is made in this column of Senator John Schmitz. Those who live outside California may be unaware of this pimple. He is a Far Right eggsucker against abortion, civil rights, feminism, First Amendment freedoms, decent treatment for prisoners...in short, the usual grab-bag of fatheaded attitudes. But Schmitz is one of those classic whited sepulchers who's always shouting about God, Motherhood, Apple Pie and the Amurrrican Way...who got slapped with a terrific lawsuit by attorney Gloria Allred for calling her and other feminists "bull dykes"... who made open remarks about "kikes and spicks" for television...and who, it was revealed to our utter delight, had fathered a baby by some woman not his wife, and the baby was removed from the mother's care because of serious abuse...a whole can of worms that, once opened, revealed the Fascistic Schmitz to be the prime maggoty example of the meat he was always condemning.

Oh my God, just *look* at you! You ought to be ashamed of your-selves. Come crawlin' back here after Labor Day in that condition, it's a goddam disgrace! You know your mothers and I have been worried sick over you. Now you come crawlin' back looking like that; where the hell have you *been!?!* And what is that...*crap* all over your clothes. Just tell me how the hell you expect me to talk seriously to you about *anything* this week, with you in that condition? Sit down. No, not there, not with that *crap* all over you. Here, lie down on these brown paper bags. I'll get the K2R later.

*Now* what am I supposed to do with you? I was going to do some heavy duty ruminating about a statistic I heard the other day, about how 55,000 GI's were killed in the Vietnam War and how 60,000 have successfully committed suicide since the war ended, and how they don't expect that figure to peak until 1990, and about this being the ongoing cost of an immoral war that none of those sanctimonious Hallelujah Patriots want to face up to when they continue to spout off about "we coulda won if we'd really wanted to."

Yeah, I was *going* to dwell on that ugliness, but in your condition I doubt if you'd be able to *blink* at the appropriate places. And I sure as hell couldn't even get a decent tsk-tsk out of you.

So okay, this week I'll let you recover from your debauch, and I'll just do my flea imitation, jumping from item to item, in hopes your little pink eyeballs don't just roll up in your heads. Try to pay atten-tion. (Jeezus, your mothers're gonna have a cardiac when they see you. *See* you...? Wait'll they *smell* you!)

You look as though you spent four days locked up in a motel room in Visalia with Senator John Schmitz and a diseased goat.

Occassionally a typo creeps into thx colhum.

Once they fired the est graduates and Scientologists, though, things improved considerably. You must realize the *Weekly* has a wonderful humanistic policy of hiring the handicapped for these sensitive jobs, so they won't feel demeaned. Most of the time (since so many of you already speak in tongues and random squeaks), the errors aren't hard to figure out. But it has been brought to my attention by The Woman With Whom I'm Goofily, Desperately In

Love, that one typo a month or so ago gave an entirely different meaning to an important quote. Herewith, a rectification. *"Chance favors the prepared mind."* As spake by Louis Pasteur. That's *chance,* folks, not *change.*

Speaking of the Los Angeles *Weekly*—this great gray eminence that brings you not only my ramblings every seven days, but also brings you such profundities as this one from Elliott Solomon's letter to the editor last week, "like others (Ellison, et al.) who pass as writers..." which is hip-deep in profundity because after almost thirty years of making my living behind a typewriter, with thirty-eight books published, translated into eighteen languages and millions of copies sold, not to mention having won enough awards to stuff a *piñata,* Solomon the Wise is the first one to perceive that I've been *passing* as a writer (actually, I'm a bricklayer...imagine your surprise at having been so thoroughly flummoxed)—take a walk, Elliott; off the Venice Pier preferably—speaking of this paper, I am surprised to learn how few of you realize that the *Weekly* is the fourth largest paper in L.A., that its readership is somewhere between 185,000 and 212,000, that it has won *almost* enough awards to stuff a *piñata,* and just because you get it for nothing on the L.A. Basin side of the hills (while equally nifty folks in the Valley and South Bay and at newsstands all over the place pay 50¢ a shot) does not mean it is a throwaway like those mailbox stuffers offering you pullets at 62¢ a pound.

What I'm trying to tell you here, gang, is that the *Weekly* is not just another pretty face. Nor is it a tool of Reagan. Nor is it an outcall service. Nor does it even restrain Free Speech to the extent of suggesting that Elliott Solomon wouldn't know a writer if one came up and tattooed the *Rubaiyat* of Omar Khayyam on his sternum. Moving right along....

I never heard back from that guy who offered to buy me a $300 pipe in exchange for two limericks. Imagine my surprise.

For those of you who followed up my invitation to hear *Dry Smoke and Whispers* on KPFK's *Hour 25* show a few Fridays ago, and whose enthusiasm for the work of those two Florida kids was made known to Mike Hodel of KPFK, you'll be delighted to learn that the response was so great that KPFK will begin regular broadcasts of the adventures of alien detective Emille Song sometime in October. Stay tuned.

For those of you who accepted my invitation to hear Susan Rabin sing at the club called At My Place in Santa Monica five Sundays ago (where I met The Woman For Whom I Would Crawl Through Monkey Vomit On Hands And Knees Clutching A Rose Between My Teeth), be advised Susie Rabin returns this Sunday the 12th at 8:00 PM for a one-performance showcase. If you missed her last time, you'd better call for a reservation early this time: the joint was booked solid the last time.

*Please* stop sending me Hydrox! That column—as has been the case with so many columns that Elliott Solomon hasn't understood—was intended as a paradigm. For the way our taste is bastardized. Yes, I *know* you can get Hydrox at Gelson's on Riverside, Michael Schlesinger of North Hollywood. I know, I know! It was a trope, Michael, a metaphor, irony, satire, a bit of reverse-entendre; it was supposed to make you laugh hollowly, make you look over your shoulder while chuckling. *Jeezus,* Michael! (On the other hand, when you ask the countermen at Trader Joe's on Riverside at Hazeltine why they are ass-deep in Oreos without a single Hydrox anywhere on view in that "gourmet" emporium, they get a frightened look in their eyes, their voices drop, they begin to sweat and stammer, "Uh...uh... we're...stocked by Nabisco." And then they change the subject. Fast.)

Well, that looks like about all you can handle this week. I won't even get into wondering why it is that menus in Chinese restaurants are in English but the check is always written in Chinese so you can't tell if you actually had all those dishes or not, and when you ask the waiter what that little squiggle across from the $12.95 is, he always looks at you as if you'd insulted his ancestors and calls the tiny Oriental woman who takes the check from him, stares at you with narrowed eyes, snarls something that sounds like "shaoh-mee," and thrusts it back at you with a movement that makes it clear you'd better not give her any further shit if you want to continue wearing your nose under your eyes. I won't get into that.

And before we get together again next week will you fer chrissakes clean yourselves up. We run a class column here, and we reserve the right to refuse service to anyone lying on brown paper bags with all that...that...*crap* on them!

**INSTALLMENT 43:** 9 September 82

# Interim Memo:

This column may not be as sociologically important as some of the others—which may not be as sociologically important as I like to think—but it's part of the run, and we hold nothing from you, nothing. Also, this column was heavily edited by the publisher of the *Weekly*. Not the first time he'd played patty-cake with my copy, and perhaps not significant in this instance, but there was a pattern emerging, and it led at the end, to my killing the column in the *Weekly*'s pages. But for posterity, this installment appears complete here for the first time. Alert the media.

All phone numbers are, of course, in either the 213 or 818 area code areas.

The drummer to whose beat I march this week is the Editorial Gestalt, a syncopater decked out in perfection. "This issue of the *Weekly* is devoted to 'The Best in Los Angeles,'" I was told. "So if nothing has you too grouchy this time, why not give us a list of Ellison's Best," I was told.

You have but to command, effendi. Herewith: idiosyncratic, but amassed from twenty years' joy and pleasure living here in Baghdad, a random selection of unqualified recommendations.

THE BEST WAITER IN TOWN: Carlos at Pacific Dining Car.

THE BEST (NON-BLACK) BBQ: Dr. Hogly Wogly's Tyler Texas Pit Barbeque, on Sepulveda near Roscoe, in the Valley.

THE BEST DENTIST: Robert P. Knoll, in Pacific Palisades.

THE BEST FINISH CARPENTER & MASTER WOOD-WORKER: Phil Blake of Design Innovations (P.O. Box 2297, Toluca Lake 91602).

THE BEST PICTURE FRAMER: Tommy Sand of Pesha's, on Melrose.

THE BEST MATTE-DESIGNER TO GO WITH THE BEST PICTURE FRAMER: Michael Craven (466-5810) whose art deco mattes defy description.

THE BEST ATTORNEYS: The world-renowned kneecapper Henry W. Holmes, Jr.; Gloria Allred and her Doom Patrol.

THE BEST ELECTRICIAN & LIGHTING WHIZ: Dennis Smith of Pacific Architectural Design, Inc.

THE BEST CONSTRUCTION GUY: Leon Opseth (761-8329), who also takes the title of MOST HONEST CONSTRUCTION GUY.

THE BEST CUBAN FOOD IN TOWN: The Versailles on Venice Blvd.

THE BEST BICYCLE SHOP: Beverly Hills Bike.

THE BEST TYPEWRITER REPAIR: Jesus Silva of Hi-Brand Office Equipment in North Hollywood who, amazingly, makes house calls!

THE BEST FANCY TILE LAYER: Earl De Castro (353-4239), who does with stone what Louise Nevelson does with wood.

THE BEST ISRAELI FOOD: Tempo Restaurant in Encino.

THE BEST CROISSANTS: Michel Richard on S. Robertson and on Ventura Boulevard in Studio City.

THE BEST STAINED GLASS WINDOWS TO ORDER: Barbara Hunsinger on Magnolia in Sherman Oaks.

THE BEST PLACES TO BUY ART DECO: H. Frank Jones and Thanks For The Memories on Melrose.

THE BEST HOT DOG IN THE WORLD, INCLUDING L.A.: Pink's, *naturellement.*

THE BEST TCHOTCHKE SHOPS: Fantasies Come True on Melrose and Propinquity on Santa Monica. Selections arrived-at by totalization of vast sums dropped by your columnist for useless-but-spiffy items over a five year period.

THE BEST OVERALL BAKERY IN TOWN: Brown's Victory Bakery near Coldwater Canyon on Victory in the Valley.

THE BEST LOAF OF CORN RYE WITH CARAWAY SEED: Nate'N'Al's, in Beverly Hills. Also the best chicken soup with kreplach.

THE BEST FRENCH TOAST BREAKFAST: The Yellow House, on West Channel Road out in Pacific Palisades, down near the Coast Highway.

THE BEST CHEESEBURGER FOR THOSE OF US WHO LIKE IT NEAT AND NOT SLOPPED UP WITH CHILI, PEANUT BUTTER, DEAD MICE OR MAYONNAISE: "Raldo's" on Moorpark at Fulton in the Valley (ask for Rose and tell her Harlan sent you).

THE BEST GOURMET THAI FOOD: The Tepparod Tea House, off Vermont.

THE BEST CHINESE FOOD: The Mandarin in Beverly Hills, though the Shanghai Winter Garden on Wilshire cannot be touched for its lemon chicken, from which it is to die.

THE BEST ONION RINGS: Charlie Brown's in Woodland Hills (but you have to call ahead and ask for the Manager, Jane, and tell her you want the thick ones they just took off the menu). A near second place is the heaping plate served at Hamburger Henry's in Santa Monica.

THE BEST FRENCH ONION SOUP: Shain's, in Sherman Oaks. (Not only is it terrific, but when you get halfway down, and you've eaten all the cheese, you can ask for a fresh larding to top off.)

THE BEST HOME COOKING: Maurice and Verna's Snack'N'-Chat on Pico.

THE BEST MEXICAN FOOD (DINNER UNDER $5.00): El Rancho on Ventura Boulevard in Sherman Oaks.

THE BEST MEXICAN FOOD (DINNER OVER $10.00): Antonio's on Melrose (don't miss the beef *molé*).

THE BEST PLACE TO HAVE ITALIAN FOOD WHILE WATCHING MOVIE STARS AND/OR MAFIA BUTTON-MEN: Adriano's in the Beverly Glen Circle or Sarno's Caffe Dell'Opera on

Vermont. Matteo's and Martoni's no longer draw the heavy-duty killers.

THE BEST FAST FOOD CHICKEN: Louisiana Fried Chicken on 6th near Alvarado. The local recipe version of New Orleans's Popeye's.

THE BEST PRIME RIB WITH A PROPER YORKSHIRE PUDDING AND NOT ONE OF THOSE TOOTH-BREAKING POPOVERS THEY TRY TO PASS OFF AS A YORKSHIRE PUDDING: Lawry's Prime Rib on La Cienega and Gulliver's in the Marina.

THE BEST RECORD SHOPS: Tower Classical on Sunset and Aron's Records on Melrose.

THE MOST INTERESTING MYSTERY PERSONALITY: Jon Douglas West. Lucy McNulty and Mike Kingsley come in close seconds. But that's another column.

THE BEST WRITER IN LOS ANGELES: Modesty forbids me.

Space does not permit me to go on in this vein any longer. I know, however, with a certainty that approaches epiphany, that within mere moments of this column hitting the streets, you will be at your postcards, correcting my thinking and apprising me of the apposite selections in each category. Like all of you, be assured, I am of an open mind and only wait to be introduced to your superlative choices, each and every one of which will dwarf mine own by their Olympian wonderfulness.

Incidentally, the autograph party for my new book, STALKING THE NIGHTMARE, was so successful at Dangerous Visions in Sherman Oaks five weeks ago, that we've decided to give all of you who feel you need inoculations to visit the Valley a chance. I'll be reprising the gig at A Change of Hobbit (1853 Lincoln Blvd. in Santa Monica, phone: GREAT SF) this Saturday the 18th, from 2–5:00 PM. Buy a book; help send this boy to camp.

**INSTALLMENT 44:** 20 September 82

Nixon and Agnew finally had their way with us. Because we had been fighting for ten years, resisting LBJ and Tricky Dick, we saw the end of the Vietnam War and Watergate as the triumph of Good over Evil; and we relaxed. We rested because we were weary. Even the most reactionary of us had seen the face of Corruption, upper lip beaded with sweat, mouth saying I am not a crook, and the face had been wiped off our television sets...and we thought we were safe forever. But as the man said, the price of freedom is eternal vigilance. And we mellowed out for too many lazy afternoons. We wanted national self-respect again so badly that we invested poor Jimmy Carter with a potency of white magic he did not truly possess. And we were not vigilant, and while we dozed all on a summer's day, the Schmitzes and the Falwells and the Wattses and the Reagans slipped in and finished the job for Nixon and Agnew.

On November 3rd we go into battle again.

I am determined we will not sleep through this one.

Our implacable foe is an old one. The National Rifle Association. The battlefield is Proposition 15. California's Handgun Violence Prevention Act. Polls tell us it will pass if we marshal our efforts. Six weeks ago it was pro-passage by twenty points. Last week it was pro-passage by only four points. In the interim the NRA jumped the gun—as is their wont, gun-wise—and rather than waiting till Labor Day, the traditional date for political campaigning, began a million dollar mixed media advertising saturation campaign to plant early doubt in the minds of the electorate.

They are frightened. The banning of handguns in Morton Grove and Evanston, Illinois has shown them that their throw-down grip on us may be loosening. And the money is pouring in to stop Prop. 15. As of August 16 the anti-15 forces had received $565,500 in support funds from gun manufacturers (all but one out-of-state).

The California gun lobby has seen the moving finger taking aim. As one with the NRA, it understands that passage of Prop. 15 in California, a bellwether state of public opinion, means an important advance toward a national gun control law, something the arms manufacturers who shadow-back the NRA fear worse than atomic annihilation.

Californians Against Street Crime and Concealed Weapons is the cutting edge of our forces. They have recently been joined by the Washington-based Handgun Control, Inc. to mount a concerted effort against the gun lobby's war chest and media blitz. They have lined up five of California's most prominent police chiefs to cut radio and tv commercials. Those spots will go a long way toward regaining the lost public opinion points subverted by NRA advertising.

But they need help. They need money, of course, Yeah, you get tapped once again. (Send a check to Californians Against Street Crime; 3315 Motor Avenue; Los Angeles 90034.) But more than that, they need you out there spreading the word. They need your fire and your determination that *this* time the babies with popguns won't bulldoze the rest of us with scare tactics.

Call for an information packet—204-6690—and send some bucks. And just to fire up your blood for this crusade, I'm departing from my policy of not reprinting material I've previously written, by inclusion here of an essay I wrote last December. On December 9th, 1980—the day after John Lennon was assassinated—I received a call from Julie Simmons, editor of *Heavy Metal* magazine. Through tears she asked me to write an editorial pleading for gun control. I sat down the next day, angry and miserable, and wrote what follows. It brought more mail to the magazine than anything they had ever published. It brought out of the slime and dust a vomitous spewing of madness and violence from members of the Klan, from neo-Nazis, from babies with popguns whose verbal insanity was more shocking than the essay; and those letters caused hundreds of readers to turn away from the gun lobby. I hope this reprinting of the essay produces the same maniacal outpouring of hate mail. The more of these twistos you see reveal themselves, the faster you'll be in sending big bucks to the Prop. 15 forces.

Between now and November 3rd we'll write more about this. It's urgent, it's a matter of life and death, and it's righteously intended to stanch the terror the NRA will try to use to confuse you. But we can win if you truly believe you need only

### Fear Not Your Enemies

John Lennon's on the menu. The worms are having him for dinner.

It's a fucking banquet: Martin Luther King, Bobby Kennedy, Luke Easter, Sarai Ribicoff, Stella Walsh, Lyman Bostock, Michael Halberstam, and one hundred and fifty assorted nonentities slaughtered each week, every week, here in our macho democracy. Nonentities, that is, to all but the mothers, fathers, sisters, brothers, husbands, wives, children, lovers and friends to whom each of those nonentities meant something.

364

I'd have included JFK in that list, but we all know *that* executive ticket-punch was part of a giant conspiracy.

And I don't want to bother with pitiful little conspiracies that include only maybe the CIA, the Mafia, the FBI, the Dallas police, Communists and anti-Castro terrorists. That kind of conspiracy is shirred eggs and squashed potatoes. What I like dealing with is the *big* conspiracy, the one *you're* part of.

Thought we didn't know you were high up in the order of the big cabal, didn't you? Thought we didn't notice, right? Well, we noticed; so don't go slobbering over the loss of John Lennon, you cowardly punk. Don't beat your breast as you stand out there in the cold behind the NYPD sawhorses across the street from the Dakota, kiddo. We're on to you, and as far as I'm concerned you're as guilty as Mark David Chapman of pumping those four shots into Lennon's back.

You didn't cry for 69-year-old ex-Olympic star Stella Walsh on December 4th when some sonofabitch left her face-down in the parking lot of a discount department store on Cleveland's near East side, wiping out the 65 track records she set in her extremely worthy lifetime. You didn't cry when Luke Easter was blown away on March 29, 1979, outside the Cleveland Trust; probably because you didn't give a shit that the old black man hit twenty-five homeruns in two months in 1949 and played a lot of first base for the Indians. You didn't cry for twenty-three-year-old Sarai Ribicoff, senselessly shot to death in the course of a petty holdup outside Chez Helene in L.A.'s Venice section; most likely because she was Senator Abe Ribicoff's niece *and* a Jew *and* a newspaper reporter and hell, that's three strikes right there; no pity for the rich, the powerful, the vocal and the members of the International Money Conspiracy. And you're probably only wailing over Lennon because it's in the air and gives you a chance to vent some of your fear and frustration. But you belong to the big cabal, chum, and we see through your disingenuous sorrow.

You started your membership sucking up the BB gun ads in copies of *The Incredible Hulk* and *Batman* comics. You paid dues every time you sat in a movie theater and watch the fever-sick violence dreams of *Dressed to Kill* or *The Texas Chainsaw Massacre* and went down the line proclaiming twisted crap like that "high art" as do some of our more prominently brain-damaged critics. You rose in the ranks every time you accepted the eloquent vocabulary of a bullet in the gut or a punch in the mouth as the final statement of any argument on *Starsky & Hutch* or *Charlie's Angels*. So now you're a fully-paid-up, card-carrying psychotic doting on the wonderful full-color panels in *Heavy Metal* that show some poor slob with his head blown apart like a casaba melon.

And you're as much against gun control and our soon-to-be-installed Chief Executive, Mr. Reagan. And you know what *he* said, mere hours after Chapman's Charter Arms .38 special had *its* say?

Well, Ronnie said, "I've never believed that gun control laws would help reduce violence. I believe in the kind of legislation we had in California. If somebody commits a crime and carries a gun when doing it, add five to fifteen years to the prison sentence."

I'm glad so many of you voted for that kind of asshole thinking. Mr. Reagan's terrific use-a-gun-go-to-jail law is so effective that Los Angeles has become Murder City: homicides for the first ten months of 1980 were over 800 in the city proper and over 1500 in the county.

Reagan, you crepuscular old fart, what the hell is wrong with you!?! Who gives a damn how long Chapman lies up in the slam? *Lennon is dead,* you puddingbrain. *Dead.* Revenge don't beat the bulldog. Chapman wasn't some amoral mugger making his living in the streets ripping off wallets and tv sets. He was a nut. Like all the other nuts who commit a murder every 24 minutes, night and day, every day of the year in this country. When the hell will you read the statistics, Reagan? When will you realize that over fifty percent of all the gun slayings every year are committed not by the dreaded composite darkie-mestizo-latino alley killer but by friends and relatives, by angry lovers and total strangers when you screwed them out of a parking space or give them the finger in a moving car. Fifty percent and more: stupid accidents where a ten-year-old kid sprays his brain matter across the bedroom wall playing with Daddy's surrogate penis, the bureau drawer Luger; heat of passion arguments in which your girl friend opens up your stomach so your intestines start unwinding on the carpet like a Duneworld sandworm; deadly misunderstandings like the one that killed baseball star Lyman Bostock, a case of mistaken identity that didn't mean a damn because Bostock was on the menu.

How about that, gentle reader, out there crying because Lennon bit the dust, how about that you're a member of the big conspiracy headed by Uncle Ronnie? You like the tag?

Don't give me no shit about how *you* ain't in on it, Chuckles. You're *in* on it! Because if you weren't, you'd be doing something about it, instead of sitting there on your ass growing lesions on your brain watching television and putting all that good dope down your neck and reading half-witted sci-fi trash and eating junk food till you're too lazy to get out of the chair to take a dump. If you *weren't* part of the conspiracy to keep the National Rifle Association one of the biggest goddam lobbies in Washington, you'd be sending all your spare cash to Handgun Control, a *citizens'* lobby in Washington.

And don't hide behind that god-fearing gobbledegook, either. I've had it up to here with the Rev. Jerry Falwell and Ernest Angley and Billy Graham and all the rest of those tv clowns perverting the tenets of the Judeo-Christian ethos with their non-specific mumble about moral rectitude. They want to censor books and movies and tv and magazines to fit some ancient worn-out idea of purity, but all those fundamentalist millions who'll deluge a sponsor with vengeful letters because some model exposed her thigh in an advertisement won't lift a finger or a buck to beat the NRA lobby at its own game. And *you* know why: because all those whited sepulchers own guns...or if they don't, they actually believe that the Constitution gives any dip who can sign his or her name to a handgun application the right to own a .357 Magnum.

Because that's all the same game.

It's removal from reality. And only a step or two from "Vengeance is mine, sayeth the Lord" to seeing oneself as the instrument of that vengeance. Who knows what leper's soup steams in Chapman's cauldron of a brain? And who cares? If he hadn't been able to get a gun in Hawaii so easily, he might not have been able to get Lennon so simply. Yeah, I know: he could have knifed him, garrotted him, hit him with a 2x4. But not from five feet away. Yeah, people kill people...with guns.

I have no tears in me for John Lennon. I've used them all up on King and Kennedy and a woman I once loved who was raped and then murdered—with a handgun—in the parking lot of a bowling alley in the San Fernando Valley.

So you can dry your public show of misery, li'l heavymetal babies. When it's fashion time for roller disco or cowboy boots or electronic wargaming or freebasing or whatever the panhandlers have in store to separate you from your bucks next season, you'll forget. And you'll renew membership in the big conspiracy.

Let me leave you with these words from the Polish poet Edward Yashinsky, who survived a Nazi prison camp only to die in a Russian one. "Fear not your enemies, for they can only kill you; fear not your friends, for they can only betray you. Fear only the indifferent, who permit the killers and betrayers to walk safely on the earth."

And on November 3, vote YES on Prop 15.

Or cop to being one of the indifferent members of the big conspiracy that killed John Lennon. Goo goo goo joob.

Or, as John once wrote: *Happiness is a warm gun.*

**INSTALLMENT 45**: 24 September 82

## The Road to Hell, Part I

New Horrors! It may be, to my chagrin and your disdain, that I have created and unleashed a Frankincense Monster.

What this is about (in two parts so relevant correspondence can be run uncut) is midgets, attacking innocent bystanders, being politically correct, knowing the true face of the enemy, and the sorry realization that merely because one subscribes to worthy ideals and noble causes does not necessarily mean that the supporter of these ideals and causes is any less likely to be personally wrongheaded or an asshole.

371

Passim this week's column you will find an advertisement, reduced in size from its full-page incarnation in many national magazines (including *California*), an advertisement for CasaBlanca Fans. Take a moment and read the ad. Let's all start together.

Now we come to Ms. Joanne Gutreimen, whose name has appeared in this column several times in the past. Ms. Gutreimen is no ordinary peruser of "An Edge In My Voice." She is an informed, erudite, intelligent woman fully deserving of our condignity for her frequent postcards suggesting topics for discussion. I have, at least twice, flown high on the wings of her suggestions, and thanked her profusely for her good offices. Having slathered that butter, it now falls to me, onerous task, of baring my fangs against this card-carrying Saint.

Along about the 8th of the month I received in the mail from Ms. Gutreimen a copy of the advertisement you've just read, and the following letter, reprinted *in toto:*

"Dear Harlan:

"How about a story with not one, but two happy endings? First happy ending: never again will I underestimate the efficacy of writing letters. Contrary to what I'd always thought, large numbers of (protest) letters are not always needed to make a point. You had said that, but I couldn't quite accept it.

"Enclosed is an ad that appeared in the June '82 issue of *California* magazine. Take a look at it. Notice the blatant sexism in the copy (and not-so-obvious racism in the photo). Envision yours truly, seeing the ad, reading it, and going into conniptions as I scrawl out an enraged letter, pen in fist. I didn't even take the time to Xerox it. You don't think of Xerox with hot lava coursing through your veins. Mailed it right off the the vicious no-good offenders, the CasaBlanca Fan Company (address & zip is right in the ad)!

"After I calmed down, I figured they probably wrote me off as a crackpot and trashed my letter. (It was not a nice letter, Harlan. I called names. I told them they were (1) sexist, (2) racist, and (3) stupid, because why offend women in any ad that was trying to push a product that mostly *women* buy? That was the gist of it.) But no! About a week or so ago, I received a letter from the CasaBlanca Fan Company on their fancy-Delancey gold-embossed letterhead (doesn't show in the Xerox I'm sending you). The letter is kind of hilarious but made it clear that (1) the entire Board of Directors read my poison-pen letter (I cringe now), (2) they received about 30 letters similar to mine (at least *some*body's awake), and (3) on the basis of (2), decided to pull the ad.

"Just 30-odd letters. I would've thought more were required. Anyhow, you won't see this dopey ad *anywhere* (2nd happy ending).

"Thank you for the inspiration. Sincerely, Joanne Gutreimen."

We pause. Go back and reread the advertisement, in light of Ms.

372

Gutreimen's reactions.

Now for the second piece of correspondence. Ain't it fun reading other people's mail?

This second item, dated August 20, 1982 (sans the fancy-Delancey letterhead) comes to us as it came to Ms. Gutreimen on CasaBlanca Fan Company stationery, signed by Edward F. Hart, who is identified as Vice President of Marketing & Sales for CasaBlanca. And here is what Mr. Hart said to our stalwart Joanne:

"Dear Ms. Gutreimen,

"This is in response to your June 2, 1982 letter in regards to our advertising program as it appeared in *California* magazine. I want to assure you that your letter has been read by all the officers of the CasaBlanca Fan Company and its advertising agency. At least 30 other writers complained similarly, and we regret that this ad has offended so many. We extend to you our most sincere apologies.

"Our 1982 brand awareness advertising campaign uses actor Robert Sacchi [star of Andrew Fenady's film *The Man With Bogart's Face*] to recreate three famous scenes from the film *Casablanca*. The 'Rick and Sam' ad was based on a particularly sad, but memorable scene from that film. In recreating this classic scene, we tried to 'lighten it' with a blatant exaggeration of Rick's remorse. We believed that we had positioned the statement so absurdly that no one could take it seriously. We now know that we failed badly in this regard.

"Our product does have considerable technical merits that make it worthwhile. However, we chose a brand awareness campaign aimed at getting maximum impact. It worked. Unfortunately, if 30 people took the time to write to us, then perhaps thousands protested by simply refusing to buy our product. That's not the reaction we had in mind at the outset of this campaign.

"As you might suspect, more than 80% of CasaBlanca's retail sales involve a purchasing decision made by women. To set out intentionally to offend these buyers is a poor way to run a business, at best. We regard ourselves as a progressive company, and women fill key roles in sales and middle management in the firm. There is no question that we *momentarily* lost our sensitivities with regards to women's issues.

"Thank you for taking the time to write us. I can assure you that the advertisement will *never* be seen again in future publications.

"Sincerely, Edward F. Hart."

Copies of this letter went to the Chairman of the Board and the President of CasaBlanca, as well as to two of the principals of Casa-Blanca's advertising agency, Davis/Johnson/Mogul & Colombatto, who must have been absolutely vivisepultural with ecstasy at Ms. Gutreimen's attentions to their handiwork.

(I hate explaining 'em, gang, but vivisepulture is the act of burying people alive.)

373

Now all of the foregoing Ms. Gutreimen sent to be because, as she said, I inspired her. In much the same way, in my view, that Gilles de Rais inspired Charlie Manson.

Which brings us to our final piece of correspondence, my letter of September 9th to Ms. Gutreimen which, due to space limitations, we must put on the if-come till next week, after which a few closing remarks about midgets and other stuff.

Please salt this week's installment away so we can count on fresh memories and you can refer to it next week without my having to vex the *Weekly*'s editors with a 2000 word recap in THE ROAD TO HELL, Part 2.

(Concluded Next Week)

**INSTALLMENT 46:** 1 October 82

# The Road to Hell, Part II

Last week in this space you began the adventures of Joanne Gutreimen, a reader of this column who found in an advertisement nationally run by the CasaBlanca Fan Company, parodying the classic film *Casablanca,* what she took to be flagrant sexism and racism. We ran the ad last week. Ms. Gutreimen's letter to the company, one of a group protesting the ads, and the company's response advising they were pulling the ads, were also here last week. We pick up the adventure with my letter to Ms. Gutreimen dated September 9th, in response to her sending me all the foregoing material. Gee, I hope you saved last week's installment.

"Dear Joanne:

"You're not going to like this.

"Since you sent me the ad with a copy of their response, and your letter crowing about this grass roots defeat of Utter Evil, with the clear implication that I'll applaud your action, I'm sure my opposite reaction will startle you. But the simple truth of it is that what you did is no better than what the Moral Majority does. You intimidated without genuine cause, based solely on a tunnel-visioned view of something you chose to misinterpret.

"The advertisement is in no way racist. It is only the barest, most vaguely sexist, if one lacks any sense of humor whatever, and if one has somehow escaped the mythic grip the film *Casablanca* holds over several generations of filmgoers, both here and abroad. It isn't even, as you claim, a stupid ad. It is a clever conceit, elegantly and tastefully put together.

"Look, Joanne: I know college women who want *Gone With the Wind* banned from their university film group because it portrays both blacks and women in 'subservient roles.' They are as muddled as you. History cannot be changed. As a portrait of women and blacks during the Civil War it is accurate; and no amount of overcompensatory revisionism will change that. As a portrait of a period, it is correct, and should be seen; as Art it should be seen. The same for *Casablanca* and the same for the character of Rick, as regards his feeling about women—in this case the one who left him standing in

377

Paris as the Nazis marched in. Doing a parody advertisement of that deeply affecting scene from the film was sensible and innovative on the part of CasaBlanca Fan Company and its ad agency. No harm, no insult, no sexism, no racism, no stupidity.

"All of those, in great measure, are what *you* have evinced. And you should not for a moment think you have done a good thing.

"You have overreacted in a destructive way. You have made the company feel it did something insensitive and incorrect. But in a world where we cannot chuckle at the *serioso* knee-jerking of those dedicated to even the most worthy causes, those who choose to hold on to their wit and their sense of the ludicrous become targets for True Believers.

"That's the stock in trade of the Moral Majority, those bluenosed, straitlaced and anal-retentives whose own souls are more than likely cesspools of sexual repression and lasciviousness. They rail against that which they perceive in themselves.

"You are too bright a woman, and too sensible, to carry on like this. If, in fact, as you say in your letter, you went into conniption fits, with hot lava (which is a redundancy) coursing through your veins...then you've got a problem. You *know* my credentials as regards racism and sexism: I was working with King in the South long before it became fashionable; I've just spent six years touring the country lobbying and lecturing for the ERA; my columns frequently take racists and sexists to task. While I may not be as sensitive to sexism as you, a female, may be, I like to think I'm considerably more aware than most folks, male *or* female. If this advertisement were offensive, I'd have written you congratulating you on mobilizing your anger for a worthy end.

"But you're wrong. Dead wrong. And you've contributed to the unnecessary shaming of a company that has committed no offense. I don't give a damn if they received thirty letters or three hundred. It is pure and simple reverse-logic and overreaction.

"In the past you've written to the column, and to me, with solid and sensible comment. I've grown to admire you and the social conscience you demonstrate. But this time you're way off base.

"I'll be sending a copy of this letter to CasaBlanca so they can take some small solace. I may do a column on it...it seems to me a subject that needs discussion. I'm sorry it had to be you, one of the stalwarts, who comes in for reprimand. But if I were to ignore your chortle of glee, if I were to permit CasaBlanca to think their ad agency and their own Board of Directors were insensitive assholes, I would not be serving the commonweal.

"I told you this wouldn't be to your liking. Sorry about that, Joanne, but we're definitely on opposite sides in this one.

"All best otherwise, Harlan Ellison."

With Jesse Helms and Orrin Hatch out there, with Phyllis

Shitfly still trumpeting her victory over the ERA, with insurance companies lobbying their rates against women, with the feminist-backlash rise in rape, with the endless and constantly mutating anti-feminist virus that infects America, it seems to me incumbent upon all of us who perceive these inequities to know who the enemy is. Please notice Mr. Hart addressed Joanne as *Ms.* Gutreimen. Also please take under advisement the highly responsible and sensitive tone of Mr. Hart's letter to Joanne, fancy-Delancey letterhead notwithstanding. And know that Hart was not blowing smoke up Ms. Gutreimen's skirt when he said women hold many and responsible positions in the company, such as the recent appointment of Elaine Pondant as Director of Sales, responsible for all national sales of their fans.

Also understand that 30 letters (the actual total was 55) *is* enough to scare the bejeezus out of a company that has to remain responsive to its potential market, but that in conversations with the writers of these letters, Hart discovered that at least *half* of them had never *seen* the film. (Several of them went fully into looneytune behavior by saying they never *would* see the motion picture *Casablanca* because Bogart was in it!)

In its way, the ad agency's use of Bogart and Sam (and in other ads Ingrid Bergman and Sidney Greenstreet lookalikes) was inspired Art. It used mythic stereotypes we know or *should* know and manipulated them with good humor and a fine satirical sense.

For Artists of any persuasion these days, the curse of not offending *anyone* becomes a crippling problem. David Denby, in *New York* magazine (18 June 79) pointed out, "An artist trying to create a powerful atmosphere can't be expected to embrace the banal method of tv documentaries, which always illustrate both sides of a situation and leave you nowhere." If you doubt the truth of that observation, consider the tv docudrama about Kent State.

For an Artist working in these days of heightened consciousness by even the smallest minority, writing with power and impact becomes difficult to the line of impossible. (I had one guy, who said he was from Malta, rail against the general equation of his homeland with the Maltese Falcon.)

It gets to a point of unnatural hypersensitivity where an Artist can write about *no one* for fear of offending; and then we wind up with television.

Let me put it this way: a year or so ago, I received a letter after the publication of one of my books, from a man who said, "You are always using midgets in your stories as heavies. They are always evil and terrible people. Well, I am three feet tall, and I want you to know we don't like being called *midgets!* We want to be called *little people!*"

That letter unmanned me. I was taken aback and gave it long

and serious consideration. Finally, I wrote him a response, as follows:

"Dear Sir: I am five foot five. *I* am a little person. *You,* sir, are a midget."

An outstanding event is scheduled this Saturday, October 16th, at Bovard Auditorium of USC. It is called THE DAY OF THE IMPRISONED WRITER, it is dedicated to freedom to write, freedom to read, and is sponsored by the P.E.N. LA Center. An afternoon (3:00 to 5:00 approximately) of drama, readings, poetry and music keynoting the hundreds of writers condemned to darkness around the world. Among the passionate artists who will be in attendance are journalist A.J. Langguth, whose book on terrorism in South America may be familiar to you; members of the Latino Writers Group presenting work of the famous Cuban poet Angel Cuadra who, through P.E.N.'s efforts, has been freed from prison; the "jazz priest" Malcolm Boyd, one the remarkable men of our time; Lester Cole, one of the blacklisted "Hollywood Ten"; and your humble columnist, who has written and will read a special essay on writers in chains. All under the direction of Jan Dorin, the Bulgarian director and film-maker who was in prison and escaped to this country. The donation is $8.00 (students: $2.00), all monies to be used by the P.E.N. Freedom to Write Fund to aid imprisoned writers around the world. I urge you to come and say hello.

# INSTALLMENT 47: 18 October 82

*Letters reprinted with permission from the* L.A. Weekly

He has nothing to do with this, except for something he wrote. His name is Eric Hoffer, an ex-stevedore turned philosopher, and he set down these words: "What monstrosities would walk the streets were some people's faces as unfinished as their minds."

The quote drifted across my mind as I started this week's advisement in terror. I thought about that ooze-dripping Thing from Carpenter's recent film, and the sleek scorpion-tailed Alien, and all the other supernatural and extraterrestrial horrors we see on the big screen. And I smiled with something like a death rictus when I realized that they would seem street correct with the rest of the strolling pedestrians in Winifred, Montana.

Because in Winifred, Montana the monsters wear Levis and farmer straws, and their minds are more alien than the most bizarre tentacled visitor from some far galaxy. Don't take my word for it: ask Kathy Merrick.

You'd like Kathy Merrick. She's shy, and polite, and intelligent. She and her husband, Happy Jack Feder (that's his name), are the sort of quiet country young folks you'd instantly call *decent.*

And she walked the streets of Winifred in 1976, never realizing she was surrounded by monstrosities. When the knowledge came, it shattered her life.

She was single then, and teaching junior and senior high school English. Fairly fresh from receiving her degree, in her first job, and blissful about opening intellectual doors for the children of that rural community. Innocent. Untenured and vulnerable.

I might never have heard of Kathy, and you would not be reading these words today had she not been turned onto a fantasy I wrote titled "I Have No Mouth, and I Must Scream" discovered by her younger brother in one of my books in 1970. Kathy read it, thought it would be exciting for her students, and proceeded to teach it in a sophomore English class.

When they refused to renew her contract, they told her it was because she was teaching godless pornography, and they cited my story as the chief example.

You won't find a word of self-defense for that story in this column. It's one of the ten most reprinted stories in the English language, and if you have never read "godless pornography" it'll be easy enough for you to locate. Judge for yourself.

Because she is, and was, shy, polite and decent, Kathy Merrick was bewildered. She had never come up against the specter of censorship before. Still reeking of blood from the Spanish Inquisition, the Scopes Monkey Trial and McCarthyism, the specter threw its shadow over Winifred, Montana and, as always, its victim was someone too innocent to move a counterattack as ruthless as the one leveled in the name of "Decency, God and Country."

She appealed to the school board. The Billings, Montana papers picked it up. The Montana Association of Teachers of English tried to come to her aid, as did the Montana Education Association and the American Civil Liberties Union. She wrote me, and I wanted to be on the next plane, to appear before the kangaroo court. But they sent word I would not be permitted to speak, nor were any of the *amicus* groups allowed to speak. So, like Peter Zenger and Galileo and Giovanni Bruno and Arthur Miller and Lillian Hellman before her, young Kathy Merrick made her appeal to the unfinished minds of the Winifred school board. To those God-fearing, bible-spouting, righteously sanctimonious church-goers, sanctimoniously swaddled in their Christian charity.

Life is tightfisted when it comes to dispensing happy endings.

Kathy Merrick was fired. Her teaching credential was tainted in Montana. She was forced to move out of town. For six years a woman who wanted to open doors for children had to wait tables to support herself.

In 1980 she married Happy Jack and this year she gritted her teeth and decided she was not going to let the Pod People keep her from her true purposes. She and Happy Jack live in Fairfield, near Great Falls, and she is teaching again.

But her innocence is gone.

On Tuesday, October 5th, I was invited to a screening of a half-hour documentary on The Moral Majority, produced by People For The American Way, an organization I've mentioned in these pages previously as the only streetwise outfit, on-line in Washington, D.C., that is fighting back against these grim reapers. The film is called "Life and Liberty...For All Who Believe."

It is one of the most terrifying half hours of television you will ever see. And see it you will, tomorrow night, Friday, October 22, 8:30 PM on Channel 11. It cost $35,692 to buy that half hour.

See children throwing books onto flaming pyres, singing and laughing and clapping their hands in glee. Hear their parents saying this isn't desecration, it's a celebration of God. See James Robinson, the video preacher, exhorting his congregation with the idea that The Moral Majority must raise up a tyrant to *make* us think as they do. Hear Falwell tell you that it doesn't matter what the *real* majority of

384

Americans want, that this is a holy war and the rest of us must be *made* to believe as they do. See it all, friends, the freak show of the beatific! The three-piece-suited manipulators who have had their way so completely with this country for the past eight years that Double-day, a major New York textbook publisher, will issue this fall a biology text in which the word *evolution* does not appear. See school teachers who have been fired and their lives crippled because they said to kids, "Well, what is your opinion of...." The Moral Majority wants narrow teaching, by rote, and opinions are not permitted.

See it all, narrated by Burt Lancaster, long a champion of free speech, the shiny face of that coin which sports, on its obverse, tarnished and scarred, the visage of Charlton Heston.

As I stood there on that Tuesday night, trembling in horror—it's that sort of film—I heard Norman Lear ask the wealthy assemblage to pledge monies to buy airtime in the expensive video markets across America. Paul Newman bought Cleveland for $12,078. Stanley Shein-baum bought Medford, Oregon for $1032 and Lansing, Michigan, $7680. Stanley Marcus of Neiman Marcus bought Austin, Texas for $3468. Vice-Chairman of Warner Bros. Ted Ashley bought a run in New York for $29,351 and a second run in L.A. for $35,692. Music mogul Jerry Weintraub, manager for Sinatra and John Denver among others, gave you tomorrow night's screening here in Los Angeles.

Goldie Hawn has just bought Baltimore.

And there I stood, with mostly dust in my pockets, readers, because I was way out of my financial league with those people, and I heard someone say, "I'll buy Billings, Montana because a woman who taught one of my stories there was run out of town."

And it was me. I did a lecture last week, out of state, and they paid me $1500, and I gave that $1500 to People For The American Way so they can buy a half hour to show this urgently needed program in the area where Kathy Merrick's parade got pissed on.

Except, flustered and broke as I was when I said I'd take Billings, the area that services Winifred, Montana is not Billings, its the Missoula–Butte market, and it costs a mere $744...and I ain't got no more to give.

But if you'd like to fight back against the 11% of far right fanatics who think they can order our lives for us, then please watch Channel 11 tomorrow night at 8:30. Burt Lancastser will give you 800 numbers to call to make a pledge.

Five bucks, ten, a big twenty-five...even in these times when none of us has escaped Reaganomics...it all adds up. And if you earmark it for the Missoula–Butte, Montana market, then Kathy Merrick can turn on her set one night very soon and know that someone out here gave a damn that her life was fucked up by the alien things walking the streets of God-fearing America.

Because, for God's sake, we've *got* to start fighting back before they set up concentration camps for all the rest of us Hell-condemned heathens.

# LETTERS

## Gun Control

*Dear Editor:*

As a gun owner, I take offense at the ravings of Harlan Ellison [Sept. 24–30, 1982] on the subject of gun control. His slander of gun owners is unconscionable. The vast majority are reasonable and sane, not the right-wing Neanderthals he purports us to be.

The arguments against gun control, which he so often decries, "guns don't kill, people kill" and "if guns are outlawed, only outlaws will own guns," may be old slogans, but they still ring true. I grew up in New York City, which has one of the toughest gun control laws in the country; so tough that it is virtually impossible to buy a handgun. But it is obscenely easy to purchase a cheap firearm from any dealer at the "midnight gun store." This fact makes a farce of the law and of respect for it.

There are presently enough laws on the books to punish anyone using a handgun in a crime (a person who would, of course, run out and register his "job tool" as soon as the law is enacted), without imposing unreasonable burdens on responsible citizens.

One more slogan to think about: "The difference between a long gun and a handgun is a hacksaw."

To ease Mr. Ellison's conspiratorial mindset, I am not now, nor have I ever been, a member of the NRA or any other "gun lobby."

As a taxpayer and regular voter, I urge every free-thinking citizen to vote NO on Proposition 15 on Nov. 3. Your freedom is in your hands. Don't give it up.

—Bob Beberfall
West Hollywood

## Letters
## Prop 15

*Dear Editor:*

I am sure Harlan Ellison [September 24–30] is well motivated; we would all like to see an end to violent crime. Yet it is not clear that legislation like Proposition 15 would help. Unfortunately, Harlan's frantic diatribe does nothing to clarify the issues.

I do not own a gun, though I certainly want the right to: Ellison's contention that anyone who might want to own a handgun is a raving lunatic from the fringes of the far right; a neo-Nazi, a Falwellian fanatic, a gun-racked NRA desperado, a supporter of James Watt; or worse, is a specious proposition that appeals to our desire for simple solutions and to our most bigoted fears.

The simple fact is, today's criminals do not purchase handguns through legal channels! The convicted felon is not allowed to, and the as yet unconvicted one is not going to give his name, driver's license and gun serial number to the police. Moreover, a felon cannot be charged for not registering a handgun, because it violates his fifth amendment protection against self-incrimination. Catch 22: Proposition 15 would only serve to create technical criminals—otherwise law-obeying folks who own a gun.

Our own history has shown amply the futility of outlawing the things that people want. Prohibition created a booming black market in alcohol and a vast criminal infrastructure to support it. Ellison knows that many of his own readers are violaters of a different prohibition: "putting all that good dope down your neck...or freebasing or whatever...." Since a large peer group does not disapprove, many people in California use drugs. The laws against drugs exist, but does the flow of contraband cease? Hell no, and the people who support this black market (your friends and mine) are not nearly as determined to "score" as is the criminal seeking a gun.

So tell me, Harlan, how do you expect this law to stop criminals from getting guns? It will probably work as well as it has in other states, where it hasn't done a thing to stop gun-related crimes anywhere: not in Massachusetts, not in New York City, not in Washington, D.C. Why should it work in California?

Do we really need to create another large, expensive bureaucracy to administer this law? Perhaps those millions of dollars annually could be better spent, for instance, on more police, so that we might *really* have a chance at stopping all this crime.

Finally, our constitution guarantees us the right to bear arms. That right may sound a little dated in 1982, but let us not take this venerable document lightly; it has served us well. Perhaps the framers of the constitution knew a thing or two. Remember, there is gun control in Poland.

—Michael Lawler
Los Angeles

# INTERIM MEMO:

Naturally, in a nation where functional illiterates with virility problems continue to misread "freedom to bear arms" as meaning they can own, pack and use guns at their whim, Prop. 15 was defeated. And the slaughter goes on and on and on and on and . . . .

Every 2 minutes a handgun is manufactured in America.

Every 13 minutes the cops take a gun away from someone in America.

Every 20 minutes someone is killed by a handgun in America.

During the time of the Vietnam War, more Americans were killed by handguns, in America, than died in the war.

Every year, 350,000 people are injured by handguns. In America.

So stop all this bullshit about "guns in the hands of criminals." Enough lies, already! Enough of those sleazy (and uncredited) posters showing Nazis machinegunning people and shoveling them into mass graves under the legend GUN REGISTRATION EQUALS MASS EXTERMINATION or FIRST REGISTER THEIR GUNS, THEN REGISTER THE JEWS. Enough of those duplicitous tv commercials with the little old lady cowering in her bed as an intruder turns the knob of her bedroom door, and the police dispatcher she's got on the phone tells her they can't come to her aid because all the cops are out registering handguns.

Enough, already.

Enough of people like Bob Beberfall of West Hollywood and Michael Lawler of L.A., who wrote in the last issue to scare the hell out of you by saying freedom means having a gun. Don't swallow any more lies, for God's sake!

It isn't the guns in the hands of thugs we're talking about, though guys like Lawler and Beberfall and their mentors at the National Rifle Association and *their* mentors at the arms manufacturers have skewed the question so everyone talks about guns in the hands of criminals. What we're talking about are the 80% of all deaths every year that are caused by snubbies in the hands of people as ordinary as Beberfall and Lawler. The ordinary citizens. You and me. *We're* the ones who have to be protected from *ourselves,* not from the thugs.

Don't try to con yourselves into believing that 350,000 people are maimed and crippled by thugs! There ain't that many crooks in the whole country. The police tell us, over and over again, that you are ten times more likely to be killed by your own gun, in your own home, by someone you know, than you are to be killed by a gun in the hands of a thug.

A few weeks ago a woman trying to back into a parking space was aced out of the parking by a guy pulling in from behind in a VW. She promptly got out of her car with a .22 Police Positive she carried in the glove compartment "for protection," and she proceeded to blow the guy away. For stealing her parking space.

Two weeks ago every Los Angeles newspaper featured a story about a man who shot his six-year-old daughter through the head demonstrating "defense" with the household handgun.

It's not the criminals. They'll have guns one way or the other. But we can cut down on the *accessibility* of guns to those criminals by registration. Because the police tell us, over and over, that thugs and street hoods get the guns from *our homes* when they rob us. And "protection" is an ephemeral lie because most robberies occur when *no one* is home.

So who is it that has turned nice guys like Beberfall and Lawler into paranoids who think freedom emerges from the barrel of a Saturday Night Special? It is the gunmakers. Charter Arms Corporation (manufacturers of the gun that killed John Lennon) has contributed $10,000 to the anti-Prop 15 campaign. Pachmayr Gun Works, Inc. has spent $14,000 in California. Hernady Manufacturing sent in $8000. Charter is located in Stratford, Connecticut. Hernaday is in Grand Island Nebraska.

But they're only pikers. Tune in to this:

The money to spur the No on 15 campaign, marketed on tv and in the newspapers as in defense of your right to bear arms, has come from the following: $100,000 from Smith & Wesson of Springfield, Massachusetts; $170,000 from Sturm, Ruger & Co. of Southport, Connecticut; $50,000 from Harrington & Richardson of Gardner, Massachusetts; $50,000 from Remington of Bridgeport, Connecticut; $50,000 from Omark of Idaho; $50,000 from Winchester in New Haven, Connecticut.

Hey, Lawler; hey, Beberfall—try and convince us that all these gun manufacturers, who don't contribute hundreds of thousands to fight pollution, or buy books for libraries, or fund the arts, or buy milk for schoolchildren, that all of these death merchants have nothing in their hearts but a love of the Second Amendment to the U.S. Constitution. Try to explain why they're so goddammed interested in what's going on here in California...if it isn't to stop a nationwide movement by those of us you consider "hysterical" because we're saying enough is enough. Hysterical? Hell, yes! What does it take to get the rest of you hysterical enough to vote YES ON 15?

Don't you understand, though the cops have told you, over and over, that half of all the guns in circulation are *stolen* guns? Where do you think those pistoleros *got* the firepower? From our homes, *that's* where!

We've got to stop the NRA. We've got to break up that massive

392

Washington D.C. lobby that allows the death merchants to make us a little more terrified every year, that permits the big profits selling things intended for no other earthly purpose than to kill.

Are they worried, the NRA...the gunmakers? You bet your ass they're worried, because Prop. 15 is a "shot" they're afraid will be heard around the country. They're so damned scared they are getting careless. They're coming out in the open. How? Try *this* one, and consider if you want to vote in favor of people who'll do this kind of thing:

Various police chiefs around California are strongly supporting Prop. 15. Last week a "promotional item" from the NRA-backed Citizens Committee for the Right to Keep and Bear Arms was received by (among others) Police Chief Kolender of San Diego, Chief McNamara of San Jose, and Chief Con Murphy of San Francisco: targets filled with bulletholes, with the bullseye reading NO ON 15. The moneyraising gimmick promised those who shot out the targets that the money would go to defeat YES ON 15 and the targets would go to those no-good Commie police chiefs.

Read the arguments in your voter's handbook. Read how sane and sensible Prop. 15 is. Turn away from those scare tactic tv commercials. Consider the mentality of people who'll show Nazis killing Jews just to make you crazy when you come to vote. VOTE YES ON 15. Enough is enough.

You may not have heard me. Let me say it again, so you'll remember it on November 2nd. VOTE YES ON PROP. 15.

Last year, handguns killed 48 people in Japan, 8 in Great Britain, 34 in Switzerland, 52 in Canada, 58 in Israel, 21 in Sweden, and 42 in West Germany.

Last year, handguns killed 10,728 in America.

Hey, Lawler; hey, Beberfall...how much blood does it take to buy your idea of "freedom"?

Hey, everybody: let's get hysterical! Enough is enough.

# Interim Memo:

I'm not sure this will make much sense. But if I don't take a wild stab at explaining it, this *column* won't make any sense. What happened was that Tom Nolan, who writes the *Mr. Los Angeles* restaurant review column in *Los Angeles* magazine, felt snubbed by me because I'd met him a few times but didn't remember what he looked like, and so I didn't say hi to him one night in a dinery where we crossed paths. Now, Tom Nolan is a nice man, and I freely confess to brain damage when it comes to remembering names with faces. I guess what actually happened was that I was preoccupied, didn't see him, and walked past him. Meaning him no slight. In any case, along about late October of 1982 I started getting calls from my friends saying, "Have you seen the *Mr. Los Angeles* column in the magazine this month?" No, I replied, what's going on? Well, I was told, Tom Nolan has written a rather snide column satirizing you as "Hubbel Nordine." Their ire had been aroused, as they read the column to be well along into meanspirited. Knowing Tom Nolan is not a meanspirited man, I picked up the issue of *Los Angeles* in question, and read what was a combination restaurant review–satire, written in Tom's distinctive breathless style. So for my column published in the 5–11 November 82 *L.A. Weekly* I wrote a parody of *Nolan*'s style and subject matter, recommending a couple of restaurants and a satin jacket manufacturer I'd been meaning to plug, utilizing the mythical figures of Hubbel Nordine, Mr. Los Angeles and non-existent actor Dane Trevor. Those who'd read the Nolan column got the gag. Those who didn't...didn't. Nolan and I made contact, got everything squared away, more or less, and that's what all this is about. You'll find the syntax and said-bookisms inconsistent with my usual writing style, and they were done for parody effect, so don't chide me for it.

I was working on the screenplay when the phone rang, and I had a pencil in my mouth, having just made a correction on page 134, and when I snatched off the receiver I forgot the No. 2 Ticonderoga and said, "Grzzmpf?"

"Is Harlan there?" It was the voice of my pal Tom Nolan, who writes the "On the Town with Mister Los Angeles" column for *Los Angeles* magazine.

"It's me Tom," I said, removing the pencil as I recognized his voice. "Talk about telepathy, I was going to call you today about your buddy Mister Los Angeles and that little sf writer, Hubbel Nordine."

Tom groaned. "Please! No more," he said.

"Look," I said, "Hubbel's a sometime friend of mine—though God knows he could make an itch nervous—and Mister Los Angeles is a friend of yours, and if he's driving *you* as nuts as Hubbel is driving *me,* then it's in the service of our mutual sanity to get together and see if we can find some way of building rapprochement between them."

Tom laughed. "I wished I'd never written that damned column about the two of them." It had been in the October 1982 issue of *Los Angeles.* "You know," he added, "it was a much longer column; and they broke it in half. Second part is in this month's issue."

"I read it," I said. "But it seemed to be about a run-in Mister Los Angeles had with an actor named Dane Trevor. I've never heard of him."

"Doesn't surprise me," Tom said wearily. "No such person. I got such static on the first column, that I caught the second part before it ran, and rewrote it using a mythical actor instead of Hubbel Nordine. At least I don't have to go through this maelstrom twice."

"Smart move," I said. "Anyhow, let's go have some lunch together. . .and see what we can work out between us to pull the fangs of these two clowns."

"Great," he said. "In fact, that's why I was calling. I figured you must be pissed at me or something."

"Why'd you think that?" I was surprised. Tom and I had been friends for years, always on good terms.

"Because you looked right through me at the party last night." The night before had been Halloween, and I'd gone down to Lydia

Marano's Dangerous Visions Bookstore for a little while. I didn't remember even *seeing* Tom there. But then, I hadn't recognized most of the people: they'd been in costumes that included masks.

"You've gotta be kidding," I said, chagrined. "Jeezus, I'm sorry, Tom. Did we talk?"

"No. I didn't want to impose. You looked distracted."

"Yeah...well...it's been a couple of the worst weeks of my life." I said. "Not the least of it being that this woman I was in love with gave me my walking papers a week ago Saturday. And I've spent most of the time since all doubled over. I hadn't expected it to hit me so hard, but I'm really desolate. So please forgive my seeming rudeness. But you should have *said* something, man. Never gunnysack that kind of feeling, specially with good friends."

"Forget it," Tom said. "No need for petty pique between us. Where do you want to eat, at *Shain's*? Or maybe we can do *Fran O'Brien's Restaurant* out in Santa Monica. I hear the Greek food there is terrific."

"I ate at Fran's last Thursday," I said. "The reports are accurate. The pastitsio and the moussaka are brilliant. Also, the portions are big enough to stun a police dog. Nice to have a top line Greek joint as friendly as that so close to home. But I can't do Greek so soon again. Why not the Maryland Crab House. It's just up the road on Pico from Fran O'Brien's."

There was a catch in Tom's throat. "*Fresh* crab?"

"Absolutely. I'm surprised you haven't heard of this place. They opened in July, and if it isn't one of the ten best joints in town, then I'm not the winner of the all-expense-paid trip to the next Slim Whitman K-Tel recording session."

Tom has one of those larky, terribly infectious laughs, and he gave me a *primo* sample. "Okay, how about this afternoon?" I said okay, and told him the Maryland Crab House was located at the corner of 25th and West Pico in Santa Monica. I told him to ask for Judy or Herb Cohen if he got there before me, to use my name and they'd put him at a good table. "Will I *need* your name?" he asked.

"If the crowds haven't abated you will. The word's been spreading about this place and even though the wait isn't a long one, they know me and it might help. You'll recognize Judy: she has a head of hair that looks like the Malibu Canyon fire."

"How'll I recognize Herb?"

"He looks like a guard for the New England Patriots. Also, his head looks like the *aftermath* of the Malibu Canyon fire."

So at 1:00 (which was too early for Tina from Wessex, just abaft Stonehenge, to be serving the tables, dammit) I walked into the Maryland Crab House to find Tom Nolan already gorging himself on the incredible rum buns filled with raisins and cinnamon, drizzled with the faintest angel's touch of sugar glazing. The menu—only slightly smaller than my faith in the Three Mile Island nuclear reactor—was open in front of him on the Formica-top table, and the glaze on the rum buns vanishing down his neck was reflected in the glaze of his eyes; eyes as soft and brown as a Pooh bear's soul. Confronted by the shellfish cornucopia contained in the bill of fare, he had slewed into a raptus as deep and profound as nitrogen narcosis.

"Hey, Tom," I said, standing above him. He reached up with a vague gesture and touched the sleeve of my hand-embroidered 100% satin tour jacket. The message of sensual grace his fingers received shocked him back to reality. "My God," he demulcented deitifically, "that jacket is gorgeous! Turn around. Is it, perhaps, hand-embroidered?" I spun on one toe, permitting him the full vision of the leaping tiger done in a freshet of colors, applied by mastercrafters in a variety of subtle stitches. (I'd wanted *Over the Hump to Burma, 1941* stitched in, but hadn't had a chance to go back to The Cloth Tattoo in Silverlake to have them do it.)

"Sensational workmanship," Tom vociferated. "Where'd you get it?" I told him, pointing out that I'd seen the ad The Cloth Tattoo had placed in the *L.A. Weekly* and, determined to ascertain the reliability of some of the *Weekly*'s advertisers, had run my own consumer research project. "I only went down there to look at their shop," I said, "but the jackets they make are so dazzling I wound up buying one. You should see what they can do with parachute silk. The operation's run by the Krupnick family, and if you see a knockout satin jacket on some rock star or sitcom heroine, it's probably one of theirs."

He asked me if he could wear it, just through the meal, and I peeled out of it to the envious stares of the gourmandish horde. Tom slipped into it, purring like an infant whose bottom has just been buttered. All through the meal he kept touching the satin in a manner only James M. Cain or Raymond Chandler could have metaphored. "I was afraid you wouldn't recognize me," he quipped.

"Listen," I said, "about Mister Los Angeles and Hubbel Nordine. . . ."

"Wait, wait, wait!" he stacatto'd. "Tell me about this menu first. I can't believe this. Fried jumbo softshell crab; fried clams; backfin crab cakes; crabmeat and shrimp Norfolk; my God, I haven't seen a shore menu like this since I was last in sight of the Chesapeake. I'm utterly at sea, pardon the pun. Don't know what to order. What do you recommend?"

"Start with a cup of the clam chowder. Not a bowl. Bowl's too much. You'll be porking out with other goodies, don't toss it all away on the pottage. Besides, the clam chowder is thick and chockablock with pieces of clam bigger than the potato cubes. Then, for an appetizer, try the Backfin Hard Fry."

"Which is what?"

Salivating like an Aztec priest contemplating a freshly ripped-out heart of virgin, I said, "The backfin of the crab is the hump cavity. They produce the most delectable meat in there. Well, Elio the chef adds even *more* backfin lumpmeat to the already bursting cavity, then they dip the whole schmeer in a heavenly batter and deep fry it. What I mean, it is to die!"

"Yes, yes, go on, you silver-tongued balladeer!"

"For the main course you can't go wrong with the spiced shrimp, absolutely heady with the taste of ginger. They try to serve them to you cold, but take my advice, Tom, get them hot. Or just buy a half dozen or a dozen hardshell crabs, done up with the famous Old Bay seasoning. They give you a mallet to crack them, they spread butcher's paper on the table so you can make a Visigoth of yourself, a roll of paper towels...and it's suck and smash and savor till your stomach shrieks *'Kamerad!'*"

When we revived him, Tom ordered *all* of it, and we sat there in unfettered camaraderie for two hours, smiling and gulping. And finally, when all about us was mere debris, he said, "Now. About our friends."

"Yeah...what're we going to do about them? Mister Los Angeles really has his nose out of joint about what he thinks is snubbery from Hubbel. And Hubbel is bewildered and upset even though he cops to meeting so many people that some of the less wonky faces slip out of his memory. What's to be done to reconcile these two wonderful galoots?"

Tom Nolan picked a bit of buttery crab from between two molars, thought about it for a second, then said, "Why don't we just ignore them?"

And that seemed peachykeen to me. Life's too fucking short.

**INSTALLMENT 50:** 7 November 82

## INTERIM MEMO:

Credit for the quote in this installment goes to Andre Gide.

Because my nausea threshold is woefully low, I will not dwell long on a postcard I received from someone named McAuliffe in Hawthorne. It was vaguely in response to the two columns recently about CasaBlanca Fans and Joanne Gutreimen's successful one-woman crusade against their advertising. The card was one of those "You're a sexist asshole, Ellison" beauties. (Response to the columns has run pretty nearly 50-50 from women. Half understood and agreed, half understood and didn't agree. I can live with that.) But the card said something like "A kike will always let you down, but a CasaBlanca Fan will never hang you up." Or something.

The reason I can't quote it exactly is that I did with that missive what I learned to do with similar mail about ten years ago. (And, yes, this is a long-overdue dip-into-the-mailbag column you reivers have been asking for.) Most mail requires no response: people praising or panning and simply wanting to be heard, which is swell. A few pieces I answer personally, usually if there's some human pain in it, or a particularly kind thought that compels a private thankyou. Much of the mail gets dealt with in these columns, openly and at length. But every once in a while something arrives that is so exemplary in its ugliness, that I give it the special treatment, which I commend to your attention for use when such a pustule arrives in *your* mail.

I return the offensive item with a form letter that reads as follows: *Enclosed please find a dismaying item I·received in the mail today. I felt you would want to see it. Clearly, some certifiably brain-damaged idiot is writing crazy letters and signing your name to them. I thought you might want to have this so you could contact the appropriate postal authorities—in an effort to stop this clown before your good name is further devalued. All best wishes, Harlan Ellison.*

You'd be surprised how little one hears from such communicants thereafter.

Robin Podolsky, along with several other readers, took me to task for saying *Gone With the Wind* should not have been lobbied against by collegiate women's groups who didn't want it included in university film programs, because it was sexist, on the grounds that it was an accurate portrayal of the position of blacks and women during the Civil War. Ms. Podolsky made a strong, if occasionally paralogical,

403

case for *GWTW* being a sentimentalization of the situation. I agree, but still contend that a film such as *GWTW,* made in 1939, probably reflects the attitude of America *at that time,* even if it isn't historically correct about the Civil War period, and for that reason has significance for us today. Her carp that *GWTW* isn't Art I choose not to deal with. I've never liked the film, though I recognize its continuing impact on generations of filmgoers.

What Ms. Podolsky *does* grind my gears by saying is as follows: "Your fucking *credentials?* Since when does a list of yesterday's accomplishments (even one as genuinely impressive as your own) protect us from today's complacency? By the way, I usually have a good memory: when was the last time you devoted a column to an exposure of racism?"

To pull your fangs for one moment before I go at the underlying text, Ms. Podolsky, my last column on racism was three or four weeks ago when I reprinted that first gun control essay, the stated and implied thrust of which was that it is the racist fear of Californians at the stereotypical image of blacks and Latinos that scared them into voting down Prop. 15. When the NRA talks about "guns in the hands of killers" they sure as hell ain't talking about all those good old redneck boys who hang out in beer bars and will off you with their snubbie should you accidentally spill a Miller Lite on them. Those guys all go to make up the 250,000 members of the NRA who live in California. What they're talking about, but are too hypocritical to put right out on the plate, is the shadowy racist fear of that great, lumbering black beast whom they believe actually exists in amoral deadliness. What they're talking about are all the swarthy *vatos locos* who live only to rape their jukebox roadhouse Dolly Parton–surrogate girl friends.

An *exposure* of racism? Where the hell have you been living, Ms. Podolsky? Richard Wright and James Baldwin and Chester Hines and Piri Thomas and Ralph Ellison and Langston Hughes all exposed it thoroughly, fifty years before you wrote your letter. What more is there to say that hasn't been said, save to keep writing about specific instances that occur every day? I wish I could find the author of that quote I've used before in these pages, that "Everything that can be said *has* been said; but we have to say it again, because no one was listening." I'll do a column on racism when something very special and horrible comes to my attention, lady.

As for my credentials as a card-carrying knee-jerk humanist, well, I'm forced to agree with you again. Yesterday's good deeds only buy so much. The coin is good, but time dulls its luster. One does the best one can. I'm not going to keep running a litany of my activities in service of the commonweal just so you can find it in your heart to trust me. What went down with Cesar Chavez and Martin Luther King, Jr. was yesterday's payment on my right to sleep peacefully.

What I did today and what I'll do tomorrow—which you'll never know about—are my business. But I suggest before you come with claws at someone whose past credits stand up, that you consider *I* write this fucking column every week, and all I hear from you is that I haven't dealt lately with what *you* want dealt with lately. At least I'm out here every week, Ms. Podolsky. Match my credits, Ace.

Now for something completely different. Terri Mitchell of Los Angeles sent me a postcard about the Great Hydrox/Oreo Cookie Conspiracy a while ago, and I've been hanging on to it for just such a moment as this, when levity is needed.

"Harlan, honey: I'm truly impressed by your taste in cookies. When I was little, my father divorced my mother when she brought home Oreos one fateful afternoon. He railed against Oreos over & over. I'm not kidding. Hydroces are definitely the way to go. But you missed an absolutely vital aspect. That is, you do not simply eat a Hydrox—oh noooo! What you do is tenderly, carefully pull the contraption apart and *lick* the white stuff off—then you pop the soggy chocolates into your mouth quickly before the spit grows green stuff. For people like you who don't like the white part, what you do is flake it off onto the floor & step on it & track it around the kitchen. Incidentally, you said the white stuff looked like elephant cum. How do *you* know what elephant cum looks like?"

Your faithful columnist chooses not to reveal the specifics of his sex life here in front of god and Podolsky and everyone. But, after that business about licking off the white stuff, you got a lotta nerve even bracing me on the subject, Mitchell.

I'll be calling for a date later this week.

Right now I'm getting ready to fall down on the floor in a paroxysm of laughter at a coupon I received in the mail offering me 25¢ off on any package of Schick Blades that will give me a "Macho Close" shave.

Hoping you are the same....

**INSTALLMENT 51:** 15 November 82

# INTERIM MEMO:

A letter from Mr. Michael Lawler, the chap who objected to my gun control columns, appeared in this issue of the *Weekly*. Mr. Lawler was upset that I took him to task for his pro-weapon stance. What Mr. Lawler never seemed to notice was that I never specified him as a gun-crazy. What I said, repeatedly, was "people *like* Mr. Lawler." Nonetheless, he took umbrage, which was fine by me, and he wrote that I was a nasty sod for holding him up to public contempt, which I didn't. I do think it's interesting to note, however, that he suggests violence (spanking me soundly) as a proper response to my public utterances. I rest my case.

*Letters reprinted with permission from the* L.A. Weekly

If, like me, you find the onset of Major Gift-Giving Holidays a pressure more in the fundament than in the fun-producing center, then perhaps you, too, have adopted the policy of bestowing largesse all-year-round, when a certain item glimpsed in a store cries out to be purchased for this friend or that lover. It has been my passport to sanity in these parlous times of economic laryngitis. Coupled with an unrelenting stricture to my friends that they eschew any buying of gifts for me, it has made the slide through the holiday season an easy one.

Something about being morally blackmailed into placing oneself deep in frivolous debt for the five months following December 25th has turned me, over the years, into a cheery Scrooge.

The preceding Novembral remarks function both as preface to my annual Decembral *Fuck Xmas* column (I'll warn you again several times before it appears...contrary to Accepted Wisdom I do not write these screeds intentionally to piss you off...unless you were one of those who voted against Prop. 15 in which case bad cess to you...and so the warnings will serve to help you avoid that particular upcoming polemic) and as apologia for interdicting my own non-Xmas-gift-giving policy.

Or as Walt Whitman put it: "Do I contradict myself? Very well then I contradict myself (I am large, I contain multitudes)."

Which is to say, if you *must* give a gift this year, there is a way you can do it elegantly, spectacularly, intelligently...and stay solvent. I have come up with two gifts of such uncommon wonderfulness, so reasonably priced, that in service of the commonweal I must bring them to your attention. I do so in mid-November because you may have to order ahead, and if you want to have the goodies on hand at the Yule moment, I must tell you about them now. Stop backing & filling, Ellison, and get to it!

Both gifts are intended to uplift and enrich the recipients; and both have that ambience of being selected with painstaking care marked by rare good taste and awesome intelligence. They are that *special* gift that says not only did you care enough to send the very best, but you are innovative enough to *know* what is the very best.

The first is a book. The gift of art and literature.

The University of California Press has published a popularly priced edition of the absolutely stunning Barry Moser-illustrated ALICE'S ADVENTURES IN WONDERLAND based on the $1,000 per copy Pennyroyal Press (of Northampton, Mass.) limited edition. It can be purchased for $19.95 until December 31st ($24.95 thereafter) and mere words cannot convey the joy of leafing through this magnificent version of Prof. Dodgson's immortal rampage in the world of the Mad Hatter, the Dormouse, the Cheshire Cat and the Red Queen's race. Unless one were to indulge oneself by shouting "O frabjous day! Callooh! Callay!"

If you ask yourself—and *do* try to answer without spilling your tea—how long it's been since you reread ALICE, actually sat there smiling and chortling with glee at "Twinkle, twinkle, little bat! How I wonder where you're at!"—then you can make book (this one, I hope) that the person you decide to decide to treasure this year hasn't gone back to Wonderland too recently, either.

And what a good time it is to fall down that rabbit hole all in the golden afternoon. If the year has been as burdensome for you as it's been for John DeLorean and the NFL and tourism in Lebanon and the makers of Tylenol, then a verdict from a jury composed of a deck of cards, no matter if they're screaming *off with her head,* is a lark by comparison; and so condign for that treasured one who managed to get through 1982 without the loss of mind or having to file in Chapter 13 bankruptcy court. It is a time when the inspired jabberwocky of a Lewis Carroll seems a linchpin between us and sanity.

And oh what a splendid edition. No, make that a !

Though I have in my library copies of ALICE illustrated by Tenniel and Ben Shahn and Dali and Ralph Steadman and Arthur Rackham, none of them, not even the traditional Tenniel versions, surpasses Barry Moser's seventy-five miraculous engravings. His Caterpillar on page 68 is aloof, elitist, urbane and bears a marked resemblance to William F. Buckley. The monocle'd March Hare on page 85 is a portrait of every slightly wonky college professor you've ever had to suffer with.

If you dash out now and invade your nearest *good,* well-stocked bookstore—Book Soup on Sunset or Westwood Book Shop seem good bets—you will fall so in love with the U. of C.'s edition that all in a moment your gift needs for those treasured few will be satiated.

It'll be nice having you owe me one, because you'll thank me for apprising you of this frabjous delicacy. Ignore this advisement only if you cannot bear the thought of your friends covering you with gratitude and sloppy kisses.

The second gift you may have to order (though the classical music annex of Tower Records on Sunset has a good selection). It is the gift of fine music.

Each of you must have one dear friend on the gift-buying list who

410

is a killer to shop for. Mostly because that sole atavistic personage claps his/her hands over his/her ears when you put on the latest aural gangbang by Missing Persons or The Human League or Roxy Music. For that dear lover of what we used to call "good music," I have the *perfect* answer to your conundrum.

If those worthies really enjoy classical music, they have no doubt already discovered the cornucopial wonders of the Nonesuch and Musical Heritage Society catalogues. But they are less likely to have been exposed to the Louisville Orchestra First Edition catalogue. Beginning in 1954–55, as a result of innovative policies that saved the Louisville Orchestra from bankruptcy and dissolution, this series of over 150 discs (110 hours of new, specially-commissioned modern classical works, 356 compositions by 233 composers), is as splendid a treasure trove of rare finds as anything you might dream in a laudanum fog.

Just selecting at random from the dozen or so First Edition albums at hand as I write this column, I can recommend the light-as-air architecture of Hector Tosar's *Toccata,* to be found with other modern pieces by Ernst Toch, Jacques Ibert, Yoav Talmi and Camargo Guarnieri on LS 702. I'll wager you've never heard *any* of these pieces, the *Miniature Overture, Tres Dansas Para Orquestra, Overture on Mexican Themes,* the lyrical *Bacchanale* by Ibert. And if you, quixotic and ever-seeking as you are, have never heard them, think of the pleasure your aurally cognizant friend will have.

Or venture into uncharted territory with Gene Gutché's *Genghis Khan,* Op. 37 (LS 722), or Karel Husa's *Music for Prague 1968* on the same album. If this latter composition does not make you wonder where, in fact, John Williams came up with his score for *Star Wars,* then you've lost the ability to spot grand larceny.

We're talking here Villa-Lobos and John Addison (LOU-695); Ibert's heart-rending *Ballad of Reading Gaol* based on Wilde's poem (LS-736) coupled with the banquet of Charles Koechlin's *Partita for Chamber Orchestra*; Jolivet and John Vincent (LOU-572) with *Suite Transocéane* and the *Symphony in D.* We're talking contemporary classical music that surges and enthralls, that uplifts and demands, that restores to your technopop-blasted brains the sense of what is immortal in music, not merely that which can be pushed by a billboard on the Sunset Strip.

This is a catalogue of wonders, every disc an open sesame of intelligence and wit and manifestations of the highest musical ambitions of the human race. It is, in short, the perfect way to demonstrate respect for those who expect a gift at the end of December.

At $7.98 per disc, ordered directly from The Louisville Orchestra, Inc. (609 West Main Street; Louisville, Kentucky 40202), you can consider yourself a sumptuous gift-giver, and you won't have to take up lodgings in Tap City. I suggest you send them a fast letter asking for the catalogue. Or take a run over to Tower Classical on Sunset and see what they have in stock. I don't think you'll be upset to pay the slightly higher price (they charge $7.99 per disc) for the availability of these titles. But I'd make the move soon: when I stopped by Tower the other night, their stock was low on First Edition releases. But if you can't get what you want, well, at least I've given you the address in Kentucky.

In a world where the plastic fripperies we're told via tv and four-color lithogrpahy are the *ne plus ultra* of what we need this second, persiflage that lies dusty and unused three weeks after the holiday, these two gifts I suggest will bring repeated pleasure to the one or two people you really think deserve something special.

For the rest of them, there's always a McDonald's gift certificate for a Toadburger and Fries, all those swell Judith Krantz and Sidney Sheldon paperbacks, the new Bruce Springsteen album, botulism, herpes, canker sores, chaffed thighs, *Monsignor* starring Christopher Reeve, and a parsnip in a pear tree.

# LETTERS

### Go To Your Room

*Dear Editor:*

I do not feel that expressing an opinion on an issue of public concern to your paper ought to subject me to unreasoned, personal attack by Harlan Ellison on its pages [Oct. 25–Nov. 4].

Mr. Ellison really broke the rules of civilized debate when he moved from discussing the issues raised in my (and another) letter, to snide character defamation. He has never met me. How dare he imply that I support advertising concepts too absurd and inhuman to bear repeating? I remind you that these atrocities sprang from Mr. Ellison's mind, not mine. This man is on such an emotional hair-trigger, no wonder he wants laws to protect him from himself.

The next time you allow Mr. Ellison to respond publicly to letters from your readers, you might remind him to address the issues broached in the letters, and not to take potshots at the characters of people he neither knows nor has researched. Otherwise, you should spank him soundly and send him to his room without supper.

—Michael Lawler
Echo Park

**INSTALLMENT 52:** 16 November 82

By the time you read this I'll be back from a lecture gig at Centenary College in Shreveport, Lousiana. As I prepare to fly out tomorrow afternoon, going into a state that failed to ratify the Equal Rights Amendment for the first time in, oh, maybe six years—save for those occasions when, under the aegis of NOW, I made forays into unratified territory to promote the ERA—I sit here commencing my fifty-second conversation with you, deep in a brown funk at the demise of the Amendment; and knowing you'll be reading this on Thanksgiving Day or shortly thereafter, I wonder just what there is to give thanksgiving for.

And because it's that kind of a night, and because the mail has been a bit too full of the sort of people who like to pick nits, I choose to flee the present. I choose to tumble back into the past to remember moments that shine, therein to find cause for a smile. To find reasons for thanksgiving. The memory mist parts and if you like, I'll take you with me . . . .

Eight or ten years ago, as winter slunk in across the Eastern seaboard, I was reluctantly called to New York on some business now forgotten. I do not return to the Apple with much enthusiasm these days, and it has been so for almost fifteen years. Very small part of the malaise that settles over me when it becomes inescapable that I *must* return to Manhattan is that bi-coastal rivalry, more regional chauvinism than pragmatic assessment of relative merits. No, I suffer trepidation about my feet touching the pavements of NYC more out of a Proustian sense of loss than fear of lurking dangers. The City seems so sad these days. There are lines in the faces of the people and the buildings. A weariness. A stolid clinging to survival against a soulfire-leaching winter perpetually slinking in.

And so it was, eight or ten years ago, that I checked into my hotel, called some friends as midnight descended, and asked if they wanted to come out for a late evening snack. Several old buddies thought that would be pleasant, and they named a small restaurant on Lexington in the lower Fifties. I said I'd meet them in half an hour, wrapped myself in muffler and topcoat, and went out into the street. I decided to walk. Cold, nasty wind wielding its scythe up Lexington, snow beginning to float down to melt instantly on my shoulders. At half-past midnight the Avenue was almost deserted. The halated dimness of shop lights left burning as futile deterrent to smash&grabbers seemed like wan beacons of some lost and sunken undersea civilization. Winter in New York produces in me all the worst attributes of bad poetry.

I began walking up Lexington, hunched over against the wind that drove snowflakes past the muffler and down my neck.

Between 44th and 45th Streets, huddled on the steps of the huge Lexington post office substation, was a pile of debris from the center of which a pair of eyes marked my passage. No more startling a creature than one of the city's shapeless bag ladies, swaddled in sweaters, pages of the *Post* laid against her skin as insulating layers. No feet, no hands, no shoulders or thighs. A mound of dark fabric from which wariness radiated.

Her eyes followed me as I passed her, perhaps my stride breaking just barely as a vagrant thought occurred to me; but I was walking, and the thought had no form. I knew that she would observe only till it was obvious I was not going to stop or accost her. The sensitive antenna of the survivor.

I walked another block. And stopped. The wind picked at my hair. The thought had firmed at the edges. It was that terrible scene from the film *Zorba the Greek* in which the sweet old Lila Kedrova character is dying, and the shrikelike Greek women from the town, all swathed in black, crouch around the perimeter of her room, waiting for the final exhalation of breath so they can divest the bedroom of its furnishings. It was a scene that had repelled me when I'd first viewed the film, and so profoundly had it affected me—I do not know why—that it had soured me on ever visiting the wonders of that gorgeous and terrible land. And now I stood in the middle of Lexington Avenue, seeing that tableau in my mind.

I turned and went back a block to the woman in the rag heap. She had moved slightly. I could now see the outline of a lower leg, a knee. I stood at the edge of the sidewalk, leaving safety space between us so she would understand I was no jackroller, come to take her secrets from their plastic shopping bags. She seemed not to be aware of me; but I knew that was not so.

Over the sound of the wind, I said, "May I help you?"

And reply there was none.

"It's beginning to come down," I said. She knew that. "They say it'll be freezing by morning." And she knew that, too. "Let me help you," I said again.

There was no movement from the pile, and had it not been that her eyes were open—staring away into the mid-distance—I would have thought she was sleeping.

I moved closer, stood near her, looking down. Though ill and living in Florida, my mother was still alive in that year; there was no resemblance.

"Here," I said, extending the twenty dollar bill I had taken from my pocket as I'd walked back that long block, "here, take this and get yourself a room at the Y. A couple of meals."

She made no move to take the money. I felt the fool.

I felt, suddenly, a diminution of the pity that had overcome me. In its place was an equally saddening respect for her sense of self-posses-siveness. Perhaps it was only that she had been too dulled by too many years on concrete to accept the gesture; but perhaps it was that she was self-contained and needed no cheap offerings intended to balm my soul. She would not take the money. Choosing to believe it was pride that kept her motionless, I laid the bill on the shape of knee and smiled and said, "It'll be warm again soon."

And I walked away. She had not moved once.

I met my friends at the restaurant, we drank coffee and talked about another world than the one in which the shape with eyes lived. At two-thirty I took my leave, and pulled my collar up, and went out to retrace the path to my hotel.

When I passed the post office, she was still there, in the same position. She had not moved, but her eyes watched me again. The twenty dollar bill was still there on her knee, now wet from the snow.

It would be there tomorrow morning when she chose to change her locale of residence. Or it would have been plucked from her knee by a passing stranger. Or it would fall off and lie there when she stood up, and she would walk away from it.

But I knew she would not put it in her pocket.

There is a liquid moment in our life when all that torments us solidifies in reality, like a fly imbedded in amber; and we understand that there are those without hope, without limbs, without beginnings and endings that matter. A moment when we fly out of our domi-nating thoughts and the shell of our body, and look down from a great height at the rest of the world.

In those moments, even if we do not believe in deities, we hear the hushed whisper, "Thank God," and we slip like smoke back into ourselves, and move on, smaller and safer and quite ready to accept the paper cuts and stubbed toes the universe does not know we suffer.

In those moments we give thanks.

At this contemplative time of the year, a year that has not been as kind as we might have wished but that nonetheless has been a year through which we maintained, I wish you some peace, an hour or two of ease, and the hope that you have had a liquid moment looking down at the rest of your kind.

**INSTALLMENT 53:** 29 November 82

*Letters reprinted with permission from* L.A. Weekly

I have seen the light. The logic of his arguments has just turned me around and opened my eyes. Ronald Reagan emerges as one of the Great Thinkers. The worldwide Nuclear Freeze Movement is a Communist Conspiracy. He said so. He did, he really did; and I believe it. You're all Reds, every one of you.

It's all part of the Commie takeover through the use of fluoridation of the water and questioning Bill Buckley's syntax.

You think I'm kidding, don't you? A lot of you think I say something for effect when I mean just the opposite, don't you? You think I'm using satire as a literary device, right? How quick you all are to spot it when I do it. (Which is why I get some of the dumbest correspondence ever penned by paw or claw.) Well, this time I'm being *real* serious. I've come to adore Ronald Reagan, purely on the basis of his illuminating the dark side of this mass social movement.

I never understood, during all the years I was part of the Anti-War Movement, that I was nothing but a well-meaning, deluded Pawn of Moscow. My thinking was all wrong. I hated J. Edgar Hoover and General Westmoreland and even Barry Goldwater (who was recently proclaimed a saint). Little did I suspect I was aiding the International Bolshevik Menace.

Fortunately, I heard our President in one of his recent fireside chats, and he made it all clear to me...about the Communist influences in the Nuclear Freeze Movement, that is.

He sat right there and, though I couldn't see him on the radio I know he wouldn't lie about it, he said he held in his hand the reports that *proved* the Movement was being directed out of the Kremlin. When one of those snotnosed reporters asked, uh, just what *are* those reports, our President said just the right thing. He said, "Well, young fellah, I'd sure as shit love to let you see these reports, but they're very secret stuff, and it would compromise National Security if I permitted you to peek at them." And then he said, with a lower tone, "And besides, how do I know *you're* not one of them?"

Well, let me tell you, friends, *I* was convinced.

'Cause, if you can't trust the *President* when he says he's got the goods, well then, who *can* you trust? He said it: he said he had the facts right there in his hand. Reminded me of the times Senator Joe

421

McCarthy held up those skinnys and said he had right there in *his* hand the names of 312 card-carrying Communists in the State Department; 165 card-carrying Communists in the movie industry; 944 card-carrying Communists in the Pentagon; 1181 card-carrying Communists in the Toledo, Ohio Department of Water & Power. It has the same sense of reality about it.

And when I stopped to think about it, I could see that our President was right. This whole Nuclear Freeze thing *must be* Red-directed. I mean, what right-thinking American doesn't lie awake nights worrying about first strike capability, the necessity for dense-pack missile siteing, nuclear retaliation shortfall, massive destruction parity? Bothers me a lot.

When some Pollyanna goes all treacly and says s/he isn't worried about a Nuclear War because for the first time in the history of the human race there's existed a kind of weapon that no one has used after its first demonstrations, even though its been around for almost forty years, I say, "Muddy thinking, youth!" Okay, so the only other example of human beings abstaining from using an available weapon was when the Japanese, a long time ago, decided they didn't like what firearms could do, and they said forget it, we'll go back to the sword to kill each other, and nobody used the gun for two hundred years or something like that, till Admiral Perry came steaming into Uraga harbor and brought culture at the muzzle of gunboat diplomacy.

Apart from the Japanese eschewing the use of the gun for two hundred years, there's never been a weapon available—from the pointed stick to the arbalest to smart bombs—that *some*one hasn't used against an enemy, usually in "self-defense."

(I saw a wonderful bumper sticker on my way to LAX two weeks ago. It was on the ass-end of a camper, naturally, and it said: MY WIFE, YES: MY DOG, MAYBE: MY GUN, NEVER!)

So these Luddites get all mushy inside when they observe that here we've had the A- and the H-Bomb for almost forty years and, apart from the first demonstrations at Hiroshima and Nagasaki that thrilled and delighted all of us, *no one* has used nuclear strike potential even though we've had about a hundred and six wars in that time. Not even the French have used it, and we all know how weird *they* are. Or the Israelis, or the PLO, or even that kid from an Eastern college who made one in an attaché case. So the Appeasers who don't understand that we have to be *strong,* Jack, real real *strong,* they say, "Oh ain't we a glorious species, how sane and reserved we are...there just won't *be* a Nuclear War, because we've learned better."

Well, sir, let me tell you those people just don't know which way the wind blows when the cow craps, and I say that they're just misguided tools of a sinister intelligence.

They're part of those millions and millions of dopes who've voted for Nuclear Freeze Initiatives in states from coast to coast, each person of whom is a Commie dupe!

Are you a dupe? Well, I've been a dupe; watching those rivers of humanity on television newscasts, those endless hordes of dupes protesting in front of the White House; seeing the baby Bolsheviks with their mommies, carrying banners that say A NUCLEAR WAR CAN REALLY FUCK UP YOUR DAY; unquestioningly believing all those people who voted for Freeze Initiatives knew what they were doing. Now I understand that *most* of them were outright Commies, and the rest were just dumb fellow travelers.

I'm glad our President sounded the first clarion note of the forthcoming purge of Freeze Fanatics. No longer will I stand by as civil disobedients climb the fences of nuclear power plants and cause grief to the power company. No longer will I turn away in embarrassment from the sexism of the sandwich board worn by the pimply guy at LAX, the sign that reads NUCLEAR PLANTS ARE BUILT BETTER THAN JANE FONDA. No longer will I sign those petitions suggesting that because millions of Americans want a Nuclear Freeze they should be listened to as a constituency of our President. No longer!

Because sometimes our President knows what's best for us. Even if we don't. Sometimes he has to treat us in the way other Presidents have treated us, as exemplified by Mr. Nixon, who once said (Washington *Star-News,* 9 November 1972), "The average American is just like the child in the family."

Yes, I can see Mr. Reagan's early warning remarks as the first step in the necessary propaganda campaign that will surely manifest itself in the next months. The subtle campaign that will begin to throw doubts into the minds of the children in the American family, as doubts were thrown into their minds about the gun control initiative, so they will come to understand that paranoia is *good* for them, that the Nuclear Freeze Movement is just one more sneaky attempt by the godless heathen Commies to weaken us.

I'm all for it. I intend to be right there at Mr. Reagan's good right hand, helping him dissolve that sinister conspiracy of clergymen, scientists, doctors, housewives and radical college students who get their orders directly from the Proscenium of the Supreme Soviet. Those millions and millions of Americans who get their orders through the mail and by word of mouth from what must be the millions and millions of Russian spies needed to infect so many people.

Why, just thinking about it, I wonder if there are any good Americans *left* in this country, what with how many must have been co-opted already. I know of at least *two* good Americans: me and my President. And if you can't belive *us,* well then, just who the hell *can* you believe?

You certainly can't believe the will of the people! I mean, that would be too radical to consider.

# LETTERS

## Bite Your Tongue!

*Dear Editor:*

Regarding Harlan Ellison's Nov. 12 article, is it possible Harlan is just another dictatorial, hypocritical closet redneck?? It's long been my understanding that *real* liberals fight to preserve the individual liberties guaranteed us by the U.S. Constitution. Yet through his advocacy of Prop. 15, Harlan actually endorsed the destruction of *five* amendments.

Obviously Harlan did not have time to divert from his rigorous schedule of making big bucks (of which he so often and openly brags) to actually read and comprehend all 33 pages of Prop. 15.

Because if he had he'd have seen the three sections which demanded outright confiscation of handguns without compensation. Surely, as a great liberal, Harlan would have recognized the confiscation of private property without just compensation is more than slightly unconstitutional.

On close examination, Harlan would have discovered Prop. 15 also violated the Fourth Amendment by giving police the right to make searches and seizures without probable cause or warrants.

He'd also have noticed it violated the Eighth Amendment by imposing excessive fines and making cruel and unusual punishment the norm for honest gun owners.

And Harlan would have seen that Prop. 15 established the "rebuttable presumption of guilt." In other words, the honest citizen is presumed to be guilty by the court and must prove innocence, rather than vice versa.

Then Harlan would have discovered that the 14th Amendment would have been destroyed by insuring unequal treatment of citizens. Harlan has made it clear in many articles that he makes a lotta bread! But surely he hasn't become so callous as to believe that he has more of a right to self defense than a lower income person not nearly so fortunate as he?? If Prop. 15 had passed, the basic economic law of supply and demand would have forced the price of handguns sky high!

Just because multi-billionaire-millionaires such as Otis Chandler, Armand Hammer, Justin Dart and David Murdock donated $50,000 each to Yes on 15, it doesn't mean that Harlan had to blindly join their attempt. If Harlan had read the initiative, he would have questioned why some of the world's richest men were trying to

disarm the individual citizens of this state.
Say it ain't so, Harlan !! Please. . . .

—William Keys
N. Hollywood

**INSTALLMENT 54:** 6 December 82

Photo by Fritz Ptasynski

Back from the dark and smoldering interior of a strange land, I come to tell you of the quaint native customs.

On a day when the NAACP conferred its 15th annual Image awards; the SANE Education Fund Peace award was given to Ed Asner at a dinner in Philadelphia; Ronald Reagan presented the 5th annual Kennedy Center lifetime achievement honors to Benny Goodman, Lillian Gish, Gene Kelly, George Abbott and post-humously to Eugene Ormandy; and the National Women's Political Caucus honored Valerie Harper for her years of service to the feminist movement with their first annual "Bread and Roses" award. . . I was serving as one of five judges who crowned Miss Tush of 1983.

We pause for a moment of reflection.

When acquaintances ask me why I married my fourth wife, the best response I can give, six years after the divorce, is this: It seemed like a good idea at the time.

Like all but an aberrant few of you, I love roller coasters. Even so, on the day that Mike Moorcock and I went to Magic Mountain, soon after they opened the Colossus, specifically to ride that great beast, I declined all importunities to join my friends along those winding trestles and steep inclines. But the next night, when the park had closed, I dressed all in black, melodramatically smeared my face with soot so it would not shine in the moonlight, and like Paul Muni in the 1942 *Commandos Strike at Dawn,* went over the fence at Magic Mountain, avoided the guards, climbed the Colossus, and walked and crawled every inch of that wonderful cyclone.

When acquaintances whom I told of this asked my why I'd done such a thing, I told them: It seemed like a good idea at the time.

In the course of almost thirty years as a writer, I have willingly put myself in the middle of race riots, youth gang rumbles, protest demonstrations, twisted liaisons, doomed romances, dangerous occupations. There is nothing of *machismo* in it, they simply seemed like good ideas at the time. To report the quaint native customs of my bewildering species I would go to black masses, crucifixions, Chinese weddings, six-day bicycle races, Australian rat fucks, dolphin birthings, civil wars, jai alai tournaments and the executions of mass murderers.

When acquaintances asked me why I had been a judge for the 1983 Miss Tush of the Year Lingerie Beauty Pageant, knowing my active support of the feminist movement, this is what I said: It seemed like a good idea at the time.

But I am returned from that journey into the uncharted heart of the South Bay mentality, to report what I thought would be a lark... and I have no answers. Only observations and some questions about who we are as 1982—near to the turn of the century—comes to a close. And I do not know if it was a good idea or a bad idea, at the time I decided, as it happened, and as I write these thoughts. The only thing I know for certain is that, for high or low, the Miss Tush of the Year Pageant is as down home American as beer drunk from the bottle, sock hops and credit cards.

Begun in 1979 as a promotional device by Pauline Barilla to exploit her Tushery lingerie shops in Hermosa Beach and San Pedro, in merely four years the spectacle (and its allied Mr. Tush Pageants) has become a proletarian South Bay social event that generates not only vast expenditures of money, but vast enthusiasm. It is an unqualified crowd-pleaser.

So irresistible is the lure of this *mise en scène* in adoration of the callipygian esthetic that no banquet facility in tthe South Bay exists large enough to contain it. The 1983 Miss Tush Pageant was held on Sunday the 5th at the Proud Bird Restaurant on Aviation Boulevard near LAX. The doors opened for buffet and No Host Bar at 6:30; by the time I arrived at 7:00, the foyer was already impacted, the lines were twenty deep at the bar, the Grand Ballroom was packed to the walls, and all that was left of the buffet was a bowl of what seemed to be potato salad that no one had defiled because there were no forks. (They came later.)

The crowd was spectacularly well-dressed: coats, ties, tuxedos for men; cocktail or evening dresses for women. The style of acting-out attire that used to be reserved for thespians; that in a time in which we have *all* become attention-seekers, draws little attention, no matter how chartreuse the hair or high up the thigh runs the skirt slit. It was a youngish crowd—even those members with gray hair and the faint white scars of having had an uplifting encounter with an anaplastist. A smattering of black faces: not enough to alarm a hip, white crowd.

Were one to sweep into a giant's hand an even dozen. Marina Del Rey condos and singles complexes, upend them and shake out the residents, it would approximate the handsome velvet crowd that jammed the Proud Bird that Sunday night.

I went into the Grand Ballroom.

Men outpopulated women by eight to one. I was told the attendance was over 750. I was told the attendance was over one thousand. I doubt neither figure. There wasn't enough unused space to change your socks. And apart from comps, reservations for each of those statistical elements was twenty dollars a shot. *There's nothing amateur about this action,* I thought. *A promotional Einstein has invested some good moneymaking ideas in this caper.*

As I threaded my way among the tables I was impressed by the size of the crowd again and again; and it became obvious that all of the women were with dates. Though there was a plethora of spiffily turned-out young men (most of them sporting Tom Selleck moustaches) who had come stag, there were no unattached females. If any guy had come for a singles event, it was lousy cruising.

I found my way to the judge's table and introduced myself to martial arts actor Chuck Norris and Mary O'Connor, Executive Assistant to the Chairman of the Board of Playboy Enterprises (i.e., Hugh Hefner). I was never introduced to, nor spoke to, the two other judges who sat at the table—actor Stan Ivar of *Little House on the Prairie* and KFOX-FM's "morning man," disc jockey Steve Lehman. In front of me on the table was a rating sheet listing the fifteen "Tushette" finalists who would be competing in order. The sheet was divided vertically into three "passes" on stage. It was indicated I was to grade each of the women on tush, legs, grace and general appearance.

Conversation was impossible save by leaning in close to the nearest ear, which limited my social intercourse for the next four hours to Chuck Norris's right ear and Mary O'Connor's left. (I am pleased to report both parties are amiable and decorous individuals who use Q-Tips.) The reason for this aural limitation was a popular South Bay band called Wizard & Co. who seem never to have learned that a decibel count in excess of 180 is no substitute for artistry. They had to be asked at least twice to lower the gain on their amps, which were the size of Latvia; and if one made the mistake of passing directly in front of those units, one had the less-than-salutary experience approximated only by being exposed for several years to the kind of verbal cacophony engendered by screaming bouts in Italian and Jewish families.

It was horrendous enough to make me reflect with admiration on the previously-abhorrent tea dance music of Lester Lanin and Lawrence Welk. I pray for the return of civility in popular music. Or the Apocalypse, which would be more soothing.

Unable to carry on normal human congress, and having been asked not to leave the judges' table until the break after the second parade of contestants, I spent my time examining the crowd that had, by this time, filled the Grand Ballroom.

I was to learn later that many of the tables had been purchased by the companies that had ponied up the sponsoring fees for the fifteen finalists. These tables, for the most part, were tenanted by groups of men, as would be expected. Since I saw no one who was less than attractive, I had to assume these men had wives or lovers whom they had chosen to leave behind for this evening of ogling. A compendium of the alibis, rationalizations, obfuscations and outright lies that gave wind to these solo flights would certainly fill a good sized notebook.

Then the entertainment commenced. A quartet of deliriously energetic dancers calling themselves The Bod Squad charged onstage and hurtled through six muscular minutes of an in-place dance routine that vibrated more in *hommage* to aerobics than to either Martha Graham or Bob Fosse. By the time they bounced off, apparently no worse for wear, the *audience* was exhausted and sweating. At which point television second banana Lyle Waggoner mounted the stage to function for the rest of the evening as host, emcee, interlocutor and commentator on passing flesh.

For those who may be unfamiliar with Mr. Waggoner, his three most outstanding credentials are his onscreen familiarity as a foil for Carol Burnett and as Wonder Woman's main squeeze, Steve Trevor; as a man so blindingly handsome that not only çan he wear a tuxedo in a manner that would make Noël Coward and Cary Grant seem like Okies, but looks as if he should be on a pedestal somewhere in Thrace; and exudes charm in what can only be called a slow charisma leak. He made several introductory remarks about Carol Burnett's chest measurements that dribbled over into smarmy, and then introduced his wife Sharon, who was to share commentary responsibilities during the pageant. Sharon Waggoner, a former Miss Missouri, rivaled her husband for gorgeousness.

Then began the parade of fifteen finalists. The first pass across the stage and down the runway among the tables, with a 90° turn that brought the women directly in front of us at the judges' table, was done by the numbers, each contestant called Miss Maureen or Miss Cindi or Miss Laurae. No last names.

The first pass, the women were clad only in shorties, teddies, bikini briefs and other diaphanous undies for which I do not know the proper nomenclature. High heels, body stockings and spectacular hairstyles credited in the program to Michael J's Hair Force completed their ensemble. And here they come, fellahs!

We pause for a moment of reflection.

How do you grade a woman's ass from 1 to 10? Which nylon-clad leg is a 4 and which an 8.5? No doubt someone who spends eight hours a day photographing exquisite women—say, Helmut Newton or David Hamilton or Francis Giacobetti—can discern the subtle variations in parallel muscular fasciculi forming competing glutei maximi, or accurately substitute eyeballing for calipers in gauging the relative esthetics of the dear little popliteal space...but not I. And when confronted by fifteen women, the least of whom is what my friend Shelley calls a "to die," by what yardstick of goddessdom do you presume to estimate another human being's grace at 3 rather than 5?

It may seem berserk even to have to put oneself in a position to *have* to do it, but as I said earlier, there I was and: It seemed like a good idea at the time. So I took the job as seriously as my co-judges were taking it, as seriously as if we were selecting a Nobel prizewinner. One can do no other. As Thomas Carlyle said, "Whatsoever thy hand findeth to do, do it with thy whole might."

And so, as Sherée (26, 5'5", French and Italian ancestry, 112 lbs., degree in Business Management from El Camino College) pirouetted up there on the runway in front of me, wearing a red and white fringed baby doll and panties, I forgot that I was made of mere mortal clay, and ran the line of thigh and hip through the caliper computer and graded her.

As Cindi (5'9", brown eyes, brunette, married) passed before us, ethereally turned out in a two-piece hand-painted emerald-green toga and briefs, I graded her.

Debbie (5'8", 125 lbs., 36-26-35, actress, waitress, softball pitcher) in her tuxedo teddy; Hope (blonde, blue eyes, 110 lbs., "Miss California Bikini," "Miss L.A. Bathing Beauty," "Miss Jose Cuervo") in her sheer pink nylon baby doll, doing erotic little movements with her hands, her hips, her candy cane; Shallan (26, 5'8", 120 lbs., journalism degree from Cal State, Long Beach) in a sheer strapless lace teddy....

I graded them. God help me, I graded them. Here a 4 on the basis of knobbly knees, there an 8 for the humanity of a leg trembling with nervousness at the turn; here a 6 for too much fleshiness, there a 10 because I felt my groin stir.

We pause for a moment of reflection.

Nearly three hundred women turned out for the preliminary selection of contestants. One of the contestants told me that the turnouts are equally as large for the Mr. Tush contests. She also told me that the female turnout for the male pageants is overwhelming. The women come and ogle and hoot and scream and whistle. She said it made a night at Chippendale's look like meditation hour in a nunnery. I asked her why she thought male-watching was so popular. She chuckled, with an edge in her voice, and said, "Maybe we're just paying the men back."

Maybe so. Because as one after another of the women passed silkenly before the crowd, the men lost control of their cool. Decorum went south for the winter. There were more glassy eyes in that ballroom than in a doll factory. The whoo-eeee that you hear in crowds at rock concerts. Behind me and to the left I turned to see a guy in a tux, with his jacket off, his tongue actually hanging out of his mouth. I have seen a great many things in my life: I have seen a blacksnake water moccasin kill a ferret; I have seen a Cessna plow thorugh a dozen cars on a turnpike; I have seen John Steinbeck up close. Never, till Sunday the 5th of December in 1982 had I seen a man watching women in their underwear, with his tongue hanging out.

Let's cut to the shootout.

There was another pass of all 15 beautiful contestants, this time in peignoirs, nightgowns, hostess sheers; there was a fifteen minute break in which a comedian named Denny Johnson performed well, I am told; I wouldn't know how well he did: after seven Perriers, I had more pressing considerations; there was a final run with the women stunningly attired in Merry Widows, nylons, garter belts. Then we toted up our grades, passed our sheets to the tabulator, and waited while the Waggoners introduced Madame T., Pauline Barilla, who thanked everyone who needed thanking; as Edie Webber, Her Honor the Mayor of Hermosa Beach, presented a proclamation to Madame T. praising her and the Tushery as pillars of the South Bay community and declared December 5th "Miss Tush Day."

And then, against all odds, Shallon Ross was named the winner. Miss Tush 1983. All but one of the other contestants seemed genuinely delighted. There was clearly a sense of good wishes, of camaraderie among them. Miss Tush won an all-expense-paid trip for two for a week in Hawaii, plus $500 cash, plus a wardrobe valued at over $1100, plus a modeling contract for 1983 with The Tushery, including featured presentation on the Miss Tush Calendar.

Then I went home and began to write this column. I thought I'd have it ready for publication by Monday morning. Last week I was not represented in these pages, because I found I could not simply write of my evening at the Proud Bird as an amusing lark. I have returned

434

from the dark and smoldering interior of that strange land, one duchy of which is my own erotic male sensibility, and I have no answers.

What might have seemed a silly and socially indefensible hype to promote a couple of lingerie shops, resisted that easy a pigeon-holing. Even with the bear pit sounds of the male honkers still ringing in my ears, I could not simply dismiss what I had seen as the atavistic preening rituals of superannuated postpubescents. Something more was going on with the Miss Tush Pageant. Parts of the puzzle don't fit, no matter how hard I whack them with a hammer of intellect.

To write of my bewildering species I would even go to be a judge at a beauty pageant. It seemed a good idea at the time. And once there, having taken on the job, I did it with all my might. But now I come back to you, to report what I found out about a sizeable segment of the South Bay population, about what they do on a Sunday night and pay twenty bucks a head to do.

Each of the contestants with whom I spoke about motivations for having entered the contest, spoke of the experience in glowing terms. Each rhapsodized about Pauline Barilla, saying she was determined that the women conduct themselves "like ladies." Not one of them felt used. Some few of them had been pushed into it by their boy friends. I leave that aspect of the puzzle to conjecture. But each of them felt enriched by having done the Pageant. Shallon Ross, in particular, an intelligent, thoughtful young woman whose decency and bemusement were so obvious up there on the runway that I'm sure they were the deciding factors in her winning the crown, told me that her self-image had always been lower than she might have wished, and she had entered the Pageant as an amateur because she had always been intimidated by *Playboy* centerfolds, by models in *Vogue* ads, by the ideals of womanhood that had always been held by the male-dominated world.

And when I asked her if it didn't give her pause now to *be* one of those icons that might intimidate *other* women, she said softly, "Yes, I've thought of that. I've wondered if I just became part of the problem."

The problem. Even Madame T. thinks about it. Is the Miss Tush Pageant—and all the other public parades of women as objects—something intrinsically vile and demeaning? Is it a well-staged, commercially-exploitative excuse to afford concupiscent louts a chance to let their tongues hang out of their mouths in a socially-acceptable setting? Or is it simply good fun? Is it, from the other side, an opportunity for male and female to do the time-honored and arguably honorable dance of the sexes? Have we overintellectualized ourselves into a place where we deny the primal urges birds and deer and fish and monkeys enjoy? Is this sort of display merely the attitudinal breeding ground for the rape fantasy, or is the woman on a pedestal-as-runway, being eternally feminine?

Half of you, as you read this, will be on one side. You will know goddammed well what the Miss Tush Pageant means. The other half of you will be on the opposed side. And *you* will get madder than hell that I could even pose the question, because you *know* what's at stake here.

But let me put it to you this way. I stopped going to a well-known Valley restaurant because the management made the lovely wait-resses wear costumes that exposed body parts that a man would be considered a boor if he ogled elsewhere. Little ruffled panties peeping out from under short, puffy skirts; corded bodices that provided dark, interesting cleavages into which eyes were drawn. I stopped going there because I didn't like being manipulated by businessmen. If a woman in my company chooses to dress that way, to attract my attention, that's her choice, and if I respond, I respond to *her*. But to be manipulated at the level of my groin for the mean purpose of ordering more booze, is to demean the waitresses and give me over to excessive feelings to which I'm not entitled *at that place* or *with that stranger,* with whom I have no connection apart from good service and a proper tip.

Notwithstanding that view, there is this to consider: if I go to a cannibal culture, by what right do I tell the natives it's evil for them to chomp human flesh? When I marched behind a great man who was later shot for his beliefs, I was confronted by natives of those Southern Lands who called me "an outside agitator," who demanded to know by what right I came to their homes and told them how to live their lives. I said to them that I was not an "outsider," that I was a member of the Human Race and a resident of the planet, and thus I was entitled to make my voice heard in protest against their denial of human rights to that great segment of others who also abided in their states. But in what way are the women who willingly, even joyously, enter the Miss Tush contest being denied their rights? They're not drones, and they're not stupid. They may be under some pressure from boy friends, in some cases, but how much pressure does a boy friend have to apply to get a woman to parade around in front of nearly a thousand men in the scantiest, sexiest of undergarments? They're not even being exploited by a man. And Pauline Barilla says, with some truth, "The only way a woman can be taken off a pedestal is if she steps down by herself." Some truth: because the question should also be asked, why the hell should women *be* on pedestals? Isn't that one of the reasons women have been kept so dependent for so long, because the image of them was that they were Dresden figurines? And hasn't the major gain of the feminist movement been to demonstrate to women that, like Pauline Barilla who is indepen-dent and has raised four kids and is one helluva sharp business-woman, no woman need base her worthiness on pedestaldom?

I have been to a strange land, where men hoot and sweat, where women preen and strut, where buffet with and without forks is proffered in service of eyeballing. And I do not know whether the several erections I had on the night of December 5th were okay because I'm still human and would be seriously troubled if I had been utterly oblivious to what was going on in front of me...or if I was manipulated as nearly a thousand other men were manipulated... if I was in the midst of something professionally corrupt...or if I was in the middle of a bunch of healthy people engaged in a form of art appreciation.

It could be said that even the Miss America Pageant, as basically dolorous and boring as it is, makes some small nod to recognizing the contestants as whole human beings: they must have a "talent," and they must give a little speech about how much they love God and America. And even though it is clearly eyewash, even though we all understand it is an excuse to see beautiful women in bathing suits... at least the nod is there. It could be said that the Miss Tush Pageant reduces women to nothing but walking clothes hangers, that the insipid questions asked by Lyle Waggoner and the rehearsed answers by the Tushettes are insulting as well as humiliating.

It could also be said that in our sincere desire to bring equality to half the population of this country, that we are becoming ashamed of our own basic drives and the Eternal Romantic that trembles between men and women, between men and men, between women and women.

All of the above can be said. And as my report from the darkest interior of that strange land...has been said.

It is not necessarily incumbent on one who perceives the nature of the problem, to have the answers to the problem.

It may simply be that the only answer that makes sense is this: It seemed like a good idea at the time.

# Interim Memo:

This one, sadly, is my favorite of all the columns I wrote. I have read it, from time to time, on the lecture circuit; and I've yet to be able to get through it without breaking down and embarrassing myself with tears.

They killed him because he cared too much. He hurt no one but himself, and no doubt his dedication *had* driven him past the point of socially acceptable behavior; but his death brings shame to us as a nation, because it demonstrates that both common sense and compassion have been leached out of our national character to a degree heartrending to consider. We are, finally, no better than Richard Nixon, who went to the windows of the White House, saw hundreds of thousands massed in the streets to protest, snickered, and went back to watch the Super Bowl.

I tell you his name because it has been just two weeks since Wednesday, December 8th, and already you've forgotten who he was: his name was Norman Mayer, he was a mad saint, and he loved us enough to die for our sins.

He was the man in the blue jumpsuit and motorcycle helmet who, at 9:30 AM, Eastern Standard Time, drove his white 1979 Ford van up close to the main entrance of the Washington Monument, stepped out, and began a ten-hour act of humanism that culminated at 7:23 PM with his needless death.

Professionally-lettered on the side of Norman Mayer's van was a placard that read #1 PRIORITY: BAN NUCLEAR WEAPONS.

He drove past the Park Service rangers, a little more than two weeks before Christmas, the time of celebration of the birth of the Prince of Peace, and he handed one of them who had come running a manila envelope on the outside of which was written his determination to speak only to a reporter. He told the ranger he had 1000 lbs. of TNT in the van, and if we didn't begin a "national dialogue" on the threat of nuclear weapons, he would reduce the 555-foot-high obelisk to "a pile of rocks." He held in his gloved hands what the saturation tv coverage kept referring to as "an ominous black control box."

It was, in fact, a harmless joystick mechanism used to fly model airplanes. There was no "radio gear in the knapsack."

There was not, as any fool with common sense knew from 9:30 AM on, even one stick of TNT in that van. Nor, as simple logic would have shown, was there ever a moment's danger from "the menacing terrorist who held the Monument hostage."

Everything he did, from the moment he pulled up to the obelisk, till the moment he lay handcuffed to the steering wheel of his van, shot four times and dying from a bullet wound in the head, was the action of a compassionate man who understood just how bloody we have become. And who gave his life to prove the point.

At seven AM Los Angeles time on that Wednesday morning, after having written all night and being unable to sleep, I was tuned to Ted Turner's Cable News Network, as the first live on-site pictures of the "emergency" broke in on regular telecasting. I saw the van tight to the main entrance of the Monument, I listened to the explanation of what had happened, *was* happening, and the first thought that came to me was, "It's a bluff. He hasn't got any dynamite in that truck!" I *knew* it. Common sense dictated the conclusion; it didn't take a Sherlock Holmes and deductive logic to know the truth. Everything the man in the black helmet *did* led one's reason to the conclusion. It was a bluff.

Within an hour of the start of the siege, the police and FBI knew who he was. They knew he was an old man, 66 and deeply committed to the banishment of nuclear weapons. They knew he was no international terrorist, no crazed killer, just a wild old man trying to make a point. More important, they knew that a half ton of TNT would barely scratch the surface of the Monument. But property is more important than human life.

He demanded nothing for himself. No ransom, no great sum of money, no fast plane to take him out of the country, no release of Red Brigade assassins. He merely wanted us to *talk*. He just wanted to plead with us to expand the dialogue. He was as one with the millions across the world who have marched and pleaded this last year. Marched and pleaded for the right of the human race to live out its days without the mushroom-shaped shadow blighting our joy. Yes, he was an extremist; yes, he was bereft of his senses; but he did not deserve to die.

Within a few hours his actions bespoke that intention. Had there been a scintilla of compassion, rather than macho posturing, in any of the authorities handling the situation, it need not have ended as it did. But there was none. Not on the part of Associated Press reporter Steve Komarow, who spoke to him five times; not on the part of Capt. Robert Hines, commander of the Park Service police, who preened and pontificated before tv cameras like one of those satraps on a road repair crew who is given the red flag to stop traffic and becomes a martinet with that puny power; not on the part of the White House advisors who moved Ronald Reagan's luncheon out of the room facing the Monument. And not on the part of our noble President who, like Richard Nixon, saw what was going on and shrugged, and ignored his responsibility.

And when, shortly after seven o'clock that night, Norman Mayer came to his senses and was terribly frightened by his own boldness, and tried to flee, to return to the anonymity from which he had emerged...they blew him away. When the first FBI special agent reached the van, the old man was lying there mumbling, "They shot me in the head."

And no one has protested the violence. He deserved it. He was a threat. He was a terrorist and we can't bargain with terrorists. "We couldn't take a chance he'd be driving around Washington in a van full of TNT," is the standard explanation for his death.

But common sense would have informed the conclusion that there *was no* threat, that there *was no* TNT. Common sense and a dollop of human compassion would have softened that killing posture. Had he been a man with death in his heart, he would not have walked into the Monument at 9:30 and told all the tourists, "Please leave quietly." He would have held them as hostages. He would have kept those seven people trapped at the top of the obelisk. He would have threatened the SWAT teams with instant explosion of the mythical TNT if those seven people tried to walk down the 555-foot structure. But he didn't. He *asked* that they be escorted from the Monument by Park Service rangers, and some of them even nodded to him as they passed him. He nodded back. I saw it on the news.

Did the police and the FBI even seek the advice of a good psychologist? Did any of them sit and sum up the realities...not the maybes and the what-ifs...just the *realities* of what Norman Mayer was doing? Nowhere in the reports do we hear of such action being taken. Just the gunslinging bravado of the O.K. Corral. Ending in the hail of rifle fire that killed old, crazily-committed Norman Mayer.

Were we not one with Richard Nixon, someone would have said, simply, "He wants to make his point. He wants to be heard." And in my deranged fantasy I see them telling Ronald Reagan that one of his people is in pain, is hurting with fear so much for the rest of his species that he wants a chat. And Ronald Reagan would have said, "I understand. Let's take a walk." And he would have crossed that short distance across the Mall, and he would have walked up to Norman Mayer, and he would have said, "Mr. Mayer, I understand what you're trying to do; but this isn't the way to do it. You're scaring people, Mr. Mayer. And you're getting yourself in terrible trouble." And Norman Mayer would have been so amazed that for the first time his existence had been validated, that he would have put aside that pathetic model airplane control box, and he would have walked back to the White House for a cup of tea and a quiet conversation with the leader of his nation, who had demonstrated that even the least of his countrymen was worth postponing lunch.

But that's a fantasy. And kindness is a fantasy. And common sense in the face of cocked guns is a fantasy. We are a nation of SWAT teams and too little open conversation.

I know I am foolish to suggest Ronald Reagan might have had the personal courage to end the "emergency" by bold leadership. I hear the snickers and the repeated phrase, "We couldn't take a chance," even though they *knew* they were in no danger of the bluff being genuinely threatening. I know I am alone in feeling that there was something noble and courageous and infinitely humane in Norman Mayer's act. Nonetheless, I have cried for him since I saw them open fire on his van.

And I cannot but consider the irony of his having died so near a monument to the President who said, "If men are to be precluded from offering their sentiments on a matter which may involve the most serious and alarming consequences that can invite the consideration of mankind, reason if of no use to us; the freedom of speech may be taken away, and dumb and silent we may be led, like sheep to the slaughter."

SANE is worried that Norman Mayer's strange behavior might "tarnish the image of the entire antinuclear movement," but in every progression of social reform, from Joan of Arc to Martin Luther King, it is the mad endeavor of a John Brown or a Spartacus that demonstrates the depth of angst most of us can only pay faint obeisance to.

Norman Mayer was presented to us by tv and by the authorities as a bad man. He had been arrested in Hong Kong in 1976 for trying to smuggle a small amount of marijuana; he was a drifter and a low-class hotel handyman; he had been jailed for civil disobedience distributing antinuclear leaflets on college campuses in Miami Beach; he had tried to buy dynamite in Kentucky; he was a deranged fanatic. All that may be so...and common sense tells me it is so. But as I see Ronald Reagan seeking to discredit the Antinuclear Movement in this country and across the planet, I cannot fight back the certain knowledge that Norman Mayer was a Great American. He died as he lived, futilely; but at least for me his death was a martyrdom that illuminates with a sickly pallor the cowardice and inhumanity, the inflexibility and disregard for the plight of our people that keynotes Reagan's administration and the Imperial Presidencies that have preceded it.

And though I know you won't, I would be remiss if I did not suggest that at this holiest of holiday times, whether it be Christmas or Channukah, that you light one extra candle this year. For Norman Mayer, a sad and driven mad old man who cared enough to take a few too many steps in our behalf.

Maybe that should be *two* candles. One for him, and one for us. Because as Norman Mayer knew, we are in terrible danger.

**INSTALLMENT 56:** 22 December 82

# INTERIM MEMO:

The letter following this installment, objecting to my takeout on the Miss Tush Contest (Installment 54), is of small historical note because at the same time Ms. Giegerich was upbraiding me for writing a conundrum column which was actually about the lines we draw between group minority rights and personal human rights (more than it was about a lingerie contest), I was being awarded a medal by the National Organization for Women for eight years of service in support of the Equal Rights Amendment, in a public ceremony at the Century Plaza Hotel.

*Letters reprinted with permission from the* L.A. Weekly

They're killing me with these deadlines, folks. No sooner do I hand in installment 55 than Phil Tracy is on the horn telling me that this issue of the paper has to go to bed the next day. Would that profundities came to me unbidden; but the truth is that epiphanies happen only once every fortnight for your columnist; and so this week's ramble is precisely that: fill-in. Perhaps it's time to answer some mail and correct some stupid errors I've made, and clean the slate for the New Year. So rest easily...I won't trash anyone this time.

One point I would like to make, however. I attended the *Weekly*'s annual Christmas bash last week, at which gathering I met, for the first time, many of the people who put out this estimable journal. To my surprise and considerable pleasure they were all, with one exception, affable and complimentary about these auctorial outings. The one exception was a harridan whose name does not appear on the masthead (nor will it appear in this column) who braced me and began giving me stuff. Her cavil with me, considerably slurred either from the effects of too much bad dope and booze, or from tertiary brain-rot, was that I was posing as "an '80s person" (her phrase).

I don't really know what she meant by that. As the decade is barely two years gone, I doubt that a stereotype, or even a viable somatotype, can be projected as prototypically "'80s." But whatever it finally turns out to be—and if *she's* the model we are definitely on our way to joining the dinosaurs as an unworkable biological experiment—I ain't a candidate for inclusion. I was born in the middle Thirties, was a kid in the Forties, stumbled through the horrible Fifties, reached belated puberty in the Sixties, and began to grasp some small part of what life was all about in the Seventies. Though I wrote for the *Free Press* in the '60s and '70s, I was *in,* rather than *of* the paper or that milieu. I have too much history in my skin to identify much with any Now Generation.

So the croaking by the Fedco Discount Wicked Witch of the West utterly bewildered me. If others of you out there share a *folie à deux* with her, and perceive intimations of my trying to shoehorn myself into the punk technopop spiked hair *shmatah*-clothing negative affect ingroup, please reread. I'm too old and cranky to run with a gang.

Not to mention that if my compatriots in such a pursuit turned out to be this high priestess of the intellectually destitute, I would rather spend my remaining years as a caretaker at the Crystal Cathedral.

Onward. A minor glitch two weeks ago caused the deletion of the photo credit on the Miss Tush of 1983 picture. The photo was taken by Fritz Ptasynski, who broke his butt, or tush, or whatever, getting the photos of Shallon Ross to me before deadline. Apologies for the oversight herewith tendered.

Cindy Little of L.A. points out, much to my chagrin, that I referred to Eugene Ormandy as "the late." She writes, "If he is, then the photograph in *Time* last week had him stuffed, sitting next to Gene Kelly on a couch." She is correct, and I'm fuddledly wrong, of course. My brain did one of those skip-logic tricks and I was thinking about Arthur Fiedler. I think parts of my head need a long vacation. Papeete, here I come!

Two letters blown in on a Santa Ana personify the extremes of opinion re the Miss Tush essay. I quote them without comment, save to hope the mid-range of responses yet to come will elicit somewhat more intellectually-searching considerations, which is what was intended by the column. The first letter is from Don Morris of Santa Monica, who writes:

"Cease and desist and perhaps refrain from ignoring then denying the biologically-determined, physiologically and psychosexually conditioned characteristic differences between the sexes that are as different as cats and dogs, Mr. Tush contests and Chippendale's women's nights notwithstanding.

"Despite your excellent writing gifts, try to climb out of that quagmire of quasi-liberal social causes (Feminism, etc.) that cause you and your Reader (me) such terrible Tylenol-of-Chicago headaches.

"There is no great Philosophical Contradiction to hold over men's heads when a small segment of our masculine grouping takes a vacation from the preoccupation with our mistresses' G-spot, and perhaps slobbers and salivates (as rutting animals) over 'hot' chicks in fetishistically tantalizing sweet nothings."

The other far outpost of comment comes from Diane Street of Los Angeles, who wrote, crumpled, threw away, and then decided to send a note that reads:

"Ellison, don't let erections fool you. You were *used*. We aren't ashamed of our basic drives, but crap like tush pageants make us want to be. You know it's quite one-sided in this country (planet). There is no artistry in oppression. 'Pedestal' femininity is a hoax. Those events show women who are used to satirize being female, and they don't even realize it's happening. There are no questions in my mind on any of these things."

Received in the mail a dandy little booklet of some 66 pages titled

EVERYBODY'S GUIDE TO NON-REGISTRATION. Written by attorney Carol Delton and community economic planning consultant Andrew Mazar in late 1980, this publication is an exhaustive information primer that provides military draft age persons, counselors, teachers, parents, etc. with all the data one needs on how *not* to register for the draft. While I advise no one either way on registering or avoiding doing same, I must tell you that I was drafted for two of the most ghastly years of my life in 1957, and were I of the ominous age today, I would send $2.50 (including postage, handing & tax) at once (check payable to EGNR) to 2000 Center Street, #1091, Berkeley, California 94704. At *once* I'd send it. Or run like hell.

Continuing interest from a substantial number of you anent the kind of monies being paid for freelance writing in America prompts my reprinting the following figures from the *Authors Guide Bulletin* of last February-March. The freelance life, whatever its other rewards, is no way to get rich. What many writers don't realize is that pay scales only *seem* to be getting better. Actually, when inflation is taken into account, the freelancer is much worse off than twenty years ago. The fees magazines really pay are frequently different from (and usually higher than) the rates that they announce as standard in writers' reference sources. This chart may be outdated already. I understand the *N.Y. Times Magazine* is now starting out at $2500 for first acceptance.

| Publication | 1960 | 1980 | 1960 dollars | Percent change |
|---|---|---|---|---|
| *Cosmopolitan* | 1,000 | 1,500 | 540 | —46% |
| *Family Circle* | 1,250 | 2,000 | 719 | —42% |
| *McCall's* | 2,500 | 2,150 | 773 | —69% |
| *N.Y. Times Magazine* | 300 | 1,100 | 396 | +32% |
| *Popular Science* | 400 | 725 | 261 | —35% |
| *Reader's Digest* | 2,000 | 2,850 | 1,025 | —49% |
| *Redbook* | 1,400 | 1,950 | 701 | —50% |
| *Woman's Day* | 666 | 2,300 | 827 | +24% |

Several people inquired what happened to my romance with the woman for whom I said I would crawl through monkey vomit. It ended. Nice of you to ask, though. Maybe the grail is out there for me, but as of this writing...the search goes on. You see, we're not very different, you and I.

Some of you in the music industry noticed that on the preliminary Grammy ballot there was a nominee in the Spoken Word category labeled *Jeffty Is Five,* read by Harlan Ellison. Yes, that's your columnist, delighted and trepidatious about being this close to a Grammy nomination. As I'm up against Sir John Gielgud and Sir Ralph Richardson, I don't hold out very much hope that when they hold the big Grammy spectacular in February I'll be picking up any awards; but I must confess to a genuine thrill. I'd try and buy your votes, but I'm as tapped out as those of you who work full time in the recording industry.

Don't you hate those form letter hustles from the publishers of magazines to which you subscribe, urging you to re-up *at once,* before you lose even one precious copy...and then you notice on the computer replication of your mail sticker that you have eight months, or two years, or a decade to go before your previous sub runs out? Don't you hate it? Don't you wish they'd knock off that shit? Gee, I sure do.

Well, I see by the albatross on the wall that we're coming to the end of the year, as well as nearly a full year's installments of this column, so I'll invoke that mystic power I acquired in the Orient which enables me to cloud men's minds, so they cannot see me, and wish you the following for 1983:

Chances.

That's all you need, kiddo.

# LETTERS

**Jill Sez...**

*Dear Editor:*

Harlan Ellison is a pretentious, dim-witted, cliche-minded jerk. I can't stand it anymore! His last article on The Miss Tush Beauty Pageant was too much. Listen Harlan, do us women a favor and from now on stay off our side! It's no joke, Harlan. Women's rights are serious business and you clearly aren't up to it. Being such a devil-may-care, rebellious, crazy, walk on the wild side kind of guy must make it hard to take life seriously. So why don't you just step down from the podium and go about your business? We don't need the aggravation. Seriously.

—Jill Giegerich
Los Angeles

# INTERIM MEMO:

The turnout for the radio script reading described in this column was sensational. They filled the restaurant and had to set up video cameras for the overflow in other rooms. It was one of the best evenings of my life. You shoulda been there.

You are isolated on a remote plantation in the crawling Amazon jungle. And an immense army of ravenous ants is closing in on you... swarming in to eat you alive! A deadly black army from which there is no...ESCAPE!

Tired of the everyday grind? Ever dream of a life of romantic adventure? Want to get away from it all? I offer you...*Escape!* Designed to free you from the four walls of today for an evening of high adventure!

Next Wednesday night we escape to the Amazon jungle...and to a creeping, crawling *terror* as the Variety Arts Radio Theater presents the classic adventure tale, "Leiningen Versus the Ants" by Carl Stevenson, featuring in the title role...your terror-stricken columnist.

When you pass a record shop and see a sign in the window advertising the latest Who album for $1.98, and you dash in to save three dollars on the purchase, that's called a loss-leader. When Cal Worthington shows you a 1982 Lancia Zagato with the fold-down rear-roof section on *The Late Late Show,* and he swears on his sainted mother's name that it has only 3000 miles on it, was driven by a quadraplegic who only took it out to attend Agent Orange protest rallies, and it's down there at Worthington Motors for $2395, that's called a loss-leader. When a schmuck no sensible woman would go out with manages to con a traffic-stopper into a date by waving third row center seats to the Itzhak Perlman concert under her nose, that's called a loss-leader.

In service of introducing you to the joys of the Variety Arts Radio Theater, a group that performs Golden Age radio scripts *live* all through the year, I have happily, willingly, even enthusiastically consented to be a loss-leader by performing in their production of "Leiningen Versus the Ants" next Wednesday in the Tin Pan Alley cabaret theater of the Variety Arts Center at 940 South Figueroa.

Let me tell you about the Variety Arts Radio Theater, the Center, and about this moment stolen from the past.

Some time ago I began receiving invitations from a nice man named Bob Farley, to come down to The Society for the Preservation of Variety Arts, to attend one of the performances of this talented group of actors and audial thespians who, for five seasons, have been recreating in the plush and charming environs of the Center, the lost thrills of attending a radio drama studio presentation.

Finally, on a Wednesday evening last November, in company with a few friends who were also curious about what a "live radio show" might be like, we drove down the Harbor Freeway, got off at 6th (and found ourselves close enough to The Pantry, which is catty-corner to the Variety Arts Center, to have a late night T-bone), and entered the sumptuous, festive building, which was worth the trip itself. The Variety Arts Center was built in 1926, in a much more elegant era, and was converted into its present form in the mid-Seventies. There is a spiffy Vriety Roof Garden restaurant on the top floor, a W. C. Fields bar, an Earl Carroll lounge, a library of irreplaceable theater tomes and memorabilia, the Tin Pan Alley cabaret theater where old films are shown, and a 1200 seat theater on the main floor.

It is a splendid building, oozing eclat, lustrous and gorgeous, resonating to memories of times gone by when the ash had not settled quite so thickly over good taste in this land. It's the physical manifestation of scenes from Jack Finney's superb novel TIME AND AGAIN. It is the sound of Louis Armstrong playing "One of These Days" with Fletcher Henderson's Orchestra on an 80-groove-per-inch 1924 shellac disc. It is a world away from Chuck E. Cheese videogame parlors and plastic paraphernalia. It's the sort of place to which you would wear a Borsalino hat, where you'd sit quietly reading poetry by Hillaire Belloc, tales of archy & mehitabel by Don Marquis or a James M. Cain novel.

And it was there, one Wednesday night last November that my friends and I ascended in the little elevator to the third floor where, in the Tin Pan Alley cabaret theater, with its tiny bar set into one wall, we saw a splendid group of performers under the direction of Roger Rittner recreate episodes of *Doc Savage* and *The Green Hornet.*

We sat at the cabaret tables as Art Dutch and Daniel Chodos and Kimit Muston and Robin Riker stood before the blocky old-style mikes, holding their scripts; and David Surtees worked out of his cornucopial suitcase of sound effects; and once again as I had been pleasured as a kid, I was taken into the magic realm of radio drama. Once again the owner of the *Daily Sentinel,* Britt Reid, put aside his public persona, took up the mask and sleep-gas gun of the Green Hornet and, with his faithful Filipino assistant, Kato, cruised the streets in the Black Beauty, seeking evildoers beyond the reach of justice. Once again Doc Savage set out to unravel a baffling mystery: the enigma of the green ghost.

For my friends, who had grown up in the age of television, it was a wonder. If you doubt me, just call Lydia or Arthur at 986-6963 and ask them. They've become addicts of old-time radio, and consider an

454

evening at the Center something rare and special.

Next Wednesday night, at 8:00, I am privileged to work with these dedicated and antic spirits, in presenting for the first time in more than thirty years, a *live* radio performance of one of the most memorable dramatic productions ever aired. Carol Stevenson's "Leiningen Versus the Ants" is a program that no one who has ever heard it can forget. If you'd like a small sample, tomorrow night (Friday the 7th), I'll be asking KPFK's Mike Hodel to play a bit of the original show from the Forties program *Escape,* on "Hour 25" from 10–12 PM. That's 90.7 on the FM dial. Listen in, get hooked, and come out to the Variety Arts Center next Wednesday.

Dude up. Come early and have a good dinner in the Roof Garden restaurant, where former Musso & Frank's chef Victor sets out a good meal for between nine and fifteen dollars (including beverage and dessert). Stop by and have a drink in the W. C. Fields bar, and then amble down to the Tin Pan Alley cabaret theater. It's free. Won't cost you a sou. One note of warning: The Tin Pan Alley cabaret is only a 99-seat theater. Right now, as you read this, you'd better call 628-7782 and make reservations for the 8:00 performance. Or you'll wind up sitting on the floor.

But you *will* spend the sort of evening you mean when you mumble to your friends, "I want to do something *different* tonight, something exciting."

It can't get much more different and exciting than being trapped in the middle of the Amazon jungle as the voracious tide of the *marabunta* oozes toward you. In short, bored and exhausted readers, tired of the same old cable tv bullshit, what we are offering you, free of charge next Wednesday, is . . . *Escape!*

**INSTALLMENT 58:** 10 January 83

# INTERIM MEMO:

This was the last column of *An Edge* to appear in print in the *Weekly*. My dissatisfaction with the petty harassments of the publisher (but never the editor, Phil Tracy) had been growing, and we were having regular telephone arguments about what I should be writing about, the ways I was writing what I *was* writing about, the length of the columns, and etcetera etcetera. The reasons for my pulling the column are described in fuller detail in the afterword to this book. But this was my goodbye column, though no one—myself included—knew this was the kiss-off.

Ignorance ain't no way bliss. It is a condition of extended infancy; it is balm for inactivity. Confucius tells us, "Ignorance is the night of the mind, but a night without moon or star."

When the weight of knowledge grows oppressive, when the world is too much with us, we drop head into hands and think how much happier we would be if we were like those mythical drones we picture working on assembly lines, who know not...who know not that they know not...and whom we perceive to be always as cheery as bunny rabbits *because* they know not.

But that is another of the free-floating bits of distractive philosophy engendered and sustained by the paladins of the Status Quo to keep us from looting when the power grid overloads and the world is plunged into darkness. It is as much of a shuck as "Poverty is ennobling," the line fed to aspiring artists so they don't demand decent recompense for their efforts.

With all my soul I deny the dehumanizing subtext of ignorance being bliss. The ignorant are femur and cranium and sinew, even as we. They suffer and ache and yearn, even as we. They know they are beleaguered and unable to cope, beset by unfathomable Forces that keep them poor, that make the goods they buy fall apart before the time-payments are completed, that drive their children to bad street dope and ValleyGirl dialogue. The only difference between those with wisdom and those without is that the former have an inkling of who is responsible for all that angst. The ignorant hurt just as much; they just don't know who's holding the hammer that keeps knocking them in the head.

Inexplicably, ignorance frequently does not produce the expected condition of humility; but rather a towering arrogance, in which state the uninformed clings to the justification of unknowledge like a doomed soul sinking in quicksand clutches a rotted vine. Ah'm an Okie frum Muskogee an' damn proud tuh be as smart as a pencil eraser.

Trust me on this one: ignorance produces nothing even passingly close to bliss; what it encourages, tragically, is a condition of manipulability in the ignorant. Thus, when Ronald Reagan reaches an impasse with the MX missile, he employs the tactic of semantic

459

pollution, renaming the weapon "The Peacekeeper," and the malleable uninformed puff up with Hestonlike patriotism and simper their approval. The wool has thus been pulled over.

But the travail wrought by ignorance affects us in a hundred tiny ways on a personal level every day. In an effort to make the point on the most mundane level possible, consider this:

Several weeks ago I mentioned *en passant* that receiving resubscription hustles from magazines as much as a year before one's previous subscription has run out, pissed me off mightily. It was one of those idle Erma Bombeck comments that I thought would get a cursory mumble of agreement from others who'd been likewise lumbered. . .but nothing more. Imagine my surprise at receiving a dozen cards from readers who were as incensed as I was. Apparently, it is an imposition that angers a great many of you.

So I did some checking with the subscription manager of a national magazine, who has been a friend of mine for many years. He asked that I not use his name, but this is what he wrote in response to my query:

"Renewals are the life-blood of magazine publishing. When the renewals are pouring in, our president walks around smiling; it makes his day. New subs are usually offered at a low discount rate just to hook the reader: we don't make a dime on them. Renewals are where we get fat; they're the best and easiest way to make money. They are the reason we exist.

"I looked you up in our computerized subscriber files and, as I suspected, approximately three times a year you receive what is called an 'advance renewal.' It tells you that we are giving you the opportunity to extend your sub and alleges that in this way you are being protected from inflation. That, of course, is bullshit. All our subscribers get those letters, regardless of when the sub expires. Nowhere does it say the sub is running out; but people get confused and think that's what the letter *must* mean, so they just keep sending those offers back to us and they keep paying for year after year after year. We *love* people who do that. We think they're jerks, but we *love* them. Loyal subscribers. Some people actually don't expire until 2003 AD. It absolutely convulses me: we probably won't even *be* here then; not with the trouble we're having getting available ad space filled. Damn television!"

He went on to explain that six months before a subscription expires, they start sending out regular renewal notices. If they get the usual money return for "advance renewals" from the blissfully ignorant, it will be between 2 and 3% of the notices sent out, which he estimated to be between 5000–8000 renewals at $24 a shot. And so, even if it's only six months premature, it means his publisher can invest between one hundred and twenty thousand/one hundred and ninety-two thousand dollars in a money market account at 9½–10%

interest.

Unless you wish to lay claims to being a philanthropist, letting someone else play with even twenty-four bucks of your money at those kind of rates, makes you a patsy. Ignorant. But how much bliss attaches to not being able to buy twenty-four dollars' worth of food for the family?

He went on to say, "You'll receive up to six efforts, each pretty much saying the same thing, just packaged and worded a little differently than the ones directly preceding or following it. The 5th and 6th efforts tend to sound a bit more dramatic, if not hysterical and panic-stricken; but people are actually paid a lot of money to write these packages for us."

There is surcease from this hustle, fortunately.

Just send a note, along with your mailing label, to the circulation director of the offending magazine(s), asking to have your name removed from all mailing lists, mentioning in particular resubscription appeals. By law they must honor your request. Just don't write the note across the front of a bill or renewal notice. Only a computer will see it.

Now that we've shone light into *that* corner of your ignorance—hoping that by arguing from the smaller to the greater you will perceive the value of taking note of the tiniest incursions into your privacy and well-being—we are ready to move on to the next annoyance: those ugly glued mailing labels that deface the magazines you want to keep for reference or rereading later. Those labels that obscure the fine art or expensively-commissioned photography that you are prevented from enjoying in an unmarred state, that if you try to remove leave the cover of the magazine adhesive with remnant glue that rips off the back cover of the next issue stacked on top of it.

From the smaller to the greater. Next week you will discover that something as seemingly unimportant as which cover—front or back—the magazine uses to affix the label is a manifestation of Big Business's disrespect for you as a consumer.

Next week I will ask you to enlist in one of those small crusades that will do nothing more than improve your life in an almost imperceptible way. But it may give you a feeling of having some power, of getting a little more respect from those you support with your money and your loyalty.

Next week, for your pleasure, we begin the Addressee's Crusade. Bring your grail and your lionheart.

# INTERIM MEMO:

I wrote this one, and the publisher of the *Weekly* wouldn't run it. No one, he contended, wanted to read 2500 words about (are you out of your fuckin' mind, Ellison?) mailing labels. So I reminded him that our deal had been a simple one: "I write 'em; you run 'em." No changes, no directions about what I should say, no bullshit. If that policy didn't sit well, then adios, muchacho. By this time the publisher was getting static from inside the *Weekly* organization, from the punk *poseurs* who were filling the paper with endless reviews of heavy metal and New Wave bands that formed and folded within weeks of their rave notices. The newspaper was doing very well now, the circulation had jumped considerably (by all reports from the circulation department in large part because of my column), and my "tone," one of commitment to action and a sort of battlement mentality, rankled the shit out of many of the postteens more concerned with Def Leppard and the Gang of Four, how spikey and aqua-tinted they could get their hair, how surly they could pretend to be (what we call "copping an attitude"), and how many advertisements for hair styling salons they could squeeze into the *Weekly*'s pages, than they were about publishing unpopular personal opinion. But then, what else do you expect me to say? In any case, this column, which ain't really about mailing labels, if you've got the simple sense to read the greater rather than the lesser, appears here for the first time.

The panic was on. Deadlines were coming due in bad karma job-lots. There simply were not enough hours in the day to do it all; and everyone was screaming. I'd been at the typewriter for thirty hours trying to do three jobs at once. The coffee was going through me without passing go, without collecting two hundred dollars. The word *cranky* would ennoble my attitude.

Then I came to a place in one of the pieces I was writing that required a specific fact about the new use of Doppler radar in monitoring tornadoes.

Samuel Johnson once noted, "Knowledge is of two kinds. We know a subject ourselves, or we know where we can find information." I'm blessed with one of those packrat intelligences that remembers vast amounts and varieties of seemingly useless minutiae. But I can't remember it all. What I *can* do, is make a mental note of where the information was published. Which is why my home and office creak under the weight of something like 47,000 books, magazines, tracts, pamphlets and assorted incunabula. I may not know what I need to know, but I have at my fingertips the sourceworks that *contain* the knowledge.

And I remembered that Doppler tornado detection had been featured on the cover of an issue of *Science News* about two years back. So I went to the *Science News* files and started leafing back through, knowing I'd find it on the front cover. All I had to locate was that color radar display. Forty minutes later, with time to accomplish the crushload of work slipping away as I went insane trying to find a magazine that *was not there* where it should have been, I gave up and faked the data.

Naturally, I got caught. The one error I'd made in the article was in relation to the fact I couldn't find.

A month later, trying to find something else entirely in my files of *Science News,* I came across an issue whose cover had been ripped loose. The cover was sticking to the back of the issue that had been laid on top. I peeled it loose, and naturally it was the June 7, 1980 issue with the tornado essay.

And for the millionth time since I'd started subscribing to magazines in my teens, I cursed the sonofabitchin' address labels they affix to the face of periodicals.

When last we got together in this column, I used the paradigm of resubscription demands months ahead of your expiration date as an example of how we are "used" by big business to our detriment. A whole lot of you wrote in to say that had been pissing you off, too. So on the theory that these petty impositions fry you, and you say nothing because you figure they're too niggling to worry about, that others will scoff at your fussiness, I propose this time to apprise you of yet another one that may have been making you grit your teeth for years, but about which you've taken no action because you don't want to seem like an anal-retentive old fart.

I speak, of course, of address labels on magazines.

Now, if you're one of those who haven't the faintest idea what I'm going on about, if you get magazines in the mail and just toss them on the coffee table with the labels still affixed, and cannot understand why anyone would even *give* a shit about something so beneath notice. . .move along to some other section of this newspaper. *But!* If you are one of the millions who peel the label off the beer bottle as you sit chatting, if you are the sort of fussbudget who removes the price tag from the aspirin bottle before it goes in the medicine cabinet, if you are someone who saves the magazines you buy on the off-chance you may need to refer to them sometime later. . .you're nodding your head and muttering, "Sic'm, Ellison!"

Thus, you are ready to join me in the Addressee's Crusade.

As a reader, I subscribe to the following periodicals (this is a partial list): *American Film, New York, California, Los Angeles, TV Guide, The Skeptical Inquirer, Zoom, Playboy, Heavy Metal, Parabola, National Geographic, Gourmet, Science News, Esquire, NY Review of Books, Time, Atlantic, Omni, Twilight Zone, The Underground Grammarian, Maledicta, US News & World Report, ARTnews, Business Week, Sport, Ms., Commentary* and *The Washington Monthly.* Do you have any idea how many man-hours and foot-pounds of energy I expend removing those bloody goddam labels?

*Why* do I remove the labels? Because, to begin with, they're ugly. Now I realize many of you consider esthetics in the same class with studies of the pore-patterns in early New England stone walls, but for some of us the sight of a gummed label festooned with incomprehensible strings of numbers and code-letters, plastered smack in the middle of a fine art painting or a lovely Bob Peak portrait of Sally Field is an affront in the eyes of GOD AND/OR WO/MAN! In the second place, if you've been saving, say, *Horizon* since the very first issue, when it was a handsome history and art publication bound in boards and tending more toward essays on Léger and the excavations at Ur than it does in its present form as slapdash magazine with curiosity about, say, "The Art of the TV Sitcom," then a full run of said periodical becomes a reference treasure no less valuable than the morocco-bound set of THE LEATHERSTOCKING TALES you occasionally wipe with saddle soap.

But when you try to peel the labels, you find they don't put them on with a light-application glue that frees the paper without damaging the magazine. You wail at discovering they use a hideous concoction I suspect is made of unequal portions of flour-and-water mucilage, Elmer's Glue, stucco epoxy and (the single most adherent substance in the known universe) cassowary jizzum.

What is left on the cover are (a) bits of attenuated label paper, (b) ripped slick cover stock and (c) at least two thick, sticky lines of blue-or pink-tinted glue. And when you lay that magazine down or put it in the rack, it binds to the one beneath—waiting to be lifted so it can rip the next in line.

After thirty years of this aggravation, the best I've come up with by way of solution is first to peel the label as slowly and carefully as I can, leaving as little of the glue as possible. Then, if one pours a bit of talcum on the glue, it can be wiped off leaving only hideous discolorations of the artwork beneath. Unsatisfactory, but the best I've come up with. Don't use lighter fluid: it bleaches out the artwork.

Okay, let's get away from the obsessive nature of this undertaking. Just register your faithful columnist as a whacko with a need to remove labels, and let me ask the following question, which is, in truth, the nub of the problem:

Magazines are forever bleating about not publishing this ad or that article because "it might offend." They constantly revamp layouts, tables of contents, logos, in an effort to serve the needs of their readers and, they hope, hold onto them in an era where more and more readers simply tune out the print medium and tune in the glass teat. They institute service columns. They slant toward ever narrower demographic groupings.

So the question is this: if mailing labels in the front cover annoy some of their subscribers, why don't they put them on the *back* cover, where they can be left affixed, not marring the expensive photography or artwork commissioned at staggering prices in hopes of snagging an audience?

If you cannot answer that question instantly, merely turn over the nearest magazine in your home and look.

There is an advertisement on the back.

They won't put the label back there, because it might piss off the advertiser. That's the simple of it.

When I put that question to five different magazine circulation directors, in preparation for this column, each one of them tried to snow me with the Accepted Wisdom that by postal regulation they *can't* put it on the back cover. They swore it was the truth. Now, since each of those people makes a decent wage at the respective publications, and one presumes the paycheck is so substantial because they know the job, I am left with the choices of them being uninformed...or they lied.

Because according to the Domestic Mail Manual, section 464.36, no preference is stated as to front or back cover. It is clearly indicated, in fact, that *either* cover will suffice, as long as the label is readable. So sayeth 2nd Class Mail Specialist Ed Biles.

So I called them back and read them the section. Then they went phumfuh phumfuh and said it was physically impossible, or at least hideously difficult, to do the job at the printing and binding plant. Uh-huh, I said.

So I called Larry Moshier, Jr., one of the customer reps at Pacific Press, which is the largest printer and binder on the West Coast, and maybe the biggest in America. Pacific Press handles 300,000 copies of *California* each month. Every week they run through a million copies of *Time*. (Six million more are processed through five other plants across the country.)

Larry tells me, in answer to my query about the impossibility of putting labels on the back cover, "Hell, no. No problem at all." Uh-huh, I said.

You see, the way they do it is this: The magazines are printed in signatures, then they're run down a conveyor belt from binding straight to mailing, non-stop. It's called "in-line mailing." The magazines are fed, *cover up,* into the addressing machinery, loosely termed a Magna Craft (though the wizards at Pacific Press have mutated the original Magna Craft behemoth with their own appendages) and they come out in a stack with the label stuck on the front.

Larry tells me the glue they have to use is as strong as it is because it has to bite through four color inks. Those suckers are, therefore, on forever, or until you break your fingernail trying to pry them off.

The line can run between 5–8000 individual units an hour. And all they have to do to put the label on the back, instead of the front, where it rankles us, is change the initial press layout for all the forms. In other words, all they have to do is send those units through *upside-down*. According to Larry, it costs not one cent more, takes no additional time, and makes no difference to the staff or the machines.

I asked him if any magazines *do* put the label on the back. He said yes. *Alaska* magazine does it. That's because they have some beautiful photography on the front. There are a few other magazines that please their subscribers in similar fashion; but the instance that gave me the clincher I needed for this column was *Westways*. That venerable publication prides itself on its cover art. And apparently they got some beefs from subscribers who didn't like their copies defaced. So *Westways* decided to put the label on the back cover.

No advertiser would go along with it.

So they didn't do it.

And when I approached Lou Harris, Executive Editor of *Los*

*Angeles,* for which I sometimes write, and made my case for treating the loyal subscribers at least as well as the casual, capricious newsstand buyer, he said no chance. I asked him why, and suggested he was afraid of antagonizing the advertisers who supplied the money to keep the magazine solvent, while angering the subscribers who provide the circulation figures that the Audit Bureau of Circulation publish that enable *Los Angeles* (as it is with all magazines) to *get* those advertising dollars. Lou said, "You got it. We prefer the bucks."

May I quote you? I said.

I'll kill you if you do, he said.

But you didn't say it wasn't for the record, I said.

Wait'll you see the rotten letters I run about your latest article, he said.

Sticks'n'stones, I said. Go ahead, run the crummy letters. *Los Angeles* only comes out once a month. The *L.A. Weekly* is out every Thursday. Instead of the letters demanding labels be put on the back instead of the front going to your Production Manager, or the Circulation Director at *Los Angeles,* I can arrange to have them sent directly to your home.

"You are not a nice person," Lou Harris said. "You are deeply disturbed."

Which is why you asked *me* to write the article on anger and revenge, and not Erma Bombeck, I said.

The point, gentle readers, is that Toyota, knowing *Alaska* was going to put a label on their ad, designed the layout so the label would lie along the spine, interfering not one whit with their hustling vehicles. Advertisers *will* accede, if the magazine owns it own soul.

But most magazines don't. They want your subscription bucks, which are nearly as important as advertising bucks, but they would rather short-change *you* than the advertisers. If you are a loyal subscriber, entitled to enjoy the art and photography on which the magazines spend millions of dollars obtaining the best, then *too bad chump.* If you are a passerby, maybe you buy and maybe you don't, then you get a pristine copy, unbesmirched by label. You see, folks, once they *got* you. . .you ain't worth worrying about, because it's the free-floating bucks and the advertiser's clout that *really* carry the freighting of concern.

So I propose we initiate an experiment. The Addressee's Crusade. Let us all pick one magazine that we want to convert. Let us decide which of the local magazines best needs to learn who's paying their way. Maybe you *don't* give a shit about the label, but do you also feel terrific knowing you couldn't do anything about being considered second-class subscriber, even if you wanted to?

Don't it anger you, kiddo?

Don't it make you feel impotent?

Wanna see if we can start a trend?

Okay, tell you what let's do. Let's pick a magazine. The best choices for us here in Los Angeles are *California* or *Los Angeles* magazine. Drop me a postcard. Put on it either one name or the other. I'll tote'm up and let you know in a couple of weeks which of these two miscreants slavering for the dollar instead of our approbation is the target. And then we can start sending letters to the Circulation Director.

I'll have sent copies of this column ahead, so they'll know what's hit them. Ed Biles of the Post Office and Larry Moshier, Jr. of Pacific Press tell us there's no good reason why a mailing label can't be stuck on the back cover. Let's see what *California* or *Los Angeles* do in response to a direct appeal from their readers.

Let's see who owns whose soul.

# L.A.WEEKLY

*The Publication of News, People, Entertainment, Art and Imagination in Los Angeles*

January 29, 1983

Dear Harlan:

I thought I'd send you a note on this occassion
to tell you that, with the exception of our
arguments over space, your column has been an
appreciated, positive force for the Weekly and
that I wish you well.  As you know, I always
enjoyed the politically-oriented columns best
but found a lot of them valuable and fun.  It's
too bad we had to disagree over space, but there's
no hard feelings and I do wish you best of luck.

Yours truly,

Jay Levin

5325 Sunset Blvd.    Los Angeles, CA 90027    (213) 462-6911

# INTERIM MEMO:

After I left the *Weekly,* I'm told that inquiries continued to come in for several months: what happened to the Ellison column? The publisher's line was that I'd just decided to stop writing *An Edge in My Voice,* which was codswallop. When I'd go out on the lecture circuit in the Los Angeles area, invariably I'd be asked why I'd decided to stop writing the pieces. I explained that such was not the case, not that simply explained. And in far places I'd occasionally encounter someone who'd subscribed to the *Weekly* so they could read *An Edge.* I tried to explain why I'd vanished from those environs. But, on sum, I felt good about two years' worth of occasional pieces. In the *Weekly* of 28 January 1983, a letter from an Alex Cox appeared. I never saw it. I was elsewhere by then. Apparently it stirred some residual interest and, in a spirit of completism, you'll find Mr. Cox's letter and several responses to him from the 4–10 February issue of the *Weekly.* These were the last times my name was taken in vain, or any other way, in that newspaper.

*Letters reprinted with permission from the* L.A. Weekly

# LETTERS

## Creeping Cultism

*Dear Editor:*

This is to inquire if other readers have noticed a strange slant creeping into the *Weekly*'s once-excellent editorial coverage over the last year or so: something one might call "the cult of personality reporting."

While other local rags contrive to publish interesting issues virtually devoid of star-status by-lines, the *Weekly* seems determined to thrust its pet reporters—specifically, Ginger Varney, Michael Ventura and columnist Harlan Ellison—at us in a manner so brazen as to put even Ben Stein or Andy Rooney to shame. To wit:

"There are two versions of Nicaragua—Ronald Reagan's and Ginger Varney's." (*Weekly,* 10th December). Two versions—really? What about Jaime Wheelock's? Or Eden Pastora's? Or Gabriel Garcia Marquez'? Or the Mizquito Indians'? Or even Thomas O. Enders'? Varney may be *right on:* that isn't the point. If you juxtapose Varney's name with Reagan's you reduce the whole Central American question to a conflict of personalities. Whom do we prefer—the actor/president or the film critic? This Point/Counterpoint approach is TV-feeble and will only convince those who don't need convincing. Is this enough for you? Or do you actually want to change some minds out there?

Similarly, a couple of months back you ran an excellent piece on the CIA's use of subliminals in the Latin America media. I showed the article to a sharp but skeptical acquaintance of mine. Unfortunately for my credibility, she turned the page—and was confronted by Michael Ventura's hommage to a hippie girl who picks up stones and *ommms* on Venice Beach. My friend shook her head and put the *Weekly* down. "And you take any of this *seriously?*" she asked.

Either you want to change minds or you don't. If you do, you can't afford this kind of lamebrain rambling undermining major cover stories. Now we are partway into Michael's major epic, a six(?) part series on the Screenwriter in Hollywood. Let me ask you this; does L.A. need another one of these? Does anyone, other than Mr. Ventura, who thinks he is a screenwriter, and likes to write about himself? [sic]

Harlan Ellison, finally, was washed up and discredited in science fiction circles years ago. A once-interesting writer (*once* being the late '60s), his readership deserted him as he drifted into egomania and the relentless detailing of his daily *minutiae.* I know of no magazine that would regularly print his stuff until the *Weekly* picked him up. And there he sits, part of the pantheon, informing us at length about the kind of car he drives, how he wrecked it, which good causes he supports this week, and how, above all, Harlan is not a sexist. *This* from the author of *A Boy and His Dog*.

As you can probably tell, I read the *Weekly*. I read it every week. And it makes me Goddamn mad that some of it is *very good* while so much more is *garbage*.

Might I suggest a small experiment? Give your Strategic Triad two months off. Send them to look for yellow rain in Laos and Afghanistan. And while they're huntin', look around for other work from other writers. Maybe they'll be sadly missed. But on the other hand....

—Alex Cox
Los Angeles


## Defending Harlan

*Dear Editor:*

I've just finished reading Alex Cox's rather sour-grapish sounding letter (*L.A. Weekly,* 28th January), and while Harlan Ellison is admirably suited to defend himself—what the hell. I've got a few minutes to spare.

First, Mr. Cox complains about Ellison's column as a responsible, legitimate forum for journalistic endeavor, decrying "the relentless detailing of his daily *minutiae*...informing us at length about the kind of car he drives, and how he wrecked it, which good causes he supports this week," and so forth. Perhaps someone should inform Mr. Cox that the personal essay—yes, *minutiae* included—is most assuredly a valid literary form. Just pick up either of the big local dailies and check out the Op-Ed page. Read Mike Royko. Or Hunter S. Thompson, Mark Twain, Kurt Vonnegut, Tom Wolfe...the list goes on, but why waste space?

Second, a flat-out error of fact on Mr. Cox's part. To say that "...no magazine would regularly print his stuff until the *Weekly* picked it up," is just plain untrue. "An Edge in My Voice" ran in the monthly national magazine *Future Life* for something like a year prior to the *Weekly* getting it—and even then, the popular column only stopped in its original incarnation because the publication disappeared from the newsstands. That he has done other columns in recent years for a number of publications is recorded fact.

And leave us not forget Ellison's column for *The L.A. Free Press,* entitled "The Glass Teat," which wound up anthologized in two volumes that have been reprinted several times and are *still* regarded as some of the best observations on TV by Walter Cronkite and *Publishers Weekly,* to name only two.

Finally, to say that Ellison was "...washed up and discredited in science fiction circles years ago," is a misreading of the facts that borders on outright fabrication. Much of Ellison's work, by his own admission (and insistence) does not fall under the heading of true SF. Most critics and published appraisals of his work—including the prestigious reference work *Contemporary Authors*—describes Ellison's work as "magic realism," on a par with some of the fantasy-oriented writings of Mark Twain and Jorge Luis Borges. In addition, Ellison makes no bones about keeping his name more-or-less disassociated with SF because to do otherwise is a terrific way to get pigeon-holed and, as a consequence, slapped into a lower standard of living and income. But this still doesn't stop publications like *The Magazine of Fantasy and Science Fiction* from purchasing stories of his like "The Hour That Stretches" *sight unseen;* nor does it prevent his work from being nominated for, and winning, Hugos, Nebulas and the like. So much for being discarded and washed up!

Mr. Cox's greatest single charge is that of egotism. Which is really rather amusing. It never fails that, if you live a varied, interesting life, people will grudgingly go ahead and permit you the right to live as you choose. But as soon as you start to *talk* about how interesting and varied your life is, you get hit with the charge of egotism.

Perhaps people like Mr. Cox don't like to hear from those whose lives are rich enough and fulfilled enough so that they don't have the time or inclination to attack those who, by way of printed word and resulting comparison, cause them to feel dull, inadequate, or bored.

Just a thought.

—J. Michael Straczynski
Glendale

*Dear Editor:*

In response to Mr. Alex Cox's letter (January 28) concerning the "cult of personality reporting" in the *L.A. Weekly,* I submit the following statements;

1) Having been associated with a similar type paper as the *L.A. Weekly,* in northern California, we found that irresponsible critics when offered a chance at a regular column would not, or could not, offer any copy whatsoever.

2) Hooray for Michael Ventura's series of continuing articles on "Surviving in Hollywood." As one involved in screenwriting for the last six years I can testify that, so far, the insights are fairly much on target and the writing style and enjoyment excellent. Once the series is complete, I hope the *Weekly* encourages and publishes a *full* response from the readers.

3) Mr. Cox's comments on Ginger Varney's Nicaragua series is well taken. The articles were meaningful, but the title ("There Are Two Versions of Nicaragua—Ronald Reagan's and Ginger Varney's") is a total mis-fire. *Weekly,* take note, this criticism did catch you with your pants down.

4) The reference by Mr. Cox to his "sharp but skeptical" friend that found disagreement with both the article on the CIA's subliminals used in Latin American media and Michael Ventura's feature on a particular woman poet as somehow connected is flam, non-specific and a self-serving anecdote of the embarrassing first kind. Let this "sharp but skeptical" person present her view forthright to all concerned.

5) Harlan Ellison's stature as an SF writer is well-established and well-earned, irregardless of the latest pronouncements by the newest clique of self-appointed experts. As far as Mr. Ellison's column is concerned (and I don't agree with Ellison all the time), he has always said it will be rambling and discursive. Submit your own column, Mr. Cox, for consideration. Perhaps you can do a better job.

—Michael Kerwin
Hollywood

**INSTALLMENT 60:** 23 June 82
(published in *The Comics Journal*
cover-dated October 1983)

# INTERIM MEMO:

The column seems to want to cling to life. Gary Groth continued to reprint the old installments every issue (or nearly every issue) in his specialty magazine (for information or subscription write: Fantagraphics, Inc.; 196 Haviland Lane; Stamford, Connecticut 06903). This essay, not originally an installment of *An Edge in My Voice* as it regularly appeared in the *L.A. Weekly,* was originally commissioned by—and in an unauthorized edited version appeared in—*Video Review* magazine (volume 3, number 6: September 1982). It was written in June of 1982 and was updated with an addendum for its October 1983 appearance in *The Comics Journal.*

As further update, a front page article in *USA Today,* the national newspaper, on Thursday, March 22nd, 1984 was headlined with the legend: 3000 VIDEO ARCADES ZAPPED. The piece went into detail of a self-fulfilling-prophecy sort (to my smug pleasure) anent the failure, in the nine months preceding this item, of more than one-third of the 10,000 videogame arcades in America. Game machine sales plummeted 65%, from 480,000 in 1982 (when, at the peak of the boom, I wrote this essay) to 170,000 in 1983. Income per machine at many arcades has dropped in half, from $120 to about $60 a week. And the Chuck E. Cheese Pizza Time Theatres and Video Arcades, based in Sunnyvale, California, franchisers of 247 pizza restaurants with arcades attached, lost $16 million in the fourth quarter of 1983 and have indicated they may well have to reorganize under Chapter 11 bankruptcy proceedings. You all know what's happened to Atari. I hope I never run into Bruce Apar, editor of *Video Magazine,* who made it clear he thought I was a know-nothing because I suggested he was making a buck off the weakness of kids. I'm not sure I'd have the nobility to avoid laughing in his face. History quickly *got'im!*

# Rolling Dat Ole Debbil Stone

Nothing in this world beyond the first 16 seconds of a baby's birth is innocent. Nothing is precisely what it seems to be. Anyone who believes otherwise spreads the marmalade of folly on his daily bread of reality. Anything can be a paradigm of life's important lessons.

Parker Brothers's Video Game Cartridge—*Star Wars: The Empire Strikes Back*—seems, at first encounter, merely another of the seemingly endless permutations of the callus-producing rage that has swept an entire generation of Orphan Annie-eyed, over-financed, leisure time-surfeited teenagers into electronic game arcades from Tampa to Tacoma.

But even the botulism bacterium looks innocent at first encounter. And *The Empire Strikes Back* videogame is an analogue for the Myth of Sisyphus.

Never having played a videogame, having stared with creeping horror at the legions of silent, intense kids mesmerized in front of Pac-Man, Space Invaders, and Donkey Kong machines in Chuck E. Cheese pizza & videogame parlors, I greeted the request to review this new cartridge with mixed emotions ranging from fearful curiosity to outright dismay.

I had no reason to think this fad was any more dangerous than swallowing goldfish, phone booth-stuffing, Hula Hoops, or wearing one's hair in imitation of Farrah Fawcett. Yet the vast amounts of money being poured into these games, the accumulated years of time lost playing them, the apparent absence of any benefit to the players, had produced in me a *frisson* of concern. In a nation where reading is becoming an arcane lost art, where television has become the universal curriculum, where the lemminglike pursuit of mindless "entertainment" has taken on the noble obsessiveness of a search for the Holy Grail, the inspired exploitation of the *Star Wars* totem in videogame form had, in the realm of possibility, the potential to emerge as the most virulent electronic botulism of all.

The Atari console system was rigged to a television set in my home, I read the simple instruction brochure, and proceeded to bore

481

my ass off for the next hour becoming as adept at *The Empire Strikes Back* as I cared to be.

(Kindly refrain from *kvetching* that a ten-year-old can become more proficient at one of these twiddles than I, an adult at least in years, could ever be. Yes, he or she very likely *can* beat me 99 out of a hundred times; but no ten-year-old I've ever encountered can write MOBY DICK, create a Sistine Chapel fresco, or fuck with any degree of expertise. And none of those are taught by videogame.)

The extremely simple-minded parameters of Parker Brothers's *Empire Strikes Back* are consistent with virtually all other video-games. Destruction is the object. A line of two-dimensional Imperial Walkers plod toward a Rebel power generator on the Ice Planet Hoth (if you can believe those mundane pastel readouts represent an Ice Planet). You, as player, have to blow them up with blasts from the five Snowspeeder aircraft you are given. The "object" of the game is to destroy as many of the Walkers as you can (it takes 48 direct hits to neutralize a Walker) before they reach the power generator and blow up the entire planet. Terrific object-lesson for kids to learn; invaluable for everyday life in a world where Nuclear Holocaust paranoia already immobilizes us.

The Walkers fire missiles at the Snowspeeders. They can track the zipping aircraft, fire "smart bombs" that loop and follow a Snowspeeder, blast fore and aft of themselves, and otherwise cause you aggravation. Occasionally a "bomb hatch" will open—as indicated by a minuscule dot of light that strobes too briefly for anyone to hit—save someone who has devoted his life to playing this game—and the Walker is off'd at once. Your Snowspeeders can be repaired and go back into action, but only twice. If you knock out a Walker, another one appears. Smarter, stronger, with new abilities. Points are amassed for various degrees of destruction to the Walkers; and for every 2000 points scored, you get an extra Snowspeeder.

There's a lot more hurly-burly. Walkers change color and are weakened as a result of amassed hits, you can crash your Snowspeeder into a Walker, sometimes you acquire the Force and cannot be destroyed...32 variations of one- and two-player games.

But here's the bottom line, quoted directly from the rules brochure: "END OF THE GAME: The game ends when the lead Imperial Walker reaches the power generator—or—when the last of your Snowspeeders is destroyed."

In other words, you cannot win.

The game ends when you lose.

It may take you ten minutes or 15 years. The level of your expertise may grow to be so elevated that the game will have to be concluded by your grandchildren, but...*you cannot win!*

In classical Greek mythology we find the familiar legend of Sisyphus, founder and king of Corinth who, because of his avarice and fraudulence, was condemned to the lower world, eternally to roll a great stone to the top of a steep hill, whence it always rolled down to the bottom again. This ghastly punishment, perceived through the ages as a paradigm for the worst eternal fate that could be visited on an errant mortal, is spoken of thus in WEBSTER'S DICTIONARY OF PROPER NAMES:

"Hence, a Sisyphean task, an unending task on which immense energy is expended with little to show for it."

Hence, playing Parker Brothers's *The Empire Strikes Back* videogame.

An unending task on which immense energy and great gobs of money are expended with little to show for it.

To be played by urchins incapable of reading a book, parsing a sentence, thinking an original thought; rationalized as valuable in establishing eye-to-hand coordination even if it's a coordination so specialized it won't help you sink an eight-ball in the hip pocket; costing, with its cheap and sluggish joystick console, enough to buy a good set of the collected works of Mark Twain; fostering a solitude of activity that separates the player even more from the real world; this latest icon of the Imbecile Industry is a pointless, time-wasting enterprise that can instill only one dreadful life-lesson in those of a youthful intelligence who play it.

And the lesson is the lesson of Sisyphus. You cannot win. You can only waste your life struggling and struggling, getting as good as you can be, with no hope of triumph. As one with governments in power, the chief reason for the existence of this game is to *stay* in power. To keep you playing. Over and over and over, rolling that great rock up the hill, killing Walkers, only to have the rock roll down on you again, only to have faster, cleverer, more destructive Walkers come to life on the screen. And you play, and you play, and in the twilight you find the cobwebs have smothered your imagination, your leg has gone to sleep, your money is gone, your friends have grown up and achieved immortality and died; and you are all alone there in the gloaming, with the radiant screen and its two-dimensional electronic death-machines...firing, firing...lumbering... making no progress, winning no awards, enriching life not one whit.

But does it really matter? Clearly not. Because life—as viewed by this and other videogame Body Snatchers—is a pitiless congeries of rocks being rolled up a steep hill, only to fall back. This is the lesson one learns from Parker Brothers and their shamelessly exploitative little toy. Unless one has the presence of self to become rapidly bored.

What a helluva recommendation: the best one can hope for is that one yawns before one's soul is snatched.

# Postscript

What you have just read was my first and last encounter with videogames. It was altered and presented in an unauthorized manner by the editors of *Video Review,* one of the leading magazines in the industry, who had commissioned it. (For those who may feel *Video Review* acted courageously in soliciting the writing of one whom they knew would probably disaffect their prime advertisers, not to mention their drone readership, be advised that the commission was tendered by one of their junior editors, a fan of my books, who caught sheer hell from the publisher. Parker Bros. did, however, pull its advertising from the magazine.)

Subsequent to its publication, I got a call from the office of the President of Atari in Sunnyvale, California. He wanted a copy of the original manuscript to frame on his wall, having seen a framed copy in the offices of Dr. Alan C. Kay, Atari's chief scientist.

That was the first that I knew of the amazing ripple effect my humble efforts were causing. Apparently the essay was the first dissenting piece ever published in the videogame community, and the screams were loud and long.

Within a month, the number one magazine in the industry, *Video Magazine,* featured an editorial by Bruce Apar, its head honcho, lambasting anyone and everyone who dared to suggest that videogames might not presage The Second Coming or some other portent of Utopia. It was titled "Video-game Critics & Cranks." And though it lashed out to all points of the compass in hopes of striking a target, the big blast was reserved for your self-effacing columnist as follows:

> *Adding to the strident rant of these cockeyed pessimists* [Mr. Apar wrote] *are irresponsible periodicals, one of which recently ran a review of a new game that insulted readers' intelligence by virtually ignoring the game. This so-called review was in truth a diatribe against all video games and people who play them. The writer, who freely admitted to never playing a video game before, was operating on that familiar premise, "If I don't like it, it's bad for everybody."*

Well, imagine my pleasure at discovering the behemoth was capable of a bleat now and then! Further enhanced by information that reached me later, the content of which was that Apar and his magazine had commiserated with Parker Bros. to the extent of telling their advertising department that *Video Review* was a nest of Bad Guys, and that they should convert all their advertising bucks spent with the magazine that had published such a dreadful bit of heresy . . . to the righteous venue of *Video Magazine*.

I wrote a letter to Mr. Apar. Here is most of it:

*Dear Mr. Apar,*

*Though referenced blind in your recent editorial, I suspect the name on the letterhead above will strike a familiar note.*

*One of your readers, recognizing the referent, sent along a Xerox copy for my attention, with the words, "Looks as if you pinked the bull." It would seem so.*

*I was advised, when I wrote the piece for* Video *Review (at their behest, and with considerable reluctance on my part), that it was the first dissenting view of videogames to be published in magazines whose vested interest is, of course, to keep as many kids goggle-eyed in front of Donkey Kong and Missile Command games as possible. And was further advised that it would bring forth the apologists for the industry in force.*

*They were correct in their estimation, of course. Your sally is estimably off-the-point and no defense of what I wrote from observation in the Real World seems required. The studies are beginning to be published on the effects of videogames on kids, so I take your umbrage as similar to that of the tobacco industry when it's suggested that cigarettes might not be good for people. But if you're going to rebut your critics, I suggest you find other grounds than that a reviewer had never before played such games. For that was* precisely *the reason I was chosen to write the review (apart from my literary and critical credentials, which even* Video *would have difficulty assailing). I had no preconceived opinions, and was ready to deal on the square.*

*It's a shame* Video, *and you, don't have such a lack of self-service. My, you do get upset when someone suggests the Emperor ain't got no clothes, don't you?*

Never received a reply. Didn't expect to. Just felt like sticking it to him. Keeps balance in the universe.

But little more than two weeks later, on November 10th, 1982, front page headlines all over America announced:

*U.S. SURGEON GENERAL C. EVERETT KOOP SAID TUESDAY THAT VIDEO GAMES MAY BE HAZARDOUS TO THE HEALTH OF YOUNG PEOPLE, WHO HE SAID ARE BECOMING AD- DICTED TO THE MACHINES. "THEY ARE INTO IT BODY AND SOUL," KOOP SAID.*

485

Naturally, I wrote a follow-up letter to Mr. Apar, the gist of which was: "Posterity seems determined to have its say rather more quickly than usual on this disagreement between our positions. How many 'cranks' does it take to make a consensus?"

He didn't respond to that one, either. Thank god I handle rejection with equanimity.

I could not, in my most power-drenched fantasies, have postulated how speedily posterity was bearing down on the videogame Eden and all its leech apologists. I like to think I have a cultivated talent for helping to redress the balance in the universe, but not even Zorro had the power to decimate an entire multi-billion-dollar industry so quickly. On two days in the following month, December, 1982, Warner Communications, Inc. (parent company of Atari, Inc., as well as of DC Comics) watched its stock plummet 45% as Atari went into the toilet.

Atari, whose revenues were nibbling at the edge of $2 billion a year, with 10,000 employees in fifty buildings all across Silicon Valley, announced on December 8th that they had been hit by massive order cancellations, and in the next two days (as reported by the *Wall Street Journal*) stockholders lost a collective $1.5 billion to $2 billion on paper. Soon after there were rumors of insider trading, rumors that certain Warner and Atari executives had jettisoned huge blocks of Warner shares just before the price tumbled. Stockholders filed suit to find out what actually happened inside the company, and the Securities and Exchange Commission is investigating.

All over America, landlords who only a few years ago were forcing Mom&Pop grocery stores and boutiques out of their locations so the shops could be converted into videogame arcades, are finding they have echoing emptiness to show for the sudden drop in clientele. As quickly as it dominated the scene, the videogame craze has receded.

At moments like these, I find my reluctant acceptance of the transient nature of the human race ameliorated. Perhaps the cockroaches *won't* take over in my lifetime.

On the other hand, the miasmic spirit of James Watt is still with us.

INSTALLMENT 61: 21 August 84
(published in *The Comics Journal*
cover-dated September 1984)

# INTERIM MEMO:

Mr. Smith became a self-fulfilling prophecy. He read the reprints of Installments 18 and 30, and he wrote a letter to *The Comics Journal*. I've mentioned this twice earlier in these pages. It was supposed to be a one-paragraph reply. But Mr. Smith pulled his own covers, he revealed himself, and he told us something we need to know; and once we have learned it we must never forget it. What started out as a flippant reply to a letter turned dark and ominous as it became an unexpected 61st *Edge*.

First, Mr. Smith's letter, exactly as it appeared in print...then an ominous dark message from beyond the campfire. How Fate does take a hand. This book might have ended on the trivial note of videogames. But there is a dark force out there that never lets us forget we are prey. It waited more than a year and a half to make its presence known again, even as this book went to the typesetters, but it came in at the finish line. Maybe that's why we aren't laughing.

*Letters reprinted with permission from* The Comics Journal

PETER CATHRO

The smiler with the knife. The flesh that always smells of soap. The good book, called the Good Book, seldom seen opened but held tightly to the chest by a hand with clean fingernails. Assassins with shined shoes.

There is nothing wrong. We repeat, listen carefully, there is no reason for fear. Ignore the faces pressed against the window. It's cold out there, and out there is where they belong. In here, everything is *all right*. We repeat, for the last time: our way is the right way, the only way that maintains order and warmth. Pay no attention to the man with the noose.

---

## Ed Asner: Paranoid, Ego-Crazed Yahoo

BRIAN SMITH, Marshalltown, IA

I feel compelled to introduce some personal insight into the argument of "Hysterical Paralogia," part one, by Harlan Ellison. I have no quibbles with his painstaking ratiocination, and do not question the validity of his conclusions within the limits of the data at hand. But...

Until very recently I worked as administrative support to the command staff of the Defense Intelligence Agency (DIA). The duties of my office included handling the sort of crank mail the paranoids of the world love to send to military intelligence organizations. Another duty was the processing of Freedom of Information Act (FOIA) requests.

Roughly a year ago we received a FOIA request from none other than Mr. Ed Asner. It made for interesting reading. It:

a) Demanded the DIA turn over to Mr. Asner all files, memos, recordings, photos, etc., relating to Mr. Asner or *Lou Grant.*

b) Demanded that any "lost" files be diligently searched for and produced at the earliest possible moment.

c) Demanded that the files search, copying, and time costs be charged entirely to the government, as the effort was clearly in the public interest.

Everyone in the DIA who saw this letter thought it hysterically funny, because:

a) We did not have anything on Mr. Asner outside of the *TV Guide* in the lounge.

b) The tone of the letter made it obvious that this simple truth would not be believed.

c) It was thought incredible that he considered himself important enough to warrant our attention.

Specifically, the silliness of the letter included the unwritten assumptions that:

a) We were the enemy. This was obvious from the tone and the explicit assumption that we would lie (the quotes around "lost" in "lost" files offended most everyone in DIA).

b) That the DIA, having been badly burned ten years ago, would violate federal law and keep files on a US civilian (and would comply with the FOIA to turn over self-incriminating files, had there been any).

c) That the DIA, like Mr. Asner, might confuse "Lou Grant" with a real person (every time the name Ed Asner was used it was carefully followed by a "Lou Grant").

A quick poll of the staff revealed that most watched *Lou Grant*, and all that watched it enjoyed it. They considered the letter as further proof of the media myth that the military are somehow (frighteningly) different from the rest of the populace.

I myself, did not think that Mr. Asner singled out the DIA. I think that every investigatory (read that as reactionary, of course) arm of the US government received a similar letter, and that every one of them found it as funny as we did.

I also noted a striking similarity between Mr. Asner's letter and those we often get from people who accuse us of breaking up their marriage with microwaves.

So, Mr. Ellison, although it does not really invalidate your thesis, I submit that your case was not well chosen; Ed Asner *is*, in fact, a paranoid, ego-crazed yahoo.

Mr. Smith opens his letter with praise for my column and seems to agree with my conclusions about paralogia. (As a refresher for those who may not recall what paralogia is: "preoccupation with subjective thoughts and fantasies that give answers to questions either wrong or beside the point...interests are narrowed to a point where thinking becomes restricted and unrealistic...the drawing of false inferences...Paralogia may also take the form of distorting reality to conform to personal desires or delusional ideas.") Unfortunately, Mr. Smith becomes, with his letter, for all of its pleasant support of my work, a self-fulfilling example of paralogical thinking. Go back and re-read Mr. Smith's letter.

All he *really* has to work with is Ed Asner's perfectly okay request for any DIA files that may exist relating to him. (And as we don't have Asner's letter for evidence, we must take Mr. Smith at his word that he represents accurately that letter.) This is not an act of ego or paranoia. It is a right *every* American citizen has under the Freedom of Information Act. Like Asner, I have made requests for similar files from the FBI, CIA, California CID and any number of other governmental agencies. I am not alone in having done so. Others who have so requested include Leslie Fiedler, Jane Fonda, the family of Martin Luther King, Jr., Saul Alinsky, Tom Hayden, Art Kunkin (ex-publisher of the L.A. *Free Press*), and thousands of others who have reason to believe that either proper or improper, legal or extra-legal or illegal files have been amassed in their names. History assures us that such files existed, continue to exist, and may continue to be brought into existence by such outfits as the DIA. Through the FOIA, in the last few years, we have seen startling revelations about wholly unjustified invasions of privacy and groundless suspicions of vast numbers of Americans. An entire cache of papers—plus restricted films—concerning Charlie Chaplin was turned up; the silly but dangerous file kept on John Steinbeck simply because he was a liberal made headlines throughout the USA; Albert Einstein, it turns out, was under surveillance because he had the most peripheral flirtation with Hollywood during the Forties.

No, there's nothing necessarily paranoid or ego-crazed about wanting to know what snoopers like the FBI, CIA, and DIA had to say about oneself. Anyone who thinks otherwise ought to get hold of a book (one among many) titled LOW PROFILE: *How To Avoid the Privacy Invaders* by William Petrocelli (McGraw–Hill, 1982, $5.95). Or send away for the United States House of Representatives Committee on the Judiciary, Subcommittee on courts, civil liberties, and the administration of justice report titled SURVEILLANCE (2 vols.) (U.S. Government Printing Office, Washington, D.C., 1975). I'm aware that many people who read only lightly in the available material—those who overload their reading time with fantasy, comic books, science fiction, spy novels, other perfectly acceptable but essentially trivial matter—are not fully cognizant of the amount or degree of information amassed by such *apparat* as the DIA. But I digress.

Let me get back to Mr. Smith's "analysis" of Asner. And I'll deal strictly with Mr. Smith's words, and how he uses them, rather than indulging in paralogia by making assumptions. Precisely the opposite of what Mr. Smith has done here.

a) We all know that files are cross-referenced, we all know that many people file in a weird manner or ineptly (I had an assistant once who filed half the material on The Smithsonian Institution under "The" and the other half under "Institution."). We also understand that the more referents you provide for a standard computer search, the more likely you are to get what you're looking for. So asking for files that might have been misentered under the name *Lou Grant*—the character Asner portrayed in his series, and a name that became so associated with Asner that many people called, and still call, him "Lou"—doesn't seem at all extraordinary or foolish. In fact, it seems sedulous and reasonable.

b) "Lost" files are not uncommon. Take a look at any article in any newsmagazine over the past ten years since the FOIA was effected. You will see endless representations by information-gathering agencies including the SEC, FTC, ICC, FDA, EEOC, CAB, HEW, HUD, DOD, INS, LEAA—as well as the three biggest snoopers of them all, the CIA, FBI, and the IRS—that files are "restricted," "out of the office," "under review," "for eyes only," "unavailable due to National Security," or otherwise "denied" in whole or in part. When the files *do* come through, after a long while and with many roadblocks having been erected, they are invariably blacked out in vast sections, show gaps in sequence, stop in the middle of a sentence so the preceding phrases make no sense . . . or are otherwise rendered useless. Asking for "lost" files is standard legalese (hell, it's a matter of course procedure in *any* legal action, whether civil or criminal). It means, "we don't know if you're dumb enough to shred or conceal evidentiary material, but this puts you on notice not to, and we give you an out to wiggle through, that said material was temporarily 'lost.'" Nothing out of the ordinary here, either.

c) This is a matter of law, and if Mr. Smith were being cards-on-the-table with us he would have said so. *If* such files exist, and *if* such files were illegally obtained or impair Asner's civil rights (as the Supreme Court has held), then it *is* "in the public interest" that he requests such files and, *res ipsa loquitor,* it falls to the agency that amassed such files to foot the bill for reproducing and providing said files. This is another perfectly standard legal device, though Mr. Smith makes it seem as if Asner is behaving in a paranoid or egocentric fashion. In fact, from what Mr. Smith has presented to us, I would be willing to bet the request letter didn't even come from

Asner personally, but came through his attorneys. Because what Mr. Smith gives us here is the sort of attorneytalk we've all confronted in the real world.

Now we get to Mr. Smith's paralogia. As we don't have Asner's (or Asner's attorney's) letter to hold in evidence as to the "tone" of said letter, what we're dealing with is Mr. Smith's *perception* of that letter. This is called hearsay evidence, and is not permitted in a court of law. But we're not *in* a court of law, we're in the court of public opinion, a letter column of opinions, and Mr. Smith is trying to get us to believe something. He is trying to get us to believe that Asner is "a paranoid, ego-crazed yahoo."

I hope I've demonstrated in the preceding paragraphs how and why Asner's request is perfectly rational, particularly when it concerns a man whose political statements were so outspoken and controversial (not to mention embarrassing to the Administration) that his tv series *may have been* cancelled, in large part, not on ratings grounds, but because of political interference. Many reputable observers of the situation, from Walter Cronkite on down (or up, or sidewise) voiced such concerns. So for the subject of such a controversy to seek as much data as he can get, is merely enlightened self-interest, not paranoia.

But even if Asner *is* paranoid, don't forget—as Dr. Richard Kimble, *The Fugitive,* proved—even paranoids have enemies. That's supposed to be levity, folks.

If you look at the second series of lettered paragraphs in Mr. Smith's letter, you'll see that b), c), and in the third set a), b), c) are all paralogical thinking. Smith assumes attitudes and draws conclusions that do not manifest themselves in what *he* has presented as Asner's bill of demands. Nowhere did Asner say or infer that the truth wouldn't be believed (though I hope no one reading this rebuttal is as naive as Mr. Smith wanted Asner to be...or are we to take it from Mr. Smith's copping of an attitude that no one in government lies to us); nowhere did Asner demonstrate the hubris Mr. Smith infers when he says Asner thinks himself "important enough to warrant our attention."

(And let me deal with *that* arrogance for a second. Mr. Smith may, like many another civil servant, think he and his agency are so importantly engaged that *no one* is big enough to command his attention. But he is wrong. *He* works for *us.* Like cops who see the world in terms of Us-vs.-Them, with "them" being anyone not in police uniform, Mr. Smith gives himself away when he gets on his high horse assuming Asner thinks he's important enough "to warrant our attention." Though Asner didn't seem to suggest any such thing by making a simple request to which he is entitled *by law*, Mr. Smith and his cronies took umbrage at anyone even *asking* them to be accountable. This is an example of the institutionalized ingroup thinking of these little petty officials. They have their bailiwick and god help anyone bold enough to suggest they are accountable to the body politic. Mr. Smith gives himself away. Asner isn't ego-crazed, but perhaps it might be suggested that civil servants who think they're too important, busy or above reproach to obey the law without getting their noses out of joint are.)

I won't even deal with Mr. Smith's "unwritten assumptions" because if they're unwritten they are as likely to be Mr. Smith's assumptions as Asner's or mine or Eleanor Roosevelt's or Dr. Crippen's. This is just pure flummery and need not concern us.

One last thing. Mr. Smith offers us as validation of his paralogia and "unwritten assumptions" the fact (reported as fact by Mr. Smith, but unverifiable) that others in his office thought all this was "silly" or "paranoid" or "ego-crazed."

There is a concept in psychiatry (and in law) known as *folie à deux,* which is the sharing of a delusional idea by two people who are closely associated. Two members of the Klan who *know* that blacks are inferior is *folie à deux*; two members of the same street gang who *know* that a certain section of their turf is theirs is *folie à deux*; two believers in an assassination conspiracy theory *know* the government is covering up. And that's *folie à deux,* too.

And the people who cover each other's asses in a government agency under attack by a random segment of the body politic who want them to cough up their secrets (if any), can well develop what Mr. Nixon toe-scuffingly still refers to as "the bunker mentality." And that's a *folie à deux* that might result in someone like Mr. Smith seeing Asner's request—like thousands of others under the FOIA— as threatening. And so it is no validation at all of what Mr. Smith *assumes.*

And I suggest Mr. Smith, as well as you readers, look up the meaning of the word "yahoo." One does not call a well-spoken, well-informed, socially-concerned, literate and talented man a "yahoo." But I can see how Mr. Smith might think Ed Asner is such a thing. Which says more about Mr. Smith than it does about Mr. Asner.

I hope I've responded satisfactorily.

P.S. Holdit! A couple more things occur to me. Not that I want to level Mr. Smith—after all, he had the good taste to enjoy my column and say nice things about me—but his letter absolutely refuses to be ignored, it is so perfect in its wild surmises. The statements Mr. Smith makes all go to the point that Asner is paranoid because he thinks there *might* be files on him, and he's ego-crazed if he thinks he's important enough to have such files amassed on his activities. But if the readers will recall, as I'm sure Mr. Smith does, there looms large in recent memory the instance of CIA files being kept on a

494

ten-year-old schoolgirl from the Midwest, who performed the highly suspicious act of writing a letter to Yuri Andropov. I'm not referring to the little girl who actually went to Russia last year, but yet *another* urchin several years earlier. If the CIA can cobble up a file on a kid like that, I don't think Asner veers particularly far from an accurate perception of possibilities where his own highly-publicized activities are concerned.

But more than that, after I'd finished writing this response, I went back yet again and read Mr. Smith's letter, and what struck me on a third pass, which I'd missed the first two times, is the unconscionable behavior of Mr. Smith in showing Asner's letter around the office *and then talking about it in public print*!

It's okay for Mr. Smith and his DIA buddies to make fun of a private citizen making a lawful request, to label him paranoid and ego-crazed and a yahoo (careful, Mr. Smith, there are folks out there who sue people for calling them crazed, even in jolly hyperbole), but heaven help him if he asks for some information.

What, exactly, does "administrative support" mean? Is that governmentese for "Kelly Girl"? Does it mean: "Pull us a schlepper from the typing pool, we're overloaded with scutwork"? Do we have euphemism here? How does Mr. Smith *know* there are no files in the DIA on Asner? If he was "administrative support," that sounds to me as if he was an office flunky. That would mean his clearance isn't high enough to accord him access to any restricted files. And if he *does* (or did) have a clearance that high, isn't he running the risk of being censured or even sued by the agency for writing his letter to *The Comics Journal*? (Who do I know in the DIA...hmmm.)

So we have someone who very likely signed a covenant with the DIA not to reveal what passed his eyes while he worked there, running his mouth in print on a departmental matter, ridiculing a private citizen in what might be conceived libelous terms, thereby opening not only himself but the agency to legal action. And at bottom, how much are we expected to respect, sympathize with, agree with, or love Mr. Smith and his DIA coterie when we perceive that they look on us as "yahoos" infringing on their valuable time? It's very much the way we feel when we call telephone information for a number and the operator tells us the number is listed in the book. "Yes, I know," we say, "but I'd like to have *you* look it up...that is, unless you're involved in something more momentous, such as discovering radium." Mr. Smith demonstrates in his wonderful letter an attitude that serves as litmus test for the very belief we, the public, hold that outfits like the DIA are filled with petty tyrants who think they have the right to pry into our lives as they choose, deny us the right to hold them accountable for such infringements of our rights, and make fun of us in print if we are not cowed by the might and rectitude of an office filled with paper-pushers who mistakenly believe they have the power to rule us in their picayune fashion.

Mr. Smith probably did not realize, when he sat down to tell us the truth about Ed Asner, that he was saying so much about himself, his former employer, our government, and ourselves. He probably thought it was all a giggle.

So why aren't we laughing?

# AFTERWORD

The slug-date on the edition of the *Los Angeles Weekly* in which my final column appeared was 14–20 January 1983. As that column went to press, I was writing installment number fifty-nine. It never saw print. "Irreconcilable differences," one of those great dissembling phrases, impelled me to advise the publisher of the *Weekly*, one Jay Levin, that we had come to the parting of the ways.

In the following edition (21–27 January) the following line appeared under *Addenda:* "Harlan Ellison is on vacation this week."

That was news to me.

In the *Weekly* dated 11–17 February (vol. 5, no 11) a boxed notice appeared on the editorial page stating as follows: "Harlan Ellison has decided to discontinue his column. We'll miss him. The column was vigorous and fun and unique, if controversial. We wish Harlan the best."

As Tennessee Williams's Big Daddy said in *Cat On a Hot Tin Roof* (excuse my repeating myself from the interim note to Installment 28), "There's a pow'ful stench of *men*dacity heah!"

Yes, I suppose if we want to be strictly technical, it was I who decided to discontinue *An Edge in My Voice*. But it was a decision forced on me by ever-deteriorating relations between the publisher and the columnist. How it all came to an end—with a grace note concluding the mystery of "Jon Douglas West"—is the subject of this afterword, by way of denouement. I know how much you all love a happy ending.

But to understanding the ending, we must go back to the beginning. How these columns come to be written in the first place.

From 1968–72 I wrote *The Glass Teat* columns, ostensibly on the subject of television though tv was merely the lens I employed to comment on Life in Our Times. Those columns appeared in *The Los Angeles Free Press* and *Rolling Stone*. They have been collected in two volumes, available in paperback. From 1972–73 and from 1976–77 I wrote a more general column of personal essays called *The Harlan Ellison Hornbook*. Those pieces were published in *The Free Press, The L.A. Weekly News* and *The Saint Louis Literary Supplement*. The spirits willing, one year soon Jack Chalker's Mirage Press will publish that run of forty-six essays.

Between 1977 and 1980 I was silent. The sigh of relief from the

Body Politic was as deep as the wind between the stars.

In the April 1980 issue of *Starlog* magazine, I was represented by a long essay-review of *Star Trek—The Motion Picture.* It drew considerable mail from the readers of *Starlog* and in February of that year I was approached by telecon (as we say in the world of big business) by Kerry O'Quinn, publisher, and Bob Woods, editor, of *Starlog*'s companion magazine, *Future Life,* as to the possibility of my doing a regular column along the lines of the *Star Trek* piece for that journal.

(If it seems time-out-of-joint that I was called to do the column three months before the review appeared, do not be overly confused. The cover date on *Starlog* was April, but I wrote the piece early in December 1979, proposed a film review column for *Starlog* in mid-January 1980—and was turned down on the idea—and was recontacted on 20 February to write a column for *Future Life* rather then for *Starlog,* which already had its complement of columnists, not the least of whom were David Gerrold and Bjo Trimble.)

The columns ran in *Future Life,* with a few lapses for missed deadlines and breathers, from August 1980 till the demise of the magazine in December 1981.

At that point, *An Edge in My Voice* was dead.

Early in January of 1982 I received a phone call from Jay Levin, a man who represented himself as the publisher of the *L.A. Weekly,* a free newspaper subsidized by advertising that was distributed throughout the Los Angeles area. Though I had never read the paper, I was familiar with it, and was interested enough in his suggestion that I write a *Glass Teat* sort of column for him, that I agreed to a meeting. Then I did some checking around, and learned that Levin had been a respected reporter for the *New York Post.* He had been a liberal covering, among other areas, the "New Left." So I checked a little further and learned he had been hired by the Larry Flynt organization to come out to California to edit a national version of the L.A. *Free Press,* which Flynt had bought when Art Kunkin went bankrupt and the paper folded. Like so many other good and reputable people who've passed through the revolving door of Larry Flynt's publishing paranoia, Levin was left afoot in L.A. when his deal with Flynt fell through; and the national *Freep* never happened (though I hear Kunkin is now on Flynt's payroll trying to revivify the old warhorse publication).

At 1:30 PM on January 4th, on a Monday in Los Angeles in which the heaviest rains in ten years began, I met Jay Levin at Jerry's Deli on Ventura Boulevard in the San Fernando Valley. I had a cup of coffee.

We talked about my doing a continuing version of *An Edge in My Voice* every week, and I gave him copies of the columns that *Future Life* had published. He skimmed them and said he liked the tone, but he wanted columns that ran not much more than a thousand to

498

twelve hundred words. I explained that the kind of rambles I took in the world of the essay were more often than not an arguing from the smaller to the greater. (See Installment 61 for a perfect example.) I told him that for me, the best essays were the ones that illuminated large societal problems by progressing from an everyday discomfort. And that sometimes took two thousand words to set up properly.

Levin was vague about how strictly he wanted to enforce such space limitations, and so when it came time to discuss what kind of remuneration I was to receive for these weekly emanations, and Levin blanched at my suggesting two hundred bucks a shot, I traded off: I'd take a hundred dollars per, with a reevaluation of salary after three months, when the worth to the *Weekly* of my writing had been established, in exchange for a policy of flexibility where length was concerned. He agreed.

The one ground rule I insisted upon, however, was set at that meeting. And it boiled down to this: I write 'em, and the *Weekly* publishes 'em. No rewriting. No editorial infringement. No "suggestions" about avoiding subjects that might be troublesome. Short of libel, I could go where I chose, and report what I'd seen. He agreed.

Therein lay the seed of our destruction.

We agreed that a good lead-in for the column's appearance in the *Weekly* would be a reprint of my final column for *Future Life,* the brouhaha attendant on my piece about knife-kill movies. I suggested it be published intact, but Levin had some space problems, so we decided to break the longer version in half, and to use it in successive issues with some brief rewriting to make it flow for continuity.

On January 14th, 1982 the first column appeared. Then the second part of the knife-kill essay the following week. By that time most of the uproar about the Writers Guild Film Society decision not to book slasher flicks had gone down, and on the 25th of January I wrote the first new column. It went in to Jay Levin and I see by my daily log that the next day, Tuesday the 26th, that I was already having trouble with "The Man." My note reads: *Jay Levin of L.A. Weekly gives me a hard time re the column—I tell him to cut it as he pleases. I'm so disgusted, don't intend to do column much more.*

Jay was a man who liked to play at being editor, I feel. It was not enough for him to be the publisher of a successful newspaper, he also wanted to be Maxwell Perkins or Punch Sulzberger. Ben Bradlee, maybe. He was not, in my view, systemically capable of maintaining our bargain—I write 'em and he runs 'em, no interference. But I was abruptly gifted with the presence of an intermediary for whom I had instant respect and affection, the actual line-editor of the paper, Phil Tracy.

He was, and is, a newspaperman out of the old school where precision and imagination and getting the spelling right counted for a lot. He understood in a way that made me love him, that too much gonzo journalism had produced a generation of sloppy reporters, that in their star-bedazzled attempts to emulate Tom Wolfe or Hunter Thompson, hordes of minuscule talents had avoided learning the craft in deference to producing writing that was fast and smartass and essentially uninformed.

Phil Tracy was born in Manhattan in 1942; he had sixteen years of Catholic education which, miraculously, he was able to transcend. He was a former social and civil rights worker, a labor organizer for the Welfare Workers Union (and served as shop steward), worked in the 1968 presidential campaign for Bobby Kennedy, and was a staff writer from 1971–76 at *The Village Voice,* specializing in political and labor union coverage, in which areas he did solid investigative reportage. He was what is commonly known as an honest, hardnosed newsman. He was respected.

In the summer of 1976, tired of New York and remembering with fondness the two years during the sixties in which he had lived in San Francisco, Tracy accepted the offer of Clay Felker (then owner of *The Village Voice,* which is now a Rupert Murdoch possession) to go to work for *New West* (now *California* magazine) in the Bay Area. Felker's problem with the magazine—which he had spun off the successful *New York* magazine empire on April 26th of that year—was that he could not, in his view, find reporters on the West Coast who knew how to dig up stories.

(Those of us who had memorably horrendous experiences with the inept and arrogant staff initially manning *New West,* those of us here in Los Angeles who swore we'd rather undergo root canal surgery than be further demeaned and jerked around by the dolts Felker had dispatched to our town, knew that there were muckrakers and investigative journalists galore. We simply did not choose to waste our time and efforts in service to a publication that manifested an obvious dislike for California. It was another confrontation with that East Coast Literary Establishment provincialism that contends anything that happens beyond the Hudson River simply ain't worth taking seriously.)

So Tracy volunteered to fry Felker's bacon, and he came back to San Francisco in the summer of 1976, in the capacity of contributing editor, picking his own shots and writing about whatever caught his interest. He was 36 years old.

In July of 1977 Phil Tracy became one of the best-known reporters in America: in the July 18th issue of *New West,* eighteen months before the Peoples Temple tragedy in which Congressman Leo Ryan and four others were murdered on that airstrip in Guyana, before the Reverend Jim Jones induced 933 of his followers to drink cyanide-laced Flav-R-Aid—including more than 200 of their own children—in a death-pact that stunned the nation, Phil Tracy broke the story. In a city where the mayor had been so convinced of Jim

500

Jones's worthiness (and political clout) that he had appointed the man to chairmanship of San Francisco's housing authority; in a time when Jones was being lauded and courted by Vice President Walter Mondale, First Lady Rosalynn Carter, Governor Jerry Brown and Mayor Moscone, the voices of Phil Tracy and his collaborator, Marshall Kilduff of the *Chronicle,* were the first (and for a dangerous time the *only*) voices raised against Jim Jones and the evil that was the Peoples Temple.

The story was a bombshell. And within two weeks the *San Francisco Examiner* was running articles that backed up Tracy's findings and suppositions. Within those same two weeks, Jim Jones began the massive pullout of his operation, from San Francisco to Guyana. Fifteen months later Jonestown was major news.

And like the pilot of the *Enola Gay,* whose existence after the dropping of the A-bomb on Hiroshima was a nightmare of assimilated guilt, Phil Tracy went temporarily bugfuck. He was a hero, a media authority widely quoted and frequently interviewed, a pundit who appeared on television explaining what had gone down at Jonestown, a reporter whose name was mentioned in the same breath with the Pulitzer Prize. Yet in some deep place in his soul, where a reporter's pathological devotion to seeking out the truth wars with his guilt about being responsible for the betrayal of those he has written about, Phil Tracy savaged himself. In a terrible reach from beyond the mass graveyard of Jonestown, Jim Jones extended his evil to claim the man who had been instrumental in bringing him down. Tracy's life began to fall apart. He told about it in an article titled "Confessions of a Hero" in the November 1983 issue of *California* magazine.

By June of 1980 he could not write, his marriage was raveling, he had gained 80 pounds, he had become withdrawn and reclusive, and he was doping heavily. At the end of that month he quit *New West.* Sometime later that year, in his own words, "I began to consider suicide. I think the thing that really stopped me was the realization that if I actually did it, I would be joining Jones and all his followers, somehow confirming their view of the world. No matter how miserable I felt, I wasn't prepared to give the bastard that satisfaction, even if he was already dead. Still, it was close."

In 1981 he became the managing editor of the *L.A. Weekly,* and it was there, having read the original piece on the Peoples Temple years before (but never making the link-up in my mind that this was *that* Tracy), that I met Phil Tracy. It was not until late in 1984 (having fallen behind in my reading of issues of *California* magazine) that I caught up with "Confessions of a Hero" and realized the torment that Tracy was undergoing during the time we worked together. He never spoke of it.

We got along famously. He became a friend on the only basis I have ever been able to validate people: trust and respect. I listened to his suggestions and seldom disagreed with his assessments of how the column could be improved. When something troubled him, it was usually because I hadn't thought it out properly, or because I hadn't gotten my verifications, or—several times—that I'd been superficial and needed to dig deeper.

Had I been able to deal only with Tracy, I'd probably still be writing *An Edge in My Voice* for the *Weekly.* Maybe. Possibly.

But my problems with Jay Levin (or, as some might say, *his* problems with *me*) went on. Two weeks later, on February 5th, I wrote my third new installment, the one numbered 16 in this volume, the column about why everything is fucked up. In that column's original version, in a paragraph discussing the ethics of planned obsolescence, I wrote: "We *expect* the toaster to go on the fritz in thirteen months, just after the warranty expires. We *expect* the digital watch we bought at The Akron to begin running backwards, widdershins like the White Rabbit's timepiece, after a year of faithful service. We *expect* the screws to come loose in the lawn chair after one summer in the sun."

In the 12–18 February *Weekly,* that paragraph reads as follows: "We *expect* the toaster to go on the fritz in 13 months, just after the warranty expire [*sic*]. We *expect* the digital watch we bought at some chain store to begin running backwards...." Etcetera and unchanged (though badly typeset) for the balance of the paragraph.

Now it may not seem like much of an alteration to the copy...after all, the meaning is as clear using the phrase "some chain store" as it is using the name of The Akron, a Los Angeles chain that deals in rattan and antimony, job lots from Siam and Korea. And had Phil Tracy called to suggest that singling out The Akron (from which I'd actually bought a digital timepiece that gave out on me within days of the expiration of the "guarantee") in an essay where I singled out no other retailer might be a bit unfair, I'd no doubt have switched to "some chain store" without hesitation. But Phil *wasn't* the one who called. Jay Levin called. And what he said was, "We're having a tough time getting big advertisers, and The Akron takes an ad every issue, and why should they be singled out when you don't go after any other stores?"

To my chagrin, it was the only time I can remember when I allowed myself to rationalize the disgorging, the bowdlerizing, the acceptance of weaseling in these essays. Well, I thought, for whatever reasons I thought it at the time, maybe he's right. By what mandate do I assume I can damage the newspaper that supports my remarks, just because I happened to type "The Akron" rather than some other specific store, or even the "some chain store" generic? Do I serve the commonweal by demanding high-flown artistic integrity when it's been made clear to me that I will cause the *Weekly* serious

502

uifficulty? Is not the continued publication of this newspaper, a small voice of liberal opinion in a town dominated by the Voice of the Establishment, the *Los Angeles Times,* a cause worth bending one's arrogance in aid of? Haven't you bought a hundred items from The Akron in the last twenty years that worked perfectly well? Why pillory this otherwise respected chain because of one purchase that went awry? Who the fuck do you think you are, Mr. Righteous Columnist?

Thus do we subscribe to floating ethics.

I changed the line. Or, I let Jay Levin change it.

But not once during the months that followed, did I sit down to write these essays without remembering Levin's demand, to which I'd acceded. And as my readers came to trust me, as time passed, and their letters and phone calls thanked me for my sense of responsibility in what I praised or damned, I felt a gnawing shame that I'd been so easily co-opted. And it never happened again, though on three other occasions similar requests were made by Jay Levin to excise specific references. Nonetheless, I had done it once. And I hated the memory.

And the adversarial relationship with Levin persisted. Not only because he often questioned "the importance" of what I chose to write about—culminating in the refusal to publish what appears here as Installment 59 (see Interim Memo page 463)—but also, in large measure, because the columns were getting longer as I loosened up and felt comfortable with the way the readers were responding. The first two columns were 1500 and 1800 words each. The first new one was 2800 and thereafter through the first three months they grew longer: 3200, 3000, 5000, 5200, 5000, 2800, 4000, 4000, 4300.

But the response to the column was overwhelmingly positive, and the circulation of the *Weekly* continued climbing; and both from Phil Tracy's championing of the work in-house, and from the general community approbation (which at its peak netted me the P.E.N. award for journalism, an accolade that Levin took pride in, and which he praised editorially), Levin gritted his teeth and continued running the installments. (Every once in a while he'd attempt to remind me of my "station," however, by apprising me, strictly *entre nous,* that many of the kids who worked on the paper hated *An Edge in My Voice,* that it was, to them, too "committed," that it had too many resonances of the Sixties, the Seventies. He gave me to believe it wasn't punk enough for them. That bothered me, I confess. Never tried to be trendy, but hoped I was *au courant.* The staff was, in large part, new wave casual surly streetsmart. I worried it, but it didn't get in the way of the writing.)

(Long after I'd departed the *Weekly,* it chanced that I found myself, one evening, in the company of a bunch of people who'd worked at the *Weekly* during my tenure. I asked them about what

503

Levin had told me. They were quick to tell me that had been bullshit, that they'd enjoyed the columns. So much for worrying needlessly. But it didn't help me in loving "The Man.")

As for having written "trivial" columns, I stopped fretting *that* one when I read a piece on Andy Rooney in which the television essayist said, "It vaguely bothers me to be dismissed as insignificant, though it may be true. I think of myself as writing in metaphor. When I talk about cereal boxes or the excess of salesmanship in toothpaste tubes, I'm talking about the fact that in America we're generally selling things better than we're making them. And I suppose it bothers me to be dismissed as an inconsequential, amusing little fellow who affects a curmudgeonly air."

The writer of the piece on Rooney concluded with the observation that Rooney is anything but dismissable to those who believe a good laugh—whether it be insightful, metaphorical, or just good fun—is well worth waiting for.

As one who has been accused of affecting a curmudgeonly air, I felt a whole helluva lot better after reading them words. Thanks, Rooney.

During the year 1982, with only eight issues in which the column did not appear, *An Edge In My Voice* poked its twitching little pink nose out of the pages of the *Los Angeles Weekly* fifty-seven times. And then it was done.

Phil Tracy resigned from the *L.A. Weekly* in 1984. He now teaches journalism at USC in Los Angeles. He won't discuss why he left Jay Levin's employ. He is rigorously mute about the particulars, offering only this: "Managing the paper was too time-consuming. I had left off writing for myself when I became staff at the *Weekly,* and I found a need to get back to doing what had given me pleasure in the days before Jonestown . . . writing. There were projects that intrigued me, and I just didn't have the time to work on them."

He's lost weight, he's productively involved with passing along what he knows about being a responsible journalist, he's doing some writing, and he gets together with close friends for dinners of barbequed ribs at Dr. Hogly Wogly's Tyler, Texas Pit BBQ and at Diamond's. He won't confirm or deny my contention that a person has to be quite a bit nuts to go to work for Jay voluntarily; he just says, "Pass the hot sauce," and grimaces at me. Tracy's like that: he remembers good deeds; and Jay performed a good deed when he offered Phil the job on the *Weekly* when Phil was going through hell.

So I pass the hot sauce, and we don't talk about the days in the trenches. We got through the war without taking a slug; we remain; and this book exists. That's enough.

\* \* \*

There were a few things left undone when I stopped writing *An Edge*. . . . I never got around to writing the column about Ridley Scott

504

and his contention that "the time is ripe for a John Ford of science fiction films to come along, and I'm going to be that guy." Never wrote it because I never saw Ridley again. And once I'd written that quote, it said just about everything I'd have put in the column. Never got around to writing the long essay on attorney Gloria Allred and what a Force for Good she is, how her Women's Equal Rights Legal Defense and Education Fund is a wonder, and about how she defended the guy who ran down the rapist who'd attacked his girl friend. Never wrote it because, well, I just never got around to it. With regret. I never got to do the column about the world's most indecently delicious hot fudge, a purely felonious confection guaranteed to drive any chocolate junkie into paroxysms of twitching and slavering, a magical stuff made by Narsai's of Kensington, California 94707 with the truth-in-advertising name *Orange Chocolate Decadence.* Mere a jar of this stuff could have convinced the Inquisition that the Earth does, honest Injun, move around the sun. Never got to do that column.

And I never got to tell the conclusion of the infamous "Jon Douglas West Mystery." But that's what the Afterword to a book is for; and so, for the terminally curious, here is the part that usually follows *and they lived happily ever after.*

September 1982. The private eye had given up trying to locate someone who had signed his letters "Jon Douglas West." I'd been told in print by West that he lived in Burbank—just down the road from where I live—and that if I wanted to come kick his ass, I'd find him listed in the phone book. Of course, no such thing. There was no Jon Douglas West in any Burbank records; not telephone, not water and power, not Southern California Gas Company, not postal delivery, not DMV, not tax rolls, not property.

Back in July the *Weekly* had received several letters from supporters of West, and one of them, signed "Lucy McNulty, Informed Citizen," had been written on the same typewriter as the West missives. Some of the same typos appeared in the West and McNulty correspondence; *complement* for compliment, and *Zionests* for Zionists come immediately to mind.

The West/McNulty comments re Beirut and "High Society Zionests" [*sic*]—both in the sections of the letters as published, and in portions deleted by Phil Tracy due to restrictions of space and good taste—were sufficiently hysterical for me to write the following response which, because I'd thought back in July that I might scare them off, I never used in my column.

*Both West and McNulty seem so startled that the editors of the* Weekly *would run letters that disagree with my column. How many of you* were startled? I sure as hell wasn't. What I write is *open to fire upon; that's been obvious from the first installment.*

*But West and McNulty (who may be the same person, neither of whom is named West or McNulty) treat this run-of-the-mill freedom of access to the press as a rare and courageous act. One wonders—if the person behind these letters bears a more, how shall I put it delicately, Middle Eastern name and background—what sort of cultural heritage leads our indefatigable letter writer to think newspapers* don't *give equal time to the opposition? Is it possible that the party who would have us believe his name is West, is actually someone from the East...where media censorship at gunpoint is the commonplace, making the publication of his/her letters in the* Weekly *seem so courageous and unusual.*
    *I'm just asking.*

But by late August, with all tracking efforts having come up empty, I was resigned never to knowing who lurked behind the West monicker. Then one night, as I mentioned in Interim Memo number 40, I received an anonymous phone call from a woman who said, "I understand you're looking for Jon Douglas West."

It was late. It was dark. I spoke slowly. "That's right; maybe. Who's this?"

"A friend of his." Then she paused and said, "Anyway, I *was* a friend of his."

"He seems to have some trouble making and keeping friends," I said. She made one of those sounds midway between a snort and a sneer, and said, "Damn straight."

"You don't have to worry about it," she said.

"Worry about what?"

"Worry about finding him. You already met him."

I felt a chill.

"You even shook hands with him."

"That so? When?"

"Last weekend. He came to your autograph party. I was there, too."

The chill wouldn't go away. On Saturday, August 21st, I had sat from 2:00 until 5:00, signing books at the Dangerous Visions Bookstore in Sherman Oaks.

I had met Jon Douglas West, had in fact touched him; and hadn't known it.

"Which one was he?" I had the sudden paranoid feeling that he was right there with her, listening in on another phone, having put her up to it, not at all a former friend.

Then she described him, and I remembered the guy. No, he wasn't a Middle Eastern *émigré*. He was one of those guys named Sonny, or Buddy, or Bubba. The kind of guy who played nose guard in high school, who went into his father's plant to work alongside Dad on the line. The style of mean furniture that John D. MacDonald

506

always uses as the villain in the Travis McGee books. One of those chunks of meat who, when he's having a public fight with his wife or girl friend, grabs her bicep a little harder than is called for; nobody notices, but she's black and blue for two weeks afterward.

When we'd clasped hands, his mitt covered mine till the fingers met in the back of my wrist. He hadn't applied any special pressure.

I didn't remember her at all.

"Fan of mine, is he?" I asked.

"He just wanted to get up next to you, to see what you looked like. It made him glad, your not knowing who he was."

I felt my jaw muscles clenching. "Doesn't seem fair, does it? Him knowing me, but me not knowing him."

So she told me his name, and where he lived. It wasn't West, and he didn't live in Burbank. He lived in Van Nuys, about fifteen minutes from my house.

"So how come you're telling me this?"

She was silent for a moment. Then she said, "If I didn't do it, my sister would. I just beat her to it."

I didn't go after that one at all.

Over the next few weeks I made it my business to check out "West's" situation. My private eye, delighted to have the puzzle solved, found me everything I needed to know about the large, unmarried, working-class gent with pretensions of literary ability who had taken such a ferocious dislike to sweet little me. I knew more than I cared to know about this joker. But I was patient. I did nothing. I just waited.

Then in early November, after publication of what appear here as Installments 44 and 48, two columns about the gun control initiative Proposition 15, I received via the *Weekly,* in an envelope postmarked Van Nuys, addressed to Mr. Harlen [*sic*] Ellison (Personal), return addressed only with the initials J.D.W., a Xerox copy of a letter he'd written to the paper on October 4th. Attached to the letter was a personal note.

With permission of the *L.A. Weekly* (a permission that extends, by letter on file with Donning Publishers, to *all* correspondence used in this book), that note and letter are reproduced on the following pages:

DEERE HARLAN:

No, I HAVEN'T FORGOTTEN.
I WAS FEARFUL THAT
YOUR DICTATORIAL-EDITORIAL
STAFF MAY HAVE KEPT
THIS FROM YOU. SORRY
ABOUT PROP 15.

YOURS,

4 October 1982

To the Editor:

"Guns are not the only weapons. Control the guns and somebody
will think of another method. It's not the weapon that creates
murder, it's the mind...it's too simplistic to say, yes, if we
have gun control everything will be okay." Yoko Ono, John Lennon's
widow (10-1-81 issue of Rolling Stone Magazine)

I just had to write and thank the Chicken Little of hypocritical, yellow-
journalism for enlightening the unenchanted public on the virtues of
Proposition 15. (September 23-30) Thanks, Harlan! But, no thanks...

Again, serving judgement and attempting to do our thinking for us from
your security-tight estate in Encino (or wherever). Again, anguishing
and accusing us for lethargy and insensitivity, clouding the reality of
a very serious issue with your paranoia and persecution complexes and
very few facts.

I would imagine your juvenile conspiracy theories are quite meaningless
to many California merchants and citizens who are forced to make a decision
involving an impending robbery or assault because they do not have the
luxury of waiting for a black and white to appear or cannot afford robbery
insurance. I certainly think the use of deadly force is their decision
and their's to live with (not yours, or some idle-minded committeeof fat
cats). You seem more concerned with a fetish for the "Celebrity Dead"
than any concern for "John Q. Public" or his dire circumstances. You
can't expect Dean Martin to drive around West Los Angeles drunk without
his .38, can you? Now really, Harlan, do you expect David Crosby to
protect his cocaine or assault women without his .45's? And Dave was
at Peace Sunday, too! Oh, the irony!

Do you really believe that a state-wide ban on handguns will reduce the
nature or degree of crime in L.A.? Of course, it's well beyond your
dignity to question the professional police officers (on the streets,
not in the law enforcement bureaucracy) who openly reject Proposition 15
as any deterrent to crime or violence. I hardly think the average
"boost artists" buy and register their hardware from Big 5 or any
legitimate gun outlet. I also challenge your assumption that the limited
availability of guns could stop a person who is quite willing to destroy
a human life. Bremer, Chapman and Hinckley stalked their victims with
premeditation and would have pursued their goals of violence with or
without a gun. Some of Southern California's most notorious "stereotypes"--
William Bonin and Lawrence Bittinger -- tortured and murdered many young
men and girls in the most heinous and sadistic manner beyond imagination
without even possessing a gun. Wirehangers, ice-picks, pliers and sledgehammers
are probably available in most hardware and discount stores and, to my
knowledge, don't require an investigative waiting period or registration.
(Have you used any Tylenol or eyedrops lately?) I'm sorry, dear Harlan,
but my surrogate penis has saved me at least once from serious bodily
harm (in my own apartment) and I'd kind of like to keep it. Unless,
of course, you have room for me in your security bunker?

Blaming film, the media or authors is another weary escape route. I
suppose you could incite someone to murder with a Stay-Free Maxi Pad or
a can of Lemon Pledge under the right psychotic circumstances. For that
matter, could Son of Sam have gotten his telepathic dog from the film,
"A Boy and His Dog"? Can you live with that?

In closing Harlan, shed a tear or two for those hundreds of mutilated,
butchered (none were shot) cats and their owners in Westlake Village
and Thousand Oaks. Of course, that apparently unbalanced stereotype
doesn't discriminate as to whether the cats are female or journalists
or Jewish. I hope he doesn't graduate to humans... Hopefully, they'll
shoot the son-of-a-bitch when they catch him.

Yours dearly,

Jon Douglas West

Jon Douglas West. Dear god, what an iniquitous man.

Here is what happened to him. I report it as it was told to me.

Apparently, sometime late in December someone broke into his apartment. Peculiarly, nothing was stolen, nor was anyone ever tagged for the break-in; but shortly thereafter, on a probable cause warrant requested by the office of the Assistant District Attorney for Van Nuys, Mr. West was visited late one evening by plainclothes detectives representing the LAPD, who entered and searched his premises. Mr. West was taken into custody for possession of unregistered firearms. Other, printed, materials, named in the warrant were also confiscated.

Subsequently, after interrogation resulting from his possession of the printed material, Mr. West was connected to the defacement (swastikas, references to "another Holocaust") less than a month before of Temple Beth Torah on Woodley Avenue in Sepulveda.

Mr. West went away for a while.

It is my understanding that he's out now. He no longer lives at his former address. Though his true name and a copy of the police report are enclosed with a registered letter in the caretakership of a friend of mine who is renowned for his suspicious nature (he sees assassination conspiracies under every cabbage leaf), the whereabouts of the man who called himself Jon Douglas West are unknown to me at this time.

Lucy McNulty, informed citizen, has not been heard from.

According to the most recent Ford Foundation study, sixty-four million Americans are functional illiterates. That's better than 28 out of every 100.

I have been asked repeatedly why I write essays such as those appearing here, why I'm such a pain in the ass, why I seem cynical and troublemaking. I respond: we are in a time of crisis.

Here are some words from a long-ago issue of *The New Yorker* (unsigned as to authorship) on the subject of crisis:

> This is notoriously a time of crises, most of them false. A crisis is a turning point, and the affairs of the world don't turn as radically or as often as the daily newspapers would have us believe. Every so often, though, we're stopped dead by a crisis that we recognize at once as the genuine article; we recognize it not by its size (false crises can be made to look as big as real ones) but because in the course of it, for a measurable, anguished period—sometimes only minutes, sometimes hours, rarely as much as a day—nothing happens. Truly nothing. It is the moment of stasis between a deed that has been performed and must be responded to and the deed that will respond to it. At a false turning point,

we nearly always know, within limits, what will happen next; at a true turning point, we not only know nothing, we know (something much more extraordinary and more terrifying) that nobody knows. Truly nobody.

The more you agree with what a columnist has to say, the less effective the columnist is for you. The more closely the opinions of a columnist coincide with your own, without his/her raising questions in your mind, the less valuable the work is to you. Every column that you read, during the course of which you experience no anger or contentiousness, is a column you never needed to read.

> "I believe that we should only read those books that bite and sting us. If a book we are reading does not rouse us with a blow to the head, then why read it?"
>
> *Franz Kafka*

The value of a columnist, of an essayist, is in his/her viewpoint; the quirkiness of his/her insights; the originality, the freshness of his/her sense of what may underlie the obvious. Reading one more review in praise of, say, Lucas–Spielberg films...is merely the use of paper. But reading a column in which a cinema critic suggests that films by these men vacillate between a supersweet, lachrymose sentimentality that is as cloying as a Sammy Davis, Jr. *hommage* to his show biz buddies or Richard Nixon, and a genuinely vicious cynicism and fascination with violence, as demonstrated in the scenes of brutalization of children in *Indiana Jones and the Temple of Doom* and nakedly, blatantly in most of *Gremlins*...is to look at the received world in a different way.

As John Simon noted in 1981: "...there is no point in saying less than your predecessors have said."

(It should be noted that I don't think merely being negative in one's insights necessarily makes for valuable criticism. Crankiness is unbecoming and unproductive. For instance, most of the attention garnered by the recently-deceased comedian Andy Kaufman, during the last five years, was negative. No one seemed to notice that he was our most *valuable* comedian because, like Lenny Bruce, he was our most adventurous, our most dangerous funnyman. He expended more courage, took more chances, developed more unsettling original forms of presentation of his material—which dealt exclusively with aspects of the human condition we'd rather not acknowledge—than anyone working in the medium of stand-up humor.)

As John Le Carré has pointed out in terms of writers—and it goes doubly well for columnists—"A good writer can watch a cat pad across the street and know what it is to be pounced upon by a Bengal

511

tiger."

This has been the week-by-week record of the world as I saw it for more than a year. It was your world, too. And though I would not have you deface a synagogue, or bomb the Washington Monument, or reveal in print the secret affairs of the government agency for which you work, or even smile were you pounced upon by a Bengal tiger, I would hope these random thoughts unsettle you and move you to informed disagreement. And what about that edge in *your* voice?

Harlan Ellison
13 October 84
Los Angeles

512

# Index

518

528

Moshier, Jr., Larry, 468, 470
*Motel Hell* (1980), 129
*Mother Jones* magazine, 267
*Mother's Day* (1980), 129
Motion Picture Producers Association (MPAA), 150
Motor Avenue (Los Angeles), 364
MPAA. *See* Motion Picture Producers Association
*Ms.* magazine, 466
Mulligan, Gerry, 63
Munday, Anthony, 39
Muni, Paul, 430
Munoz-Perou, Miguel, 245–246
"Murder on the Huddleston Ferry" (radio), 335
Murdoch, Rupert, 502
Murdock, David, 424
Murphy, Con (Police Chief), 393
Murphy, George, 178
Musical Heritage Society (record label), 411
Muskogee (Oklahoma), 459
Musso & Frank's Grill (restaurant), 17, 455
Muston, Kimit, 454
Mutual Network (radio), 94
Mutual Radio, 49, 55
MWA. *See* Mystery Writers of America
MX missile, 459
*My Bloody Valentine* (1981), 129
*My Bodyguard* (1980), 112, 184
My Lai, 156, 159
Mystery Writers of America (MWA), 225

**N**
NAACP. *See* National Association for the Advancement of Colored People
Nabisco (National Biscuit Company), 326, 327, 353
Nader, Ralph, 11, 205, 207
Nadler, Eric, 267
"Guiding TV to the Right", 267
Nagasaki, 50, 422
Namath, Joe, 205, 207
Napoleon, 165
NARAL. *See* National Association for the Reform of Abortion Laws
Narsai's (confection manufacturer), 507
NASA. *See* National Aeronautics and Space Administration
*NASA News* magazine, 52
Nash, Ogden, 316
Nate 'n' Al's (delicatessen/restaurant), 358

*Nation, The* magazine, 76
National Aeronautics and Space Administration (NASA), 47, 49, 51, 52, 171
National Association for the Advancement of Colored People (NAACP), 111, 429
Image awards, 429
National Association for the Reform of Abortion Laws (NARAL), 346
National Biscuit Company. *See* Nabisco
National Coalition to Ban Handguns, 104
National Football League (NFL), 410
*National Geographic* magazine, 466
National Guard, 249
National Hot Air Balloon Races, 178
*National Lampoon's Animal House* (1978), 184
National Museum of Natural History, 78
National Organization for Women (NOW), 104, 201, 280, 347, 415, 445
National Rifle Association (NRA), 92, 179, 347, 363, 364, 386, 387, 391, 392, 404
National Women's Political Caucus, 429
"Bread and Roses" award, 429
*Natural History* magazine, 85
Natural History Museum (Los Angeles), 287
Nazi/Nazis/Naziism, 92, 93, 212, 241, 242, 304, 329, 340, 364, 367, 378, 387, 391, 393
NBC, 49, 92, 243, 264, 265
Neanderthals, 83, 85, 386
"Neanderthal the Hunter" (Guest), 85
Nebraska, 203
Nebraska Man, 83
Nebraska State Department of Education, 101
Nebula Awards, 16, 17, 477
Neenah (Wisconsin), 251
Neiman–Marcus (retail store), 385
Nelson, Ozzie and Harriet, 270
Nelson, Willie, 63
Nesmith, Mike, 63
Ness, Norman, 56
Nestlé, 69
Nevada, 171, 277
Nevelson, Louise, 357
New England, 466
New England Patriots football team, 398
New Freedom, 250
New Haven (Connecticut), 392

535

ONE IN 300 (McIntosh), 17
*One Million B.C.* (1940), 76
"One of These Days" (song), 454
O'Niel, (Space) Marshal, 106, 115,
  116–117
Ono, Yoko, 511
"On the Town with Mr. Los Angeles"
  (column) (Nolan), 395
ONTOGENY AND PHYLOGENY
  (Gould), 85
O'Quinn, Kerry, 66, 500
Orange Chocolate Decadence, 507
Orange County (California), 250
Oreo cookies, 326, 327, 328, 353, 405
Ormandy, Eugene, 429, 448
Ormsby, Sondra, 315
Orwell, George, 10
Ory, Christy, 68
Osmond, Donny & Marie, 171
Ospeth, Leon, 168, 357
Ostrom, John, 83, 85–86
Ostrow, Larry, 229
OTHER GLASS TEAT, THE (Ellison),
  67
O'Toole, Annette, 318, 319
*Outland* (1981), 104, 106–107, 111,
  112–118, 135
Oval Office (White House), 211
Ovaltine, 37
*Overture on Mexican Themes* (1969)
  (Talmi), 411
Oxnard, Charles, 83
Oz, 347
*Oz* books, 257, 286
*Ozzie and Harriet* (tv), 270

**P**
Pachmayr Gun Works, Inc. (arms
  manufacturer), 392
Pacific Architectural Design, Inc., 357
Pacific Coast Highway (California 1),
  358
Pacific Dining Car (restaurant), 357
Pacific Palisades (California), 172,
  357, 358
Pacific Press (printer), 468, 470
Pacino, Al, 315
Packard, 1949 (automobile), 166
Packard, 1950 (automobile), 253, 258,
  315, 316
Pac-Man video game, 483
Page Museum (Los Angeles), 287
Painesville (Ohio), 94, 294
Pal, George, 15–18
  *Destination Moon* (1950) (producer),
    15

*Doc Savage: The Man of Bronze* (1975)
  (producer), 15, 16
*The Power* (1968) (producer), 15
*The Time Machine* (1960), 15, 18
  (producer/director)
*When Worlds Collide* (1951)
  (producer), 17
Palestine/Palestinians, 290, 300,
  302, 320
Palestine Liberation Organization
  (PLO), 301, 302, 317, 321, 329, 420
Palmer Raids, 213
Panama Canal, 100, 102
Pantry, The (restaurant), 453
Papeete, Tahiti, 448
*Paper Chase, The* (tv), 325
*Paper Moon* (1973), 22
*Parabola* magazine, 466
*Parallax View, The* (1974), 134
paralogia, 259, 261–264, 270–272,
  493–496
Paramount Pictures, 18, 24, 69, 70,
  104, 184
Parasaurolophus, 87
Paris, France, 377
Paris of Troy, 326
Parker, Gary E. (Dr.), 76, 77, 82–86, 88
Parker, Richard, 209
Parker Brothers, 483–485, 486
  *Star Wars: The Empire Strikes Back*
    video game cartridge, 483–485
Parker/Dodd and Associates, 209, 210
Park Service police/rangers, 441, 442
parole board (California), 261
*Partisan Review* magazine, 269
*Partita for Chamber Orchestra* (1945)
  (Koechlin), 411
*Partita No. 3 in E Major (for
  Unaccompanied Violin), BWV 1006,*
  (Bach), 64
Parton, Dolly, 404
Pasadena (California), 49, 283
Paschal, Richard, 244
Pasteur, Louis, 41, 257, 352
Pastora, Eden, 475
*Paths of Glory* (1957), 70
Patriots football team. *See* New
  England Patriots
Patukas, Gus, 2, 3
Paul, Frank R., 56
Pauling, Linus, 40
Peacham, Henry, 5
  THE GARDEN OF ELOQUENCE, 5
Peak, Bob, 466
Pearl Harbor, attack on, 50
P.E.N., 253, 380

537

538

7-Eleven (convenience stores), 33, 218, 226
*700 Club, The* (tv), 45
*Seventeen* magazine, 269
*SF Chronicle* magazine, 67
SFWA. *See* Science Fiction Writers of America
Shahn, Ben, 410
Shain, Don, 189–191
Shain's (restaurant), 187, 189–191, 358, 398
Shakespeare, William, 39
 "Hamlet", 11, 39
 "Richard III", 118
Shanghai Winter Garden (restaurant), 358
Shapiro, Judy, 227
Shapiro, Marty, 229
Sharon, Ariel, 301
"Shatterday" (record) (Ellison), 95
"Shatterday" (story) (Ellison), 155
Shaw, George Bernard, 5
Shaw, Irwin, 2
Shaw, Robert, 25
Sheinbaum, Stanley, 385
Sheldon, Sidney, 33, 217, 325, 412
Shelley, Mary W., 11, 32
Shelley, Percy Bysshe, 326
Sherman Oaks (California), 187, 189, 315, 358, 359, 508
Shinn, Eric, 68
Shockley, William Bradford, 39, 178
Shreveport (Louisiana), 415
Siam, 504
Sihanouk of Cambodia, 191
*Silent Scream* (1980), 129
Silicon valley (California), 488
Silliphant, Sterling, 68
Silva, Jesus, 357
Silverberg, Robert, 32, 56, 346
Silverlake district (Los Angeles), 399
Silver Pen award (P.E.N.), 253
Silverstein, Eliot, 22
Simmons, Julie, 364
*Simon & Simon* (tv), 250
Simon, John, 5, 113, 141–142, 183, 207, 318, 319, 513
Simon, Neil, 142, 295
 *Seems Like Old Times* (1980), 112
Simpson, George Gaylord, 85
 THE MEANING OF EVOLUTION, 85
Sinatra, Frank, 385
*Singin' in the Rain* (1952), 293
Sirhan, Sirhan, 257
Siskel, Gene, 157

Sistine Chapel, 197, 245, 484
Sisyphus, 483, 484–485
*6th and Main* (1980), 112
6th Street (Los Angeles), 359
*Skeptical Inquirer, The* magazine, 466
Skinnerian behavioral modification, 262, 272
Sky, Kathleen, 286
 THE BUSINESS OF BEING A WRITER (with Goldin), 286
Skywalker, Luke, 32
Slatzer, Bob, 230
SLAUGHTERHOUSE FIVE (Vonnegut), 213
Small Claims Court (California), 227, 228, 229, 230, 231
Smith & Wesson (arms manufacturer), 392
Smith, Brad, 51, 52, 56, 57
Smith, Brian, 175, 176, 489, 491–498
Smith, Dennis, 357
Smith, Gerald L. K., 210
Smith, Valentine Michael, 92
Smithsonian Institute, 493
*Smokey and the Bandit* (1977), 184
*Smokey and the Bandit XVII,* 293
Snack 'N' Chat (restaurant), 358
SNCC. *See* Student Nonviolent Coordinating Committee
Snow Summit, 173
*Snow White and the Seven Dwarfs* (1937), 134
Snyder, Tom, 243
Social Security, 203
Society for the Preservation of Variety Arts, 453
Society of Vertebrate Paleontology, 82, 88
Soft Cell, 325
Soleri, Paolo, 10
Solomon, Elliott, 352, 353
*Sonata* (Poulenc), 64
Song, Emille, 333, 334, 335, 352
Son of Sam. *See* Berkowitz, David
Sontag, Susan, 325
Sony tv, 31
Soul, David, 296
South America, 61, 380
South Bay area (Los Angeles), 352, 430, 432, 434, 435
South Carolina, 277
South Central Los Angeles, 44
Southern California, 32, 297, 511
Southern California Gas Company, 507
Southern Governors Conference, 280
Southern Poverty Law Center, 104

543